COME BACK TO ME

EDMOND MANNING

WARNING

This e-book contains a shitload of sexually explicit scenes and adult language that may be considered offensive to some readers. Main characters have mind-blowing sex. Please store your files wisely, where they cannot be accessed by underage readers.

Author: Edmond Manning
Editor: Jonathan Penn, Romantic Penn Publication Services
Cover Artist & formatting: L.C. Chase
ebook Typesetting/Formatting: Beaten Track Publishing
http://www.pickwickink.com
pickwickinkpublishing@gmail.com general inquiries

ISBN#: 978-0-9978608-1-8

Also available in ebook
ISBN: 978-0-9978608-8-7

COME BACK TO ME

EDMOND MANNING

Trigger Warning

If you're the kind of person who wants trigger warnings, read this page. If not, move along—these warnings contain serious spoilers.

I respect the need for trigger warnings. I do. I have learned I have no stomach for graphic descriptions of kids being hurt or killed. I mean, yes, that could happen in a book about a war, or a book about sick kids in a hospital, and I'd read both of those without trigger warnings. But in those situations, you know and accept what you're getting into. I appreciate that you're reading this section to avoid being unexpectedly triggered. Here goes.

In the Prologue (less than a page long), the narrator—Vin Vanbly as a child—is being bitten by rats. Gross, I know. But it's a part of his childhood alluded to in the previous books.

In Part III, *The Lost Ones*, two adult men engage in consensual role-playing: a fake kidnapping and forced sex scenario. Actually, there is no forced sex. One of the men ends the scene just as he is about to be penetrated—he can't go through with it. The fantasy is not as fun and sexy as he had hoped. The story is very anti-rape. Once the reader knows that this entire story is consensual (revealed at the beginning Chapter Five), you can see what's really being discussed and what's really at stake. You might appreciate the story from that perspective. But if you don't want to read it, don't. However, you should read Chapter Five because there we learn Vin Vanbly's real name. Of course, first read *No Kings* (Part I) and *King Fitch* (Part II).

In Part IV, *King Malcolm the Restorer*, the narrator recalls a rape he overheard many years earlier. Much of that story deals with the sad consequences of that rape.

There! All trigger potentials revealed.

I've written an entire series of books about a man (Vin Vanbly) whose childhood was warped by what he had to do to avoid being raped by adults. I take the idea of forced sex very seriously and did my best to handle this topic responsibly. I'm open to your feedback if you want to discuss it with me. As always, thank you for reading.

—Edmond, pickwickinkpublishing@gmail.com

To the men I have loved.
You held my heart. I held yours.
Didn't last.
But it was love.

TABLE OF CONTENTS

PROLOGUE

Once upon a time, a—ow!

...upon a time, there was a mighty—ow!

No, I *like* the dark.

I like it.

Dark, dark, dark, like a dog's bark.

Once upon a time, there was this man who—ow!—traveled the world with a superfancy car, lots of awesome cars, and he was very rich and—ow!

I like rats. I like them. Cold tails. *Cold tails!* If Billy wouldn't feed them, they wouldn't— ow! Dark! Dark! Dark!

When I grow up, I will be rich and live in a big house with many rooms and have lots of cars, and—ow!—I will give myself a cool name, like Vin.

Ow!

I will become Vin.

No Kings

The events of this story take place in 2005.

ONE

H ere he comes.

Walking across the parking lot, he appears lost in his iPod world. He looks up, and his eyes jump wider, catching me staring at him. Jeans and a T-shirt, both flattering his light, muscular frame. Pleasantly plump biceps indicate he lifts more than twice a week, but this kid isn't entering any competitions—not yet at least. But he's young. His life could take any number of directions.

His face hints at a swarthy ethnicity—definitely Italian. Or maybe...Greek? His features present as strong, masculine even, yet pleasantly curved. Closer now, I see his five-o'clock shadow and shiny black hair—short, but long enough to curl slightly behind his ears, an overall appearance suggesting he is older than twenty-five. He's not. He's twenty-four. People can't hide their true age from me. I know.

He's a hottie. Anyone would agree.

He affects nonchalance as he swaggers closer, as if he can't feel my penetrating stare.

Bullshit.

I'm watching you, kid.

Over the years I have cultivated a few useful skills, including letting someone feel the weight of my presence. When I stare at you, you know it. He draws near me—he has to—to enter the convenience store.

Look up again, kid. Glance my way. I'm right here.

I parked my truck right under the fluorescent lights, closest to the front doors. I stand between their glow and true darkness in the parking lot. As he approaches, his reflection ripples in puddles, the last hour's rain still shivering in lopsided circles across the surface. When he passes he smiles feebly, a friendly grimace.

I lean in his direction—a slight change in my posture—forcing him to decide whether to alter his trajectory or ignore me. He ignores me. I inhale him. I don't smell anything particular, but that wasn't the point. I want him to sense my interest.

He pushes open the glass door with the flat of his right hand. A chime *bings*.

There! His hand shakes.

I draw a thick cigar from my favorite outdoorsman's jacket—brown leather lined with red flannel—and light up, continuing to lean against the tailgate.

I should have time Sunday afternoon to tune up this piece of crap before returning it to the rental place. I heard a few odd sounds when I drove it here from the motel.

He may not face me in this moment, but I believe he's aware I'm checking out his ass. Pretending to ponder some purchase from the front shelf. I think he's too nervous to move. Pretending to ponder, ponder a purchase, pretending to ponder a purchase, *possibly pretending* to *ponder—*

Stop it.

Look at the ripe curves of his ass.

I'm an ass man. I love ass.

Seconds ago, when I saw those muscular cheeks filling out his worn jeans, I knew I would spend significant time tonight coaxing those twin mounds to part for me, to welcome me inside. I can't stop thinking about his body. I've never met this kid before tonight. I haven't stalked him online. I haven't been to his home or somehow insinuated myself into his life. The newness of this feeling thrills me. Anything is possible. I can already imagine this ruggedly beautiful man stretched naked on my motel mattress, atop the shitty, threadbare bedspread, goose bumps making tiny ridges along—I can only guess—his otherwise smooth ass. But who knows? Maybe he won't give himself to me.

We're about to find out.

He receives change for the bottle of water purchased, and ambles toward the exit. He stumbles for a second when he sees me exhale a thick cloud above my head, and I breathe in the sweet burned scent we cigar smokers fetishize. When he opens the door, the dull mechanical *bing* recognizes his humanity and passing presence. He stands outside, almost unsure, and nods at me, preparing to stroll by with affected ease.

I want this kid's ass. *His ass in those worn jeans.* I'm not hard, but I am sure my dick is plumping out.

I glance down. Yup. I'm tenting.

Suck in more smoke.

When he's a foot away, I exhale, swirling mists of cigar smoke right into his face.

He freezes, a deer in headlights. That trite expression never seemed truer. At this moment, as a car enters the parking lot, its headlights sweep across the puddles and fill his black eyes with white, reflected light. His entire body goes rigid.

Got him.

"Boy," I say in a low tone meant to be remembered.

He blinks a few times, unsure what to do, and I see a muscle in his neck tense. I want to caress it, to kiss it. He stumbles beyond me, my next cloud of cigar smoke chasing after him. He crosses the parking lot, moving faster the farther he gets away from me, until I can't see his ass anymore.

Damn.

I smoke my cigar, trying to enjoy this unique New Jersey night. It's warmer in November than I assumed it would be. The sky remains sullen, pouting after its outburst, thick gray clouds obliterating and obfuscating any source of moonlight.

Obfuscating. Obfuscation.

Wait, that's strange. Why isn't my brain playing word games with *obfuscate*? Never mind.

His lips were thick, full with a dusty-rose color when he licked them, right after the smoke hit his face and his eyes filled with light. Within the hour, I intend to drag the head of my fat dick across those lips, wiping precum on them. I'm sure he's gonna taste my load tonight. This makes my dick pulse. I haven't jacked off in a week.

But if we fuck, no condoms. I'm going to fuck him raw. Can I really fuck him bareback? What would a Lost King do, Vin? You know. You always know. Fuck him raw. Come inside. I steel my resolve. I'm a Lost King. Why not sink into it?

Three minutes pass. Four? Probably only two. It always seems longer when you're waiting for someone. There—the edge of the parking lot—the tip of his shadow appears, and he's standing still, hesitating before returning. He knows if he comes back, he will submit. Come on, kid.

Come back over here.

Another car pulls in.

On Foster Avenue, a few cars plow by at a reduced speed, respecting the wet pavement. Not too much traffic in this neighborhood after nine at night. I arrived three days ago. Those out this night live here, the ones who accept this neighborhood's mostly undeserved reputation. It really is a cool neighborhood. Just not a fancy part of Newark. Four blocks away, the city morphs into industrial parks, two or three rogue bars, an abandoned church, and another more desolate convenience store. The yellow sign announcing the convenience of this particular store flickers in and out of existence, unable to commit to living.

Here he comes.

I ensure plenty of cigar smoke creates a fog for him to walk through as he strides purposely toward the front doors.

He flashes an embarrassed smile, and under his breath says, "Forgot something."

I say, "I'll bet. Stop walking."

He halts. A young woman sprints from the newly parked car toward the entrance. She is chased by an equally young man, who yells something unintelligible at her.

"Wait for them to pass," I say.

He stays.

I blow more cigar smoke in his face. He inhales it and coughs. Once they are inside, I speak.

"What you forgot...it's not in there."

I stand right behind him.

Speaking low, I say, "What you forgot, kid, is to thank me."

He shivers. "Thank you? For what?"

"For deciding to fuck you."

Still staring straight ahead, he says, "Oh."

I wonder how many other older bears he's wandered by, hoping they'd recognize the light in his eyes, the furtive glance to see if they recognize him—a man who wants to be controlled but doesn't know how to express such a desire after an initial "hello."

"Thank me, buddy. Go ahead."

Another car pulls into the parking lot.

"Thank you?"

"No." My voice makes him jump. "'Thank you, *sir*,' is how to say that."

"Thank you, *sir*." He whispers into the wet night, and he trembles. Now he knows. The battle is over and I have won. I place my hand on the back of his neck and grip it.

"Good boy. That's my man..."

He squirms. "Someone looking out...they might see us from inside."

"They might."

My thumb massages his neck, and I stand close enough for him to feel the heat of my strong presence. Despite the very public circumstances, he moans.

With gentle pressure, I guide him around the truck to the passenger side.

"Get in."

He tugs on the door handle and it relents with a squeaky groan. He climbs in and pulls the door shut while I take my time returning to my side. Crush out the lit cigar on my boot heel. He watches me with nervous surprise through the windshield. *Do you know what you're doing, kid? Are you ready for this?*

When I hop in and slam my door, he touches the case of beer bottles between us and shyly asks if he should move it.

I ignore him.

He blushes and moves the bottles to the floor, stabilizing them with his feet on either side.

The engine flips over with husky grumblings as if questioning his logic, his decision. Last chance, kid.

"My name is Mark."

I nod in acknowledgement.

We drive in silence.

I know he wants to talk, to ask questions, to know me better. His brain will make this entire scene more okay once he can validate I'm a regular guy, a nice guy even, someone to be trusted. It's a little cruel, keeping him in silence. But he already knows everything he needs to know. He's going to get fucked.

The motel is a run-down piece of crap, a haphazard construction in a *U* formation, individual rooms cut from the long rows, like stingy pieces of birthday cake. Or maybe this place washed ashore from the nearby ocean, perhaps after a few years rotting at the bottom. The siding's fat vinyl slats evolved into tired gray yet remain colorless at the same time. A weak orange neon sign blinks VACANCY, and the poor sign must get no rest because there's no way this place would ever be fully occupied. I wanted a cheap motel with cheap walls. I want temporary neighbors to hear him groan and beg and howl when it happens. I want this night to be trashy and mind-blowing.

I'm gonna bareback him. No condoms.

Shit. Can I do this?

I navigate the parking lot, avoiding plastic take-out containers and splatters which may have once been food.

"Is this place even open?" Mark chuckles nervously, trying to initiate conversation again.

"Bring the beer."

We walk the wet, black pavement in silence, him trailing me, following my lead. Even the parking lines are geriatric, faded to the point of irrelevance.

Using the motel's one concession to the modern world, I stick a plastic card into the slot to unlock Room 1_1—what I assume is meant to be Room 111, since the middle digit has gone AWOL. I send him in first. Get in there. Feel it. Absorb the squalor of this skanky room where you lose your virginity.

Once inside, he pauses, unsure what to do with himself. Should he sit on the bed, or will I pounce on him there? Set down the beer? But where? Or maybe he should start out kneeling...he just doesn't know. He glances around the room, stalling.

I like his confusion.

He sets the beer on the tattered floor, and several bottle necks clink together nervously, expressing hesitation regarding whether they themselves should stay. I left a dim lamp on, a beaded brown lampshade missing as many beads as it possesses, but it might have been more of a kindness to leave the room dark. The wide, sunken bed does not inspire comfort; the stained carpet does not encourage going barefoot. Nothing in here suggests relaxation. Cigarette burns aligned atop the cheap plywood desk, suggesting someone waited impatiently. The whole history of seedy, gritty residents has conspired to leave behind their indelible print and oily residue. It's disgusting. I love it. I belong here. The perfect home for a Lost King.

From behind, I breathe against his neck. It's too dim to see the tiny hairs rise, but I feel them against my stubble. My arms fold around his stomach, thick hands meeting on his belly, and I pull him in to my chest.

"Relax," I whisper. "It's okay...it's okay..."

He doesn't relax; he isn't relaxed.

While his brain is likely screaming, "Why am I here?" the rest of his body seems compelled to stay, if not relax.

I kiss the soft, olive-colored skin on his neck, rubbing the same square of flesh with my chin, while simultaneously massaging his stomach in tiny circles, letting him adjust to the feeling of me wrapped around him. He tenses when he feels my lips against him, but then he breathes, and pushes back a fraction. He melts a tiny, tiny bit. The degree he relaxes is so small, but matters so much.

After another minute of my comforting presence, my hands move in fluid motions, go under his shirt, and slowly drag it over his head. He's shirtless in a cheap motel room with a man he met only minutes ago. His body stiffens. My hands return to his smooth, brown tummy, circling the wispy trail of hair leading to treasure below.

He's self-conscious and nervous again, anxious about what I think of his body. I know this because I know. It's cute, really. This adorable muscle boy is into bears... and he's nervous about how I'll perceive his body. Worried I might judge him and find him lacking. I feel his sudden anxiety through his shoulders, in his taut breath, in the way he shifts his legs uncomfortably.

I kiss his neck with wet lips, and he shivers.

My left hand travels his chest—more hard muscle than his shirt revealed, that's for sure—up his neck to his chin, and I tip his head back onto my shoulder. I stroke the front of his neck, like a dog's, while kissing him, the rough texture of my tongue tasting him, taking his measure. He tastes clean. In a room this layered with dead skin and unidentifiable odors, that's saying something.

He's never been with a man before. Hell, he's never been with anyone. He's a virgin.

I'm going to fuck a virgin without a condom.

My dick rises instantly, as if responding to an alarm. Ready.

A virgin.

No condom.

Do it, Vin Vanbly. Be the Lost King you've always been. Fuck him. Fuck him and come inside him.

With my right hand, I unsnap his jeans.

His body stiffens. "I'm—I've never done this."

"I know. Your body already told me."

He moans, less moan than soft air escaping him, a secret exposed with a quiet vocalization.

My left hand joins my right and I unzip his jeans, holding him close to me. I allow the back of my thumb to graze his pouch, bulging now, lumpy and semihard if I'm not mistaken.

I'm not mistaken.

"It's okay, baby..." I coo into his ear, "You want this...you want this..."

I push his jeans to the floor and command him to step out of them and his shoes.

He wears sexy low-rise briefs, white ones, and as he leans over to remove his jeans, I see the deeper cleft of his ass crack. My dick throbs. I can't believe I'm going to fuck a virgin. I can't believe at my age my dick can still squirt out precum without being jacked. This kid is really doing it for me.

"Turn around. Face me."

He obeys.

Instinctively, my left hand reaches under his balls. With fingertips, I stroke them. My right hand reaches around to cup his perfect ass. My god. It's flawless, a combination of muscle and plumpness curving into ripe perfection. *No one has ever parted these cheeks!*

He breathes awkwardly, staring into my eyes, trying to understand my silence.

"Will you...undress?"

I don't answer him.

His eyes plead with me already, wondering how rough I'll be, how gentle, where our mating will fall in between. Our lips are already close, but I move my head closer, and his eyes widen, as if scared we might touch. My right hand finds the crack of his ass, and I swear it's taking all my self-control not to rip off this underwear and bite his damn ass cheek.

I speak into his parted lips. I want him to smell my warm breath.

"I'm going to give you an order. Turn around—face away from me, and slowly pull down your briefs. When you do that, Mark, you're mine. Do you understand? Your submission is complete, and your nudity is a contract agreeing you freely give me your body to use for the night."

"But—"

"All night. All mine. No resistance. Think carefully. This night and this opportunity will never come again. Are you ready? If not, get dressed. I'll drive you back."

He stands before me, bewildered, recognizing a way out of this, but not sure he has the power to take it. I remove my hands from his body and take a step back.

"Strip."

He regards me again, and his face reveals reluctance melting into imploring. *Don't push me too far. I'm new to this.* Oh, Mark. You've no idea what I planned for you.

He faces away and hooks his fingers around the band of his bone-white briefs. I can't tell if he's deliberately putting on a show for me or he's truly reluctant. I don't see his hands trembling. The way the fabric slowly reveals the roundness of his butt is like a sculptor revealing Michelangelo's *David*, the muscles, the marble innocence captured in a single smooth curve. I am not sure if drool actually leaves my mouth, but I wouldn't be surprised. I lick my lips to make sure. He pulls the briefs to his knees, forcing him to bend in front of me, then kicks them free. As suspected, his ass is smooth, no hair in the region until the backs of his thighs, fuzzing his legs with black curls which makes him appear to wear assless chaps.

He's naked.

His perfect, brown butt, taken from the oven just in time, golden brown. I'm definitely drooling.

I haven't bothered to check out his junk. It'll be perfect, I know that.

My lust yells at me to throw him on the bedspread and punch my dick so deep inside that the cashier at the convenience store hears him scream...but that's not what happens. That's not how this goes down. He deserves better for his first time.

"Get us both a beer. Bottle opener on the desk."

While he is engaged, I cross to the bed and sit, leaning against the headboard with the saggy pillows propped beneath my back. I pull out the cigar and lighter so they lie next to me on the bed. When he comes to me, his cock bobs in front, a proud hard dick rising from the black thatch of the carefully groomed base. I missed the opportunity to watch him bend over for the beers—and I regret that—but I trust another chance will come.

"Put your head on my chest."

He's embarrassed at first, awkward, but I compliment him on his body, ask him how he works out, while I stroke his thick shoulders, his neck, and kiss the top of his head. He begins to let go and soak in the masculine energy between us. He stretches out and dares—yes, dares is the right word—to drape his leg over mine, muscled and shapely lying across my jeans. He rubs his naked toes against my booted ones, the foot equivalent of holding hands.

We sip our beers and I ask him questions. Listen attentively to his answers. Sometimes it's quiet between us, and it makes him a little nervous, but I don't mind.

By his second beer, he's buzzed. He answers questions in more detail, and his true voice flows out of him more naturally.

I raise his head and angle it toward me.

His heart starts beating faster—I feel it pounding against my chest.

I spend the next fifteen minutes kissing him, guiding him with soft whispers. With my lips, I instruct him in the art of pressure and insistence, and knowing when to relent. He learns to accept my chewing on his lower lip at the end of a long kiss, to suck my tongue while I fuck it into his mouth, and to meet my strong, rough kisses with his instinctive passion.

His hard cock rubs against mine while he's on top of me. His is roughly seven inches, cut, and it bounces with nervous excitement. His hand wanders down to his dick, and I knock it away.

I throw him off me and he lands on his back.

I'm on top of him instantly, holding down his thick biceps, and he must realize in this moment how strong I am, how powerfully I've got him pinned. He can do nothing. I lift weights, too, Mark. I've been lifting for years.

I lean down to kiss him. Tenderly.

He moans and squirms, apparently not noticing I have positioned myself between his legs and forced them wider apart with each lunge. Every shade of meaning you can experience through kissing, he has already mastered, as if someone handed him a clarinet and forgot to explain it would take years to learn, so he is amazing from the onset.

I lurch forward, and his legs are suddenly around my waist.

"Oh!" His eyes go wild again.

My spittle is on his upper lip, and his eyebrows arch high in surprise. How did we end up here so quickly? This makes me feel incredibly dirty.

I grin, my twisted, lascivious grin. "You're a virgin."

My hard cock strains against my jeans, eager to touch that soft pink spot…a week's worth of semen weighing down my heavy nuts, bouncing against his tight button.

Even wearing his surprise face, he still looks strong. Strong and yet vulnerable.

I throw his legs higher and dive for his hole. My first kiss is a wet tongue kiss, and I slobber all over it.

The kid gasps.

I dive deeper, running my tongue and scratchy goatee up and down his tender anus, licking, slobbering, coating my spittle over him, his twitching butthole.

He tries to twist away but I grip his thighs and continue my assault. Virgin ass. I'm eating *virgin ass*. This drives me into a saliva frenzy, and he cries out several times when I nip at the succulent flesh. I want this to be memorable. A week from now, I want him to jack off remembering this. I slobber and slurp over and over, assaulting it and kissing it, licking it like ice cream, long strokes with the broadside of my rough tongue. Soapy. Clean. He did a good job of cleaning his butt.

I manipulate him onto his stomach so I can dive deeper. I prop exhausted bed pillows under him, and he whimpers as I suck his hole into my mouth. I don't want to distract him from the sensation in his ass, so I shuck my clothes discreetly while glued to his adorable butt. He doesn't realize I'm naked until I land on his back and align my hard cock with his ass crack.

He cries out in surprise, shocked all those tiny steps taken landed him right here, my cock hungry to tease his virgin ass and also hungry to open it up. I've enjoyed this honor twice in my life—taking a man's virginity—not enough to make me an expert but enough to feel privileged to participate. Yes, it's an honor. Despite feeling noble and poetic, I want to fuck this ass hard and blow my seed as deep as I can. The dinginess of this skank room and the stink of beer works as an aphrodisiac on me.

I reach for my cigar and the lighter. I have to lean down to reach them, which glides my shaft right between those muscle cheeks, and his whole upper body jerks in surprise. He says, "Was that it? Did you just enter me?"

"No," I say.

He flops down hard. He groans, exhausted.

He deserves to know the moment when it happens. If done right, impossible moments like that can be remembered and savored for years to come. Even as a Lost King, I will do right by him. I pull back and my cock slides away. I'm not sure my cock is suited to breach him first. Eight and a half fat inches. The amount of precum I'm drooling is amazing, so that will help, but am I really going to fuck him bareback? Can I go through with that?

I don't know.

I know my status and STD results. He's got nothing to worry about from me. But it sends the wrong message. Bareback fucked by a stranger for your first time? What kind of precedent is that? I absolutely cannot do this. It's wrong.

But I can make sure he has a good time anyway.

I light up. Puff out some clouds of smoke and lean forward again. I pull back and glide forward until he learns how to dance with me, to move when I move, following my lead. For someone who has never fucked, he's a virgin virtuoso, a master of this nonverbal communication. Who is this kid?

"Shouldn't we use a condom?"

My slick cock glides against him. "No. No condoms."

Did I just say that?

He shudders and then grumbles as if he wants to protest. I squirm. He sighs, possibly with resignation. I can't get a solid read on him. I'm sure he's feeling everything in this moment, a thousand sexual personalities exploding out of him like Pandora's box, everything unbound, creating more chaotic love in the world.

How could I say *no* so quickly? Am I going through with this? I can't. I won't. It's not right.

My cockhead stops on his hole, the puckered wet feel of it, and the invitation is now. This is now. This is happening.

"Turn over."

He says, "Should we pull back the sheets?"

"Nah. When we splatter the bedspread, we will sign the genetic guestbook of this shitty room, adding our names to its history."

He snuggles back, great affection glowing in his eyes. He's ready.

I lean into him. "Let's make history."

In halting words, he asks, "Don't people normally use condoms when they first meet?"

I know what he wants.

I say, "This isn't going to be normal."

Okay. I'm doing this. For a minute—bare for a minute and then I pull out.

I lift his legs. The cigar cloud hangs over us, protecting us from the room's other smells, scenting our oxygen with something stronger.

As I lean in to kiss him, the tip of my wet dick kisses his ass, a tandem kiss which makes his lips twist in an unfamiliar pattern. He huffs into my mouth.

Am I really doing this? I brought condoms. We need lube—

My cock sinks into him, an inch. Two inches. His eyes fly open, staring into mine.

What are you doing, you fucking Lost King?

I say, "Now. It's happening now."

Our eyes lock. I nudge deeper and his face twists. His eyes accuse me. He's either saying, "How could you do this?" Or perhaps "Please keep doing this!"

He leans back into the pillow, pulling me with him, and tears squirt out both of his eyes.

He says, "Oooohhh."

I should stop fucking him, that seems like the polite thing to do, but my cock is not feeling polite, and instead, I feel myself edging deeper into him, a little at least, a depth which should stop soon but it doesn't seem to happen, and I find his ass gripping me, welcoming me with surprising grace. I don't think those tears were from pain. I'd stop and get lube if he were in pain. I spit a lot into his ass, quite a bit, but it may not be enough.

Quietly, I speak. "You're no longer a virgin."

He arches up, pushes back against my thick shoulders, and drops down again, unsure which way to pull himself. His head flips left, then right, and he lets out a low moan, all *m*'s, a *mmmmmm* so soft it sounds like each letter attempts to sneak out unnoticed.

Haven't thought of a letter or word thing in a while.

Interesting.

I'd reflect more on this, but he's riding me or I'm pushing inside him, the last few inches convinced to comply.

He thrashes, and one of his arms shoots out from my grasp, flopping to the right as if seeking a way out.

I shouldn't do this. I shouldn't do this. This is irresponsible.

Get a condom. Get a condom. You're sending the wrong message.

Also, I don't know how long I will last fucking a virgin ass. Do other tops hunger for virgins? Is this a fetish of mine? He should not let me come inside him. He should save himself for love, someone who loves him back. Not a stranger. Not me. Love must guide him to wait until the right time.

Oh god.

Stop fucking him!

I need to explain about love before it's too late. How you can't take for granted the beauty of our sexuality, that is yes, you can take it for granted—that's sometimes beautiful too, in its own odd way. I'm not sure my explanations will make sense. What am I going to say to this kid, how about explaining there's nothing wrong with casual fucking if that's what your heart desires, but your virginity is sacred—

Oh man, I have to say this immediately or it's going to get messy and globby inside him. Very soon.

I'm dimly aware of the lit cigar in my right hand, ash on the pillow, and the strong curl of acidic scent wafting over us, and he breathes it deeply, a wispy finger curling around the nape of his neck, his short black hair, those big eyes, shining—he should wait for someone he loves. To love someone, to love the person you're with, is what matters and what I must tell him. *Hurry.* Tell him about love.

I eyeball him hard. "Love—"

He jerks and tightens his legs around my back, causing my cock to get squeezed hard, gripped by the strength of him, the inside strength of Mark, and, I can't stop it.

I come.

Our eyes lock onto each other's, speaking a language without words.

My semen shoots out of my dick like gunfire, blasting shot after shot.

This wasn't supposed to happen!

Pull out! Pull out!

Instead, I keep jackrabbiting, fucking my semen into him, pushing it deeper, deeper, and what am I doing, my god—now he screams at the top of his lungs, his powerful voice ringing through the room with a ferocity sure to attract notice. Eyes wide open, we scream into each other's mouths.

Good god, pull out!

His cock squirts me right on the forehead, and he howls again with surprising alarm. Maybe that's not alarm but joy that doesn't quite yet know how to be joy, so the surprised alarm infused into his voice is his expression of a new reality.

His eyes search mine, his question obvious by the shock on his face. *Did that just happen?*

My eyes search his. *Did that just happen?*

We ping-pong this question between each other, over and over, and the proof is my still-hard dick inside him, sawing more slowly, still pumping—and pushing my sperm deeper. My god.

Vin, what have you done? You absolute selfish moron, what the fuck have you done?

We're afraid to break eye contact, he and I. I am afraid to speak. What can I say? He didn't insist on a condom, and he could have. No. This is on you. You're the Lost King. Now you're really sinking into it. You fucked a virgin without a condom. You denied him a condom.

You came inside him!

My cock keeps pumping him.

Fix this! Fix this you shitty, stupid waste of a man!

He wrenches his head to the side, ripping away from my gaze as if desperate for escape.

I can speak again. I have to fix this.

Fix this!

Mark! Mark! Mark!

I take a deep breath. "Once there was a tribe where every man was the one true king. Odd you may think, and ask yourself how any work got done. But these were not those kinds of kings."

"No," he says, and the word oozes out of him, like semen from—no.

His eyes remain closed. His chest rises and falls as he takes longer breaths, and his legs unclench from my back.

I'm still fucking him.

Breathing shallowly, he squeaks out more words. "No kings, Vin. No kings."

He pants in the half shadow from the beaded lampshade.

Okay, Marky.

No kings.

Two

What have I done?

What the hell have I done?

Vin Vanbly, you selfish asshole, what have you done? Vin, you just bareback fucked a virgin, a man you physically met—first time—earlier tonight in a convenience store parking lot. Then, after getting him drunk on two beers, you fucked him raw in a cheap motel while smoking a cigar. Yup, that sums it up. An impressionable man with no prior experience. A man you've only known through emails and IMs. You're a horrible person. What kind of man does that? A selfish asshole.

I'll explain—

Oh.

No, I won't.

I *can't.*

I can't because he's...snoring. Is that possible? Yes, he's snoring.

My cock is still buried inside him. I should pull out. I mean, Jesus, he's unconscious. Why am I fucking an unconscious man? Pull out, you psycho! Did I fuck him unconscious? This must be illegal—you can't fuck an unconscious person. I'm breaking the law.

Boy, you fucked up this time, Vin Vanbly. He's fucking unconscious, you asshole.

I slowly begin to withdraw.

"Nooooo," he groans, and turns to me, eyes still closed. "Don't pull out if you don't have to."

Despite my intense reservations, his half-pleading tone makes my dick get harder again. Damn it. Why am I not getting softer? I have to quit being turned on by this.

Almost immediately his shyness returns, and his eyes flutter open.

"I wasn't asleep."

"You snored."

"That's not proof." He gazes at me with bleary earnestness.

I can't believe my dick remains inside him—still—and I'm not doing anything to remedy that. What's wrong with me?

His hands rise to my shoulders as if he wants to push me off, but instead he grips them. "I told you I have narcolepsy. It doesn't mean I'm really asleep. I mean, technically, yes, but I'm usually awake again right away."

We stare at each other in mutual surprise. How am I still inside him? Why is my cock still hard? This almost never happens. Hell, I'm thirty-eight! My dick doesn't—oh god, that feels good. He squeezed again and it's so wet.

"You're still fucking me," he says.

"I am."

I want to explain this is not okay—you can't chat up someone online, meet them in a parking lot—but wet squishy sounds between us drive me crazy, and I can't think of anything but how we smell. Yes, okay, fine, I won't deny it was very possibly the greatest orgasm I have ever known, ever. And yes, that's a big fucking deal because I've exploded amazing orgasms with phenomenal men. Perry on Mount Tam. Mai in the corn. But a few moments ago...his eyes locked on mine. Neither of us could free ourselves. I need to remember every second, play it over and over.

And yet, what have I done? Stupid, selfish fuck. Why the hell didn't you whip out a condom? You brought them, you idiot.

Ow!

Cigar. Ash burns my thumb. The cigar's orange glow burns my fingers.

Ow!

"Hang on. I need to stub out this cigar." To reach the nightstand, I lean forward and push farther into him. This close, I smell him—the scent of his skin, the spice which is his own. It's better than the cigar smell.

He groans and hikes his hips as if to retreat, but he doesn't, not much, and by the time I stub out the cigar on a pizza takeout menu, he wakes up, which means he had fallen asleep again. Boy, that happened fast.

"Was I defensive about my narcolepsy?"

"Yes, a little."

He nods, taking this in.

We watch each other's eyes for clues on what to say next.

"I get defensive," he says solemnly.

I'm afraid if we stop fucking, we'll have to talk, talk with words, and our bodies feel so attuned already. I lean over to kiss him because he seems to need kissing, and this kiss leads to more kissing and more kissing and the sounds becoming wetter and the kissing becomes fiercer, and his legs lock around my lower back again, his heels on my ass, pulling me into him.

He's a virgin. He can't take much more of this.

I can't resist basking in his masculine beauty, the half-light reflecting off his coal hair, the almost curls behind his ear, the tantalizing scent of him. I'm not one to fuck a second time, not immediately. Yes, I have with certain kings, Jamie, and

Dewey, who—come to think of it—was a virgin as well. So, that's three... Maybe I do have a virgin fetish?

"Oh," he cries out, as if he'd forgotten our connection and a deeper jab has reminded him.

I might worry I'm hurting him, but following his cries, he squeezes and pulls me deeper, and I come to understand his outbursts are moments of surprised pleasure. He cries out and arches up, his body moving with muscular grace as he writhes and twists around my cock. My brain debate rages on—demanding I pull out, this is the wrong message to send—but even while I cajole myself to do the right thing, I feel those internal triggers—knowing my orgasm is imminent—and push as deep as I can.

Into his open mouth, I gasp when I speak. "I'm coming."

I shouldn't do this!

I unload again, staring into his eyes, the depths of them impossible to fathom. I cannot imagine what he's thinking, what he's seeing. He confounds me. Is that why I didn't pull out? Because I couldn't tell what's happening inside him? That's a terrible reason. I fuck him harder as I shoot, hoping to understand his eyes and what he feels in this exact second. As the last shots blast through me, I fuck harder.

With the final spurt, I cry out because I cannot believe this is happening. I've enjoyed lots of sex, amazing sex. Why does this feel like my first time as well? This is happening, and I'm not even fighting it. Meet a virgin online. Fly out to New Jersey to fulfill his parking lot fantasy. Fuck him raw. Come inside him. Truly, I've sunk as far as a Lost King can sink.

He looks at me with surprise. "Oh! Vin!"

My hands push his biceps deeper into the mattress, and he cries out, shooting a small river of sperm on his stomach and almost up to his pecs. This kid comes a lot.

We return to a state of breathing in synch, each of us returning from our meander through physical bliss, we rehash the experience though eye contact alone. Without actual words, he tells me he is all right, he's doing fine, and he grins this sexy smile that suggests better than fine.

Okay. Okay.

I pant. I pant and feel sweat drip down my back.

Fuck. I fucked him twice.

My dick shrinks. Almost involuntarily, I pull out.

Aaaaaaaand, he's asleep again.

He told me about the narcolepsy. I read two books about it, the chemistry behind it. Not everyone gets the same symptoms. Not everyone spontaneously naps. But I didn't know how it would feel in this moment, staring at his sleeping—

And, he's awake!

His eyes shoot open as if he closed them only to better recall a forgotten detail. His hand reaches to my face, tracing sweat along my cheek. "Is it always like this? Sex?"

"No."

I want to explain how this was special, unique, impossible—but no words come out.

He nods as if we'd concluded a much longer conversation. I think he understands. Does he?

Still holding him in my arms, I transition from on top to his side.

Shit.

Now, we'll have to talk.

"It didn't hurt," he says, his face studying mine. "Everyone says your first time hurts. It has to."

"It doesn't have to."

"Well, my best friend said it would. Of course, she never had butt sex, so she didn't know firsthand."

I smile at the idea of his having discussed his upcoming deflowering with his best friend. I'm not gonna initiate the bareback conversation. I'm not going to ruin this moment. But we will have that conversation, and soon. I can't part ways with him without warning him and extracting a promise he'll use condoms in the future. I owe him that at least. We shouldn't have done this. It's my fault. I sent him a very wrong message, and I'll have to fix this.

"You look worried. Does it bother you when I fall asleep?"

Don't stress him out. Say *no*. "Yes."

Goddamn it.

"What I meant was, I know you're not sleeping intentionally. But I want you here with me. Awake. Looking at me. Sleep steals you."

He nods at this answer. "My sister Patty used to say that, when I was little. She would get mad at me for leaving our conversations. At her tea parties, she would line me up with her dolls, and I would fall over, asleep. She organized us by height."

I smile. "I'm not mad."

He touches my face. "I would know if you were."

He probably wouldn't, but the thought is sweet.

I roll him on his side and maneuver behind, wrapping myself around him. With one hand on his stomach, stroking the warm puddle of his jizz, I feel his breath enter and leave him. He pushes back against me and nuzzles, making small grunting sounds of satisfaction.

"Are you cold?"

"No," he says.

After a few minutes of this intimate silence, he says, "Are we supposed to clean up?"

"It's up to us. Do you want to?"

Quietly, he says, "No."

We stay in this position until his breathing becomes more rhythmic, and I realize I truly am jealous of sleep for stealing him from me.

I can't believe I fucked him bareback. So wrong. So very, very wrong.

"I'm not awake," he says brightly, cheerfully, as if midparagraph instead of his opening sentence. "I mean, I'm not asleep."

I kiss the back of his neck. "Okay. You're not asleep."

"It's not like this happens all the time," he says. "Mostly in peak experiences created by high-intensity situations, such as extreme fear or heightened emotional awareness."

"You're quoting a book."

"My doctor," he says. "I have to explain myself sometimes."

"Are you experiencing extreme fear?"

"Duh. No." He pushes back into me for emphasis, and apparently, this is the only explanation I will receive.

Moments later, he says, "I was diagnosed young. Most narcos don't get it until they're eight or nine, but Patty kept asking Mom and Dad why I slept so funny. Not a lot of people have the kind I do where you fall asleep for short periods of time. That's a myth. My parents had noticed, but our older brother fell asleep in weird ways, and he grew out of it, so they didn't worry. But it made Patty cry, so they finally took me to a doctor to find out."

He flips over on the bedspread with the agility of a cat, and ends up in my arms, his nose inches from my face. His expression is hard to read, as if he's pondering something deep, considering the best possible way to raise the topic.

"You're still inside me," he says. "All of your sperm."

A pang of anxiety sweeps through me. It's time for the conversation. I have to tell him I was selfish and wrong. It was wrong. He should never do this again. But don't freak him out, don't make him feel he's made a big mistake. The fault is mine.

"I suppose I am."

"What do I do with it?"

"Go squeeze it out in the bathroom."

"Do I have to?"

"No, I guess not. I mean, maybe you should—"

"Yeah, but what's the accepted etiquette? What do guys do? I don't know. I'm a virgin."

"No. You're not."

He is surprised by my words and lifts himself on one elbow. "You're right. Not anymore."

My face gets serious. "I'm glad you brought this up. We should have a conversation about bareback sex."

"No," he says, and he raises a finger to my eyebrow. "Let me do this."

I am not sure what "this" is, exactly, but his index finger pushes my head back into the pillow, then traces my eyebrow, as if grooming it into place. With fingertips, he explores the space between my brows, and then grooms the other one. He traces the creases—who am I kidding, wrinkles—across my forehead, the planes of my cheek, and thoroughly brushes my goatee, quarter inch by quarter inch, as if scouring for something he knows to be hidden within. When I occasionally open my eyes, glancing his way, I see he studies me with the attention of a medical specialist. I understand what "this" is. He wants to touch me. Remember this. Remember these moments.

When he speaks, he's so quiet it's almost like he doesn't want me to hear. "You spend your whole life being one thing, thinking of yourself in this one way. And then it's over. Everything is different but nothing has changed."

This seems to require no response, so I offer none, just allow him to continue outlining me.

"I was a virgin all my life. Up until an hour ago."

"Do you feel different?"

"Absolutely. Don't you?"

I'm not sure how to respond. How do I feel? Ashamed. Guilty. Like an older, Internet scumbag, preying on innocent youth. I decide to respond with the truth. "I do feel different."

He nods, as if this were self-evident.

"Everything changed," he says, and his eyes close again.

With his fingers hovering over my right eye, he dips his head forward, resting it on mine.

That's it? That's all it takes for him to nod off? I spend my whole life trying to fall asleep, every night a challenge to forget who I am, the things I've done, the lives I've ruined, and the people who hate me. This guy, this magnificent, muscled—

"I'm not asleep," he says, his eyes still closed. "I know you think I am, but I'm just resting my eyes."

"Okay, Mark."

A moment later, he's snoring.

Peak experiences created by high-intensity situations.

He bolts awake in my arms, a miniscule jerk, but it's enough.

"Welcome back."

He pulls away from me. "I normally don't drop off this much. But I stopped taking my medication a week ago."

"Why?"

"I wanted you to see me like this. My worst. See if you'd still like me."

I kiss his forehead.

A new fear begins to gnaw inside me. I knew this would happen. You can't take someone's virginity without them falling in love with you, a little at least. His comment implies he sees a future for us when, obviously, there can be none.

Be careful in this, Vin. Do not disrespect his emotions. But it's time to change the energy.

"Who wants pizza?"

He raises his head. "Seriously?"

I grin. "It's not late. Plus, sex makes me hungry."

He sits up, his face mildly alarmed. "Where?"

"Where else? Romero's. The late-night place you always talked about in our IM chats. You said you and your roommates would chow down on their bacon and onion with garlic ranch dressing. Best pizza on the East Coast."

I extract myself and scoot to the edge of the bed, glancing around for the jockstrap I wore tonight. As I slip my legs into my jeans, he finally speaks.

"We can't go there."

"Sure we can."

"No, I mean, we can't. I know people who go there."

"Mark, do you trust me?"

My stomach twists. *You asshole, Vin! You just fucking barebacked a virgin who suggested we use condoms. How dare you ask—*

"Yes."

I'm surprised by the strength of his reply. The confidence of it. Over pizza, I'll talk to him about using condoms. How wrong I was.

"Do you trust I'm going to treat you right in your stomping grounds?"

"Yes."

"Okay. Get dressed. Don't forget who's in charge. You wanted me to be in charge of you this weekend. So, get dressed."

"Aren't we going to shower?"

"Nope. We're scuzzballs who had incredible, sweaty sex in a run-down motel. We don't take showers."

He says, "Right. Scuzzballs."

Mark's not facing me. I only hear the words said softly and with reluctance.

"Check the top drawer, Mark. I got you something to wear tonight."

The bedsprings crunch behind me, and the shifting weight tells me when he's off the bed. He wrenches the crude drawer open.

"You got me a stripper thong?"

"Yup. You wear it and it pushes your junk to the front."

"It's purple."

"Yeah."

"And sparkly. It's totally a stripper's thong."

"Yeah. I figured I'd make you strip for me later."

He laughs. "Oh my god. Do you honestly expect me to wear this?"

"Yes, Mark. I do."

Through IM and emails, he was clear about what he wanted. He wanted to be dominated. But in a loving way. I've never met someone so articulate about what they want from an experience. Keep your voice even, Vin, and keep your shit together. I barebacked a virgin and came in him. Twice. This is unnerving me more than I anticipated. It's completely irresponsible. I hate that I'm this way.

"Put it on."

Focus on him. I turn to watch.

He bends over to slip in one leg, and I stare at his ass for telltale signs—wow, that ass is perfect. I feel this incredible surge course through me. Pride? Gratitude? I was the first ever to fuck that gorgeous ass, which of course, makes me feel terrible, because only a terrible person would bareback fuck a virgin after said virgin suggested they use condoms. I'm horrible.

As he stretches the shiny fabric over his junk, he shakes his head. I see resignation and doubt in his eyes. He knows the safe word. He can say *pineapples* at any moment and end my domination.

He must feel okay with this on some level, because once he adjusts it into place, snark appears on his face. "Happy?"

"I am. How's it feel?"

"Weird. Slippery. Do I get to wear jeans, or is this it?"

"Jeans are optional. Your call."

He scoffs. "Golly. Thanks."

I like him. I can't fall in love with him, of course. Kingly as he may be, this isn't a King Weekend. It's a sex weekend. An "I-took-your-virginity" weekend. No, wait, could I still make it a King Weekend? Over pizza, I'll—no. No, he didn't want that. He expressed zero interest knowing anything about the Lost and Founds.

No kings.

He wanted me to take his virginity. Sex weekend. I have never done anything like this, but he wanted to be dominated all weekend and I decided I could help. But I fucked this up. I took his power. He suggested condoms, and I should have—*enough*. Discuss over pizza.

He snaps his jeans and examines his bulge in the room's full-length mirror. Nobody can look good in that cloudy piece of crap, but holding his socks, Mark pulls it off, a dirty janitor in his reflection, a Mediterranean prince in this world. I catch him looking at me. He shakes his head and rolls his eyes.

He's quiet on the ride across town, well, not across town actually, just a few neighborhoods beyond this run-down area. He takes my hand and looks out the window.

We're here.

As we pull into the strip mall parking lot, Romero's appears to be nothing special, wedged between a dollar store and a defunct laundromat. A few other straggler businesses—Chinese takeout at one end, a national hardware store at the other—anchor the group. Mark and his two college roommates frequent this place. Maybe he fears running into them. Or someone from the neighborhood. He grew up around here. As we park, I see every patron, all three of them, through the floor-to-ceiling front glass. Oh, there's a fourth person, a guy in a ball cap hunched over, munching away. Nobody seems to be Mark's age, but still. We can't predict who will come and go.

This may not be a King Weekend, but I can offer a few assets he will need as a fully sexual adult. Like sexual confidence. To be seen in public with someone you're having sex with, and experience how that feels. Does it make you feel stronger? Proud of whom you attract? Time for him to find out.

Hell, I'm no catch. I'm older. I've got some muscle definition, true, but also chunky love handles, which seem to have no interest in departing. I've got face wrinkles and eyes that appear bruised from lack of sleep—he could find someone much hotter than me in an instant. In fact, I wouldn't be surprised if he's ashamed of me, which is okay. This is about him and how he works through those feelings. We will find out if anything challenges him tonight. And if nothing happens, that's okay too. Taking the risk of wearing the purple thong and the possibility of friends approaching is almost the same as it actually happening. Whether friends show or not, courage was required.

I open my door. "You coming inside?"

"I dunno," he says. "This is weird."

"How so?"

"Well, my cock is all slippery in my jeans for starters. That feels weird. Kinda good. Kinda weird. When I walk, will this thong ride up? Every seat in Romero's is a stool, and if I lean over, everyone will see I'm this big whore wearing a thong. That's weird number two."

"You're not a big whore."

"I feel like it."

"Mark, you're a sexual person. You're not a virgin anymore. That's not being a whore. Allow yourself to feel sexual."

The hint of a smile flits over him but somehow butterflies its way into a frown. He crosses his arms.

"Okay. Maybe I'm pushing you too hard, Mark. You wait here in the truck. You don't have to go in with me. I'm dying to try this amazing pizza you described, so I will get two slices. One to eat there in the shop, while it's hot, and the other to go. You want me to get you a slice to go? We'll eat it at the motel. Together."

"No," he says, and I sense he already regrets the word.

"Mark."

He looks at me.

"This place is important to you. It's one of the first places Brian took you on an outing—your brothers' day out. You also told me it's where you, Brian, and Patty would eat when your parents went on a date. It's one of your regular hangouts.

I want to share a slice with you in there. That would mean something to me. If you're not ready for that, I understand."

His features soften.

"You did good, putting on that thong instead of fighting me. You didn't complain once."

"I rolled my eyes."

"You did what I told you to do. That's good enough for tonight. C'mere."

He leans over to me and we kiss.

"You're doing great, Mark."

I'm the fuckup here. Not you.

He says nothing else.

Damn.

I climb out of the truck.

I had hoped to talk to him over pizza. Explain what I did was wrong. We should have used condoms. Yet, maybe a little alone time is good. I need to privately freak and figure out what to say. How do I fix this? I know he loved the raw sex. I have to tell him he can't love it—can't do it again. For his health.

As I stroll away, he remains, watching me.

As soon as I enter, a strong garlic-and-baking-crust aroma envelops me, wrapping around my face. Other smells. Yum. I don't have a distinguished enough palate to identify each one, but I recognize the knee-buckling aroma of incredible pizza. My stomach grumbles.

Apparently, you can be an Internet scumbag and still get very hungry.

I pay for three slices of bacon and onion pizza, Mark's favorite. Two sodas, though I explain I'm only picking up one right now. I ask them to keep one of my slices hot behind the counter. I still have hopes he will come in. The air smells like butter—garlic butter. I want to rub the air all over me. I can only hope it sticks to my clothes.

They hand me my two slices, angry cheese bubbles rippling, and the smell of bacon fat punching its way into my reptilian brain. My god. I don't see how I can wait for this to cool. I'm going to burn the roof of my mouth. I know it.

I sit at the front window so he can watch me blow across the tip to cool it. I don't know if this helps the pizza get cooler. He's still—oh. He's sleeping, I think.

After an impatient thirty seconds, I risk a hearty bite and sink my teeth into hot cheese.

Oh my god.

Marky was right.

This pizza tastes amazing. Holy shit.

I scarf another two bites before I set it down, chewing happily, and pull an index card from my jacket pocket. I use my favorite pen and introduce the two, writing a short phrase.

I set the notecard facedown on the space next to me, two spaces away from the guy bobbing to the tunes blasting in his headphones.

Less than three minutes later, Mark approaches my side with his slice.

"Hey."

"Hey."

The note. I knew I'd get him with a note.

"Thanks for paying for my slice," he says quietly.

"No problem."

"I guess you figured I'd eventually come in, huh?"

"What made you come in, Mark?"

He shrugs without the full motion of a shrug, just the hint of one. A shrugette.

"You don't know? Oh, please." I kick the leg of his stool. "Give me a fucking break."

He smiles bashfully and raises the pizza to his mouth.

"No, Mark. Don't take a bite. Set it down. No pizza until you tell me why you came in."

He glances at the notecard and then to me.

He reaches for it.

I place my soda on top of it.

"What made you come inside, Mark?"

He sighs. "I saw you write that guy a note. The one with the headphones. I wanted to see what it said."

He's jealous. Be careful. I am his first serious infatuation. For him, this may already feel like love.

Which is even more reason we should have practiced safe sex. Ugh. That thought ruins this moment. This pizza is so good, so amazing. Why ruin it with that conversation now?

"What did you write to him?"

I move my soda. "You can eat your pizza now. And read the note."

In block letters, he reads, I CAME TO NEW JERSEY TO BE WITH YOU AND ONLY YOU.

He snickers when he reads this, obviously pleased, and mumbles when he says, "Figures."

He laughs to himself and swings his playful gaze my way. "You got me."

I find myself getting hard again. Wow. Three times in one night? It's not unheard of for me, but still.

This man is hot.

When we get back to the motel, I will teach him everything there is to know about cocksucking.

THREE

"**M**mmmmmmmmmmmmmm."

I hear his purring and feel him cat-stretching against me. I'm not really awake. My head feels like sludge, like I've got a hangover, but I don't. I know I'm not hungover. Three beers isn't enough. No, it's a sleep hangover. I slept so much. I never sleep this much.

My eyes pop open.

Shit, what's wrong? I never sleep this much!

I panic.

What's wrong?

The *mmmmmmmm* sound Mark makes keeps elongating, growling beyond his mere wakeup to convey other nuanced meanings, such as he feels glad to awaken, no, wait—ready to sleep again, and finally, no, I'm truly awake.

Nothing... My heartbeat slows. Nothing's wrong. I slept. Oh man, I slept for hours and hours in a row! I never sleep next to another man, except on a King Weekend, so for a split second I thought I had failed to enact some weekend activity, some protocol...but I'm not on a King Weekend. This is so eerie. No King Weekend. I didn't stalk him for a month. I didn't plan anything, other than a new suit and dinner at a fancy restaurant tonight. I feel empty. Who am I if I'm not kinging a man?

Unfortunately, I know the answer to that question. This weekend, I am an Internet scumbag. A Lost King. I preyed on a young virgin to get my rocks off. Okay, yes, the sex was amazing. Yes, it was the best orgasm—quit it. Quit thinking that way. You violated a young—god, *I'm so sick of this conversation in my head*! Tough luck, asshole. Last night, you never had the balls to instruct Mark not to fuck raw with random guys he meets online. Make that conversation happen today.

His head disappears under the sheet.

Oh god! His lips sink around my cock. My eyes spring open. Any thought of meaningful conversation flies away. His entire mouth focuses on the head, not sucking, not anything, merely holding my spongy cock head with his lips.

Just like I taught him last night.

My hand goes to his skull, gripping him.

Sometimes, I explained, this is the most effective way to get a man hard—to do nothing but wait. The inactivity will drive a guy nuts—the feeling of warmth around his—

It's working. I'm getting hard.

"Mark!" My word emerges as a gasp.

How can I be getting hard? I'm almost forty. I came three times last night. Three times. I'm not in my twenties any—oh god. *Oh god!* He's a quick study, this young king. Fuuuuuuuuuuuuuuuuuuuck.

Okay, yes, fine. I will fuck a load into his throat this morning. Suck one or two loads out of him—he's inexhaustible; he's twenty-four. And then, breakfast. That's what normal people do on a weekend, right? They go out for breakfast without manipulative plans?

Eggs and bacon. Maybe panca—

Oh god. He's using my ball rubbing techniques with wet fingers! Fuuuuuuuuuuuuuuuuuck!

Breakfast was an unmitigated disaster, between Mark asking questions about my life in St. Paul, and my lame attempts to answer. I can't talk about my life. How could I explain the odd skills I continuously sharpen are exclusively for King Weekends? How do you explain you have no hobbies but shooting pool and insomnia? He asked me how I hung out with my friends. I changed the topic. What should I have said? I have no friends? On every topic, I was elusive and mumbly quiet. I'm not good at normal conversation. I know what to say on a King Weekend. I always know what to say. Around Mark, I must fight to prevent his seeing the real me, the broken, dysfunctional mess I am.

Of course, it won't matter after this weekend.

I'll never see him again.

Despite my perverse inability to converse, our connection remained. He laughed at some of my distracting comments. He blushed and grinned as I reminded him of fucking last night. But is that a good thing or bad thing? I want him to have an amazing deflowering weekend...but I don't want him feeling *in love* after I leave. In emails, I explained he would likely develop feelings for me. I explained he should enjoy those feelings but accept the limitations. I am a one-weekend kind of guy. I explained this. He understood. He agreed.

Never mind.

Deal with it later.

One good thing from breakfast is I made the decision to deal with all of it later—his feelings for me, the bareback sex. Mark made his sausage links argue in Brooklyn accents, prompting me to decide there's no point to spoiling our time together. I mean, I do like him a lot. He's hot. The sex is unbelievable. And he's funny. Of course I like him a lot. If I didn't already enjoy him, I couldn't have shown up for this crazy weekend. Do people actually do this? Meet online for a weekend to hang out and have sex? What on earth do they talk about?

We walk in silence, watching the Ironbound neighborhood wake up. Awkward for me, but Mark is humming and unconscious of how hard it is for me to merely hang out. Not control our every conversation.

C'mon, Vin. Navel gaze later.

Newark surprises me with its charm. When I travel to this part of the country, I spend my time in New York. I don't go to Jersey. But Ironbound boasts colorful blue-collar homes, apricot and lemon on tree-lined streets. On our right, an olive-green Victorian is meticulously painted, its trim and porch spindles pink-orange and gingerbread brown, two surprising colors complementing well. For some reason, the colors inspire me to believe people from different backgrounds can be friends. The brick building on our right displays burnt-yellow mums on its front stoop, basking in the bleak November sun. The faded blue mailbox perched at the corner is slathered in layers of graffiti, true, but the streets are well maintained. Not much scattered garbage. We turn left and pass a bakery, already open for many hours according to their sign, and a bead shop, which won't open for another hour. A blocker farther, sidewalk chalk advertises an art show somewhere in the neighborhood later today. Might be fun to attend. Is that what people do on non–King Weekends? I don't know. Most shops aren't open, but a few, here and there, blink their eyes in the morning sun. Ready to start the day.

"I was right about those pancakes, wasn't I?"

I say, "You were right."

"I know my cakes. The pecan ones are their best."

"The bacon was perfect. Crispy with fat. Hey, you know this neighborhood well? Restaurants and stuff?"

Mark says, "Sorta. We didn't spend a lot of time here. The 'Guese get pissed when you try to pick their pockets, so my friends and I stuck to Penn station and a few other hot spots."

"Geese?"

"Portuguese. This is their neighborhood, predominantly. They keep it up."

He looks so innocent, smiling at me, at the sun, at everything, I forget he possesses street experience. Never in a formal gang, never that level of trouble, but when he and his buddies needed spending money, they acquired it. In an IM, he once referred to stealing as "kid stuff," but I think he might have been a tougher kid than most. In an email, he described his first true fistfight at twelve. His description made me want to puke. But the sun now beams on him, and he beams back with showy confidence. Is this his natural confidence, or does he glow from last night's sex? Don't know.

Odd to think I only knew him for an hour in his virgin state.

We pass a shopkeeper with braided gray hair, sweeping her stoop before business arrives, and it's so idyllic, the sunlight, her sweeping, I can't help but compliment her on her long skirt, Celtic tribal patterns flowing to her ankles. We chatter, me flirting, asking if she's single, and, okay, maybe swaggering a teeny bit for Mark, who laughs with his hands over his face until she shoos us away with her broom and resumes her task, shaking her head.

Mark says, "You're the worst. You know that?"

"Oh, come on. She flirted back."

"She hit you with a broom, Vin. You're terrible."

He's right. I am terrible. But even that cannot ruin this morning.

Hell, I survived breakfast conversation.

A block and a half later, we reach a local grocery, and Mark suggests grabbing bottles of water. Good idea if we continue to wander on foot. I'm not sure if we are, because I'm not in control of this. But I'm not panicking. Am I? No. Not yet. I underestimated how stressful this would be, not knowing how we will spend today. I have no script. I have no planned activities until retrieving his suit, and then dinner tonight. What do we do? Just talk? About what? I exhausted all my conversational topics over breakfast. I can't do this.

Don't freak out.

As we ponder the many water options, Mark says, "The kind of water you pick out will tell me a lot about what kind of person you are. Fizzy or fruit flavored? Are you more of a vitamin water guy or—"

"Mark? Mark Benson?"

An older man—well, not older exactly, maybe ten or so years older than me— interrupts Mark's impromptu psychology test, and Mark's reaction is to make his face blank. He's uncomfortable.

Mark says, "Hey, Coach."

His voice sounds weak and unsure.

The man regards me with a curt smile, as if trying to determine what business I have with someone he knows. I feel him evaluating me, even as he faces Mark. Instinctively, I dislike him. Something is off. He's holding two cans of Brussels sprouts, but that's not it. Though seriously, who buys canned Brussels sprouts? He looks normal enough, windbreaker, and a Newark Bears baseball cap. Black-and-gray tufts coming from either side. Little paunch, not too much.

Oh shit—do I recognize him from somewhere? Is that it?

"How've you been, Mark?"

Do I know this guy from my past life? Shit!

No...no, wait. Calm down. You're on edge. You're freaking out for no reason. You don't know this guy.

"Good. Great, really. You?"

"Good, good." The coach glances at me. "Same old, same old."

I don't know him. He looks familiar, but no. I would have remembered his unfriendly face. He's not ugly, just unfriendly.

An uncomfortable silence falls among us.

I could say something—anything—to remove this tension, but fuck it. I want to see what Mark does. Will he introduce me as his date? Will he pretend we're buddies or invent a lie of omission? I won't get offended if he does, but what will he do? He said he was out of the closet to everyone who matters. Who will he choose to be?

At last, Mark says to me, "Coach used to coach me in little league. Again in traveling league."

Coach trains his steely eyes on me. "I've known Mark a long time."

"Oh yeah?"

Coach waits for me to chime in.

Well, fuck him. I refuse to give him any information. I smile pleasantly. Nod.

He holds out his hand. "I'm Jim."

I shake it. "Hi, Jim."

Mark blushes hard, and I hate doing this to him, making him squirm, but it's important he sees who he is in these moments, when his adult life as a sexual man clashes with those who knew him back when.

"This is Vin," he says, the words rushing out of him. "We're on a date."

Coach Jim doesn't allow surprise to show on his face. "Oh, you are?"

A thrill of pride rushes through me. *Good for you, Mark. Good for fucking you.*

I nod. Smile pleasantly.

Also smiling, Jim says, "You seem much older than Mark."

Smile pleasantly. "Do I?"

"It's a first date, but it's going well," Mark says, obviously flustered. "But we should get going. We've got a lot to do today."

The man nods with an abrupt quality and I hate the judgment he's showering on Mark. He's bullying Mark. Simultaneously, I'm delighted how Mark handles this man, this judgmental prick.

Jim deliberately ignores me. "How's your mom, Mark? How's she doing?"

"She's okay," he says, obviously squirming. "Not great. I mean, not terrible, just not...just not...not well, right now."

Obviously, this former coach presses a known sore spot. Asshole. I hate to witness Mark struggle like this. I wonder what's wrong with his mom. If I had stalked him, I'd know. He never talked about her. I should ask later.

"We should go," I announce. "Lots to do, Coach."

He returns his hard gaze. "Is that right, Vin?"

What an asshole!

"Yeah, Jim. Sex, mostly. Lots and lots of sex."

Jim is clearly too surprised to speak.

"Oh my god," Mark says under his breath.

He takes my hand, and after grabbing the two closest bottles of water, says, "Good to see you, Coach. Take care."

As soon as we're a dozen feet away, Mark says, "You have, like, zero people skills."

"I didn't like how he pressured you."

"Yeah, well, I handled it."

"You did. Very well. I'm genuinely impressed."

"Oh, boy. That means a lot coming from the guy who brags about our sex life to people at the supermarket. Great job with that."

We reach the checkout line, the shortest one, which is three or four patrons deep. He hasn't let go of my hand. Mark chuckles to himself, and I sense he's not terribly upset after all.

"I can't believe you, Vin. *'Lots and lots of sex.'*" He guffaws. "What kind of person says that? Why would you—were you raised in a barn?"

This tweaks me in an unpleasant way.

"Rats. I was raised in the sewers by rats."

Why would you say that, you idiot?

I'm horrified that sentence popped out of me the way it did. I felt a sharp stab of irritation by his "raised in a barn" comment, and yet, I didn't mean to share that! *Fuck! What is wrong with me?*

"Well, my money was on raised by wolves. And don't try to gross me out talking about rats. I love rats. I owned two growing up. Whiskers and Horace the Great. They crawled all over me while I slept. It was very comforting. Patty hated them but Brian liked them. He and I used to have rat races."

Mark's not afraid of rats?

Before I can formulate any further thoughts, I ask, "Why Horace 'The Great'?"

Mark places our water bottles at the end of the conveyer belt. "Because he was *great.*"

Change the subject. *Change it!* "What does our water say about us, Mark? What was revealed?"

"That we're mortified and desperate to get out of the store," he says.

While he shakes his head with exaggerated disappointment, I see him laughing. He turns away while simultaneously leaning against me and says, "Oh, Vin."

He likes rats.

Maybe today will be a good day.

Today is terrible.

I was wrong. So wrong. I don't know what I'm doing. What gave me the confidence to think I could handle today? I don't know how to do this, to walk around casually, killing time.

We come upon a bookstore, Toppe and Earl's Used Books. Mark stops to investigate the mobile shelves wheeled out front. I catch him glancing inside, eyes exploring.

"Mark, let's go inside."

He says, "Okay."

People do this. Wander through a bookstore and get to know each other, talk about mutual interests and hobbies. He reads titles. I hover a few yards away, pretending to read. Should I talk to him? Should I ignore him, give him space? If I were alone, I might stay here for two or three hours, revisiting favorite titles or discovering new adventures. How long do we stay here? How does a person do this, this *hanging out*, without an agenda, without a king story to tell? I don't like it. There's no structure. There's no...it's chaos, is what this is.

After a while, I'm so uncomfortable, I fall back on the one dimension of human behavior where I have any skills—sex. I lure Mark to the deserted travel section, and once alone, I put my hands on either side of his face and pull him into a kiss.

His lips taste soft and exactly like him, despite the hint of strawberry leftover from our water bottles.

This calms me down. His lips taste like him.

It's odd how you feel you know someone in less than a day, how they taste, what to expect of their unique scent. His lips part for mine, and already he kisses better than most men. Of course, I wasn't his first kiss. He may have been a virgin, but in his words, "I wasn't a hermit, Vin." I kiss him as long as I dare amidst the comforting scent of old books. I don't want the shop owner to get suspicious, nor am I interested in running into additional figures from his youth, so after a respectable few kisses, we part, and a humming sound emerges from his mouth.

I don't know what to say. What do I say?

You're in a bookstore! You read travel books! Say something, idiot.

"Have you ever thought about traveling somewhere amazing, Marky?"

He smiles, and his eyes are still closed. "Just did."

We wander, aimlessly, for another four blocks, giving me time to sweat the latest development. Upon leaving the bookstore, Mark informed me he has organized "a surprise." I do not like surprises. Where is the surprise? Is it lunch? Is it a movie? I try to remain calm while my brain backflips through many possibilities.

"Can you tell me how much time until the surprise happens?"

Mark's smile is mischievous. "Nope."

"Should we hang out here or should we go somewhere to be closer to the right place? The right place for the surprise."

He grins. "Your call, boss."

I'm irked. It's hard enough not knowing what's happening next. He should give me a clue so I can help him plan for it. How can I help plan for the surprise if I don't know what it is? Okay, that makes no sense. I'm going to give myself a headache over this. A shock runs through me. Is this what men on my King Weekends feel? How do they survive?

Keep it together, man. Try to remain calm.

"Mark, I can't guess the preferable option without your giving me a clue."

"We can wait here. This place is fine."

"Here" is a baseball field. A park. I imagine this space is premium during the summer, four or five soccer fields and a baseball diamond. I survey the enormous greenish-brown grounds. It's November. Grass is mostly dead. How did I talk myself out of showing up early to study the neighborhoods? Why didn't I stalk him? If I had, I'd know the surprise. I could still act surprised while being prepared for what's to come.

I don't like surprises.

Calm down. Glance around.

Over there, someone's practicing football. High school team, maybe. We can sit on the bleachers, I guess. Look at the blue sky, and a factory chugging out smoke in thick, regular belches. Is this what we're supposed to do? How can he expect me to be in charge all weekend without knowing what he wants me to do? All I wanted to know was whether the surprise was coming to us, here, or whether we should go to it.

Let it go, Vin. And quit lying to yourself—you were hunting for a clue.

No, I—okay, fine. He caught me. I was hunting for a clue.

"Sit on the bleachers, Mark?"

"Could we lie in the grass for a while? In case I need to narc out?"

"Sure. Of course."

We cross inside a chain link fence to the infield, third base side. He leads us beyond, to the very middle of the outfield.

Taking my hand, he says, "I always thought it would be cool to die in center field. People would read the obituary, and talk about me to their friends. They'd say, 'Look at this. Some guy died in center field on a baseball diamond.'"

"This is your life goal? To die on a baseball diamond?"

"No, I'm saying, as long as we're going to lie down on a baseball diamond, I wouldn't want it to be third base. I'm outfield, all the way."

"From the grocery store encounter, sounds like you played baseball a lot as a kid."

"I did. But I didn't like it. I don't like sports."

"Really? You've got a jock's body."

"Yeah?"

He says nothing more than this, but I can hear his pleasure in my saying so.

He drops to his knees and rolls over in centerfield.

"Join me," Mark says. "Tops of heads touching."

"You give a lot of orders. I thought I was in charge all weekend."

"Vin, you are in charge. Of the main stuff. Of the small stuff, well, give me one or two little things. Brian and Patty and I used to play astronaut on a field near our house. When you're astronauts, your heads have to touch together."

When I lie down, I make sure the top of my head butts against his.

"Sounds like you were close to your sister and brother growing up."

Mark cups his hand over his mouth. "Astronaut Vin Vanbly, do you read me."

"Roger that, Houston."

"Ccckkkk. This isn't Houston. This is astronaut Mark Benson. International Space Station."

I add the walkie-talkie sound to my response. "Ccckkkk. Hello astronaut Mark Benson. Vanbly, over."

"Cckk. Say something. Talk to me, over."

I don't know what to say. "Ccckkkk." I pause. No words come. "No can do. I'm conserving oxygen. Over."

I wince. Why can't I talk like a normal person?

Mark says, "What do you suppose they talk about for fun? While they're out in space?"

Walkie-talkie time seems to be over. Apparently, one of us docked on the other's ship.

He continues without me. "Do you think they talk about Earth? Or when you're off the planet you have to leave Earth things behind."

"I don't know."

"Guess."

I don't know! I don't know! *Well, say something, you idiot.* "It may not be so bad, leaving Earth behind. Forgetting about everything down here."

Shit. I didn't mean to say something so negative.

Fix this!

"I mean, you're in space, you get to think new thoughts, make observations about life in a way most human beings never experience. Maybe it feels good to think differently, think off-planet. Maybe your brain is free for new dimensions. That's all I meant."

"Yeah, maybe." Mark is not sold on this idea.

We talk space-talk for a while longer, and he leads the conversation to other topics I find baffling, television shows, movies, friends, and funny texting stories. I have little to contribute, for I have no one to text. But I ask questions and listen deeply. I am uncomfortable when he asks me for insights. I'm the last person to offer advice. I try reflecting back his observations with new words to see if he gleans any new insights, more true than mine. I can add some value in conversation that way. That's something, I think.

A few minutes later, talk drifts back to our apparent space mission, Mark showing me with his fingertips how we should try to grab shoulders in outer space in case one of us goes whizzing past the other. We reach to the sky, fingers finding each other, and gradually traveling down our arms until our hands are on each other's shoulders.

"What happened out there? I mean, if one of us is whizzing through space and needs to grab the other? Something go wrong on the mission?"

Mark says, "I dunno. Something. You probably pressed some button. I'm pretty sure it wasn't me."

"Hey, you're the one out traipsing around outside the shuttle on your space tether. I'm stuck inside all day and night making dinner."

"You call that dinner? You add water and wham, it's dinner."

"Last week you said you loved my space enchiladas!"

We bicker through outer space, passing millions of stars, holding on to each other's arms and shoulders, heads touching.

His voice begins to fade and his grip loosens.

I panic.

I know it's just his narcolepsy, but my grip tightens.

He's leaving! Suddenly, I feel we truly are in deep space, and if I let go, he will be lost to me forever. It's just a quick nap. But I feel panic at the idea of letting go. His arms drop to his side. Mark! No! He's going somewhere farther than the stars, a place harder to follow than outer space.

I fight my irrational panic. It's a quick nap. Admitting I'm panicking is not helping. *Vin, get a grip. Don't panic! We're not lost in outer space!*

Deep breaths. Deep breaths.

"Look at the sky. It's so blue."

His being awake startles me more than his falling asleep, and my eyes jerk open to see the expanse of blue skies and white puffy trails from an airplane. My whole body is cold. I lurch up and scramble to my feet. I can't lie in the cold grass anymore. The universe is squeezing into me, and I'm already so cold.

"Cccckkkk. Vanbly, you okay over there? Over."

"Fine. Over." My voice isn't fooling me, so it's probably not fooling him.

He sits up. "Thanks for lying down with me. This is the first nap I've needed today. Well, after the one in the shower."

"You were asleep in the shower this morning?"

I'm calming down. I'm okay. I'm calming down.

"Yeah, when you were holding me from behind."

"But you were standing."

"Short nap." He stands and brushes off his legs. "Only two and it's almost noon. That's pretty amazing."

"And when you're on meds?"

"Three times a week, if that. I have more control too. I can feel it coming on and delay it for up to a half hour. Depends on the week, my stress level. Off meds is usually more than this."

"Last night you fell asleep six times."

"Yeah. Peak experiences created by high-intensity situations, such as extreme fear or heightened emotional awareness. I'd say losing my virginity counts as a peak experience in my life. I felt a tad overstimulated. Also, I didn't sleep much the night before. I was too excited you were really coming. I was getting tired of being a virgin."

I'm okay. Panic attack over. It's over.

He takes my hand. "Okay. It's time to go to the surprise. C'mon."

My heart feels warm toward him, especially after what he said. Nevertheless, I grit my teeth. I don't like surprises.

Oh, come on. Can't be that bad. Play along.

I say, "Great! This should be fun!"

We retrace our morning steps along the same streets. When we pass the market, he says, "Hey, not sure all these strangers know about our sex life. Do you want to tell them or should I?"

I grimace. "I'm sorry about that."

Mark pretends to chat up an imaginary nearby person. "Do you have a minute to hear about our sex life? How many times we fucked? No? Okay, maybe later."

I laugh, but inside I feel utterly humiliated. What a dick move on my part, even though I thought I was protecting him somehow. He doesn't need my protection. I'm attempting to mentor someone who is more resilient than me, possesses more people skills than I ever will. That's a dick move. No wonder I'll always be a Lost King.

He snickers, still remembering. "Oh, Vin."

We stop before Contelli's, the bakery we passed this morning. The yellow-and-white awnings partially hide the block lettering painted in red on the giant glass front. Elegant wedding cakes and over-frosted birthday confections vie for attention on tiers in the showcase window, competing to win votes for categories like Best Dressed, Most Appealing Interior, and I Would Stick My Entire Face Into That.

I say, "Contelli's doesn't sound Portuguese. Other people get to live and work here, too."

"It's not. Go along with this." Mark pulls the door open and says, "Hi."

I hate surprises.

When I follow him inside, I discover the object of his "hi" to be a woman not much older than him, a thick braid down her back. She directs traffic, and after confirming we are together, gives me an odd look, smiles brightly, and allows us both to pass.

Mark knows where he's going, bypassing the busy counter with its red-ticket numbers for service. We leave the front room, but not before I hear someone's shrill voice rise above the murmuring din, "No, *I'm* thirty-four. I've got the number." Popular place on a Saturday morning. Well, noonish. We follow a short hallway with a metal cart piled high with loaves of bread and other baked treats, second-string team, ready for easy restocking, I suppose. We emerge into a classroom of sorts, white-clothed tables arrayed around a teaching station, countertops, sinks, and high tech audiovisual equipment positioned over the preparation area. Obviously, they teach cooking classes here. I bet we're here for a cooking glass. Okay, I can deal with that. I can deal.

Over his shoulder, Mark says, "When you told me you'd bought your plane ticket, the next day, I signed us up."

Mark leads us to the instructor who suggests a table to adopt as our own. Is it my imagination, or did she throw me some shade, too? First, the front-room lady with the braid, and now her. Mark sits next to me, scoots his chair closer, and on top of the table, wraps my hand in his. "I'm having a good time today, Vin. Thank you."

He's having a good time? With me? I smile, still irritated and confused, but now the feelings are directed at *me*, not him. This thoughtful man planned a surprise as a thank-you, and instead of feeling gratitude, I can't stop grousing to myself.

Relax and be a normal person, you idiot. Chill. Look around.

Everyone's holding hands.

Couples only.

Young couples, mostly.

Oh shit.

I know what kind of class this is.

Our instructor speaks. "A few folks are late, but we have to start on time, so, thank you for attending Contelli's wedding cake taster. We found this class to be helpful for those of you considering different bakeries for your weddings, because you get to sample our best cakes. Of course, you'll have to sit and do a full cake consultation if you choose Contelli's, but this class really helps engaged couples discover our range. We will sign you up for private appointments after class. I'm Beatrice Duarte, and I'm one of Contelli's senior associate bakers. I've personally been involved in creating every one of these cakes many times over, so I can address ingredients and presentation, everything. We're on a tight schedule for six tastings, so rather than waste time previewing, I'll just introduce each cake as we meet it, okay?"

She pauses to smile in such a controlled way, I bet her notes say *Pause here to smile.* I recognize fellow control freaks.

"Please hold off on questions until I have finished discussing each cake specifically. We will all taste all the cakes, and I have plenty of pictures from different angles, in three tiers, four tiers, whatever you like."

I gaze around the room. They all think Mark and I are getting married.

"You should see your face right now, Vin."

I glance over in time to see him snap a photo of me.

He puts his phone back into his jacket. "I'll show you later. When you need a good laugh."

"—but first, we always stand up and introduce ourselves. Tell us when your big day is." Our instructor, Beatrice, pauses to smile. "Don't add too much more because we have to stay on schedule."

Each couple ignores these directions, regularly introducing details like, "We met in college," or mentioning the church where the ceremony will take place. A few ramble longer, detailing their careers or saying what Contelli's deli dish they love best, which prompts our Beatrice to smile and cross her arms, approaching them until they feel her presence and wrap up their introductions.

There's another gay couple in the room, Joe and Craig. The one guy is kinda bearish. Both have beards. They follow her instructions, leaving out extraneous details, clearly not interested in making a flirty impression as previous couples have done. Good job, men. I appreciate their rule-following. Maybe Mark and I can get away with saying next to nothing.

She's coming. I should stand.

Mark pops out of his chair and says, "Hi, I'm Mark Benson."

Wait!

"This is my fiancé, Vin Vanbly. It's a funny name, isn't it? Sounds made up."

Oh god.

"Vin was my high school science teacher."

Amidst a few audible gasps, I jump to my feet. "No, we never—I mean, we *never*—"

"Oh, god no," Mark says, linking his arm through mine. "That would have been creepy. I just thought he was hot, and lusted after him from the back row. I got a C in his class. No, we met online a few years later on Daddyhunt. The website."

I feel myself blush crimson red. "That's not—I like *all* ages of guys, not just really young guys. I've been with men of different ages—*a lot of men*. Also, he's kidding about meeting on Daddyhunt. I don't even have a profile on that one."

Joe and Craig dip their heads, ashamed we currently represent *the gays*. Did I just announce I'm a whore to this entire room? With men of any age? And by promising I *don't* have a Daddyhunt subscription, didn't I absolutely guarantee they all think I do? Disapproval hangs thick in the air, and Mark tugs me back down. Our introduction is over. We have killed the jubilant spirit among the soon-to-be-wed.

I feel sick.

Beatrice has been inching steadily closer, arms crossed, bearing the thin-lipped smile reserved for over-talkers. I know she senses the awkwardness we've created, and if she's truly a control freak like me, she won't allow discomfort to ruin this sales event. If I were her, I wouldn't move on until I'd cleaned up this mess.

Oh, shit.

In a thick voice, she says, "When's the big date?"

Shit.

"Oh, it *was* April 1st. Next year." Mark stands again. "But Vin cancelled it. We have to set a new date. He said he's not ready for marriage."

More gasps are heard.

Okay, now I'm irritated.

I hate surprises!

I stand up. "Look, I'm not—it's nothing against Mark. He's amazing."

"I'll bet," mutters a nearby groom, who is immediately elbowed by his red-haired bride, her face never breaking the frozen smile facing in our direction.

"Mark is an amazing man," I say stronger. "He's smart and kind. Great with people. It's not him. I'm not sure marriage is for me. I mean, I don't think I'd be good at it. And the odds you don't divorce in three years are almost, what, thirty-five percent these days? Even with both people believing in the sanctity of marriage, let alone someone like me—"

I survey the disbelief on the faces of my classmates.

I sit.

I just spoke out against the sanctity of marriage at a wedding cake tasting. One of the Other Gays drops his head in his hands, his back facing me in silent judgment. And who humiliates their fiancé like I just did? Who does that with such disregard?

I am the worst person ever.

Beatrice gives up on the salvage operation. "Next table. Tells us your names, please."

There's an extra emphasis to her saying the word *please*. Luckily, this couple is young and fun, their bubbly enthusiasm infectious, and their table close enough to ours he can clap me on the shoulder and say what everyone is thinking. "You better pick his favorite cake, because you're in the shithouse now, brother."

His accent is southern, and after the entire class finishes laughing with nervous relief—relief *someone* said *something* about the train wreck I am—he confirms he's from Alabama. She's from New Jersey. He moved here for love. He explains he couldn't live without her, even if he is a southern boy to the core. Their obvious affection makes everyone smile and remember they are here because they, too, know this kind of love.

I see Beatrice is conflicted, because Alabama and his fiancée eased us all through a rough patch, but they also talked for a longish time. She is even more impatient greeting the next couple, demanding their *short* introduction. The eighth of the nine couples are two lesbians, which I couldn't tell until they stood up and faced us all. The woman who sat with her back to me is Heather, who now looks at us directly and says, "Mary and I also met online."

Mark shoots her a thumbs up, and I nod.

Her support makes me both grateful and uncomfortable, because she is attempting kindness to us, and we are pretending to be something we are not. We are liars.

During the ninth introduction, I can't hold my tongue a second longer. Quietly, I ask, "Mark, what was that shit about me not being ready for marriage?"

"Well, if you would have let me finish, I would have explained your last husband was pushed off a cruise ship to his death, and you dove in after him. You almost died of hypothermia. I worked at the physical therapy center where you were learning to walk again. You were afraid of love. Our story was very romantical."

"I thought you said we met on a website?"

"Yes, but we had become friends at physical therapy, both of us filled with secret longings, and going online to look at butt pics and dick pics and *more* dick pics and suddenly the big dick unlocked on the Daddyhunt website was you, and we were already secretly in love, so it was pretty amazing we met there."

"Nobody would have believed that."

"I know. But it was romanticals."

"Mark, why are we here?"

"Duh. Free cake. Six slices. That's six slices *each*. We don't have to share."

"We could buy cake."

He regards me with confusion. "But it's free."

Introductions over, Beatrice now gives Mark and me her hard glare, demanding *silence*, promising everyone in the room how much fun we're going to have tasting together. We are dutifully silent for a moment while Beatrice explains the first cake.

"I planned a much longer introduction," he says, turning and lowering his head. "But I didn't go through with it. I don't think Beatrice likes anyone speaking. She gives everyone dirty looks."

I laugh, a short, loud laugh, reining it in almost immediately. Everyone jumps in their chairs. The laugh makes me hiccup spontaneously.

Great. Now everyone assumes I'm drunk.

After we taste the white cake with raspberry filling and optional mint leaves, Mark asks me who in the room I would marry, if not him. I suggest this seems an odd game for a happily engaged couple to play. He insists that for this game, gender doesn't—or shouldn't—matter. You still had to pick who you could love best.

I shouldn't play this. This whole situation is dangerous, enabling him to fantasize we're getting married. He knows. I explained myself in emails, long before agreeing to meet him. It's dangerous to believe in a false future. Sure, I could fantasize about a future with him, too, but it's a luxury I cannot afford. I say a lot of good-byes to amazing, unforgettable men. I'm still in love with them. All of them. I can't handle one more love. I can't. I will die inside.

I came for the sex.

I fucked him bareback. I blush with shame. What is wrong with me? How do I make this right?

He's handsome. Good chemistry. Incredible kisser. And let's not forget, incredibly young. Which is why I got funny looks from both the hostess and Beatrice. With their eyes, they were saying to Mark, "Really?" Mark doesn't notice. He doesn't see.

Last night, he said, "No kings."

I should have said, "Agreed. And no love. Just sex."

"C'mon," he says, "Pick someone. That's enough time thinking it over."

I'll discourage this wedding fantasy later.

The hazelnut-almond cake with an espresso drizzle is delivered.

I pick Heather, who met her fiancée online. Mark picks a woman across the room who gesticulates wildly with her hands when she's excited about a cake. "She looks fun."

"She's very opinionated. Don't you think you two would argue?"

"Yes. Of course. Then, I'd get mad and storm out of the house. Go to a bar and meet you."

He puts his chin on my shoulder. "You could be my man on the side."

Before I respond, he says, "I can't believe you'd break up the only lesbian couple we know."

We are quiet while Beatrice explains the advantages of the hazelnut-almond.

Beatrice says, "For this next cake, a lemon sponge, some people worry it won't be filling enough, and guests will want second or third pieces. Sponge cakes are easily as filling as the first two we've tasted. Add a fruit side to each plate if you want to give people more to eat, like pears or peaches. But sponge cake offers three distinct advantages."

Mark leans over and says, "Are you sad? About our having less than twenty-four hours together at this point?"

"I am not."

His face shows hurt surprise.

Goddamn it, why can't I say anything the right way?

"Mark, I don't want to waste any time with you being sad about the future. I'm having a good time with you—well, other than being your creepy science teacher. I want to focus on the now."

I cannot tell if he is comforted by this.

He says, "An alternate story I had planned to tell was we met two years after high school ended. You were tutoring my little brother in our home. I was home on college break. Some teachers still do that, you know. Tutor in homes."

"You don't think that's creepy? Tutoring your little brother in your parents' home, while secretly checking out your ass?"

Behind us, Beatrice clears her throat, and without a doubt, she overheard.

I want to die.

"Everything all right over here?" she asks brightly. She carries the platter of sponge cakes with her, setting my piece before me. I notice her assistant carries a similar platter to the other side of the room.

"No," Mark says. "I think chocolate is the way to go, a crowd pleaser, you know? But Vin wants us to be more edgy with our cake. Something unexpected."

"Unexpected—" I see her choke down whatever snarky comment rose to the surface. "—is overrated."

I cross my arms in defeat. I get it. I'm a creep. There's no disproving it. Only I could fuck up a class where the greatest student responsibility is to eat cake.

She sets the plate in front of Mark and evaluates him. "Don't decide on the chocolate just yet. The sponge cake is delicious. And we end on a red velvet that is Contelli's signature."

I fork it.

She's right. This sponge cake is incredible.

Beatrice serves Mr. Alabama and Ms. New Jersey, then two others, but returns to our table, the empty tray at her side. She says to Mark, "Do I know you? I recognize you."

Mark says, "You might. Almost a year ago, I attended a Contelli's wedding cake taster. You were in charge of that one, too."

"So this is your *second* cake tasting." The brittle tone makes her accusation clear. "What happened to your first wedding?"

"My fiancée called it off."

Beatrice is both surprised and not surprised by this news. "Oh dear. That seems to be a theme with you."

"Oh yeah," Mark chuckles and takes my hand. "I was supposed marry a woman. Back then, I thought I was straight. But Vin convinced me to play for Team Dicks."

I cough.

Mark pats my back a few times and says, "You okay, babe?"

Beatrice has no response for this and flounces away.

Two other couples, including our friend from Alabama, heard most of the exchange. Even Alabama won't reach out with support. Clearly, I am a homewrecker exercising the gay agenda. Mr. Alabama is now all about the fork and plate in front of him.

Beatrice booms her words to the whole class. "Let the lemon sit on the front of your tongue before you chew it. Really let it in."

I whisper to Mark, "You were engaged last year?"

"No. That was my best friend and me. We were pretending."

"Why?"

"Free cake. Duh."

I hate surprises.

Why the fuck wouldn't he let me do a King Weekend?

So much easier than this.

He whispers, "Beatrice is right. I'm rethinking the chocolate for sponge cake."

FOUR

At the polished-oak host stand, I readjust the knot in my tie and announce our presence. "Benson, party of two."

When I glance to my right, I see Mark is pleased I made the dinner reservation under his name. He calmly surveys the plush elegance around us, the glamour of this expensive Newark tradition—the only Michelin three-star restaurant to defect from New York. To me, it looks like the kind of expensive steakhouse that caters to an older generation, those who want to remember smoke-filled supper clubs and big-band jazz. Long, beveled mirrors, and stout chairs covered in expensive fabrics.

Our maître d' is a graceful man with long fingers, long nose. Thin blond hair. He could be within five years of my age either way. "Did you say *Benson*?"

"Yes," Mark says firmly. "We're here."

With subtlety, he evaluates Mark, finding favor in his dark Armani suit and handsome youth. When he looks at me, his face does not lose any of its practiced smile, which suggests he's hiding his true reaction. I'm used to it now. Well, more used to it after this weekend, this afternoon. People look at Mark with pleasure, and at me with something like judgmental curiosity. What could I possibly be doing with this gorgeous man? Am I his young father? His guardian? His...I see the question marks in their eyes. As we walked toward the tailor's shop this afternoon to pick up his suit, some random woman stepped up and asked Mark, "Is this man bothering you?" I thanked her for looking out for someone she thought was in danger. But it hurt. A little. It's irksome people assume I am not wanted here. I'm used to that feeling, I guess, but not when I'm standing next to someone.

"Come this way."

I steel myself for the quizzical stares we will encounter as we cross the crowded floor. I can't help but feel we're making a grand entrance at a formal state reception.

Remembering the one person who seemed supportive, I blush. We treated ourselves to Starbucks before the tailor, and as we left, the stout black woman behind the counter, barely out of her teens, gave me a double thumbs up when I glanced behind me. At the time, I assumed it was because I'd left her a twenty-dollar tip, but an hour later—as Mark and I showered together—I decided something was different about her smile, more than common gratitude. She had been applauding my sexual conquest. How humiliating. Everyone around us thinks I'm a perv.

And I am. But tonight, I must be as elegant as he is. I am his refined consort in this swanky place.

Look at him.

He belongs to a life like this.

Mark walks tall behind our maître d'. We pass red velvet curtains, gold tassels still gleaming and proud despite their proximity to the carpet. A wooden dance floor that's so shiny and scuff free, it might be virgin. We navigate clear of that. The booths are hand-carved, their standard dining chairs would be someone's best pieces in an ordinary home. The muted clattering of silver domes, demure waiters delivering food, and quiet, excited conversation create a richness of elegance, all sounds celebrating extraordinary food. Diners ignore us as we pass, but Mark saunters by as if all were drawn to him, and in some ways, he's not wrong. More than a few women—and a couple of men—check him out.

I would never demean him by explaining how to behave in a fancy restaurant. No, his glorious presence comes entirely from within, his natural kingship asserting itself. At this moment it's obvious why he didn't want me to king him. He doesn't need it. And not just his masculine grace in this moment, but his demeanor at all times. He is generous in his praise. Though he's something of a street rat, he is thoughtful about his experiences and appreciates the advantages of his middle-class upbringing, suggesting to me his parents did a damn fine job. He loves his siblings and enjoys talking about them. He thanked me thirty times for the suit and for flying here to meet him. He seemed delighted by the cufflinks I presented him in the shitty motel, although I had to explain what they were and how to attach them. Then, grateful.

At our table, Mark pauses, awaiting further instructions from the maître d', touching his cufflinks unconsciously. His five-o'clock shadow complements his dark suit, and in the soft glow of candles and mood lighting, he appears a young movie star from the 1950s or perhaps a modern mafia boss's expensive muscle. Last night, I fucked him like a whore in a seedy motel, stripping away his virgin exterior until all that remained was raw, purring masculinity. Even though he's wearing the stripper thong under the suit, look at him now, royalty in a lemon-white shirt, silk lemon tie.

Our table is a four top, with plenty of room for the large vase with a dozen red roses set to one side. Mark doesn't seem to notice them or the fact no other table in the restaurant boasts fresh flowers.

Mark turns to our maître d' and touches his fingertips to the man's arm. In a low voice, he asks, "Am I supposed to tip you?"

The man offers an annoyed smile, the kind given to novice diners who don't know how such things are done. "No, sir."

"Because, I would," Mark says in an equally quiet voice. "I have never walked across a fancy restaurant like this. I felt nervous, but it was easier with you being professional, leading the way. Thank you."

The maître d' seems genuinely touched. When he says "Enjoy your dinner, gentlemen," there's a quality of freshness. He means it.

As we sit, Mark nods politely at a few diners who catch his eye, arches his eyebrows in hello to some of those who admire him from farther away, and then ducks his head behind the roses. "Hey, how many people am I supposed to acknowledge? What's the etiquette? This doesn't happen in a Denny's."

This makes me laugh.

"I feel like the whole restaurant is staring at us."

"At you. You look amazing."

"At us," he says. "*We* look amazing."

"No, Mark. It's you."

"It's us," he says, and then hides behind the menu. "You can't argue with me when I'm behind my menu. It's rude."

I laugh to myself, delighted by his rule-making—

Wait, what's wrong? Something's off.

I glance around. Something inside me is sideways, but I can't quite put my finger on it.

This morning I thought something felt wrong as I lay in bed, but the queasy feeling passed. Today, I learned how difficult it is for me to not be on a King Weekend. I don't think it's likely I'll do this ever again. I had thought maybe I could show up and go with the flow. I thought I could. It's been hard. I thought that explained this morning's queasy feeling. Maybe the crushing uncertainty around how to act was behind the feeling something is off. Now I'm not so sure. Something is still not right inside me. A feeling.

What's happening to me?

Damn it, why don't I know?

I don't like surprises.

Our waiter appears, carrying two glasses of champagne, wearing a white shirt and black tie, a crisp white apron tied around his middle like a cummerbund. He could be in his late twenties, I bet. Black hair, slicked back. Maybe early thirties. He introduces himself as Roscoe, promises to serve our every need, and delivers our drinks without causing a single ripple in either glass. His hands free, he folds them behind him, the appropriate air of subservience expected in a money place like this.

"On the house," Roscoe says.

Mark looks at me with guarded surprise.

I tilt my head *no*. I'm not sure who sent these.

"These are with compliments from Lawrence, our maître d'. Are you gentlemen celebrating an occasion?"

Ha. My turn to be mischievous.

"Yes. Mark lost his virginity last night."

Roscoe seems startled by this declaration, but catches Mark's blushing face for immediate confirmation. His expression loses its crisp professional demeanor, and he gets down on one knee. "Are you serious, man?"

Mark scrunches his eyes closed and says, "Uh, yeah."

Roscoe says, "That's fucking awesome. Was she good? Did you love it? Wait, why now? You're good looking. You could've gotten laid long before this, bro."

"It was incredible." Mark peeks at me, still blushing. "I was waiting for the right...experience. I was very particular."

Roscoe chuckles and holds out his fist for a bump. "Well, fuckin' A. Definitely worth celebrating, bro. What were her tits like? You know what? Don't answer that. Keep it classy. Lawrence said to get you two good champagne, but he didn't say why."

I can't stop grinning.

Roscoe leans in and asks in confidence, "Was it wet? Was it sloppy?"

Mark laughs and hangs his head.

I clear my throat. "This morning at breakfast, didn't you describe it as 'jizz-tastic'?"

Mark puts a hand over his eyes.

Roscoe laughs and punches Mark's shoulder lightly.

I flinch.

As much fun as this is, I have yet to explain he can't bareback with strangers he meets online. He can never do that again. Never. The conversation looms.

Roscoe asks a few more questions, and Mark answers truthfully without revealing additional details about his sex partner. Roscoe tells Mark he admires him for waiting, and then shares details about his awful first time, an experience with a high school junior named Leslie, who—immediately upon finishing the sexual act—compared him to her last boyfriend.

"It was terrible," Roscoe says. "You were smart to wait."

"How old were you?" Mark asks.

"Fourteen."

When Roscoe leaves, Mark scowls and says, "Well, that was embarrassing."

"As your high school math teacher, I couldn't be more proud of you."

"Science teacher. I would never date my high school math teacher."

"Aha. So you did have a crush on your high school science teacher."

Mark gazes at me coolly, suggesting he will never confess. "We should toast."

I lift my champagne. Heavy glass. Real crystal.

I offer a single word. "Jizz-tastic."

Mark twists his mouth into a half grimace and follows my lead. He takes a deep sip. "Is jizz-tastic hyphenated?"

After we settle the word issues surrounding us, we discuss champagne and liquor in general, what he's tried and what he didn't like. We absorb tonight's menu. The chef's tasting menu is why you eat here; it's the experience. But other excellent options remain, steaks described in such a tantalizing way as to possess borderline sexual appeal, and several lobster arrangements with surprising ingredients. I ask him if he'd like to try caviar.

"Ew. Not a chance."

Mark asks food questions, some I can answer, and some I cannot. Our sommelier arrives, a gray-haired man, sleek, and soft-spoken, answering Mark's detailed requests for wine explanations. After each answer, Mark looks to me expecting confirmation, as if I could. At the end of his extended visit, our sommelier says, "If I may make a recommendation. Try the '72 merlot. It's perfect for someone young who needs to maintain his...stamina."

Mark's lips part.

"Congratulations, young man." He glances at me with approval. "I wish my father had taken me out to celebrate my first time."

He promises to return with our merlot.

Mark smirks.

I warn him with my eyes. "Don't. Don't say a word."

"Daddyhunt.com," he says. "Technically, it's not even a word."

"Why am I the pervy old man in our backstory?"

Mark interlaces his fingers and studies me seriously. "Well, I didn't want all those strangers knowing I found you on the Internet and begged you to take my virginity. They would have thought I was creepy."

This makes both of us laugh, and we follow up with additional snarking. Roscoe returns with a two-tiered giant shrimp cocktail, a glorious kick line of salty deliciousness which we did not order. He informs us this is a gift from himself and Charlie, the bartender.

"Charlie says he thinks it's a miracle you waited. He can't believe it. Good job."

Together, our eyes scan the enormous rosewood bar across the room, more like a cave than a bar, and one of the bartenders—presumably Charlie—waves a white cloth at us, grinning madly.

"Thank you," Mark says, in a tone betraying his nervousness. "You really shouldn't have."

Five minutes later, a new bartender—someone other than Charlie—appears at our table with a second glass of champagne for Mark, compliments of an admirer.

Mark glumly asks, "Is this because I was a virgin yesterday, and now I'm not?"

The bartender appears shocked. "No, I, uh, she just thought you were...uh... attractive. I guess. Shall I take it back?"

Mark's face is such a rich mix of confusion and humiliation, I can't help but laugh hard into my napkin. I can't stop laughing. Soon, tears run down my face.

When I can breathe again, I find Mark staring at me in horror. "You don't think Roscoe is going to bring a cake after dinner? With candles?"

I start laughing again, but this time, something's wrong. The queasy feeling. Something heavy. I feel an incredible pain in my chest. Something's wrong.

Mark's eyes go wide. "Vin, are you okay?"

Oh shit. Oh shit, oh shit, oh shit.

I do my best to smile. "Mark, I'm fine. Really."

This wasn't supposed to happen. Not on a sex weekend like this.

Sensations flood my tight chest, feelings for his innocence, his power, his smell, for fucking him, for his reactions, for eating cake together, for the way he smiles at me, the way he looks at me, for our heads touching in the grass, for our flying through space, hands on each other's shoulders, for his ridiculous insistence we both attract attention tonight, when he is the one, clearly he is the one, *the one*—

Love floods my chest.

Mark creases his face in worry. "Are you sure? Are you having a heart attack?"

I pick up my champagne glass. "I'm fine. Let's toast. To being a man."

Fuck, fuck, *fuck*! I'm the very opposite of fine.

How did I let this happen?

Goddamn it.

I'm in love.

I can't be in love! I can't. I barely choke down the avocado with quinoa and fava beans. It's amazing. The tastes are the most incredible, hard to synthesize—but I can't be in love with him. Fuck! He's a kid! I'm four hundred years older than he is. He's starting his life and I'm—I'm retiring. To Honduras.

I made up my mind to move to Honduras. To live off-the-grid. It's time to hide from the world.

Fuck! Fuck! Fuck!

Roscoe proudly delivers Mark's filet mignon, and my squid-ink spaghetti with lobster in dill sauce. Before he leaves, he admonishes Mark. "Finish it all. Keep your strength up." My meal smells amazing. But I wasn't supposed to fall in love. This is a sex weekend. Mark carves out a chunk with the skill of a surgeon.

"Hey," he says, spearing a forkful. "Roscoe said he's the beef sommelier, but he kinda snarked about it. Is beef sommelier a real thing? Or is it a made-up word to impress people."

"Both."

Damn it, I wasn't supposed to fall in love. I recognize how trite this sounds echoing around my head, stupid cliché, but when a cliché happens to you, it feels unique, like stepping barefoot in fresh green grass, and you realize how it became cliché. My brain is too freaked out to even play with the word cliché.

Say something. Don't ruin dinner.

I can't think of anything to say.

Still chewing, he says, "Are we gonna dance after dinner?"

Saved by a topic.

I say, "They don't have a band tonight. Only special nights."

"I would," he says, spearing his garlic-infused asparagus. "Dance with you."

"Well, thank you."

I study my plate so he can't see me flushed with pleasure.

"I'm serious," he says with great earnestness, carving off more steak. "You were smart last night, making me go into Romero's. Walking in—wearing a thong—was the hardest thing ever, which means everything else is easy. I'll dance with you, Vin. Doesn't even have to be music playing."

He stares at me, working those jaws on that steak, like a lion.

I raise my glass to him, trying to decide how to describe his eyes. Chocolate brown, but sometimes black, but mostly brown. Golden-flecked. In certain light, they reflect green for a split second. But naming the colors doesn't do them justice, it's the aliveness in them, the power and hunger which make them flicker with complicated intricacies—

"Can I ask you a question?" Mark swallows. "About sex?"

"Go for it."

"How does butt fucking work if you have to poop? Do you say 'Hey, poop break' or something? Yesterday afternoon, I cleaned out like you'd instructed me. Do you do that every single time? You do, right?"

Yup. I'm in love.

He says, "Honestly, it would be easier for me to eat a Sausage McMuffin with egg and cheese for breakfast the day I'm supposed to get fucked because those things clean out your system like nobody's business. They go right through you."

Definitely love.

After the last course—which Mark is happy to see does not involve singing around a cake—we discuss the décor and favorite tastes during the meal. Mark points out his favorite diners. He is drawn to the groups laughing and couples obviously enjoying themselves. I am drawn to those eating in silence, focused on the food.

It would never, never work between us. Never. It's not even a question—it was never a question. We won't see each other after this weekend. But the weekend's not over, and he's my responsibility until noon tomorrow. My responsibility to show him an amazing weekend, helping him remember his first-time experience with joy.

When he returns from the bathroom, I've paid the check. He takes my hand, holds it, and tells me how much this meal has meant to him, to dine in such extravagant luxury after his mac-and-cheese upbringing. With tears in his eyes, he tells me he really wants to sneak the remaining dinner rolls home inside a napkin. He explains he can't, of course, because it's an Armani suit. He wipes his eyes. But otherwise, he would.

I squeeze his hand with the same tender affection. Softly, I say, "They were incredible. So chewy."

"Yeah," Mark says, nodding.

He tears up again.

I understand.

They were amazing rolls.

Outside, Mark is surprised when I steer us in the direction opposite my rental truck, parked two blocks down.

"This way."

He obeys, sliding his arm through mine, leaning against me, and although I can't hear any actual noise coming from him, I get the distinct impression he is purring. This is a man who purrs.

I'm enjoying this too much. I'm enjoying him too much. This can't stand!

We can't stay together. I've discussed this. He knows this. I will be able say good-bye tomorrow—I'm used to saying good-bye to a man I love. But he—he's so young. It will destroy him. I will have ruined yet another life.

Okay. Stop it, drama queen.

We're having a great night together on a fun sex weekend that, yes, has been hard for me at times. I panicked with today's unplanned Saturday stretching before us, but now there's only tonight and tomorrow morning. Make the most of this— make the most of him—and love him with all your love, Vin Vanbly. He knows what's going on. This is a one-weekend visit. Quit being so dramaticals.

Where did that word—damn it.

He said *dramaticals* this afternoon. Dramatic. Don't be so dramatic is what I meant. It was cute though, when he said it, asking me if I thought wearing a cape with an Armani suit was too dramaticals. Heh.

A block later, he asks, "Do you think I could become a beef sommelier?"

"Sure."

"Do you go to beef sommelier school?"

"There's a private institute in Sweden."

"Sweden, huh?"

"Absolutely. They accept four scholars each year, and at least three of the four work on farms around the world, men and women for whom every ounce of meat is appreciated differently. For the final exam, you have to chop up a cow."

"That sounds disgusting. Maybe I could be the first vegan beef sommelier."

This November night gets colder the longer we're outside. That, or the warm glow we carried from the restaurant dissipates. Neither of us wears a winter jacket, suit coats only, but our destination is only two blocks away from the restaurant. Downtown Newark is surprisingly alive, or maybe I'm used to home. By nine o'clock, St. Paul rolls up its sidewalks and then sleeps. Tonight, I'm delighted by the people out walking, laughing, huddling together in couples and groups. Two women yell at each other across Broad Street, and it takes me a moment to realize they don't actually know each other.

When we arrive at Hotel Indigo, the—

Wait, what?

"Did you just say you wanted to be the first vegan beef sommelier?"

"Just hearing that now? Maybe it's time for a hearing aid, Daddyhunt.com."

I stop. "Don't say that. And who's going to trust your beef recommendations if you don't eat beef?"

"Well, if I graduate from this Swedish place, everyone will. They only accept four fucking candidates a year. Any chance we can argue this somewhere warmer?"

"We can. We're here."

I look up.

The Hotel Indigo seems to have repossessed an old bank—the cement arches and high windows with wooden framing look like old money to me, but with a boutique hotel like this, they might have deliberately built it to project the appearance of an old bank without its actually having ever been one. It's narrow, yet tall enough to count as a skyscraper in the Newark skyline. Ten stories. As one might expect, the night façade is front lit with deep indigo color, charming its evening visitors with an edgy, comic-book feel. Batman might come here to meet the Joker. For drinks.

"Here?"

"Nightcap."

I hold the door open for him, and in turn, he opens the inside door for me.

After two sparkling champagnes from the hotel bar, and with dinner more settled in us, we pass through an iconic, mismatched lobby, 1960s-designed furniture merged with the '70s emphasis on plush comfort. Classic vintage knickknacks contrast a fountain trickling down the textured cranberry wallpaper. Three indigo-blue couches with dark wooden trim form a triangle, the focal point in the lobby. Mark murmurs his appreciation for their stark beauty, and insists on massaging the rich fabric. If he is surprised we head right for the elevator bay, he does not show it.

He does, however, express surprise when we arrive at the top floor, and our penthouse reveals floor-to-ceiling windows facing downtown Newark. He races to them, pressing his hands to the glass, exclaiming he's never seen Newark like this. *Never.*

The room itself is a curious study in casual luxury—the luxury is the space itself, not the items within. The bed is large but ordinary, a comforter in their signature color sprawled across it, ice-cube blue pillows scattered near the head. A large, white desk, a high-definition television, and two black leather couches complete the attractive but ordinary furniture. These penthouse rooms are modern, which means I can't quite identify the subjects in the art on the walls. I have a few names in my head, minor painters.

Huh. I wonder how Perry's doing.

Mark races to the bathroom and reports back he found five soaps in there—five!

"Who could possibly use five soaps in one night?" he asks with excitement. "I mean, *five*?"

He crosses the room again, and instead of throwing himself at the front windows, he launches himself at me, catching me by surprise. His lips find mine, the fullness of them, and I remember. Oh god, I remember. The last time we kissed this way was earlier in our shitty motel, dressed in our suits, promising to enjoy each other's company tonight. The renewal of his lips on mine feels like spring's return after a long pale winter, lonely for green.

I love kissing him.

Between kisses, while breathing shallow, I whisper, "Marky."

He launches at me, pushing me off-balance, forcing me to push back, grab him harder.

Despite the drinks in the hotel bar, he tastes like steak, and the scent of him—him plus the restaurant, plus the smell of his suit—makes my cock awaken.

"This place," he says, looking into my eyes, "is swank."

"Go to the window. Unless it's time for a poop break."

"No," he says seriously. "I'd know if it was."

I don't touch him, just stand behind him, arms at my sides. He squirms, frustrated I'm not holding him. I wait until he quits fidgeting and really stares at the wonder of a modern city, lights glowing, thousands of lives being lived in comfort, with ease, with warm beds and safe dreams.

He says, "Newark is gorgeous. I've never seen it this beautiful."

"Look at us in the reflection."

Ghost versions stare back with elegant gloom. In this lighting, we can't see our eyes, just hollow sockets. I imagine them watching our lives, wishing for things that never come to pass.

No.

Too melancholy.

I kiss his neck, the back of his head, wrap my arms around him and squeeze, two men in suits staring over the diamond-lit skyline. I untuck his shirt, caressing his stomach, his chest, reaching as far up his flat stomach as possible without making either of us shift positions.

He moans the same "Mmmmmmmmmm" he made this morning in bed, and I remember how good he was at sucking my cock. Practice makes perfect.

I inhale the scent uniquely his and kiss him in front of his ear.

He sighs.

I had no idea we'd have this much sex. I mean, yes, I came here to steal his virginity, quench a few fantasies of his, like cigar smoke and the parking lot pickup, giving him a first experience to savor. I didn't know he'd reveal a sexual animal, ferocious in his hunger. I guess he starved himself, waiting for his sexual freedom. This weekend is his banquet. But it's more than his hunger alone. It's mine as well.

I love him.

No! Don't say that, even to yourself. Don't be a fucking idiot. Stay in control. Your feelings may be out of control, but you cannot surrender control.

C'mon. Focus on him.

After he kicks off his shoes, I find his belt buckle, and a moment later, the gorgeous charcoal slacks surrender. They glide to the floor, folding over themselves, over and over, like liquid is this cloth's other natural state.

"Step out of them."

He does as he's told and as he reaches for them, I command him to leave them.

"I have to fold them."

"Leave them."

He protests weakly. "It's Armani."

I refuse to argue this point, and he surrenders.

I'm already captivated by the way his ass moves when he bends, the redistribution of weight when he shifts from side to side. I drop to my knees to examine him closer, and decide, really, the only reliable examination tool from this perspective is my tongue. I kiss his ass, bite it gently, forcing nonsensical sounds out of him, like, "Ohhhssshhh!" and "Whaaiiiiiimmm." When I tug his thong strap to the side and rim him, his hands shoot apart and land on the glass, as if he's testifying in church on Sunday, and I suppose, in his way, he is. He does. He testifies. He spits out more original words and sounds, his latest form of prayer.

When I feel his legs shaking, I order him to get the desk chair and drag it to the window. By the time he finishes, I have joined him in lower-half nudity. Well, he's wearing a thong. I sit in the chair, facing him, and pull my shirt back enough to allow him to see my proud cock, the proudest thing I own, standing tall and drooling.

"I love your penis," he says, almost reverently. He looks to me in surprise. "Can I say that out loud? Can I say I think it's perfect and fat, and perfect?"

I laugh. "Thank you. I didn't have anything to do with how it turned out, but thank you."

He kneels and stares at it again, still mesmerized, touching the tip with his finger and pulling away a strand of goo. "Are you sure? Are you sure you didn't teach it to lift weights and bulk up?"

His adoration is an aphrodisiac, and I caress his ear for a moment before guiding his mouth to me. He laps at the head gently, as if he doesn't want to disturb the precum by accident, and he takes his time kissing and licking every exterior inch before he eventually takes it inside his mouth. I didn't teach him that. That is the product of healthy, cock-worshipping devotion.

He sucks my dick carefully, as if he's an archeologist who's newly discovered some ancient Egyptian obelisk, and must take intimate inventory before presenting to a museum. His lips follow every curve and vein with sensitivity, and I find myself closer to orgasm than I want to be. It shocks me he is this gifted already, a single day of sucking. One day! But his natural hunger, combined with those years of virginal waiting, must have sharpened his resolve to make each second count.

Before he moves me closer, I should say something. "Soak my cock with spit, because it might be the only lube you get." This encouragement makes him suck more lustily, grip my cock tighter, and that's not exactly what I wanted, to get edged closer to the endgame. I just wanted more spit.

I make a few nonsensical sounds of my own.

Stop. *Stop!* I make sure my breath is even before I say, "Okay, Marky. That's enough."

I position the chair so I face away from downtown, and he gets the view. I slide down so it's easier for him to climb on my cock, and despite my threat of no lube, he's still an almost-virgin, so I use the small packet stashed in my jacket pocket to make sure I'm slippery, and so is his anus.

I'm no longer debating the bareback sex.

Big talk tomorrow.

Big fun tonight.

I've already screwed up this kid emotionally, what's one more—*stop. Don't think about the damage you've done. You'll lose your erection.*

After he positions himself so the head is inside, he stares me down with every inch. He winces at one point, but opens his eyes wider, as if wide eyes were the key to his success. Once he lands—and we both experience the unmatched pleasure of my being fully inside—he stares at me with the same question in his eyes from last night. I'm as skeptical as he is.

Is this happening? His eyes search mine.

Is this really happening? My eyes search his.

We stare, and when he's ready, he makes small motions, never taking his eyes from me, and I make small motions too. Lifting him, pushing him away. Making my dick throb inside him. I can't believe we're not using condoms. I always use condoms.

My cock seems to recognize this and relishes its freedom, because I have been harder this weekend—more prone to get hard—than the last five weeks on my own. How many times have I come? How many times has he? I lost count. He came twice when we fucked around before dinner. That sleazy room has seen a lot of sex.

"Look at the city," I say, staring into his eyes. "Your city."

"I am," he says, never breaking eye contact with me.

This fuck is not aggressive, it's not me pounding his ass. It's him lifting and me joining him, finding a rhythm together, and it strikes me this is the best part, creating the rhythm together. His lemon-sorbet shirt feels light in my hands, his tie smooth and erotic. He tugs my tie a few times, grinning in silence, and he moans while I'm deep inside him, throwing his head back and saying my name.

After a while, I comment on how he hasn't napped in a long time.

"I took a short snooze in the restaurant bathroom," he says.

"You were gone a long time."

"I was."

This is the most conversation we have for the better part of a half hour.

We kiss.

We touch.

This is our night.

When it's time for sleep, we both know it, and I start making movements suggesting we end this form of intimacy. Neither one of us have come, but I don't think it's about that. Not this time.

"No," he says. "Stay inside me. I'll take off your clothes, and you stay inside me."

He unbuttons my shirt, attempting to concentrate while I jab him a few times, bumping his fingers away. He laughs and drives his ass down, attempting to resist my throwing him off. What starts out erotic ends as ridiculous; after mine, we fight to get his shirt off, and he twists in both directions, refusing to give me access to the front of him.

When we are naked, he relents, pulling himself off my cock. We drag ourselves to bed.

I say, "Leave the clothes on the floor. We'll pick them up in the morning."

"Vin, I'm sorry," he says, "but this is Armani. I have to hang it."

"It's only clothes."

He handles his jacket as if he'd scooped into his arms a spotted fawn from the forest floor. He looks at me with a mournful face. "This matters. This is a gift from you. *Please.*"

I nod.

He hangs it carefully, and from bed, I hear him whisper to it, "Thank you."

He joins me under the indigo comforter, and I feel for a moment we are baked in a blueberry pie. As we snuggle together, I congratulate myself on surviving an impossible day, hanging out without being in control of every moment. Letting myself be led. Enduring a surprise that was worse than anything I could have imagined. I smile at the painful memory. Although, I did love the sponge cake. Beatrice was right. Even while my fingers intertwine his, I scold myself again for letting feelings arise, for letting love flood my chest. That's bad. I'll have to fix that.

But not tonight.

Tonight, the warmth of him makes every discomfort worth it. The feel of him in my arms. My cock is now soft, but I recall the feeling of being inside him, rocking inside him, with no goal other than to pleasure him and witness the intimacy in his eyes.

His hand curls into mine.

I'm going to sleep tonight. I'm going to sleep so goddamn well.

As we're both drifting off, he says the words I've been dreading in a voice more air than sound.

He says, "I love you."

I squeeze him, but I can't say them back.

I can't.

Tomorrow, I'm leaving him forever.

FIVE

My brain feels sluggish. I can't remember where I am. I want blueberry pie. "Wake up. Vin, wake up."

I feel myself shaken awake.

Mark.

Why is the skyline so bright? Is it still the middle of the night? The room is dark. Sky is dark. It's the middle of the night.

He shakes me again. "Vin, wake up."

Fear grips me. I'm awake now. "Are you okay?"

"Yeah, yeah. I'm fine."

He doesn't say anything.

I rub my eye. Adrenaline retires before it can climb further. "What's wrong?"

"Now that you're awake, I'm kinda embarrassed. I don't want to say."

"Okay. Take your time."

I snuggle back into my pillow, pulling him closer, wanting to smell more of him, the scent of his body, the way he feels, the wispiness...

"Vin, wake up! I'm sorry. Wake up."

I struggle back to consciousness.

"Do you still have the other room? The other motel?"

"Sure."

Mark seems nervous, and this alerts me to wake up further. Is something wrong?

He says, "I want to go back there. I want to spend the rest of the night there."

I'm not sure I heard him correctly. "In that dump?"

He seems bashful. "This place is beautiful. I'm sure it was very expensive to get this top floor, and I don't want to be ungrateful. This is gorgeous. The suit sex was amazing. Better than the fantasy."

"But...?"

"I wanna go home. I want to go to our room where we fucked for the first time, where we woke up this morning. I wanna wake up tomorrow in our bed."

"Our bed?"

The look in his eyes is serious. Nervous.

We check out at two fifteen a.m.

Mark carries the five soaps in his suit pockets.

I'm so tired.

Considering I spend so much time bearing insomnia, this thick, heavy feeling of imminent sleep is a treasure, something I rarely experience. I love it. I wish I felt this every night. But tonight is special, because I'm with Mark. Back in St. Paul tomorrow night, I'll probably—*no. Don't think about tomorrow.*

Go to bed.

Let sleep win.

Mark mumbles to me as he drags across the room, and I ask him to repeat himself.

In a weary voice, he says, "Poop break."

I remind him I attached a shower douche in the bathroom.

He grunts.

I strip and throw my suit to the far side of the bed. Tomorrow's problem.

I hear the shower come on.

It's the last thing I hear.

I'm wide awake. I woke up with my hand cupping his ass.

It's still dark outside—no light seeps through the drapes. One of the panels is ripped where sunlight flooded us this morning. Well, yesterday morning.

The problem is, his ass feels so good. And I never came.

Also, his snoring is adorable. That's a problem, too. Because I can't fall asleep listening to his deep breaths, feeling the warmth of him. Not knowing his beautiful butt accommodates all of me, and with surprising ease. How can I sleep, knowing this? Having freed my body from the flimsy bedding, my semihard dick is careening around the dark room, making gestures nobody sees but I feel down in my balls.

Mark groans and twists. His butt jiggles.

I stretch out my hand over his entire ass cheek, reveling in the softness of it, the buttery softness. I don't know why the curve of his ass gets to me the way it does. It's not like you can "do something" with a curve. But Mark's ass is a geometrical wonder nevertheless, meaty muscle and a delicious plumpness of form. He's too thick to model for an iconic Greek statue—but he wouldn't get cut from the auditions in the first round.

I need to explain to my cock how it's rude to fuck someone sleeping, although I did that yesterday, didn't I? Yeah, but in my defense, he was awake when I started inside him. He only fell asleep during. Hmmm. That doesn't sound much better, someone falling asleep while you're fucking them.

You don't feel like fucking. You're tired. Go to sleep.

I'm sleepy. Very sleepy.

Damn.

Lying to myself isn't working.

He rises, pushing his ass into my hand, and it makes me think he's awake. Is he awake? His breathing sounds the same, but after a moment of silence, he pushes again, definitely pushes into my hand, and he makes a small whimpering sound. I think he's awake.

He spreads his legs farther apart.

Oh, I see how this is. I get it.

Little fucker. He's awake.

I will test him.

I grab the lube from the stand and strategically crawl on top of him—never dropping my weight on him, of course—but dangling my cock over his butt. Streetlamps in the parking lot lend enough silver light to see the shape of these globes, and looking at him is enough to keep me hard. This is a helluva lot of sex for one weekend. It's not always like this—another item to add to my list of explanations. I must leave enough time tomorrow. Don't have bareback sex. Sex isn't always this good. It may hurt for a little while, but this isn't real love. Just good chemistry. Well, sex is always good with a king candidate, but that's not, no, don't bring that up.

Let it go.

Tomorrow.

But it's not tomorrow yet, no matter how close to sunrise. Tomorrow doesn't start until we wake up together.

I squeeze my lubed cock, and rest it against the cleft of his butt, lowering myself.

Let's see just how asleep he really is.

I rub my dick against him, making small movements, sawing back and forth, keeping the motion unobtrusive on the off chance he really is asleep. But I don't think so.

He pushes back the tiniest bit, almost imperceptible, but in the darkness, it's easier to see invisible quivers.

Ha. I knew it! He's awake!

I do not change my pace. If he's awake, he will angle his butt—there. He did it. He hiked himself on the pillow, mumbling, angling his ass so my cock head is positioned right at his back door.

I lower my body on top of his, keeping my weight on my arms.

I'm not sure if this is one of his fantasies, a sleeping fuck. He sure has a lot of fantasies, though. I wouldn't be surprised if this were one. I really hope the suit sex lived up to his hopes.

I whisper into his ear. "Gosh, I hope this doesn't wake you up."

He makes no movement, no sound, and I decide to punish him.

"I shouldn't do this. It's wrong. Not while you're asleep."

He does not respond.

"So, I'll just get off you and let you sleep."

His body jerks backward enough to push the very tip of my cock inside.

Ha. Gotcha.

I take my time sliding in, inch after inch, remembering how he felt in the Indigo, how we stared into each other's eyes with longing and adoration. Well, this ain't gonna be like the Indigo. We're in a cheap motel with crappy, thin blankets and a mattress that's lumpy and uneven. He's facedown, and he's gonna get fucked.

I lose whatever patience I possessed moments ago, and slide in farther, push deeper, and he continues to feign sleep. I like this game! I take a few long strokes, and he moans in his sleep, and so I fuck a few short strokes until he grunts. This becomes another game as I lower my weight on him, and he grunts out a deep pocket of air, refusing to acknowledge he is awake. I laugh, but keep it inside my chest, making me chortle with silent glee as I fuck him harder, slapping my hips against his perfect, perfect ass.

He makes a few yelps, now making exaggerated snoring sounds, so I fuck harder until the bedsprings sing in complaint. The thin headboard knocks hard against the neighboring wall. I love this so much, this raunchy bareback fuck in a cheap motel, I start growling, fucking him harder, surprised he can handle my bouncing him all over the bed—and still—he refuses to acknowledge my presence. It's ridiculous.

Neighbors pound on the wall, and yell, "Knock it the fuck off, you goddamn faggots!"

"*You knock it off*," Mark yells in response, shocking me. "*We're trying to fuck!*"

I'm so delighted by his roar, his surprising and furious defense, I can't help myself—I come. I come hard, squirting every remaining drop, screaming loudly over the neighbor's yelling, and Mark yells too, whether at the neighbor or at me, I don't know—everything merges into one cacophonous explosion. In blinding seconds it's over. I pant hard, sweating against him, holding him, telling myself to never forget this moment, this thrill, this love.

I never will.

Peak emotional experience.

We gasp together, listening to the screaming swears of our neighbors.

Mark says, "I think you might be trying to kill me."

No, Mark. I'm trying to bring you to life.

SIX

When I return from the nearest Starbucks, I am careful to be silent as I unlock Room 1_1's door—the missing "one" hasn't returned in my absence—hoping he's still asleep. We were awake most of last night, so I slept late, all the way to nine a.m., a true luxury for me. I will set the coffees on the nightstand nearest him, and Mark will wake to their combined aroma. I will hold him, like when I awoke. Maybe he will make yesterday's "Mmmmmmm" sound again. Which is a bad thing. It has to be. I can't love him the way—

He's not asleep.

He sits naked on the bed corner, tears on his face when he looks at me.

Panic.

I set down our coffees hastily and join him at as side. I glance around the room for signs. Nothing.

"Mark, what happened? Are you okay?"

I focus my attention on the bathroom. Could someone be in there? Have to be ready for anything.

"You were gone when I woke up." He wipes his eyes. "I thought you left without saying good-bye."

Okay. Calm down. I feel my heartbeat slow. I wrap my arm around his shoulder. "I would never do that. Never leave that way."

He pushes me back. "I know that. I just...I felt it, is all."

He wipes a new tear from his eye.

I feel sick. I feel the weight of my leaving too.

I lean in, letting my head touch his.

"I know today is our last day together," he says, wiping another tear from the other eye. "At least for a while. But don't fuck with me today. I'm an astronaut in love."

Okay, calm down. This is good. He accepts that we won't see each other ever again.

He understands we cannot be together.

But to help him, I must give him whatever he wants. Anything.

I put my free hand on his thigh. "What do you want to do this morning, Mark?" My stomach feels queasy as I make the offer I must. "We can do anything. Go anywhere. You decide."

I don't want him to decide.

I want to decide.

I hate surprises.

"Anything." I kiss the side of his head.

This is not the morning I had imagined.

Why are we here?

In silence, we slam the truck doors, and the loud noise seems inappropriate. With the solemnity a cemetery demands, we tread respectfully across the dried November grass—dead grass—as if the grass respected the lifeless surroundings and quietly followed suit. I trail behind, as he navigates down a brown grass alley, thick tombstones on either side of us. It's Catholic, so the graves are showy: weeping angels and forlorn crucifixes. A granite baby, worn by time, melts into the sad rectangle honoring his short life. Souls remembered and forgotten, in every direction. Glancing around, I spy two other people visiting loved ones on this gray Sunday morning. Nobody else. The grass bristles as it bends beneath our weight.

Navigating with the experience of someone who visits frequently, Mark leads us to a grave and stops, cupping his hands in front of him. I cup my hands. We look very solemn wearing our suits. Wait, *her*? Oh my god. He told me stories all weekend, but never said she was dead. Why?

"Hi, Patty. This is Vin. I wanted you to meet him." He pauses. "We're in love."

Why did he never mention his sister was dead? According to this, she died six years ago.

Wait...wait, I should correct him. Maybe this is the moment to correct him and explain we can't be in love. I'm a Lost King. And he's...he's perfect.

My stomach hurts.

He takes my hand. "I don't think either of us expected this to happen so fast. Well, no, that's not true. Vin knew. Months ago, in an email, he said I would probably fall in love with him."

Mark gets quiet.

Far away, a bird shrieks in ugly tones that claw the sky.

"I thought he was being cocky and, yeah, he was. But he was also right. I'm in love. I think I loved him before he showed up Friday night. Meeting him in person was confirmation."

What do I say? What can I say? I want to say something, but I have no words. I'm out of words.

Wait—wait. Why hasn't my brain been playing word games all weekend? Word games and...that's what's been wrong all weekend—my word mania is gone! Why? Where did it—I already know the answer. It's *him*. When I'm around him, my brain doesn't dance and flip over words. The last time I remember censoring myself was in the parking lot before we met. Why? How does he do that?

Wait, why is he so quiet?

His body jolts, jerking my hand. I jerk in response.

He says, "I wasn't sleeping. I'm awake. I was explaining, Patty, how Vin said we can't see each other for the next nine months after this weekend. He said time apart is necessary so I could fall out of love. Yeah, right. Like nine months is enough time to forget Vin Vanbly."

I cannot let him be in love with me. I can't. I'm not—this would never work. He knows that. Still, another part of my brain screams in angry demand, *why did you insist on nine months, you idiot?*

"He says it's for the best," Mark says. "He explained it over and over. But best for me? Or for him? I don't think he knows. But Vin makes the rules, and I had to agree or he wouldn't have shown up."

Focus up. *Focus up, moron. Explain the rules are for his protection.*

"Mark—"

He looks at me earnestly. "Do you mind, Vin? I'm trying to have a conversation with my sister."

My mouth clomps shut. But before I can think or feel anything about being scolded, my brain skates around my recent revelation. Is it true? Can it be true around him—around him—my brain doesn't obsess with words? Is that possible? Why is that? Test it out. The letter, *p*. Go. *P*. Think of the very *p*-ness of *p*. *P...P...p...p...*

"I know, Patty, I know. He has his flaws. Big ones."

Nothing. No *p*-ness. Wait, what did he say?

He turns to me. "How racist would you say you are, on a scale of one to ten?"

What?

I say, "I'm not—I have black friends."

"Hoo boy," he says, facing her grave. "Here comes the I-have-a-black-friend speech. That's the mating call of liberal racists. By the way, I didn't make that up. It's from late-night television. You are missing some killer lines, Patty. Go ahead, Vin. Tell me about your black friend and how you treat him like he's white."

"I'm not racist," I say with surprise.

He glances at me with skepticism. "Once, in an email, didn't you brag about giving a New York City black man a new name? He had a name he liked just fine, but you gave him a new name. Right? Wasn't it *Rance*?"

"His name was Terr—"

"I thought white people were done giving black people names. I thought we finished that."

"Okay, yes, out of context, it's—"

He turns back to his sister. "I don't think it's racism with a capital *R*, which is good. He's trainable."

I sputter out the words, "My older brother is black!"

Mark ignores me. "Here's another flaw. He was embarrassed to be seen with me this weekend because of my age. It's stressful when your lover is ashamed of you."

I feel a stabbing pain to hear this. He saw it? "Mark, I never—"

"Yes you were. I saw it on your face. At the cake tasting. Other times too."

"You told them we were *engaged*, and I was your high school science teacher."

"So? You can bear walk through a homeless shelter, but you're embarrassed to be engaged to someone who is twenty-two?"

"You're twenty-*two*?" My brain does sour flip-flops between surprise and anxiety. "You said you were twenty-four!"

He looks at me coolly. "I lied. I lied because I knew you'd be uptight about my age. You wouldn't have come to New Jersey if you had known I was twenty-two."

Oh my god. *He's twenty-two.* What the hell am I doing with a twenty-two-year-old?

"See? You're doing it again with your face, all nervous and panicked."

"I'm not. I'm not! I just...you were—you *lied* to me."

"I did. I'm sorry about that. I wanted to meet you, Vin. I had to meet you. Can you understand that? Have you ever lied to a guy you were interested in, tried to make yourself more attractive to him somehow?"

I bark out a laugh. "Have I ever lied?"

I am drowning in lies. As if lies are stones tied around my ankles, my life rockets down into the ocean depths in half seconds. Sinking, sinking, sinking. I am nothing but lies! How dare I judge him for lying to—but it hurts to be lied to. This fucking hurts. I keep imagining me sinking into midnight waters, drown—

Wait—*wait*!

"How did you know bear walking?"

Mark shrugs. "I talked to Perry."

What?

"I talked to several of your kings, Vin. I researched you online. Did you think I would let some Internet stranger show up and put his sperm inside me without knowing what kind of man he was? What he believed in? I needed references. I found them."

How? Who—

"Vin, are you listening?"

"I am. Yes. Wait, if you talked to Perry, then you know about the kingings."

"I guess. Sounded confusing. I mostly asked questions about you as a person. Your exes like you. They kinda rave about you. That's a strength. Oh, and another flaw, Patty. He's got a lot of shitload of ex-boyfriends. *A lot.* He's been slutting around for decades."

I'm a slut? Forget that. This is more important. He knows about the kingings.

I say, "So, you know the story of the Lost and Founds."

His voice is nonchalant. "Sure. I saw your website."

"And?"

"I liked them. They were funny. And sometimes sad."

"But you wouldn't let me talk about it this weekend. You didn't want a King Weekend."

He faces his sister's grave. "Patty, I just lied again, acting all casual. Truth is, I loved his king stories. But I needed to know if I could love Vin without his stories. I wouldn't let him bring them up all weekend. And I do. I do love him. Even though he's embarrassed to be seen with me, I love him."

I'm so ashamed. My eyes fill with tears, and I cannot speak.

He's shown me nothing but love all weekend, correctly reading the reluctance on my face—and still, he loves me. Ow. *Ow*. I'm an asshole. I'm a total asshole, and he deserves better. I don't know what's happening inside me right now, the heavy boulders sinking, all the lies I tell about myself, and yet a thousand sensations of air, light, movement, explosions. My brain won't function. I can't think. I can't think of what to say. How can he say he loves me? Why would he think I'm worthy of that?

I have to say something. Neither of us is talking.

"Mark—"

Both our bodies jerk at almost the same time, his a fraction of a second ahead of mine.

He says, "I'm awake. Peak experiences created by high-intensity situations, such as extreme fear or heightened emotional awareness."

I don't know if I will ever get used to that. My heart sinks. I don't have to get used to that, because we can't ever date. I've got to convince him.

"Mark, this weekend has been amazing. You're amazing. But I am not dating material. I am very, very messed up."

"I know."

"No, you really don't. I can't even explain—"

He looks at me. "Vin. Please. When we lay in the grass looking up, you freaked out looking at the sky. Considering staring at a clear blue sky is about the most relaxing thing in the world, my guess is you're an eight point five on the Damaged Scale. Out of ten. Who freaks out looking at a clear sky? I get it. You're fucked up. All your rules, your weird word games in emails and IMs...plus, I saw it all weekend. I don't care. I'm in love."

I can't breathe. I can't speak.

He has stolen all the words from me.

Mark says, "I'm messed up too, in my own ways. Maybe it's hard to see right now, but I am."

That's not possible. He has no flaws.

He looks around. I do the same.

Nearby evergreen trees get caressed by a ghost breeze, rustling their heavy branches in an appropriately somber fashion. The monochrome tombstones endure gray November with a stoicism few living souls ever witness. The two other visitors I saw earlier reach their car. Soon, we'll be alone in this dead city.

"Also, Patty, he mostly dresses like a bum, all wrinkled shirts and old jeans, which for some reason, I happen to like. So, I guess that's not a flaw. He prefers to be in charge all the time, which, also, I happen to like. Maybe a lot. I discovered things about myself this weekend. I learned a lot about who I am."

"Mark, you deser—"

"Still talking, Vin."

His tone is quiet, firm. My mouth opens to argue, but maybe it's just best to do what Mark wants. Nevertheless, I have things to explain. *He can't love me!* Also, I have questions. He talked to the kings? Which ones? Or should I remain quiet and listen? Don't I owe him that much after what I put him through this weekend?

"You just heard him interrupt me. He's got, like, no people skills."

"*Hey.*"

Why am I objecting? He's right.

"I mean, he does have some people skills. He goes out of his way to show kindness. Twice this weekend, I started to say 'fuck off' to strangers but Vin spoke first and showed kindness to a-holes. Especially to this one lady, asking if Vin was bothering me. I would have pushed her off the pier, given the opportunity and ten dollars, as that guy on the corner used to say. Remember him, Patty? That weird guy? I think he died. I haven't seen him in a few years. Anyway, Vin ignored their rudeness. He's not an idiot. He saw it. He's just nicer than most people. See, this is the problem, Patty. I like his lack of people skills. It's funny. Sweet. Everything that's a flaw about him, I end up liking."

I want to argue these points, but what would I say? Explain my people skills aren't so charming after one weekend, that after—

"I was kidding you about the racism stuff," he says, squeezing my hand. "But boy, you get defensive fast."

"I do not."

The words fly out of my mouth before I can appreciate the irony.

He suppresses a smile, and says, "Okay, Vin."

Damn it.

"He's lonely," Mark says. "Super lonely."

I keep my mouth clamped shut. It hurts to hear him say it out loud.

"Although, I'm not sure I consider that a flaw so much as a state of being. I mean, I'm lonely too. You're gone. Brian's always busy, being a parent. I'm lonely."

The cemetery wind is cold.

"Oh, and he's rich," Mark says. "Mega-rich. And you know how I feel about rich people, Patty. They are the worst."

Okay, this one I had better correct.

"Mark, I know two hotel rooms and an expensive dinner seems—"

"Patty, before showing up this weekend, he ordered me an Armani suit, from the Askani line, double-breasted with hand stitching. It's gorgeous. Three fittings in the past two weeks. In other parts of the world, actual royal people wear these. Watch. I'll unbutton. It's very sexy. Oh, by the way, suit sex was even better than I had fantasized. We did it watching the Newark skyline. Incredible."

He shoots me an appreciative grin.

For his sister, he unbuttons with grace to expose his silky lemon shirt. He does so with the flair of a man used to wearing expensive suits, like a power move in a corporate meeting.

"This shirt? Easily three hundred dollars. Probably four hundred."

"Mark—"

"Still talking, Vin." He squeezes my hand. "It's not the price tag of the shirt or suit that makes me think he's stupid rich. The tailor put the suit's credentials and receipts in this elegant folder and Vin said, 'Toss it.' You know who keeps a receipt for an Armani suit? Everyone. You know who *doesn't* keep the receipt? I know you're thinking rich people, but nope. Rich people always keep the receipt. For insurance, if nothing else. If they suck enough, they'll try to find a way to return the suit after they've worn it. They're the worst. No, you have to be the next level up—crazy, stupid rich—to be disinterested in an Armani receipt. This is the kind of suit you pass on to someone in your will."

"The money—"

"Craaaaaaaaaaazy rich." He holds up his hand to halt me, and I stop. But he keeps his hand raised, angling his arm to highlight his wrist. "These cufflinks? Patty, they're real diamonds. Last night at the restaurant, I excused myself to go to the washroom for a short nap. Then, I waited outside the women's bathroom, and I invited this lady to have a secret with me. I told her I thought these were real diamond cufflinks, and the only way to be sure was to scratch something glass, and did she have an old compact I could use to test it? Well, she didn't. But the next lady I asked did, and we scratched it together, each of us taking turns, guessing how much we think Vin spent on these. She was really nice, and we were having fun together. Her name was Eileen.

"My point," he says, lowering his arm and intertwining his hand with mine again. "I know money. If you remember, Patty, I worked three years as a busboy at the country club."

He faces me. "Busboy rule number one: distinguish the super rich from the kinda rich. You're definitely super rich, Vin. Your only saving grace is you don't seem obsessed with money. As rich as you are, you didn't even use the suit to impress me. Anyone else would have spent all weekend bragging about it. Saying things like 'Did you see that stitching?' and 'I hear the tailor learned the craft from his father,' really douchy things. But you never did. That's the only reason I think I might be able to tolerate your wealth. Otherwise..."

He was going to ditch me this weekend? He thought about it? Am I reading into that?

He shows a quiet amusement in his eyes. "Though I wouldn't be surprised if there were a ton of rules about how you spend the money. Like, you can only spend it on charities. Your suit looks sexy sharp on you, but it's from JCPenney. Clearly, you don't spend money on yourself. But I can learn to tolerate your being rich, as long as you don't try to impress me with it."

How—how do I explain the money? Although, what's to explain? He seems to possess a surprisingly good grasp already.

"He does have good qualities," Mark says, returning his gaze to his sister's stone. "He makes me laugh. He's smart. Decent astronaut. He's got this quality which is like thoughtfulness, but bigger. At the restaurant last night, there were a dozen roses on our table. Nobody ever bought me flowers before—not ever— and I didn't know what to say. They were beautiful, but I froze. I don't know why, but I felt weird. So, I ignored them. Vin didn't point them out or make me feel small. He didn't need to take credit, not if it might embarrass me. And I know he wasn't intentionally trying to make me feel bad about my being younger. I know he's struggling with it, and he showed up this weekend anyway, so I can live with a little hurt. He came to create this perfect weekend with me. He succeeded. It's been perfect."

My eyes well with tears. I don't deserve this.

"Patty, I've been complaining to you for years now how desperately I wanted to get laid. But I had very specific kinks I wanted to explore in my first time. Cigar smoke, being picked up by a stranger in a parking lot, raunchy sex in a cheap motel. Being dominated. I mean, just because a person is a virgin, doesn't mean he can't fantasize. Extensively. My sex brain is exploding. My biggest fantasy was no condoms. I wanted my first time to be completely raw. Vin spent months online trying to argue me out of, it but I told him I would use condoms for the rest of my life, most likely, so I deserved to know at least once how it felt. That way, I wouldn't be tempted. I even told Vin, as part of the role-playing, when I suggested condoms, I wanted him to tell me 'no.' That was a very specific part of my fantasy."

I can't believe I went through with that! So fucking irresponsible.

"Two months ago, Vin finally agreed. He still argued with me, but he agreed. Last Thursday, he FedExed his STD test results. He even included a Western blot HIV breakdown, the antibody test, which was way over-the-top unnecessary. There was a chart and everything."

I should have done the right thing and pulled out, despite what he wanted.

You can't bareback in this day and age.

"Fantasy-wise, he did exactly what I wanted. Although, I can't believe he went through with it. In fact, that's when I knew I loved him. He gave me what I wanted, Patty, despite feeling so strongly I shouldn't want it. That meant a lot. You can only be that unselfish when you love someone. In fact, the first word he said to me as

Vin—not the pick-up stranger from the convenience store—was *love*. His very first word to me."

No. I said other words—

"His first words as *Vin*," he says, as if correcting my thoughts. "He loves me."

No, no, no! This can't work! I'm a Lost King! I'll always be a Lost King! Hasn't he figured that out?

I feel his grip tighten.

"I need to lie down," he says. "Just for a second."

I worry he will pass out instantly, so I ease him to the ground, but he seems to be under his own power, reclining on the dead grass. He's fading. I feel like I'm the wicked witch putting Sleeping Beauty into his glass coffin. He snuggles into the earth, as much as one can in a cemetery. I look around. As his hand slips from mine, I reach out to grab it and fold it on his stomach.

He snores, quiet little *zzzz*'s I only hear with my face near his.

I stand up.

Oh god, this doesn't look right, his hands folded on his stomach. He looks like a corpse. Should I move his hands? I feel awful, him lying flat in a cemetery, wearing an expensive suit, and me hovering over him. Mark, come back! Come back! How much time before he wakes? He looks so peaceful. Oh god! This is so fucking creepy. I want to shake him awake, I can't stand watching him like—

"Love," he says, opening his eyes and looking into mine. He smiles, almost bashfully. "I can't believe that worked. I told myself to remember that word, to say it—first thing—just like you said the word *love* to me, and it worked." He raises himself on his elbows. "How long was I asleep?"

Before I can answer, he says, "Doesn't matter. A little help?"

I clasp his arm and pull him up. While he straightens his tie, I brush the grass off his shoulders as if I am his valet. I'm so fucking relieved to see him vertical.

"Patty, I've hardly narco'd on him all weekend. That's another plus in his favor. I went off my meds to see if he could deal with my falling asleep. And yes, I crashed hard a few times, especially after we had sex for the first time. But I was in total ecstasy and overwhelmed by the feeling of him. Standing near Vin, I feel like I'm constantly getting a tan. I feel like I have to be awake every second or I might miss something he does or says. I don't want to miss anything."

He squeezes my hand asks me, "Did it bother you? My naps?"

Softly, I say, "No. Yes, sometimes. Just now, seeing you horizontal in a graveyard wearing a suit, yes. But no. I mean, mostly no. Except...yes."

I don't even know what to say to this kid anymore. Why am I a babbling idiot?

Quit calling him a kid. He's a man. Hasn't he proven it over and over?

He turns to Patty. "Oh. Back to flaws. Mom and Dad hate him."

What?

"A minute ago, I mentioned how Vin FedExed his blood work? Mom and Dad were *very* curious to know what kind of man does that before a first date."

"How did your parents see it? Didn't I send it to your dorm room?"

"I don't live in a dorm. I live in a house."

He looks at me expectantly.

It takes a second for me to make the connection. "You live with your parents?"

"Yup."

"But you said you were a college student."

"I am."

"I mailed it to Wilshire Hall or something like that."

"I told you to our address on Wilshire. You added the word *Hall* on your own."

"C'mon. You encouraged me to think it was a dorm. You implied—"

"You're right, Vin. I admit, I didn't say street or avenue. But I didn't exactly lie. I just didn't tell all of the truth."

"You told me you have two roommates who eat a lot of pizza."

"I do. Mom and Dad. You assumed they weren't my parents. Well, they are. It's just the three of us at home. Brian, my older brother, moved out years ago, and Patty is dead. They're always inventing wacky pizza flavors. They're kinda gourmet cooks. Plus, we go to Romero's as a family."

"You didn't—"

"Gosh, I wonder why I wouldn't volunteer I live with my folks to the guy I was trying to seduce. Duh, Vin. I was trying to keep it a secret. Of course, I never imagined you'd send me your blood work before our weekend together. Who does that?"

I try to absorb this latest shock, biting my tongue. I want to complain he lied to me. Again. But how many thousands of lies have I told, lies of omission, like this one? How many men were upset—or worse—to find out I had deceived them. Hell, I lied to Rance about being Vin Vanbly for almost an entire weekend. How dare I get upset by this? No wonder he was reluctant to go to Romero's on Friday night. Thank god we didn't run into them.

"Of course, after seeing the blood work thing—and I don't have to tell you how overprotective they are—they insisted on meeting Vin."

I look at the sun, well, the brightest smudge in the cloudy sky. Roughly, ten forty-five. Thank god we won't have time. "Mark, we may not have time…"

"Don't worry about your precious noon deadline, Vin. We already met them."

I feel every muscle in my face sag at once.

"Oh yes," Mark says with a sigh. "We most definitely did. Patty, Vin refused to tell dad his name."

Oh shit. Shit, shit motherfucking shitbags, fucking hell.

I try to keep my voice even. "The coach?"

"Patty, as you undoubtedly remember, Dad was my little league coach. And he made me join the traveling league to keep me out of trouble. It gets worse. After refusing to introduce himself, then, Vin bragged about our sex life. To Dad."

I want to die. I want to disappear into the ground, to become one of this dead community.

"The funny thing is," Mark says, and chuckles, "I worried *they* would embarrass *me*. I insisted they not reveal they were my parents. Boy, I worried about the wrong thing."

"Why didn't your dad say something? Or punch me in the face?"

"Because he's civilized. And he respects me. Although, I think he wanted to kill you. As we checked out, whenever you weren't looking, I gave Dad the 'give me a moment' finger, indicating I was going to take you outside and come back in. But I never went back inside. Instead, we headed down a side street and ditched him."

He pulls out his phone. "Check it out. Thirty-two unheard messages from them."

Oh my god.

"It's okay. I texted them while you were getting us coffee yesterday afternoon. I said the date was fine and you would most likely feel sorry once you realized what you had done. I told them to quit calling, and I'd see them later today. They didn't like that. I had to remind them that I'm an adult. We're going to have one hell of a fight later."

Why won't the earth open up to swallow me whole? I want to never speak aloud again. How could I ever look Mark in the eye? Or his father? I glance around as if his dad might appear around a tombstone. I try to remember his face. He looked familiar. *That's* why he looked familiar. He looks a little like Mark.

I want to die.

"Dad even asked me how Mom did with Vin. I told the truth. *Not well.*"

Oh god.

"Your mom?"

Mark shakes his head. "Mom had to beat off Vin's sexual advances with a broom. So, yeah, Thanksgiving next year should be fun times."

Oh my god. *Oh my god.*

"There's no point in getting angry," Mark says with a sigh. "It's just Vin being Vin. He is who he is. It would be nice if my new boyfriend got along with my parents and resisted bragging about our sex life, but I guess I was expecting too much. Boy, I bet they'll be glad about this nine-month separation. Nine full months of them trying to convince me never to see Vin again."

I feel sick. I'm going to be sick. "Mark, I'm so sorry."

I don't know what else I could possibly say.

"They're probably filing a restraining order." Mark turns to me with the hint of a smile. "Although, it was a tiny bit funny, your refusing to tell Dad your name. Who acts that way?" The hint becomes a smile, trying to stop itself from becoming a smirk. He lets a few halting laughs escape. "Oh, Vin. What do we do now?"

He surrenders to the laughter.

Mark! Don't leave me!

I am falling apart inside. Everything's crumbling.

No.

No, you fucking idiot, you douche bag. You asshole. The last few minutes have proven thirty times over, Mark deserves better. His kindness, his tenderness toward my shitty behavior—he's already a Found King, and I could never, ever be with a Found One. Never.

"Not everybody hates you, Vin." He squeezes my hand. "I introduced you to Nicole, my best friend, and she digs you. She gave me two thumbs up as we left the coffee shop."

Her? She was signaling Mark? Did I get anything right this weekend?

This is what happens when you don't stalk someone!

"Anyway, Patty, I wanted you to meet him," Mark says. "We can't stay long because Vin leaves at noon. That's another big rule: our weekend ends exactly at noon. I want him inside me one more time before he leaves for nine months, so, we should go. But you had to meet him, Patty. You had to see who I found."

My head is spinning. My feet feel icy in these dress shoes. A chill runs up my back. He manipulated me all weekend. All weekend, I thought I was in control—oh god, I hit on his mom.

"By the way," Mark says. "He thinks he's a ghost."

Electricity runs through me, head to toe.

"Which is funny, because my sore butt says he's very much alive."

After a few seconds of silence, he says, "Let's go."

He tugs my arm. We turn.

Without looking at me, he says, "Patty likes you too."

I jerk my head back, half expecting to see her phantom rising. Nothing. Nothing but tombstones crowding her on every side against a dead, gray sky.

"She's not there," he says, still facing forward. "This is just the last place I saw her."

He leads me away.

Away.

In our dingy room—pregnant with memories I will revisit obsessively in the coming months—neither of us turns on the light. Gray light seeps in from the cold crack between curtains, taking refuge on the thin carpeting, illuminating the occasional cigarette burn. The radiator kicks in with a mysterious sequence of clicks, a weak trickle of warmth pissing into the room. He watches me while he unknots his tie, his black eyes studying me.

I find myself avoiding his gaze, focusing on my shirt buttons, unsure how to apologize for everything—all my humiliations lined up before his naked, unflinching inspection. I glance up, and he smiles at me, the smile elongating into his sexy grin. I shamed him in front of both parents. He witnessed my shabby treatment of him—and he forgave. He loved me anyway.

The second he glances down to watch his pants hit the floor, I allow my eyes to fill with tears. He loved me. He loves me still.

I have to end this.

When he steps out of his slacks, I find my determination at war with my lust. I mean, look at him. His unbuttoned shirt reveals his muscular chest, those muscles you find only on someone in their twenties, the flesh plump with youth. Black hair in forests on his lower legs like assless chaps. His butt is not hairy. He's built like one of Pan's inner circle, a satyr insatiable and fresh. I'm too old. He deserves younger, better.

Stop.

Set that truth aside. He saw it on your face all weekend, those doubts exposed. Honor this young king by calling him a *king*, forgetting his age and letting him be a man.

My king.

I step to him, cupping his jaw in both hands. His lips. *His lips!*

His kiss reflects newfound sexual confidence discovered over the weekend. I taste his strength, the strength of a man who understands his power, his ability. When our lips mold to each other's perfectly, refusing to separate, I recognize this kiss. This is a Found King kiss. This is a Sunday morning kiss from a man who understands he is special in the world. He need not say it, he need not shout it. He never needs exposure to *The Lost and Founds*. He is content to know it within himself.

I have to end this.

This realization makes me kiss him harder and makes my dick rise against him. He feels my desperation and unleashes his own. Nine months. We can't see each other for nine months, and it's my fucking rule that—no. No. I can't see him ever again. I'm not good for him.

"I love you," he says with a gasping breath when we pull away from each other. *I can't say it back! I have to end this!*

He drops to his knees and pulls down my underwear, exposing my true feelings for him, as my hard cock bats him across the forehead. He laughs and drops his mouth over the entire thing at once, instantly down his throat. My head shoots backward, exploding in sensation, and my hands grab the sides of his head in surprise.

Breaking up will have to wait.

The only thing I focus on is the wetness of him, the insistence, as if every long suck argues why I need him, why we must stay together, why this weekend experience should elongate into something greater. I want to argue with him, and my lips move in response, but the sounds coming from me are soft grunts, not words. I clasp his head, feel the perfection of his thick, short hair, his hairline, and I urge the back of his head deeper onto my cock until I feel his drool rolling down the seam of my balls. I hear him moan, not flinching from a single inch of my cock. Nobody told him deep-throating takes practice and experience, so he just does it.

I picture us together, a thousand positions, several we've already explored this weekend and many, many we have not. Picturing him naked and on top of me, under me, to the side of me, nakedly cooking pancakes with me, all of it makes my cock harder, which makes me precome more. I cannot feel it oozing out of me, I cannot distinguish it from his saliva slathered all over me, but his happy little jerks tell me he tastes it. He likes it. This makes my dick harder.

I usually have such control over my orgasms, but around him, nothing is assured. Nothing is predictable. Where's my word mania? Where did he hide it? Clearly, I interpreted everything wrong this weekend. How come I can't read him the way I read others? How did he manipulate me all weekend without me knowing, and—why don't I want this weekend to end? It's getting close enough to noon I must figure out a way to end this—to end us—without breaking him, this golden king, bearing maturity and confidence beyond his years.

Also, I'm going to come down his throat.

He jerks his head off me as if yanked.

"Don't come yet," he says, gasping for air, kneeling before me, panting.

Can he read my mind? Is that possible? No, that's crazy. But he's always one step ahead of me—always knows what's happening right before I do. I have to keep up with him. Wait, is that where my brain has been focused all weekend instead of word stuff? I'm busy trying to keep pace with him? A warmth floods me, an awareness extending beyond rational knowledge, a sensation this is true—true—in words I cannot explain. *I can't keep up with him!*

"Move," I say, trying to recover. "I want you to sit on my cock."

Get focus. Get focus back. Don't cry in front of him. Don't start missing him already, this king.

I've got to end this.

I lie on my back, making toward the middle of the bed. With a sexy confidence, he climbs on top of me, straddles me, and within seconds, my cock is inside him as he pushes back. That incredible muscular ass descends around my thick cock, and his eyes shine light right into mine. He's an angel while his ass works me like a python. His ass has an obscene talent for this.

I buck up into him, and he smiles, grins crazily at me.

"My butt is so sore, Vin. Go easy."

Oh god, his ass!

The way he grinds against me, the way he forces me deeper inside him...I can't—I can't—I can't.

I'm going to lose myself in him, am already losing myself in him and I—*wait*. I know how to end this. He must admit he's a Found King! Then, when he can't reach me in nine months, when I am living in a small town lost deep within Honduras, he'll finally understand why we can never be together.

Stay in control. Don't let the orgasm come.

"You've been to my website," I say, trying to control my words.

I feel sweat forming. His body undulates on mine, and despite the skill in his ass, he winces, grimaces, as if he's having an uncomfortable conversation. His hands find my hairy chest, and he falls forward. When he pushes his ass back, the hardness of my cock pushes against his interior, a new angle, a new pleasure. Always a new pleasure. Go easy, Vin. He's sore.

"Hey," I say, half-panting.

"Yes," he says, at last. "Your website."

His eyes are closed.

"You know about the Lost Kings, and the Found Ones?"

"Yes." His eyes are closed, and he twists his head.

I force my pelvis up, jabbing him again.

"Oh," he says. "*Oh.*"

Go easy!

I want to grill him—find out who he spoke with besides Perry. How did he find Perry? The kings have gone underground. But none of this matters. None of it. He must admit it. It's the only way he'll understand why we can't be together.

"Mark, are you a Lost King or a Found King?"

Wow. Subtle.

Damn it, where's my finesse? Where's my fucking polish? I can't do anything right around him. Why won't he quit loving me?

He grunts and pushes himself up again, sitting upright. Oh god. I can't last too long like this. He reaches to me with both arms, hands grasping my forearms as I rise to meet him. With his eyes closed, I assume he's contemplating the question, until I realize he's snoring lightly, and my arms are supporting him much more than he's grasping me.

Again? Seriously?

How is it I keep fucking this guy into unconsciousness?

He opens his eyes, blearily, with a dreamy smile spreading over him. He's so beautiful. The shadow on his jaw, those eyes—I can't last much longer.

"I dreamed you were fucking me." His smile gets wider, and he closes his eyes again. "And then I woke up."

No diversions. He has to answer.

"Marky, are you lost or found?"

He blinks at me, smiling, and squeezes his ass.

Oh god.

"Lost or found?" I gasp.

I feel the familiar tingling throughout my whole body. It's coming. I'm coming.

"I heard you." He stops gyrating his body.

No—no, don't stop now! I'm so close! So fucking close.

His faraway look becomes more present, and he focuses his attention on me. "Which one are you, Vin? A Lost King or Found King?"

"No, you first. You have to answer first. Quickly."

"Why?"

"Because you do. Hurry."

He exhales, still not moving. "This feels very childish."

My orgasm hovers right between "very soon" and "not happening," and I find myself confused which I want in this moment. I'm ready to blast into him and jack off for the rest of my life to the memory of it—but he's got to answer the question.

"Fine." He crosses his arms.

He sits back, and the movement is enough to make my legs quiver.

"I'm on your team, Vin. Whichever team that is."

No! He has to answer!

Keeping my voice even, I say, "It doesn't work that way, Mark. You have to pick Lost or Found."

"I did," he says. "I picked your team."

"That's avoiding. That's not how it works."

"Sure it is," he says, introducing the slightest rocking motions. "You already know what team you're on—I assume—which means I'm on that team too."

I feel the sweat pooling on my chest.

He says, "I like your chest muscles. They're big."

"Mark, it doesn't work—"

"You don't get to make the rules, Vin." He pushes back, and I find my orgasm receding. "Not all of the rules at least. If every man is the one true king, well then, I am the one true king. I get to make some rules too. We all do. Which means when I say 'I'm on your team,' it counts. Are you happy? I chose."

No! No! He can't! He has to admit it.

But he picked me!

He twists to the right, his whole body, as if stretching out his lower back, and my cock twists with him. I was so close a few seconds ago.

"I think we should be Found Kings," Mark says. "On your website, they sounded like more fun. I liked their adventures. But I don't care. We could be Lost Ones too. I bet you'd make being a Lost King more fun."

Mark, you're *better* than this! Why won't you admit it?

He twists his entire torso to the left this time, stretching his arms, facing the window.

My cock hasn't gotten softer, only retreated, so the intensity of this stretch, and how it twists my cock, brings me closer to where I want to be. But where do I want to be? Am I trying to seduce him further or break up with him forever?

"Oh god," he says, still staring out the window. There's enough space between curtains to see into the parking lot.

He twists his body again, and he might jerk the orgasm right out of me, but he's off me with a wet, cold plop. My cock resumes its life in the outside-of-Mark world. He jumps to the side of the bed.

"Hurry, get dressed!" He yells with an urgency I haven't seen all weekend.

He races around the room, picking up my clothes and throwing them at my duffel bag, the fat brown one I used this weekend. I have no idea what he saw out that window, but after how much I let him down all weekend, I owe him this, to trust him, to follow his lead. I jump off the bed, grab my boxer briefs and struggle into them.

Oh god.

His father is out there. *Maybe with a gun.* Mark doesn't even make time for his underwear, sliding his sweatpants over his muscular butt, and I twist inside knowing I will never see his beautiful ass again. I will never be inside him again. Never.

This fuels my panic. I race to put on socks.

He never said he was a Found King! What will he do when he can't find me? When I'm living beyond the reach of a telephone or any communication?

"Hurry," he cries again, obviously distressed.

His father is coming. What if he tries to hurt Mark? What if it's the neighbors who called us *faggots* last night?

This inspires me to shove my jockstraps, my shoes, the rain jacket I brought in case it poured on us, and remaining clothing into my bag. No time to pack. No time to organize. But I've got to communicate it could never work between us, not ever. How? How do I do that?

Don't think, just do.

I reach into my pants pocket, hoping to find the truck keys, and instead find the folded index card, my words written at Romero's pizzeria. A note! I'll leave him a note, one sentence explaining why we can never be together.

"I'll get your toothbrush and bathroom stuff!" He disappears into the bathroom.

I grab the pen from the worn desk, and on the blank side, I write the five words that will explain everything. Instinctively, I write in all caps. I refold the note and throw it onto a pillow as Mark emerges and races to my duffel.

"What's happening, Mark? Where are we going?"

"Just hurry," he says. "I'll explain everything outside the room."

My pants are up, and I shove my left foot into an unlaced boot. My lavender dress shirt is buttoned wrong but I can fix it later. Where's the other boot? Mark already opens the door, flooding the dark corners with dirty sunlight. Mark grabs my right boot from inside the door and tosses it a few feet off the cement stoop. I grab my bag, and with a furtive look around the room, I hobble to the door. I've got everything! We've got to get out of here!

I jump into the dull outside, and three feet out, drop to one knee, wanting to remain unseen. Where is he? I don't see his dad. I don't see any cars I recognize, but

I wouldn't recognize his parents' car, would I? Of course not. I glance at my boot ten feet away. I've got to grab it if we're going to take off running.

With a hiss in my voice, I say, "What are you seeing? Who's here?"

Only then do I realize he's not scurrying behind me. In fact, he's not moving from the motel room. I stand and pivot. Mark stands in the doorway, shirtless, cross-armed, watching me.

Why is he not hurrying?

"Mark?"

"You said we had to end the weekend exactly at noon," he says coolly. "I made sure you were out of the room by noon, because, I promised you I would follow your rules."

The wind is cold, and I feel it ripple through my flimsy shirt.

He looks behind him at the digital clock on the nightstand. "I obeyed exactly as you instructed, Vin. Our weekend together is over. Although, I gotta tell you, I never understood why noon was so important. You mentioned it three times in emails and twice on the phone, so I assume noon is magicals or something. Boy, it's going to be *fun* dating someone who thinks noon is *magicals*."

My mouth is dry. My heart pounds.

Magicals isn't even a word.

"I know we only spent one weekend together, Vin, but that was my sarcastic voice."

The adrenaline flooding me has nowhere to go. There's no need to panic. I force myself to speak. "Noon isn't magic."

"Are you sure? Because you made a really big deal about it. You said it was for both our protection."

The wind flips open my shirt and tickles my love handles, but I barely notice. I mean, it's cold as fuck, but he's staring at me, evaluating me. How did I not catch him timing this so perfectly? Doesn't matter. He's right, I should go. My exposed foot is freezing. But I can't move.

"Well, good-bye, Vin," he says in an aloof voice. "Thanks for taking my virginity."

He steps back a few feet and slams the door.

What just happened to me?

My heart leaps into my throat, desperate to be on the other side of the door, to be with him, just ten more minutes, just fifteen minutes. If I could have fifteen more minutes, I'd be able to part with him forever, I know it. If I could just have fifteen or twenty minutes.

The door swings open.

Mark crosses his arms. "By the way, I didn't say anything in our emails, but I'm not a big fan of the letter *x*. I mean, *x* sounds pinched next to an *i*, or strong like an axe next to *a*. It changes to *zee* if it's standing before an *e*. Who the hell does that? *X* is shady as fuck. You know what letter I prefer? The letter *m*. Capital *M*, specifically."

I hate capital M.

"Capital *M* is the only letter to make its own babies without another letter, because it starts the word *Mmmmmmm*, which is the sound I make any morning when I wake up happy. You think I moaned yesterday morning because of you, and yes, I did, but I would have *Mmmmmmmmmm*-ed if I smelled bacon. I like bacon. Which is a problem if I am going to be a vet. Also, *M* begins the name Mark, which is another reason to like it."

What is he saying?

"Hey, speaking of kids, do you want kids, Vin? Have you thought about our future at all?"

Our future? I feel panic edging into my voice. "Are you asking me if I want to have *kids*?"

"Calm down. I only asked the question. Hey! Duh, there's a more obvious reason you should love capital *M*. It's the first letter of your name too."

Wait—

"Your real name."

Whatthefuck?

"Oh, don't look so surprised. I found your name online. I'm a millennial, Vin, that's what we do. That's Millennial with a capital *M*. We use the interwebs. I didn't do anything illegal, well, a little illegal, some basic hacking, nothing too intense."

"You hacked? You're a hacker?"

"No. Yes, a little. Nicole and I researched you. It wasn't hard to find the title paperwork to the garage you own in St. Paul. It's funny you named it Vincent's Garage considering your name isn't Vincent. We confirmed your real name with public records of the home you purchased years ago. That wasn't hacking. More like investigative skills."

He knows my real name.

"Your house is super cute." He steps back and begins to close the door. "Well, it's two minutes after noon. See ya."

I stop the door. "Wait, Marky. I can stay past noon. It just—I get—"

"No, Vin," he says with a sigh. "You were very clear about the rules." He cocks his head. "If I make an exception for you, I'll have to make one for every barebacking sex date—"

No!

"Oh, relax. I'm messing with you. I'm yours and only yours. You know that."

Despite the thrill soaring through me, my brain says, *no, no, no.* He's not mine, I'm not—we were just going to meet for the weekend. For sex! He can't be *mine.* I could never be with him. He knows that. He *knows* that.

He glances at a pretend watch. "Oh, look. Now, it's three minutes past noon. Nobody died. The sun didn't explode. Uh-oh. What if noon isn't magicals? What then, Vin?"

Cold sunlight strikes his face, making his eyes a golden chocolate brown.

"So, anyway. Nine months."

He steps back.

"Wait!"

My plea is too late. The door slams shut.

The door opens almost immediately. "I know you like to be in charge. I like it, too. I will do what you say, Vin Vanbly. I will go wherever you lead us. But you better make sure of what you want."

The door slams again.

Why did I say nine months? Why can't I—wait, does he think we could adopt kids together? How can I wait nine months to discuss what he meant? Plus, I'm moving to Honduras. I can't breathe. He hacked my real name! Which means anyone could find me. I don't think anyone's looking anymore, but still. He and his best friend found me.

I take two deep breaths and rebutton my shirt. I need to put on my right boot. My items stuffed into and falling out of my duffel bag make it appear like a twice-baked potato. It's cold! Where's my suit jacket? Did I leave that inside? Why do I make so many rules? Why am I so fucked up? I can't—

The door swings open.

Before I even see him emerge, a folded square of paper flutters to the brown-stained cement stoop.

"I found your note on the pillow. I'm not much of one for notes, Vin. I'm more of a just-tell-me kind of guy, but I love you, so I wrote my reply under yours. Hey, I've got an idea. How about if you wait nine months to read my reply, just like I'm waiting for you."

The door slams again.

A slight wind lifts the folded note, and I snatch it from the cement as if it were a hundred-dollar bill. I stare at it, uncomprehending. Can I really not unfold this for nine months? I have to explain why we will never, ever work. Fuck, what did he write? Am I going to spend the next nine months wondering how to let him down gently? Or did he dump me in the note?

The door opens again.

He emerges excited, and he bears no trace of frustration. "One last thing. When I move in, I want equal share of your closet space, and I'm talking a full fifty percent." He scans me up and down. "I suspect most of your shirts lie in piles on the bedroom floor, but I'm serious about half your closet space. I like my shirts to hang one finger length apart. In the morning when deciding what to wear, I need to see the colors. Colors are important."

Wait. He wants—"You're moving in?"

"Well, living with my parents could have been an option, but you torpedoed that this weekend. I'm flexible on shoes. I don't need a full half of the floor space. Just hanging space." His face clouds over. "But that can't happen for another nine months, so good-bye."

The door slams again.

Do I read the note? I couldn't possibly have kids. Why would he think that? Did he just instruct me to clean my bedroom closet? Should I read the note? He knows my real name! What else does he—what did he write? He only had a few seconds to scribble a response.

From the other side of the door, he yells, "*I'm not asleep. I wasn't just sleeping.*"

Mark! Mark! Mark! Like a dog's bark!

Nausea sweeps over me. Basement words. Never! I refuse to remember those words. Those words are locked up tight.

"*IT'S SIX MINUTES PAST NOON, VIN. YOU'RE STILL NOT LEAVING. I CAN SEE YOU THROUGH THE PEEPHOLE.*"

He's inches away. I squeeze the folded note until it pokes the tender inside of my right hand.

"*IS THE SUN EXPLODING? IS EVERYTHING ALL MAGICALS OUT THERE?*"

I touch my fingertips to the door. He's on the other side.

I love him.

"*GOOD-BYE, VIN! GOOD-BYE!*"

Why am I always saying good-bye?

King Fitch

The events of this story also take place in 2005

ONE

He muscles his way past me, closer to the people-packed bar, *muscles* being the operative word. Even in this darkened club I see them, spread over him like thick gobs of honey. Muscle queen. I wonder how much time he spends gym-bound to get muscles that actually bulge? I lift, but have achieved nothing compared to him. Fat, bouncing biceps glide over lesser-known muscles supporting them.

Huh.

He's not so thick he can't move with easy grace. His arms don't hang awkwardly. He's got enough muscle on his six-foot frame—just enough—for admirers to appreciate his perfection. Each time I see him, I ask myself, "Steroids?" Each time, I decide *nope*. I don't think so. He's vain enough to want every ripple to be one hundred percent his—no enhancements. He's got a seven-days-per-week workout regimen. A real regular regimen.

A regular regiment, *regular regimen*, regular regimen. No. More like, *regular* regiment, *regular* regimen, *regular* regimen. Stop it! Don't lift those *r*'s like free weights. Regular regi—*stop*. Picture the forest. Pines launch like rockets from underground silos, fully formed, piercing the letters, the words, beginnings of patterns. Boom. Trees. Nestled in the valley of the Cerro Las Minas, branches droop and unfurl, uncoiling anacondas, and a fawn skitters through the unfolding foliage, damn it, don't think of the word *foliage*, it's too ripe for word play. Mysterious birds, chirping unseen—a cacophony of chittering—drown out the sound of the letter *r*. Bushes, brambles, vines, restraining the letters, pulling them into the fertile earth. Push it away with the forest. *Think of Honduras, your future home.*

I breathe deeply, feeling relief at preventing another episode. The trees help me. They always help me. The word obsession is definitely getting worse. Trees help. But for how long? I'm running out of coping mechanisms.

Stop fixating. Look at him.

His faded cranberry tee implies he grabbed whatever was clean from his laundry hamper. Please, girl. You're fooling no one. Every piece of clothing has been carefully selected to radiate the Abercrombie vibe. He's got it mostly right too. The overly constricting, generic shirt. He doesn't want to appear vain enough to wear an actual Abercrombie & Fitch tee, no, that's too obvious. Frayed baseball cap.

An inch of checkered boxer shorts rising above the skin-tight jeans, highlighting perfect muscle ass. Hairless, I'm sure, either by nature or his salonist. He's too muscular to boast the boyish Abercrombie frame. And too old, too. I'm guessing thirty. Maybe thirty-two.

While I wait for him to get his drink, the music pounds and vibrates its way through the floor, into my shins, up my calves. I'm too old to be carousing on a Saturday night, listening to this goddamn club music. The vocals—if you can call them that—are just the word *dance, dance, dance,* moaned over and over by swollen red lips preaching from the giant monitors surrounding the dance floor. I assume this is good club music, because the floor is packed with gay men and assorted guests gyrating hard, pounding the air and squealing. Sweet-smelling coconut smoke occasionally explodes in bursts from unseen sources, filling the air with enough fog to suggest an English moor and writhing ghosts. Ugh. This crap is probably toxic, full of carcinogens. *Boy, Vin. You're fun on a Saturday night.*

Through the fog, I glimpse two shirtless guys dancing together, true Abercrombies, drawing envious stares, and I watch with a distracted curiosity.

I should be at home in bed watching *Antiques Roadshow*. Eating turtle cheesecake.

Oh man, now I want turtle cheesecake.

My quarry steps away from the crowded bar rail. How did he get his drink so fast? I wonder if the thirsty patrons parted for one of the beautiful people, or if the bartender thinks it's good for business to have a handsome man wandering the premises, and so he serves him ahead of others. Either way, another win for the beauties.

He's got strong, chiseled features, and an angular jawbone jutting out at a superhero angle. Icy green eyes; I feel their sharpness even in this pulsating light and shadow. I feel like I see his tan, though that's impossible in the blurry rainbow spotlights. Blond hair sticks out from his jaunty cap. I wonder how long it took him to position it for that precise angle of nonchalance.

After a deep pull on his cheap beer, he notices me watching him and says gruffly, "I don't fuck bears. Even muscle bears."

I nod. *My king.*

His withering glance feels like chomping a wintergreen mint. No flicker of recognition accompanies his preemptive dismissal. Tonight is the first time I let him see me. He has no idea about the other times.

He saunters away with enough casual indifference to imply intense boredom. He moves with precision, almost as if walking were somehow a feminine act, and he wouldn't want to convey that—no way—so he works to infuse each step with extra masculinity. He's a man who is aware of how others see him. He wants to appear as if he recently finished working on the farm, baling hay. *Buddy, you're no Mai Kearns.*

There he goes. King Fitch, the last king.

This is my last kinging.

I've said this for a couple years, ever since John at Burning Man. I still get emails from John. Why won't he quit trying to befriend me? He should. I am a Lost King, he is a Found King. Nothing is going to change, not ever. I know it. I accept it. Life is much easier once you accept the reality of your situation.

Damn it, focus up. You let him notice you. You're done.

Time to buy a drink.

While I wait my turn, I pull out a pen from my brown leather jacket and write him an index-card note in all caps.

DO YOU EVER WONDER HOW YOUR LIFE WOULD BE DIFFERENT IF YOU HADN'T BEEN SO INFLEXIBLE? WOULD YOU STILL BE WITH HIM?

Never underestimate the power of a good note.

I drop a pile of twenties for the bartender and hand him the card.

His eyes flash in recognition. "You again." He reads the note. "You're weird, you know that?"

I nod. I may not be one of the beautiful ones—or even a regular—but the bartender knows me.

He scoops up the twenties. "Good tipper, though. Okay, who do you want to receive this?"

"Guy got a beer here a moment ago, wearing a frayed baseball cap, cranberry shirt. Real muscular."

"Jeez, narrow it down a little."

"His name is Kevin."

"I don't know people's names. Be right back." He finishes a drink for someone else and takes their money before returning to me. "C'mon, give me something. I don't know who this is."

What do I say? Fitch is aware of how handsome he is, and he regularly breaks men's hearts. He worships at the church of his glorious physique, and he finds plenty of eager acolytes. He also possesses a streak of compassion which remains buried, as if he fears showing his love to the world.

"He's kind of an asshole," I say. "Very Abercrombie & Fitch but too muscular to be one of those twinks."

"And he was just here? Baseball cap? Got it. We call him On Leave."

"Yeah?"

Over the loud moans cajoling us to *dance, dance, dance,* he raises his voice. "We have nicknames for all the regulars. He always acts like he's on shore leave from the navy. Like this is his first time in a gay bar, and he's surprised to find himself surrounded by homos. A one-fuck wonder. Trolls for twink meat."

"Can you deliver my note to him with a Bell's Oberon?"

I know the beer King Fitch truly prefers, the one he buys for himself to drink at home.

"Sure."

The bartender studies me. "I know how you want it done. Silver tray with the classy gold napkin for presentation. Single bottle and the note handed to him personally."

I nod. "I'm surprised you remember."

"You tip two hundred dollars. Not hard to remember that."

As I back away, I point both index fingers at him. "This is why I'm naming my next car after you. Because of this. This love."

He smirks and glides away to assemble my drink order.

I'm going home. I wonder who sells turtle cheesecake this late.

The next Friday we're in a different club, Fitch and I, the one you go to on Saturday after eleven p.m. but before one thirty. Fridays, you go early. There's a different late-night bar for Friday. There are rules about these things. This Minneapolis bar—the Gay Nineties—is an institution. It began its boozy life as a no-pun-intended gangster club in the 1930s, reinventing itself in the '60s as an underground men's bar—wink, wink—until the mid-80s when it officially climbed out of the closet and accepted its own shabby-fabulous. It's now a fun house, with dark hallways leading to eight unique bars, all connected. A country-western bar, an enormous drag-show stage upstairs, a large dance floor downstairs, a stripper bar, two lounges quiet enough for conversation, and, of course, the leather room. Their wine bar is always empty. I'm not surprised. This place isn't classy enough to pull off a wine bar. I'm intrigued by the variety of people who tramp through these dank corridors, smelling stale beer and a thousand extinguished cigarettes, while searching for true love. Or tonight's true love.

After trailing him for a few minutes, I scout out the best place for our first encounter, and position myself, waiting for him to appear. Not too close to the dance floor, because Fitch and I must hold a conversation tonight. But I want it difficult to engage in quiet conversation too—should be loud enough we have to make every word count. From my position, I see anyone headed to dance as well as those exiting the floor. I'm not blocking the door, but he must pass me to continue working the fun house corridor circuit.

I wait.

Here he comes. Blue frayed hat tonight. An old Minnesota Twins baseball cap. Is he a baseball fan? I've mostly trailed him through nightclubs, but I'd be surprised. I should have followed him more during his day and weekend routines, but I found I didn't need to. Not much anyway. I can make connections faster than when I first started the kingings.

I scan the gyrating crowd—trying to make it obvious I'm looking for someone. I frown, shake my head, use my forefinger to point as if counting...*there*. He's here. Just came in through the door on the other side of the room. A moment later, he flashes recognition and frowns, as if he smells something familiar but can't recall the scent.

He's gone.

Good first contact. That went well.

He'll come back.

Thirty minutes later, he returns, standing off to the side, just beyond my peripheral vision. He thinks I can't see him. Maybe I can't at first. But I feel him near. I *feel* him. Buddy, I've been following you enough to grow attuned to your presence in a crowded room. I've seen you work out. I've watched you buy groceries. I've been to more gay bars in the last three weeks than in the last three years. Of course I know when you're near me. Of course I can tell when your curiosity has been aroused. Tonight, *you* initiate contact with *me*.

He disappears.

I don't have to wait long until he returns, sidling up to me casually.

"'S up."

I nod when he speaks to me, but I'm busy scanning the crowd.

Fitch chugs a deep pull—same cheap beer as last week—waiting for me to begin. I look at him blankly and resume my visual investigation. My brow furrows in concentration.

"Thanks for the beer. Last weekend."

I nod to acknowledge I heard him. I crane my neck as if straining to see someone on the far side of the room.

Loudly, he says, "So, I assume you're one of Jason's friends."

"No. I don't know anyone named Jason. Well, not any Jasons in the Twin Cities."

The music from the dance floor explodes louder, preventing any additional conversation. I swear, it's the same *dance, dance, dance* music from last weekend. You know you're old when all the dance music sounds the same.

I have to shout. "I'm looking for someone. I can't see him. Can you?"

Without knowing who I seek, instinctively, he skims the crowd.

"What would you wear if you were royalty?"

"Did you say royalty?" His voice expresses irritation.

"If you were a king hanging out in this skuzzy club, and you wanted to blend in with all the locals, what would you wear?"

Fitch frowns at me. "What the fuck are you talking about?"

"He's here. Tonight. He's trying to hide, and I don't want to blow his cover. I just need to warn him he's running out of time."

Fitch exhales heavily. "Okay, crazy. I'm outta here."

"He's here." I raise both hands, as if blessing these people. "The king is here. Can't you feel him? He's been here before, and he's growing desperate."

Fitch takes a step away.

I stare at him earnestly. "I know things you don't. Things about the king."

"I was just saying *thank you*, you psycho," he says, disgust on his face. "*Christ.*"

"You should go dance," I say, throwing both hands over my head. "Do that thing where you pump your arms over your head while you're wearing your weightlifting gloves. Really highlights the extra triceps work you've done, bro. Do it."

He glares at me.

"If you see him, remind him he's running out of time," I yell as he backs away. "Remind him to *remember the king.*"

For show, I resume scanning the crowd with a crease in my brow. Suddenly, the people all look like letters trying desperately to form words and create meaning. Uh-oh. That's not good. I used to just get stuck on certain words, the sound of them, the extra meaning buried in their construction. Like the word *dance*. It's a surprisingly strong word, pounding against the floor each time you say it aloud: *dance, dance, dance.* That's why dancers are some of the toughest motherfuckers around. They have to be. That word is relentless, spinning, twirling, the *-ance* pivoting around on its tough *d*. But my crazy word fixation has grown worse. My brain no longer fixates on a word, now it invents visual hallucinations. Those people look like the letters *d*, *a*, *n*, *c*, and *e*, all of them spinning and re-forming, recreating the word with new partners every five seconds.

Stop this before it gets worse.

I force the forest—the pictures I've seen of Honduras—and imagine myself surrounded by the thickest underbrush. Trees will rescue me. Animals. Colorful snakes writhing, creatures hopping. Screaming birds, swooping and eating *dance* letters. Soon. Soon I will move there, retire to a village where I cannot communicate with anyone, and nobody knows my name. I will grow old and die there. Alone. At peace.

Soon.

But tonight's mission is accomplished. I gotta go home. I have to open the garage in the morning. I hate being a mechanic. I didn't imagine it could be any worse owning my own garage.

I was wrong.

It's much worse. Now, there's paperwork.

And tomorrow, I open the shop. I should bring in donuts or something.

Another week. Another club. Pounding music blares in my ear, and I find I'm beginning to recognize certain songs, certain beats. Ah, here he comes. Good. Good. I have got to get back before Tim loses his nerve. When Fitch catches my eye, he grins. Laughs, too. Perhaps it's my lopsided goofy expression. More likely, he cares so little about me, he doesn't mind laughing right in my face.

"Hey, freak."

There's an odd affection in this greeting.

"Hey, Fitch. I'm glad you're here. I need your help."

"My help?" He laughs. "You're kidding me. You think I'd help you?"

"Fitch, in thirty minutes, come to the open area back by the bathrooms. Thirty minutes."

He smiles. "No. Hard pass."

"Thirty minutes. Bathrooms near the cigarette machine. Thanks. You're the best."

"No."

"It has to be you, Fitch. Do this for the team, bro. For the team."

I want to clamp him on the shoulder, but something tells me that's way too familiar.

I back away. "I gotta go. Thirty minutes, Sport."

He says, "You're unbelievable. I should show up, just for the crazy story I can tell my friends at brunch."

As I head toward a different part of the bar, he yells at my backside. "I'm not kissing you, you freak!"

Almost exactly thirty minutes later, he comes into my range of vision, close enough to scout the area and turn heel if what he sees makes him nervous. Fitch probably doesn't understand why he's here. He would like to ignore me, but he can't.

He assesses the situation and moves closer. "Hey, weirdo. I'm here. Make this quick."

"Thanks for coming. Fitch. Meet Tim. Tim wants to say a few things to you."

Next to me stands a handsome man, twenty-one. Cute face and a compact body. His parents originally came from Venezuela and North Carolina, blessing him with a golden brown complexion. Flat belly and jet black hair, artfully spiked. Thick glasses. He is attractive, with a generous dose of nerdy cuteness. I put my hand on his upper back to lend him confidence. He's breathing heavily, staring right at Fitch.

"Tim, say it."

"I want to suck your cock," Tim announces in a strangled voice, and immediately goes wide-eyed.

Fitch glances my way, narrowing his eyes. Tim stares at Fitch with surprised alarm, shocked how he's said—so boldly—words he always wanted to say when approaching a hot bar stranger. We spent a good part of the night discussing the quality of courage.

"I should explain," I say. "Tim works as a business analyst. He's in town for two weeks on a work trip. He saw you out last Sunday afternoon, and then again tonight, and he wants to say a few things. Tim, elaborate."

Tim gapes at Fitch, as if Fitch were the one who spoke with such directness, and Tim can't believe what he heard.

"Say it, Tim. Remember the King of Courage."

Tim sputters and says, "I wanna suck every fat inch. I know your cock is huge. I see it pushing out your jeans, and it makes me want to clamp my mouth around you until you can't stand it and you shoot cummy loads into your jeans. Then, I'd haul it out and suck your cum-covered dick."

Fitch frowns, trying to understand this strange declaration.

With less hesitation, Tim speaks again. "If I got your big cock in my throat, I'd suck out at least two loads before I let go, man. I love to suck dick. It's my favorite thing, and I'm pretty good at it. Okay, I just lied. I'm very good at it."

Fitch asks me, "Who is this guy?"

"One of your fans, Fitch. Someone who thinks you're amazingly handsome and wants your big dick."

Tim says, "Even after you finished coming, I'd keep sucking to milk out every drop. I wouldn't let go until you pushed my head away. I once sucked off a former boyfriend for three and a half hours. He couldn't take anymore."

Fitch considers Tim with something like appreciation. If I understand Fitch's tastes—and I'm sure I do—Tim fits the profile of prime candidate. Nerdy. Twinkish. Handsome. Muscular.

Fitch says, "Sounds good to me."

Tim says, "If you fucked me, I wouldn't make you use a condom."

Okay, too far.

I say, "Hang on, Tim. You gotta use a condom, every time. Even with the mighty Fitch Dick. Fitch, Tim is what you might call shy. I told him a story earlier tonight, and he decided he wanted more courage in his life, more risk-taking. He decided to tell you exactly what he thought of you, regardless of whether it inspired you or disgusted you. Because, you see, it's not about you."

"Oh my god." Tim sputters out the words, only now recognizing what he said.

"You okay, Tim? Breathe. Thanks for showing up, Fitch. You can take off, now."

Fitch jerks his gaze back to me. "What?"

"Take off, bro." I indicate with a nod of my head which direction he should go. "We're done."

Fitch stares at me in amazement. "That's it?"

"My new friend Tim didn't believe he could speak to someone he found so completely unattainable. This was an exercise in courage. And wide-awake hypnosis."

Tim fixates on some imaginary point. Whether he sees Fitch anymore, I cannot tell.

"He's hypnotized?"

"Yes and no. Tim's aware of what he said. But he needed a boost to get his courage closer to the surface."

"That's so..." Fitch's face tightens in a way suggesting both lust and mild aversion. Maybe he's wildly impressed. It's impossible to tell in this shadowed light. I'm surprised we've been able to talk this long without interruptions from the patrons all around us.

"Fitch, my power only works on some men. If they let me, I'm able to change the trajectory of their entire lives in one weekend. Tim's not getting a full weekend, just a few hours of coaching."

"You're a life coach?"

"Me? Coach? Never. I couldn't tell anyone how to live their life. But I can guide a man into the kingdom." I make my gaze hard and unflinching. "Men whose hearts are so unbearably swollen with love they act like a total asshole to the outside world. Men who know their best qualities aren't touching the surface, but they feel stuck. Afraid. Men who know they're running out of time."

Fitch shrinks away in horror. He staggers backward. I crafted those words carefully over the past week, calculating their impact. They're designed to stab him in the chest. Well, the heart.

I yell, "I can guide these men, Fitch!"

Fitch spins abruptly and slips away into the crowd behind us.

He's gone. I saw his wet eyes before he slipped away. Good.

Mission accomplished.

"You were amazing," I say to Tim. "The King of Courage would call you a friend."

Tim's breathing returns to normal. "Oh my god. Please tell me I didn't—"

"You did." I kiss the side of his head. "And you were beautiful."

My next encounter with Fitch is a week later, another bar.

Amidst the exaggerated loudness, thumping base, and nearby drunken conversations, he approaches me, sheepishly. "Hey."

He wears another tight tee, tight jeans, sans baseball cap. What was the bartender's nickname? On Leave?

"Where's your friend? The dude with the glasses?"

"He went back to Atlanta. He's well. Tim sent me an email yesterday to let me know he asked out a man on the bus. The guy said no, but Tim had never done anything so bold. He was happy."

Fitch nods. "Was he any good?"

I play dumb, though I know exactly what he means. "Good?"

Fitch shakes his head, dismissing the question as inconsequential.

"Oh, you mean, *in bed*. I wouldn't know. He wanted you, Fitch. Not me."

"Bullshit. You—"

"I saw your eyes fill with tears before you fled, Fitch."

"You saw nothing," he says with irritation. "You smug prick. You don't know me."

"Maybe not. But if I were to make guesses about you, I'd say you were searching for me tonight. You're not wearing your frayed baseball cap. Not the white one or the blue Minnesota Twins cap. You always wear one of those. Either you're a huge Minnesota Twins fan—which you might be, for casual masculinity points—or, you unconsciously use your baseball cap to protect yourself from emotional entanglement. You're not wearing it tonight, suggesting you came looking for me, specifically. You're open to the possibility. But you're confused as to whether to trust me. You're here because something has got to change in your life. Change quick. Spending all your free time at the gym isn't paying off anymore. You're over thirty—"

He takes a step away from me.

"Ah, you're thirty-two. Got it. You aren't ready to surrender your identity as a young hottie. Of course, you're still highly desirable, but even you see those days are numbered. Already things are changing inside you, and you don't know where to go next. You want love, but most of your friendships are shallow, so what are the odds of finding your true love? But then again, what could I possibly know about you?"

Fitch strides away without saying a word.

Oh, c'mon, Kevin. How many more nights do I have to chase you through bars? Turn around.

Come back.

Tonight, I make the invitation.

Then, home. *Bed.* After a long day under cars. Worse yet is managing employees. How did I get here? I never dreamed of my own business. Owning a garage. I fucking hate cars. I need sleep. This is why I'm so grumbly. But Fitch is important. He is the last king. But sleep is important. Once Fitch is kinged, I will get serious about making my Honduras plans. My thoughts are all scattered tonight. So fucking tired.

When he approaches, it's obvious from his walk he's hovering between tipsy and drunk. This is not the practiced masculine walk I saw a few weeks ago.

He clomps up to me with no practiced, measured intention. He stands next to me and nods.

"You make me nervous," he says, slurring his words. "I can't even go out to the bars anymore without worrying I'll see you. Also, I'm a little drunk."

"Here's how it works, Fitch."

He plugs his other ear and leans in.

"For thirty hours, you do everything I say. If I say bottom, you bottom. If I say top, you top. This means slow-kissing, ass-eating, and licking the crud between my toes if that's what I want. If I want you dressed as a naughty Catholic schoolgirl, you fucking do it without making me ask a second time."

His face betrays no discernable reaction.

I hope he's sober enough to remember these details.

"Expect things to get weird. I swear to heavenly Zeus, Fitch, these thirty hours will fuck you up. You will have a hard time jacking off for the next week, and I can't tell you how much of that is physical and how much is emotional. You will be changed. A door will open in your life. You won't leave with STDs or an addiction to crystal meth. No drugs or alcohol. Arrive sober. But think carefully before you show up. I've been clear about the expectations. Your arrival on my doorstep is a giant, fat *yes*. To everything. All thirty hours."

"I don't even know your name," he says.

"Names are overrated. And you're not as drunk as you're pretending."

He toys with several expressions: incredulous, scoffing, and arrogant dismissal. They all pass within seconds before he settles on glum. He sips his beer.

"You're unbelievable," he says.

"Believe this. I'm done chasing you through the St. Paul and Minneapolis nightlife. You won't see me in one of your bars again. I made the invitation. I'm done here."

"Wait," he says.

"Find me," I yell at him, transcending the loud party din.

I start backing away from him, watching his disbelief.

"Wait," he says, worry crossing his face. "I don't know your name!"

"Find me online. Search for *The Lost and Founds*. If you want it bad enough, you'll find me."

"Who are the Lost and Founds?"

He reaches out a hand in my direction, as if he might grab me. In his black silk shirt, under the club's neon-green lights, he's almost immediately lost in the sea of pushing bar patrons, headed for drinks, for the dance floor, to someone new, everyone moving, crisscrossing between us.

Right before I disappear from his sight, I yell, "Remember the king! Remember the king, Fitch!"

I check my email daily, discarding the obvious fake replies to my website and those emails from curious non-believers who want details and explanations. I don't have time for them. I receive another reply from the closeted army guy in Wisconsin who wants to control how his King Weekend unfolds, so there's no possibility of our appearing together in public. I already told him *no*, but he musters another attempt to convince me. "My buddies can't find out..." There's an email from a kid in New Jersey, a twenty-four-year-old named Mark, politely introducing himself and explaining to me why I should take his virginity. The attached photo shows a handsome man—very hot—but he's twenty-four. Sorry, Mark. I reply to his email with two words: *Too young*.

I click Send.

The next day I find an email, the subject of which reads "Fitch."

I expect the email to be many paragraphs long, demanding exceptions and escape clauses, accusations about my true intentions, and—but they aren't there.

Funny.

I'm sure they were written and then rewritten, consequences considered, debated, and maybe discussed with whatever friends he has. I'm sure he wrote fifty paragraphs—in his head at least—and debated the nature of his submitting for thirty hours. I picture him lying naked in bed, his fat biceps spilling over his flannel sheets, exhausted by their all-day effort to hang proudly off his meaty frame. Tufts of blond hair in his pits, just the right amount, of course. Or shaved. I imagined his pubes are groomed like English topiary. He wouldn't want too much hair. Fitch would lie in bed and wonder...what's the worst that could happen?

But Fitch is more ready than I suspected, because his email lacks any caveats or demands for explanation. Instead, I find his phone number and a single sentence revealing his first begrudging surrender.

ARE YOU FREE NEXT SATURDAY?

I am. But I want him to show Friday. King Weekends always begin on Friday. I write out the details of how I want him to show up, how to prepare. In block letters at the end of my instructions, I add my signature line.

WHAT WOULD YOU RISK TO FIND A LOST KING? AND WHAT IF HE DOESN'T REMEMBER YOU?

Come to me, Fitch.

Let's dance, dance, dance.

After all, you are the last in a long lineage.

Two

"**S**trip."

Fitch has barely crossed the threshold into my home when he receives his first command. He hasn't even had time to remove the frayed baseball cap. He glares at me with menace, as if unsure whether he came this afternoon to submit or attack.

But he isn't leaving.

If Fitch intended to back out, he wouldn't have been exactly on time. Fitch would have been an hour late, two hours late, and partially drunk. I would have sent him home. No, he showed as I instructed, exactly at 4:00 p.m. Friday afternoon. Thirty hours from now means we're done tomorrow night at ten. It's not my preferred Sunday noon departure, but tailored for him. Tomorrow night, Fitch will have a decision to make.

"I'm not an asshole," he says, standing in my foyer. "I don't know what you think of me, but I'm not as bad as that."

I nod.

Even under khakis and an Abercrombie hoodie, his muscular chest is obvious. He has worked hard for his body. Somehow, recognizing this makes me want a piece of chocolate cake. Or, you know, a whole chocolate cake.

"Are you friends with an ex-boyfriend of mine? Jason?"

"You already asked that. No."

"Did I reject you at some point, besides that one night a few weeks ago?"

"No."

"Did you invite me because I rejected you?"

"No. I had already decided to king you."

"Why? What does that even mean, *king me*?"

"You didn't read about it on my website?"

"No. I tracked you down through the bartender at Bar Twelve. The one who brought me your beer. He said you were a mechanic. Another bartender saw you at a garage in St. Paul. I tracked you down." Fitch pauses. "It wasn't that easy."

"You found me through my garage? Through my being a mechanic?"

"Yeah." He offers me a half smile. Conciliatory, I guess. "I thought it was hot you're a mechanic."

In a way, I'm not surprised this is a turn-on for him. Fitch is obsessed with his masculinity. From the baseball caps, to the careful swagger, it's got to be manly or it's not for him. Whatever connection he now feels has been fortified by my day job. A fuck date with a blue-collar garage mechanic must earn him some masculinity points on his own internal scale. Maybe we should do something feminizing—no. Don't second guess now. This can be addressed through everything I have planned. No last-minute substitutions.

"You got my email address from the garage's website, not from my personal website."

"Yeah. Vincent."

He says the name with relish, proud to have learned something about me.

"My name isn't Vincent."

"But you *are* Vin Vanbly. Your picture is on the website. You own the garage?"

"I do. But my name isn't Vincent. And you showed up tonight without reading about the Lost and Founds?"

Now he looks uncomfortable. "Yeah. You have to explain to me what a *kinging* is."

I consider answering him.

"Why didn't you Google *The Lost and Founds*?"

He looks sheepish. "I couldn't remember what you said in the bar. I was drunk."

Huh. I had hoped he would have read the Lost and Founds backstory. Doesn't change much, if anything. In fact, this highlights how biggish an effort he made to find me, especially if all he had to work with was the vague knowledge I was a mechanic in St. Paul. Fitch is more ready than other men. He needs this. He wants this.

"Strip, Fitch."

"First, explain this kinging situation."

"No. Strip or leave. This is the third time I've told you. There won't be a fourth."

He doesn't need explanations. Hand-holding. He'd only demand more information anyway. What he needs is to begin. When we lock in eye contact, I make sure he sees me shift my gaze to his baseball cap.

He chucks it to the floor with a dramatic flourish. If he were hoping for an accompanying dramatic *kerthunk*, he doesn't get one. He folds his hoodie and sets it carefully atop his shoes—he loves that hoodie. He jerks his tartan-plaid-shirt buttons, staring me down the entire time. Either buttons piss him off, or he's not happy with me. Shirtless, in his khaki slacks, he is suddenly the poster boy for Sexy Disgruntled Youth. Well, if he earned the crown a decade ago.

"I'm not a whore," he says, pouting.

I nod.

I will not argue. I will not draw him out. He knows what to do.

I stand before him at full attention. Not military attention, but something similar enough, a heightened awareness of the energy between us. I appreciate how hard it was for him to show up and strip on command. I'm not surprised by his sullen demeanor. I cock my head to one side, as if listening to music Fitch cannot hear.

He grumbles and unbuckles his belt.

Every submitting man tests his top. *Can you handle me? Are you worthy of my submission? Will you respect this gesture, and do you appreciate what I'm doing for you?* Well, every man *I* king tests me one way or another. They need to know I am in charge. That I can remain in control, keeping them safe. Fitch feels no different. In fact, he needs this assurance more than others. He's used to being the man in control. This probably feels very *unmasculine* to him. Poor guy.

I wonder why he chose to accept?

In the past, I needed to learn every single detail about a man to king him. Just remembering some of my insane exploits makes me want to chuckle. Following men every waking hour for weeks—months, in those early years—uncovering all their secrets before they could confess them. Not anymore. Now, I just know. I know how hard to push. I have a good idea of what's going to be revealed without needing to know specifics about the man. I just know.

Being crazy helps. Kinging men has driven me to extreme places, breaking me. Altering me. There's no doubt my word issues are worse, tangled and *rejigulated*—one of my favorite made-up words—tied to my brain's craziness. The crazy guides me. Which is why I have to move to Honduras. The crazy is taking over my brain.

Fitch says, "Underwear too?"

I say, "Don't ask questions when you already know the answer, Fitch."

He challenges me again with his gaze. "How come you're not stripping?"

"Because I'm not the one about to have a hands-free orgasm."

Fitch is taken aback but controls his surprise. "Hands-free?"

"Soon."

He smirks, his thumbs poised under the elastic band of his designer underwear, baby-blue short shorts highlighting every contour of his cock and balls. Through the thin fabric, it's obvious. Fitch is hung.

We stare at each other.

His gaze quietly penetrates me. He's a smart guy, and he's got damn-good people skills, though he pretends oblivion to others. His gleaming intelligence extends to a rich understanding of his impact, how people revolve in his gravitational pull. He knows things about himself, things he chooses not to share with the outside world.

He's like the letter *u*, which everyone assumes is an isolated, single letter, but it's not. It's a concept and has an uncommon relationship with every other letter. Not nearly as popular as its vowely brothers and sisters, but essential and uniquely understated. *U* is about me and my relationship to you, to *u*, to all the understandings *u* possess. *U* is an agreement to see and be seen, to be witnessed by the world, a loopy, exaggerated curve, which means the playfulness of—

"What are you doing? Your lips are moving."

Fitch frowns. My talking to myself is clearly a bad omen for him.

Shit.

I say, "I was thinking about how difficult it must be to be you."

Fitch stands motionless, a true underwear-model moment, fingers poised and ready to shred that last piece of clothing.

"I bet it's hard for people to see the real you, the living man. People want to use your attractiveness, for you to stand by their side and prove their innate worth. You have to validate boyfriends, strangers, people who want to impress you. Despite the fact that you love it, and encourage this Fitch-worship, you're probably exhausted being eye candy for everyone you meet. I bet you hope someone comes along who finds you hot, yes, but not so hot they aren't also seeking more from you. You want someone who demands to see the better man lurking inside. You're waiting to be invited."

He stares at me, glumly, until a single tear falls from his left eye.

He looks down and tugs the underwear over the perfect curve of his ass. At this point, what does it matter if I see him naked? Already, I've witnessed something more vulnerable than physical nudity. Yet, I must be careful. I can push Fitch harder than others, but I must respect this is difficult for him.

Ah, at last, the Fitch Dick is revealed.

I can't glance at it; I maintain eye contact with him. Or rather, when he looks at me, he will see me staring at his face. After flipping his short shorts to the pile of clothes, he finally returns my gaze with a combination of boredom, irritation, and a lets-get-this-over-with expression I find quite hilarious. You'd think he were here to take a written essay test.

Too late, Fitch. I saw your lone tear. I saw you.

I point at the thick purple curtain hung from a rod, temporarily separating the foyer from the living room.

"Go through there."

Warning flashes in his eyes.

I wish I were on the other side already so I could see how Fitch enters the room. Will he retain the Fitch Saunter I tracked through nightclubs, or will he enter as a man who has chosen to submit? Humbler steps to be sure, and yet more honest for him.

He gasps as he enters the room.

This pleases me. I follow him in.

More than one hundred candles create a giant circle—big thick pillars and dainty tea lights, misshapen candles in bad pottery, long tapers in quirky candelabras, fat and burnt-low candles, radiant orange candles, burgundy and lapis lazuli bases—dominating the entire room. I had to push the furniture back and remove a few chairs. The circle is large enough for me to pace around him while he kneels in the center.

"What is this?"

Fitch glances toward the front window, but the ordinary brown drapes do their ordinary job—exclude the outside world from my home. A crackle from the fireplace draws his gaze, and he moves a few feet closer to the blaze. Wouldn't want Fitch to get chilly. He glances around, taking in bookshelves, the hunter-green wall behind them, the beat-up leather couch I crash on instead of crawling to my bed. My home is ordinary. Books, end tables, coasters, rugs. The drapes are ordinary, the wall hangings are ordinary, and the fireplace is, well, charming—but similar to the ten thousand other fireplaces in a fifty-mile radius. It's all ordinary.

I don't want to stand out.

Fitch hesitates on the perimeter, instinctively knowing he must step inside, yet also knowing this is one of those moments similar to shedding his clothes. To step inside is to surrender, but didn't he do that already? So, what's the big deal now? His wavering betrays it does feel like a big deal, as if this single step were proof he liked how I took control in the foyer. He lifts one leg over the candle fire, testing the water—so to speak—but normal Fitch becomes aware of this indecisiveness, and he worries it might seem unmanly, so the rest of him steps inside with a hard thud, strutting proudly to the center. He faces me with a defiant grimace. He crosses his arms. Of course, maybe he didn't think any of those thoughts. I dunno. But I do like to guess what's happening inside a man. Over the years, I've become a good guesser.

"Now what?"

"Kneel."

"On the floor?"

"On the towel."

"It's a hand towel. Get me something thicker and fluffier."

"Do you have bad knees?"

"No."

"Kneel."

He grunts and obeys. I'm a teensy bit surprised how easily he caved. Once he's kneeling, his arms go instinctively behind his back, allowing a few of his fingers to interlock. He drops his head. Why not? If someone he knew were to catch him this way, Fitch wouldn't want to meet their eyes. Not like this.

From the nearest shelf, I grab a glass bottle and set it before him.

"Slather up."

"You're kidding me," he says. "Olive oil?"

"Do it."

"Are those garlic cloves floating in the bottom of this bottle?"

"Yes. Slather up."

"Too far." Fitch glares a finality at me. "I do not want to smell like a goddamn pizza."

"Fitch, nothing is too far. We haven't even begun to go far. You came here. You stripped and knelt in the circle. You're here for the experience, so quit fighting this, and have the experience."

"How do I know you're not filming this? How do I know there's not a secret camera in one of your books or over on that table?"

"No cameras. Filming this would dishonor what you came here to do. I will push you, yes. I will make you submit. But I will do so while respecting the gift of your submission, Fitch."

His eyes blaze with anger. *"My goddamn name is Kevin!"*

"I know," I say softly. "I know."

He takes several deep breaths, allows himself to return to something like normal.

"But for now, your name is Fitch."

"Crazy bullshit," he mutters.

"You're here, Fitch, in my home. I rarely bring men to my home. This means something to me. You're not just the flavor of the week, so please know I respect you. Bottom line, you came here to get something. Will you leave without getting it? Or will you do anything—whatever it takes—to transform whatever it is you need transformed?"

He scans the room again, possibly for hidden cameras.

"Kevin, what would you risk to find a lost king? And what if he doesn't remember you?"

He says nothing.

The words hang in the room.

The fire spits and crackles.

He picks up the bottle of olive oil. "No filming?"

"I promise. King's honor. And if I were you, I'd ensure every square inch of my body is covered."

He unscrews the cap, and after a brief whiff, he pools it in his right hand and begins slathering his clean-shaven chest. He must shave his whole body. I bet he permits an admirer do it for him, some semi-regular in the Fitch Fan Club. His thick muscle glistens and gleams as my nose fills with a familiar, robust aroma, almost fruity. By the time he works his neck and skull, something smells damn good in this room. I feel my dick begin to plump out as he works his thick arms.

Perhaps he's revised his opinion of olive oil, because by the time he finishes his ass—and he was quite thorough with his butthole, I'm glad to see—the mighty Fitch Dick stands straight and tall, a pillar of thick muscle which never gets worked at the gym. Well, I don't think it does. I never witnessed him fool around at the gym. He worked his routines with undistracted commitment and never spent time in the sauna. But the Fitch Dick is leaking goo, and it's not olive oil—I'm sure of that. Damn. It's thick, and a good nine inches long. Or longer. He's really got a monster.

He coats the Fitch Dick gingerly, not willing to show more of an erection if that's possible. Seems pretty fat and erect to me. The room now smells of warm, baked bread. Roasted garlic.

Watching him obey this simple command has revealed a few erogenous zones I would have uncovered in the next few minutes anyway, but the early intel is useful. Nipples, stomach, the neck in two spots, and, of course, the Fitch Dick. I suppose that one goes without saying.

"Invite me into the circle."

"Why?"

"Because this is how it's done. Respectfully. I'm here to both push you and honor you at the same time. You must invite me into the sacred space. In doing so, you give me permission to release that which has not seen light."

"Release what?"

"What would you risk to find—"

"Okay, okay. Whatever. Come into the circle."

I step over the candle barrier, approach him so my cock is almost at his eye level. He looks down again, hoping to avoid this. From my back pocket, I pull out the blindfold and wave it in front of his face.

"Put this on."

He refuses to take it from me. "No way."

"Fitch," I say, and sigh. "Can we not do this every time? Please? After some bickering, you'll eventually wear it. Get with the program and quit fighting everything. Do it now."

He snatches it from my hand. The blindfold goes on.

He inhales its scent, strong cedar, sandalwood, and pine, a special concoction I created to help me fall asleep, my personal brand of poppers. Together with the heat and crackling-wood sounds, it probably smells to him like he's in the middle of a pleasantly burning forest. With garlic overtones. He inhales deeply, and as a result, his cock bounces hard, back and forth.

"This actually smells pretty good. What is this?"

"Woodsy oils. A personal blend."

Now, the string.

I'm not normally a fan of circus sex: the flashy, over-the-top props one uses to transform sex into a three-ring spectacle. Well, that's not true. I involve food whenever possible. And maybe a spectacle is fun once in a while, I'll admit that. But I get put off by the obsessed fetish artist who can only be restrained by blue dress socks tied in slip knots, following the English tradition. Narrow parameters can kill the sacred flow. On the other hand, some of the practices born of deep tradition, grown in mindfulness, do provide value. Bondage can be quite useful for releasing trapped emotions.

"What are you doing? What's happening?"

"Is this string? Are you wrapping it around my fingers?"

"Is this necessary?"

I do not answer his questions because I wish to communicate that not everything asked receives an answer. Instead, I instruct him to lift his right arm, then his left, and I wind the string under him, around him, binding his arms loosely behind him in such a way he does not feel the constraint. Not yet.

His questions eventually die. My silence and the occasional crackles from the fireplace fill the room. I let my thumb glide across his upper back, and he moans, softly, breathes harder.

I loop around his left wrist and draw it to the big toe on the opposite foot. I pull string from the toe straight up, wrapping his bicep twice, down to his index finger, where I make two loops, then back to the original arm near the elbow, repeating in slight variations, until his fingers and toes are enmeshed in a web of interconnected sensations. It's not terribly tight. He still has a few inches to maneuver and not tug a string inadvertently. I finish my windings and make sure all twenty digits get bound in what I describe as "the orgasmic grid."

He is surprisingly patient during my calculated silence, and I feel it is now time to reward him.

"In feudal Japan, samurai warriors used Hojōjutsu, a martial art, to restrain captives. They were honor-bound to treat the prisoners well. They used different bondage techniques to illustrate the status of their captives. Over centuries, Hojōjutsu evolved into the art of shibari, which means *to tie*. It's not a martial art anymore, it's an erotic spiritual practice. The top is obligated to create beautiful geometric patterns with the bottom while attempting to—"

"I'm not a bottom."

"Fitch," I say.

I tap his left shoulder, and the surprise of the contact causes his body to jerk, twisting unexpectedly, which might not be a big deal if he weren't bound head to toe in ordinary, white twine, negating every attempt to right himself. He quivers like Jell-O, all those muscles bouncing and confused as to which way to tip over. After watching him struggle for a long number of seconds, I reach out to steady him.

He gasps. "Whoa..."

"They say there's an endorphin release associated with this type of bondage. What do you think?"

He breathes heavily, still not speaking.

"Good. How about if you don't speak until I address you, okay, Fitch? Let me talk."

His silence is acquiescence.

While circling him, I explain the patterns I've created on his body, how I matched shapes to particular spots of vulnerability described in acupressure and acupuncture. I describe the colors of these pressure points, and I test them by pushing against his skin, causing him to jerk. I describe the lemon yellows, reds, and pinks in his body. I know he can't see what I'm describing, and honestly, my words are a smoke screen. I don't expect him to recognize the shapes or the mystical intention, but to create in his mind a blurry mess of colors and strings, so once I pluck a single string, it's automatically wired in his brain to explode light and sensation.

It's all connected.

The past, the immediate present, the potential futures opening to us at each moment. The ordinary, white string binding it together is memory, and though we can't always remember what parts of us are bound, we feel it the exact instant that string vibrates. Which is why I can never escape my childhood. I have no future because every string is wrapped so tightly around the past.

Quit it. Stop. Focus up, moron.

I pick up the candle I preselected for its ability to drip just a few drops at a time.

"Fitch, when was the last time you had sex?"

"I didn't jerk off for the last three days, like your email instructed."

He tilts his head at the floor, and his right arm spasms. He's lying. I let the melted wax land on his right shoulder blade.

"Ow! *You motherfucker*!"

It's not pain he shows me, but anger.

"Try again. This time, answer honestly."

"I did."

I drip wax onto his left shoulder.

"Fucking hell," he cries out. "That hurts!"

"No, it doesn't. Not much. It's the surprise that makes you decide it's pain. I'm going to ask you one last time, and before you answer, consider this. You're bound and helpless, covered in oil and surrounded by fire. I'm holding a candle ready to drip wax on you when you lie. If you jerk and tip over, that would be bad. I'd like to emphasize how right now is a good opportunity for complete truth telling."

"You're a fucking nut job," he says. "Untie me. Right now."

"Fitch, breathe into this. Find the king inside you, the part of you who tells the truth for no other reason than it's the truth. The truth can be a weight. You lift weights all the time. This is the twenty-pound barbell of truth. Do it, bro. Bring your strength to the surface and share the truth. When was the last time you had sex?"

His whole body sags. He gets very still, and after a moment, says, "Yesterday."

"With whom?"

"I dunno. Some Mexican kid I fucked a few weeks ago."

"What was his name?"

"I dunno. Pedro."

I pour wax onto his left calf, a few drops.

He cries out and twists.

"You could have invented a less stereotypical name, Fitch. C'mon. Also, try taking some deep breaths. It will minimize the impact of the hot wax, and you won't flinch as much."

"Thanks for the tip. Asshole."

He adds the last word under his breath.

"Oh, I'm definitely an asshole. I'm not the one denying that part of myself. You are. What was the Mexican guy's real name?"

"Tim."

"Tim was the name of the guy who you met with me in the bar, Fitch. Not the Mexican guy's name."

He tenses, knowing what's coming. I drop the wax closer to his neck.

"Fucking—ow! *I don't know*! I didn't fucking care what his name was."

Now there's an answer I respect. The truth.

"Thank you for the truth, Fitch. Who did you have sex with before him?"

"I'm not sure."

I drop some hot wax.

"Chad! His name was Chad or Chase or something! From online."

Our conversation—if one can call it that, given the liquid wax's role in stimulating his words—continues to evolve as he volunteers sexual details from men he hooked up with. He tells of times he promised to call but never did. Fitch begrudgingly shares how many of those men believed a second date was possible, and he didn't correct their assumptions...he wanted the sex, and so he held his tongue.

I stop asking him questions. He takes over, volunteering stories. At the end of each anecdote, I drip wax on him, almost as if signifying I heard him.

"This one time, I made a guy ditch his parents, who were visiting him from out of town. He explained to them he needed to visit a sick friend, all so I could get blown. Over the phone, I threatened if he ever wanted to suck my dick again, he had to come over right away."

The words seem to make him sad as they leave his mouth.

I drop more hot wax on him, this time the sole of his right foot. He flinches in surprise, but no longer cries out or fights what I'm doing.

"On a first date, I made a guy give up his ass to me in the Institute of Art bathroom. He was terrified of getting caught, but I insisted."

Fitch never breaks down sobbing, but I witness through his body how it does not always please his memory, adding up the numbers, calculating the casual disregard. This is why Fitch is not a complete throwaway. There's decency in him, a gold mine untapped.

Fitch is covered in wax, drippings on his arms, his legs, his chest, his back, his shoulders. None on his face. Forced to kneel upright all this time, he droops, this Gulliver on the Island of Lilliputians, bound cleverly in their tiny ropes.

"Okay, this one is kinda bad, so don't burn my balls off over this," he says, and hesitates.

He waits for a response from me, but gets none.

"Even though I've bitched about men seeing only my muscles or my...looks, I broke up with guys because they weren't handsome enough for me." He sags again. "Which is shitty, I know. I'm a hypocrite. I don't like myself some days. I don't like myself at all."

Instead of dropping hot wax for this latest admission, I hover my hand over his shoulder—less than an inch from his skin—letting my presence be felt. After a few seconds, I lower my hand until I am touching him in solidarity.

Fitch yowls, as if this hurts him worst of all. He cries for a moment, not sobbing, life-changing tears, but his face breaks, and his shoulders heave as much as they can without pulling his whole body forward. He cries and rights himself, thick shoulders proudly straight again, as he stretches his legs and discovers the limits of his ability to move. He pulls in the tears, and shakes his head.

"Oh, man," he says, wincing. "What's happening to me? Trees are getting burned."

Trees?

"Sorry, I hallucinated there for a second." He attempts a chuckle but it sounds hollow. "This is intense."

I don't say anything in response. I step a slow perimeter around him, keeping one hand on him at all times. Shoulder. Neck. Chest. Other shoulder. Bicep. This is my blessing, a king's admiration for the time he puts in on his body. Even a Lost King's blessing must be worth something, because Fitch kneels straighter, chin up, finding strength inside him to stand tall while on his knees.

"I'll be right back."

In the kitchen, the shallow pan is still steaming, as it should be. I pulled the kettle off the stove as he rang my doorbell. I bring it and the washcloth inside the circle, setting them at my side.

I crouch so I can speak directly into his ear. "Think of the guy whose parents were in town visiting. Anything to say to him?"

Fitch asks, "Like what?"

I do not answer. Instead, I kneel at his side, and with my fingertips, massage the very top of his spine, the base of his skull, until he tips his head forward. It does not matter what he says, only that he says it aloud.

"I'm sorry, dude," he says. "I'm sorry I forced you to put me ahead of your parents."

I dip the washcloth in warm water, and wipe his forehead. He winces again, as if he might cry from this gesture alone, but he's back in control almost immediately.

"I'm sorry, Mexican guy from yesterday."

With more warm water, I rub the wax on his left shoulder until I have softened it enough to break.

He waits until I have finished the area completely.

"I'm sorry, Institute of Art guy. I'm sorry about that. I was an asshole."

"Visiting guy from Phoenix, I'm sorry. I should have used more lube. I'm usually a better top than that."

In this way, we work across his body, him remembering and apologizing, me wiping his body clean, restoring the king to his greatness, or at least a level of greatness. Fitch might consider hurrying the process because he's been kneeling for a while, but surprisingly, he does not. He does not omit names and stories or urge me to scrub faster. He accepts where he is. Sometime after the twelfth "I'm sorry," his voice gives out, midword. The callousness toward these men was easy for him. Apologizing is not.

He whispers the remaining few apologies.

I ask, "That's all of them?"

"One more," he says.

I thought he was going to say "one more rep." Apparently, he is. The weightlifter's final push.

"I'm sorry, Jason," he says. "I cheated on you, and you were a good boyfriend. I don't know if we were forever material, but I ruined us so we never found out. I'm sorry. I got scared."

We are both silent.

I step outside the circle, abandoning the crowd: Fitch and his Fitch Men. His ghosts stare, judging him, perhaps forgiving him, and maybe not. How they react matters less than this one fact—he's faced them. He knelt before them and honored the kingship he refused to see in their prior contact. A king kneels before them.

All around, the candles flicker, like the eyes of all those staring men, and this reminds me to throw another few logs on the fire. The flames burn brighter, harder, and this makes Fitch glow brighter, stronger. He appears as Apollo, the Greek sun god, receiving his assignment to bear the heavenly light of creation to the world.

"My butt itches," Fitch says.

I do not answer this. Let it itch.

I leave him. From the fridge, I retrieve another shallow pan of water, adding a few ice cubes before returning. The flames rage furiously within the sweet-potato-colored bricks containing them. The room is hot. Oh, boy. Now, I imagine sweet potatoes cooking—delicious, root smells implying autumn, not a crisp spring night. I soak a different white washcloth, wring it out, and put it over my palm, dressing my hand like a ghost.

I touch his chest, the cold water against his hot skin causing him to spasm, sending a shockwave through every constrained digit and limb.

Fitch moans.

It's time. Time to begin.

"Once there was a tribe of men, a tribe populated entirely of kings. Odd, you may think, and wonder how any work got done in such a society with everyone making rules. But these were not those kinds of kings."

His golden, glowing body shudders as my cool hand explores his pec. Shadow flames dance across his chest. His whole body jerks, making his right foot shoot to the side, causing his balls to get tugged under the strain. This orgasm has been building for almost an hour.

"They required no throne rooms, no jewels, no gold crowns. They chose to king as they went about the business of living. The gardeners, the blacksmiths, even the tax collectors were fair and just kings."

Fitch takes a deep breath and says, "Oh."

"In this tribe, all brothers were the rightful owners of the kingdom. You might come across King Ryan the Protector, or King Jamie the Dancer, on their way to visit the King of Bargains. They loved freely and with open hearts, some lying with other kings and some seeking women as their queens. I met one such king, a queen seeker, King Malcolm the Restorer, an African giant, whose powerful voice commanded love and goodness from those who had abandoned their true selves."

I dip the washcloth into the water, which has grown colder as the ice melts. Fitch almost winces when I graze his stomach with the cloth, which forces him to twist his arms, which jerks his feet, which makes him lean forward and list to one side. I have to right him while he gasps.

"The orchards were full of ripe, luscious peaches; the beer brewed amber and frothy. King Nareeb the Baker of Gifts delivered pies and fresh, buttery croissants. You could often find King Jimbo the Bruiser stomping across the countryside, tracking Kalista, his beloved falcon. His best friend, The King of Curiosity, chased them over hills and through forests—"

Fitch moans and mumbles to himself.

"Playing the most ridiculous games, like penguin marching, and—"

Fitch whispers, "Noodle toss."

What? What did he say?

Trying to fight the surprise in my voice, I say, "What was that?"

Fitch breathes heavily, his chest sagging in and out. He doesn't answer.

"Fitch?"

He jumps in surprise, as if he'd forgotten I was present.

"Vin?" he cries out, wrenching his head from side to side.

I forget he's blindfolded.

"I'm right here. What did you say?"

He cries aloud again, twists his arms, and a shiver passes through him. "I don't know where I am. There's all these people...they're...they're all around me. Vin, help me." He hesitates, and I see his Adam's apple bounce a few times as if he's fighting crying. Something's happening to him.

When he finally speaks, he trembles. "They're real, aren't they? The names?"

Nobody ever asked me that. No one. A few men hinted or wondered aloud if some men were real, but never asked, as if afraid to hear the truth.

Fitch says, "These are real men, the king names you're listing."

I remember what I learned about King Jimbo the Bruiser the last time I visited DeKalb. Randy Phinter is becoming him. The bruises were real. I didn't know that during Mai's weekend. Hell, I barely knew Randy. But he's changing. Softly, I say, "Yes. They're real."

Fitch cries out again, and in doing so, twists his body, causing every string to tug and vibrate, leaving him writhing. I put my hands out to steady him. He sobs into his chest until he gains some measure of control.

I don't want to answer any more questions. Keep talking.

"King Vladimir the Finder of Beauty, was always a favorite in this tribe, as he could uncover the gorgeousness in any man, in any woman. Those who had lost themselves sought his counsel and came from his side grinning and bashfully proud. The King Who Loved Turtles cared for his charges with the most tender affection, inspiring all to greater compassion in their lives, especially on Lime Jell-O Day."

"You have to stop," he says, tears escaping from under the blindfold. Light from the fire catches them. "I'm not ready. I'm not good enough. I'm not a good person."

I want to say "We're all good enough," just to comfort him, but the truth is, I agree. Some men can never be kinged. They don't deserve it, even if they want it. Even if they wait for decades, hoping one day it will happen to them. I would know. Some men are destined to remain Lost Ones. But it's not my decision who those men are. The Found Ones want Fitch returned. That's it. I obey.

I continue to cleanse his arms, his shoulders.

"Please," he says. "They're all watching me. I can't take it."

I glance around the room, but obviously, it's just the two of us. I don't want to take us out of the story, but if he's worried about his personal safety, that's a problem. "Fitch, I promise you, we're alone in the room. Only the two of us in this house."

"No." He shakes his head, causing the string around his neck to yank his right foot. "They're all here. You invited them into the circle."

He cries, and the sound is so pitiful I find myself tearing up.

"Vin, make them stop staring."

"Shhhhhhh."

He's wrong. We are alone. The candles surrounding us flicker to an invisible current. The fireplace crackles, the intensity of the recently added logs already fading. It's time to get back to the story.

"I can't do this," he says softly, to me or himself, I cannot be sure. "I'm not ready."

Don't listen. *Keep going.*

"Perry the Forgiver might meet you under a peach tree to listen to your struggles. He transformed men's burdens into origami swans which were floated down a willow-treed creek."

My eyes are drawn to the bookshelf bearing the snow globe he bought for me while we loved each other in San Francisco. One of my most valuable possessions, and yet it reminds me of my unwillingness to forgive—goddamn it, Vin. Not now.

"The Butterfly King's power was so immense, like a sledgehammer, it could fall upon you, and yet, at the same time, so delicate and soft, you might never see it coming, he was so...sensitive..."

At this moment, I allow my finger to touch his anus; the wrinkled flesh trembles at my fingertip and causes his knees to leap off the floor.

Fitch's head jerks back, and he bellows a bull's roar.

He weeps again. "You can't—I'm an asshole! I don't..."

I continue to rub the tender flesh with miniscule motions, making him flex and buckle in unexpected directions. His shoulder shoots forward, his right leg juts to the side, causing all his fingers to fold and expand instantly, like an anxious spider.

I squeeze the washcloth at the base of his skull, so cold water trickles down his spine. He screams and soars upward, jerking his arms, his feet. He moans and sags to the floor again, gasping for air with heaving breaths. His body draws ever closer. I peer over his shoulder to see the Fitch Dick bobbing wildly, thrashing around with a life of its own. His cock is an angry king with a furious purple crown, barking out orders, but unable to execute. His balls are tied independent of each other, both nuts straining and taut.

Oh, yeah. He's close.

I kneel behind him and let the washcloth trace the hard planes of his back muscles, down to his ass, lean and shapely, like a bicyclist's.

Fitch groans and shifts forward. "He can't walk into the kingdom," he says, as if whispering a secret to the air. "Not with those damaged legs."

I have no idea what he means. Does he? I don't dare question him—I don't want to break the spell enveloping him. He breaths heavily. I breathe heavily too. My head feels faloopy, as if his sensory drunkenness is contagious. Why is this happening?

Because he is the last king.

Keep talking, you idiot. Keep talking.

"Oh, and the gay kings, Fitch. You would not believe their power and beauty."

I inch around so I can keep one hand on his butthole while using my free hand to explore further. I allow one fingernail to slowly graze the length of the Fitch Dick, which makes his head thrash, and he swears.

"Those kings celebrated their bodies with relish, the chunky kings and the oddly thin. Those with small dicks and those with long beards. They laughed at themselves naked, laughed with joy to be in their physical bodies and feel such peace. At night they laughed at the stars in the sky, and during this laughter, they kissed and loved until each man radiated his own unique light."

He moans.

"They laughed at the stars..." I want him to remember this line. "Remember..."

He nods but does so too vehemently, sending his fingers and toes into an orgasmic dance, squirming involuntarily.

Fitch gasps when I pinch the seam of his balls. "Help me—someone help! I'm not ready!"

He's ready. Every synapse is merging, the signals confused, too much sensation to report to the brain, which attempts multitasking, managing a deteriorating central nervous system that's overwhelmed, excited, and depleted. He's been kneeling in bondage for a long time.

The heat, the fire, his drunkenness—something overtakes me, swimming through me, and I keep wondering *why*. Why is this happening to him, and *why* is this happening to me? This is a most unsatisfactory letter, *y*, who cannot answer anything, but never stops talking. *Y* is a chattery fellow, no doubt, spinning in circles, both a vowel and a consonant, vowel and consonant, vowel and consonant, and he ends so many lovely, lovely words but never quite provides the answers you want, the *y*, the *y*, the way of the *y*.

Why was I born this way?

Why didn't I become someone else?

Why am I still here?

Y doesn't care about the answers, only the—*talk, moron!*

"Questions," I say loudly, and panic, realizing I'm not sure where this is going. *Shit. Improvise!*

"One of these kings asked many questions, question after questions, a man whose king name was impossible to pronounce aloud, a king so formidable he once commandeered a pirate ship in the barren desert—and did I mention he was a power bottom? With an ass that could grip your fat dick and twist it—"

I twist the base of his cock.

Fitch howls.

He's ready. Change the story direction.

"And the dawn would cuuuuum," I say, emphasizing the last word with a low, deep growl, speaking right into his ear.

Fitch cries again, murmuring soft words I do not recognize.

"Each king greeted the dawn in his glorious king shirt, fire-truck reds, and minty greens so fresh you would catch your breath. Fuzzy, peach-colored shirts, and black silky jerseys so bold they seemed to absorb the very rays pouring out of the morning sun. Some king shirts were homemade, and at a glance appeared quite plain, but the love sewn into every stitch made the shirt glow with light not easily visible to the naked eye. *Why*?"

Quit it. I can't be drunk right now.

My brain swirls, letters forming and unforming, twisting into words I don't want to know, another attack of the craziness that seems to grow stronger with each passing year. I've got to finish him before I lose myself in this mess, the *y*'s are coming for me, and I can't drop a forest on them, not now. Why am I so fucked up? *Why?*

I pinch the head of his cock.

"And when the dawn came, spewing its light, splattering each man with the juice of raw creation, filling each man through his eyes and heart, it would awaken in them—in him—the most regal and profound feelings, the golden desire to become the best possible version of himself."

"No more," Fitch says, twisting hard away from me, as if punched. "No more. I can't—"

You can. You're about to. I dance my fingertips across his planes of flesh like feathers, forcing open his chakras and teasing his smooth muscle with a hint of fingernail.

He screams and bucks.

The Fitch Dick dribbles precum like a factory with production orders, and as he twists his legs, glistening strands stick to his inner thigh.

Fitch arrives.

I stand, preparing myself to catch him no matter which way he tips.

I make my voice hard. I am in control. "One king could make another man shoot his sperm by merely demanding it."

He pants, he heaves, he's not listening, he trembles, he tries to free himself while the mighty Fitch Dick screams his outrage he should be so constrained—

"*Come!*" I scream.

Fitch obeys.

His knees leave the floor as this first arc of his jizz leaps forward at me, shooting straight into the air as if to attack, and then splats on the hardwood between my feet. Damn. That was knee-high.

Fitch howls—which sounds more like barking—as his body convulses, and the prison I wrapped around him prevents him from touching himself, from working out the orgasm further. It doesn't seem to need any help. Arc after arc punches its way out of the mighty Fitch Dick, semen touching the air and soon landing. After a number of these jettisoning splats kiss the floor, Fitch tips with a strangled cry. I wrap my arms around him as he falls to one side. I drop to the floor, legs wide, and pull him to me while he struggles in futility and fights for air. He recoils from my contact—it's too much human touch, too raw after what he's just experienced, so he fights against me and tries to pull away, while simultaneously needing me to protect his vulnerable body.

While he huffs, I free his left wrist from the string webbing, and the orgasmic grid releases him. He could almost have freed himself at any time by going completely limp. But who among us has the strength to do that?

"Are we alone?" He pulls down the blindfold and cranes his neck around the room. "What happened? Where are they?"

"We're alone. Nobody was in the room but the two of us."

"You're wrong," he says, his voice hoarse. "We were never alone."

I'm not sure what to say to him. I glance around the room myself, not sure what he sees.

Fitch weeps, clutching me tightly.

THREE

"Well. This looks great." He mumbles the words, and yet I am meant to hear them.

We cross East Second Street, continuing on Jackson, trudging in silence toward an underpass. Trains screech by overhead, skirting downtown St. Paul on their way somewhere more important. We're not the only ones plodding along in this direction. A trickle of shabby locals join us, two of them pushing shopping carts with all their belongings. Though dark under here, the light welcomes us from the other side.

More grumbling.

Sullen Fitch is back.

Maybe it's because I refused to let him shower. I wanted the remnants of wax and olive oil all over him while we go out, vestiges of, well, whatever the fuck happened to him. He doesn't know. I don't either. After several minutes spent recovering, I asked him questions about the words he said, what he meant by *noodle toss*, but he stared me down in angry confusion, saying, "I don't know. I don't remember."

I believed him.

His storm-cloud attitude returned as I blew out candles. I felt him grow harder like melted wax cooling into its solid state. When he answered tersely, I sensed the truth of his words, his frustration. Grumbling, he asked, "What did I say, exactly?"

I didn't answer him either.

I know how this works. If the kings want you to remember, you remember. Years ago, during the first kinging, I'm sure I recognized the characters on the ancient tablet I witnessed. For a split second, through the searing pain, I knew what they meant. But soon after, the meaning melted into my brain, dissolving among a million misfiring synapses. I don't care anymore. I've quit searching for it. There's no point. At least by moving to Honduras I am finally admitting what I should have realized more than a decade ago. Not every man can be kinged. Some people are too lost.

When we emerge, I can't help but think how I love late May. Friendly green trees lounge along the Mississippi's banks and wave us forward. They are happy to use their newly minted appendages in eager hellos, and I am cheered watching them flutter. Hello, greenery! Hello! Though it's almost seven p.m., the sun bobs happily in the oceanic blue sky, blissfully unaware of its responsibility to disappear in an hour or so.

"Do we have to be here?" Fitch speaks more clearly now.

"We do."

To the right of the underpass, we find our destination, a small lot, too small for a business, and there isn't any real foot traffic here anyway. Not unless you count the homeless who gather here, congregating in greater numbers the second and fourth Friday of each month.

Free dinner.

"Right," Fitch says, once he assesses the small gathering, Styrofoam bowls piled high, and a volunteer buttering pieces of bread. "Feed the homeless. I should have known this was part of your king thing. You're a big do-gooder, and you're going to show me how much better life is when you volunteer. All right. Let's get this over with."

Fitch sounds bored. Fine. He can learn whatever lessons he wants from this experience. Or he will learn more about who he is. He will take away something, like it or not.

As we draw near, I see Father River stirring whatever stew he concocted this week, from whatever discarded restaurant food and canned goods he salvaged. He barks a reprimand at a young woman who prematurely handed out a slice of bread. One of the diners agitates the restless crowd by complaining loudly. "He got one. I should get one too." Two other muffled cries echo the complaint with vague demands. "Gimme an apple," says someone else. "C'mon, you fuckers!"

"Quiet down," Father River yells. "Get back. We're still setting up."

"Why is she handing out bread?"

"Because she fucked up," he says, continuing his preparations. "Leave us alone for five more minutes. Go."

"Fuck you," says a voice from the crowd. "I don't need this shit food."

Nobody volunteers here for the warm fuzzies.

Father River *thunks* a ladle hard on the table next to his guilty bread distributer, making her jump. "That's why. You don't hand shit out early. I told you that."

"I'm sorry."

"Don't be sorry. *Listen* next time."

He turns to frown at me. "You're late. Who's your friend? Let me guess. Another one of your weirdo dates?"

Kevin tries to introduce himself, but Father River interrupts. "Will you be back to serve dinner in two weeks?"

Fitch does not even hesitate. "No."

"I'm not going to bother remembering your name. Vin will show you what to do."

Father River assumes command again, demanding last-minute details from volunteers and guests alike.

"Hurry," echoes a man with a black garbage bag tucked into his back pocket. "I hafta get to the shelter before they close."

The college-age volunteer asks meekly, "Don't they serve dinner there?"

"I want *two* dinners," he says loudly, and then laughs, a loud gorilla laugh. "I wanna feel full!"

River hands me the ladle. "Tonight is turkey stew with refried beans. Your friend can make sure everyone gets an apple. One apple. Don't let them pick the apple."

"I'll do the stew," says the college student.

Father River scoffs. "Do you mind getting punched in the face?" After seeing her skepticism, he continues. "If you don't put the exact same amount in every bowl, people gets mad. Some of these people—high as a kite, by the way—get mad and punch." He jabs his thumb at me. "When this ugly fucker gets punched in the face, he stumbles a few feet away and vomits. Then, two breath mints later, he's back and serving. Can you do that?"

The college student offers no argument, though she is not happy about her nonglamorous assignment passing out Styrofoam bowls and plastic spoons.

I say, "I could mentor her—"

Father River says, "Shut up, Vin. Do your job. Thanks to you, we're late getting started. People are waiting."

As we get into position, Fitch says under his breath, "Nice priest. Nice attitude."

"He's not a priest. The homeless call him *father* to tease him, but also with gratitude. He's gruff, yes. But he pays for this food through donations, handouts, and his own money. He gets mad when the regular homeless skip Friday dinner. The regulars here call it 'skipping church.'"

"That's great," Fitch says. "But he seems like a dick."

We must concentrate for our first twenty minutes. I dish stew, and Fitch hands apples to people in their twenties, thirties, forties, and fifties. And sixties. And seventies. Several of the older men I serve live in nearby tenements, I'm sure of it. Their suits may be threadbare, but nevertheless, they dressed smartly for the occasion. We nod to one another without conversation. Too proud to admit they are here by necessity, I suspect they choose to believe themselves out for an evening stroll, which happens to involve stew from an abandoned lot. I try to get a sense of who might welcome conversation and who might not. A black woman and a white woman show up searching for a friend. After calling the name *Ellen* among the stew-eaters, they casually announce as long as they're here, they may as well get something to eat. Pride wears many faces.

"Some of these apples are bruised," Fitch says. Before I can stop him, he says, "Hey River, what should I do with the bruised ones?"

"Hand them out."

"No, I know, but the really bruised ones."

"Hand them out."

Fitch looks at me for confirmation.

I shrug. "People eat bruised fruit when they're hungry."

One of the women, someone I recognize as both a regular and a heavy drug user, flirts with Fitch, and when she can't generate enough interest from him, she switches off the seduction and explains all the ways to keep rats out of your hair when you're sleeping on the street. Fitch doesn't much seem to appreciate the helpful tips. This talk doesn't bother me. Eventually, you get used to the rats.

The numbers decrease. There are breaks in the line.

A veteran I know shuffles into view, hobbling on his bum leg. He pushes his shopping cart along Jackson Avenue, packed with garbage bags full of recycling, clothes, and treasures I can only imagine. His overstuffed cart always reminds me of Santa's sleigh, except this man has nowhere to go, nowhere to deposit his Christmas. It will take him another ten minutes to arrive in the food line, and he's not far away. His progress is slow. River told me he broke his ankle jumping from a train car and never recovered his mobility.

The regulars linger, sitting in the grass or talking in small knots, knowing seconds will come later, fifteen minutes before the end-of-dinner run. This policy allows latecomers to straggle into dinner camp and find a full meal. Father River circulates among them, alternatively chatting and berating them with his regular rants: wear clean clothes, use fresh needles, and wash with the goddamn soap I just handed you. I see Fitch casting a suspicious eye around the lingering mob. I'm sure he's wondering how turkey stew with refried beans is going to help his next big orgasm.

It will. Definitely.

Compassion for others opens the heart. An open heart means better sex. It's not hard to comprehend, really. Compassion moves us into surprising places.

There's enough of a break I may speak without interruption for a few moments.

"This place reminds me of the Lost Kings."

Fitch frowns at me quizzically, as if to say "Here? Now?"

"It's hard to know whose idea it was to leave the kingdom first. Probably one of the explorer types, like King Wesley the Wanderer. Or perhaps DuRay, the Best Friend King, might have been eager to meet those who dwelled outside the kingdom walls. Or perhaps King Mai the Curious. He was one of those midwestern, corn-fed bubba types. You couldn't stop his curiosity."

Fitch spins to his right, and I peer to the right to see what startled him.

"It was nothing," he says, seeing my searching expression. "I thought I saw a group of guys, six of them. A trick of shadows or something." He huffs in relief. "I thought we were gonna get jumped."

He thought he saw six men when I mentioned the King of Curiosity? The DeKalb Six-Pack? What the hell is Fitch seeing? *Vin, keep it together.* If I'm not careful, he's going to unnerve me.

Talk!

"Some argued the first to leave the kingdom was surely Vladimir Vitchnokker, the king who could see the beauty in all things."

"Because he was gorgeous. A total stud."

"Oh no," I say, pleased Fitch chimed in. "He was hideous to behold. His ugliness was legendary."

Fitch smirks. "Oh, really? You're not just saying this to contradict me?"

"His eyes were close together and uneven. One eyelid drooped. Splotchy skin with angry red zits splattered along his neck, and he had thick jowls. His teeth were crooked and inclined to yellow. His eyebrows were owlish, and his hair long on one side and poorly maintained. It grew unevenly, so there was no point to combing it or shaving it off. He might have tried harder with his appearance, it's true. Some creams, better haircut. But King Vladimir didn't care about *being* beautiful. His passion was for cultivating beauty in others.

"You'd think his hideousness would make people avoid him. But quite the opposite, kings and queens flocked his way, pressing him with dinner invitations and requests for strolls through the golden orchards. Everyone knew that to see the world through Vladimir's eyes was to witness divine love, the harmony and beauty of all living things. Nobody left King Vladimir's side without feeling more wonderful—more vivid and less gray. He might whisper what was beautiful about you *today*, which could be different than what he whispered to you yesterday. As if everything in the world were a diamond, his giftedness refracted light so all could witness the depth and power of beauty."

A few patrons shuffle before us.

A woman asks Fitch for two apples, one for the daughter hugging her leg. Fitch gives her three.

After they leave, he explains, almost angrily, "One of them was really bruised."

"Okay."

Clearly, our time serving food is eating at him. As his outward resistance grows more brittle, his compassion grows stronger.

Soon enough, we stand alone.

He glances around with raw disgust. "If this kingdom is such a perfect utopia, why'd they leave?"

"Why not? They weren't in hiding, this tribe, trying to protect their borders. They were never in danger of being attacked because only Found Kings could find them."

Fitch grunts.

"They were *kings*." I say this as if it explains everything. "Kings are adventurers and explorers. Without fear to keep them in check, *of course* they journeyed far and wide. King Vladimir might have said, 'I wonder what beauty exists beyond the purple dragon wall, beyond the ice caves facing north.' So he left one gorgeous morning, through the twisted gold and copper vines, beautiful metalwork defining the—"

My gaze falls on a man in line as he approaches me. Tonight, he's wearing a blue knit cap.

"—the southern gates," Fitch says, watching a nearby knot of diners get loud.

My head snaps to him. "What did you say?"

"I said how this doesn't seem safe. Those guys arguing. They could pull a knife."

That's not what he said at all—he said *the southern gates*. How the fuck does he know that?

Fitch is distracted. "They're fighting over who got a better apple." He turns to me. "It's a fucking apple."

"I guess when you have nothing, an apple is worth a fight."

"I'll give them another one," he says.

"Don't. No more apples until Father River rings the bell for seconds. That's how it's done here. Respect his rules."

The blue knit cap man presents me with his empty bowl, and with a sullen expression says, "I know you."

I say, "That's right. You do know me."

He flashes me his very few teeth, either as a smile or veiled warning, impossible to tell. We make small talk about topics important to those without homes. The weather, the cops, the weather, stolen belongings, the weather, and finally, the cops. I'm not sure he enjoys the conversation with me, but he needs it. He needs it to be human for a few moments.

He snatches the apple Fitch offers him before sulking away.

Our next diner is a young guy, really young. Like possibly high school or younger. He's a little chubby, with blond hair that could also be brown. He wears glasses, though it takes me a moment to realize there're no lenses in them.

Fitch asks, "Hey kid, where's the glass in your glasses?"

The young boy is nervous and mutters. "Got knocked out by older kids."

"Oh," Fitch says, embarrassed to have hit upon a sore subject. "Well, uh, where's your coat? It's gonna get chilly tonight."

May in Minnesota is no guarantee of warmth.

The kid mumbles another reply and trots away without his apple. Fitch calls out to him, but the kid loses himself in the meager crowd.

"What did I do?" Fitch's tone is worried. "Did I say the wrong thing?"

"Don't know. Maybe he was flustered by the attention. Perhaps he felt ashamed to not have a warm jacket."

Fitch stares glumly at the people with bowls in hand. "He didn't get his apple."

"I suspect he's got worse problems."

We serve a few others. At the next lull in our traffic, he says, "So what happened to the kings who left? Where did they go?"

Oh, good!

He asked. He's interested.

"They went everywhere. The faraway lands in storybooks and legends, under the bejeweled seas, and others walked through the black fields of fire—places with no names. One even went to New Jersey. When King Vladimir left, his king brothers felt dismay, because who doesn't want a king around who reminds you you're beautiful when you don't believe it? But he was definitely coming back, so while they grieved his leaving, they eagerly anticipated his eventual return."

Fitch says, "New Jersey, huh?"

"But he didn't return. Neither did others from the tribe, the Accounting King, the Turnip King, and the King Who Was Gruff. Kings who once worked the golden orchards now worked at McDonald's. More and more men disappeared, showing up in the terrible land of the Lost Kings. This is what the remaining kings called them, the Lost Kings or the Lost Ones. Men who forgot their gold, vanishing into a world which appeared much like our own."

"How did they know these guys were lost and not just out wandering like they said they would?"

"Because they did not greet the dawn."

Fitch laughs. "You've got an answer for everything."

"When King Vladimir didn't meet his brothers and queenly sisters in greeting the dawn—their one chance to connect on the ancestral field, no matter the distance—they knew something was terribly wrong. Even a king researching the Arctic Circle would still greet the dawn at least twice a year, to celebrate his kingship and greet his brothers. But Vladimir, and then others, stopped showing up. That's how the Found Ones knew they were lost."

The story is interrupted, as it must be, by more hungry diners who present their Styrofoam bowls. A man in his forties with scraggly hair demands more, challenging me by holding the bowl out even after it is half full.

"I'm hungry," he says.

"I know," I say. "Stick around for seconds. Father River will ring the bell soon."

"I'm hungry now," he says, his voice a warning.

"Then you should eat it while it's hot."

Fitch watches this exchange nervously, taking a step back, but nothing comes of it. The man grumbles about the size of the apple Fitch passes him and moves to the next station to receive his two cookies.

It's taken this long for the veteran with the shopping cart to adequately store it—safely—and find a guardian to watch over it, another college-aged volunteer now spared from cleanup duty. Father River carries the veteran's plate through the line. He trusts no one else to gather his food.

When he reaches me, the veteran says, "More."

Father River says, "No. Equal."

I ladle the same amount everyone received.

When they step closer to Fitch, Father River says, "Put out your hands."

Fitch obliges.

"Not you," he says in an exasperated tone.

The veteran—who has never shared his name with me—or Father River as far as I know—holds out his hands for Fitch's inspection. Fitch remains shy at first, nodding politely and avoiding eye contact like a good Minnesotan. But he eventually overcomes his upbringing and studies the backs of the man's hands.

The hands are aged. His flesh is wrinkled and grayish. Scratched and scarred. This man has lived too many years outdoors. I know from his stories, he used to catch trains to somewhere in southern Illinois or warmer, ideally, for the winter. But he always came back to St. Paul, hoping to restore something of his former life. As far as I know, he never has.

When Fitch's inspection ends, Father River says, "This man is thirty-three."

Fitch gasps and says, "Oh shit."

The veteran's hands belong to a sixty-year-old man. They are worn and tired of this life.

Father River says, "He served our country in Iraq."

Fitch looks to me for words, but I have none to offer. We live in the land of the Lost Ones.

Fitch says, "I'm sorry. I really am."

The man stares at Fitch, long past caring what someone else thinks. He turns his left hand over, palm up, and presents it to me.

He says, "Do it."

I must. For whatever reason, this means something to him.

I take his hand in both of mine and raise his palm to my lips, kissing the soft part under the thumb. As if speaking directly to his hands, I whisper, "My king, my king."

The veteran takes his hand back, no more impressed with me than Fitch's expressed sorrow.

"Give this war hero an apple," Father River commands, which seems an awfully meager demand. Father River carries his plate, and the veteran limps away.

Fitch faces me. "What did you say? When you kissed his hand that weird way?"

He does not need to know.

I say, "Once the Found Kings realized their brethren were missing, a battle cry was raised, for the kingdom had lost its one true king. You'd think in a land of all kings—all queens, too, mind you—the loss of a single person would mean nothing. Not true. Every king mattered, the one who made toast well, and the king who awarded college scholarships. King Derrick the Aged, a man so ancient he could not walk unassisted to his front door, was equal in importance to King Tyrol, the man who ran the largest city. The loss of any man was devastating, because what would the kingdom do without its one true king?"

"So, you're not going to tell me what you said," Fitch snarks. "Got it."

"Are you listening to the story?"

"Yeah, yeah. Kings got lost. They sent out search parties."

He did it again! He anticipated the story!

"You're right. So I take it you did read the story off my website?"

"No," Fitch says with uncertainty. "I didn't know about your website."

"But you knew they sent search parties. How?"

"I don't know. I—I think I've heard this story somewhere. Maybe on the Internet."

He's lying. He may not have visited my website, but there's nowhere else to read this online. I check regularly. The tremor in his voice reveals to me he doesn't know what's happening either. Interesting. But there's nothing more to do now, no more information to gather.

"The Found Kings sent out search parties, but often these men did not return. Once in a great while, a searcher would return with a newly remembered brother, arms around each other's shoulders, passing through the eastern gates, grinning and laughing under those ancient marble arches. Whenever a Found One left the tribe in search of lost brethren, the remaining kings met him at dawn at the kingdom's southern gates."

The story is interrupted by another newcomer. Damn it, I need to finish. The seconds bell will ring soon, and we will be swamped until the food vanishes.

As soon as we're free, I speak again. "At the southern gates, as the dawn repainted the black grass to spring green, and the gold metal leaves intertwining the gates began to shine, two questions were always asked of the departing brother. The first was this: 'What would you risk to find a Lost King?' Each king answered with what he was willing to sacrifice, and it was always worth more than anyone knew."

Fitch says, "Oh."

He looks at me with genuine surprise, as if he wants to ask a question.

I won't let him.

"The second question asked was this: 'What if you find a Lost King and he doesn't remember you?' That is to say, what would you do if you found the King Who Fixed Toys? Or stumbled on the Lavender King in some corporation's mailroom? When King Andrew, the Singer of Souls, was asked, he shouted as his horse galloped away, 'I will show him my love, I will show him all my love.' Andrew himself was so beloved, many adopted this as the standard answer to the second question."

Fitch says nothing, rotating the remaining apples, seeking the bad ones.

As predicted, the bell for seconds chimes, and sure enough, we are stampeded by the thirty remaining diners, everyone first in line, or trying to be. We scurry to keep pace with the impatient crowd, and for five minutes, we must focus all our attention on serving.

Fitch leans over and says, "Save a bowl for the kid. Leave some at the bottom." Before I reply, he adds, "Just do it. *Please.*"

I nod.

The rush for seconds ends quickly. Standing at the back of the line is the jacketless kid, wearing glasses without glass. He grimaces, as if he knew this would happen. Or perhaps it's happened before, and tonight is proof it was destined to happen again.

Fitch calls to him. "C'mere. Come over here."

Reluctantly, the kid obeys. He shuffles over to Fitch as if he is in trouble.

"I saved your apple. You didn't take it the first time."

The kid reluctantly reaches out to take what is offered, two apples, in good condition from what I see. He does not meet our eyes. Fitch remains silent, unsure how to proceed.

I ask, "What's your name?"

He glances at me. "Ronnie."

"Ronnie, do you want more stew?"

He clutches his prize apples in both fists. "I heard you tell people you were out."

"I am. But my friend here asked me to save a bowl for you. I have enough."

Ronnie looks at Fitch with one of those hard-to-tag emotions—suspicious wonder—unsure what he has done to warrant this thoughtfulness. Fitch nods and grimaces. Ronnie attempts to stuff one of the apples in a front jeans pocket, an unnatural fit. He doesn't have enough hands for the bowl and the two apples.

"Here," Fitch says, stripping off his Abercrombie hoodie. "Wear this. Put an apple in each pocket, and then carry the stew."

Ronnie will not make eye contact with either of us.

"Just take it," Fitch says with irritation, waving the hoodie in front of him.

Ronnie does and puts it on slowly, scrunching up the arms until his fingers pop through the tailored wrists. Fitch loves this hoodie. He wears it a lot. While I'm sure he has more Abercrombie at home, it's also not nothing, surrendering your favorite, comfy hoodie to a total stranger.

Ronnie carries away his bowl of stew, balancing it cautiously, the hoodie weighted with fat apples.

Fitch and I spend the next fifteen minutes engaged in cleanup, receiving orders barked at us, scrubbing pans and utensils with minimal soap and water, packing Father River's traveling supplies and loading his van. While Fitch and I fold tables, Ronnie approaches again, carrying Fitch's hoodie across both his arms.

"Here," Ronnie says.

"Keep it."

"No," Ronnie says. "I'm gonna end up trading it anyway."

"Why?"

"For food. Or for a bed one night when I don't want to sleep on the floor. Something."

"Don't trade it," Fitch says. "It's one hundred percent cotton, and it's got a thick lining. You're gonna want that in the fall when it gets cold."

"I'm not going to be here in the fall," Ronnie says, still offering the jacket to Fitch. "My dad will come get me by then."

Fitch doesn't ask about Ronnie's father, and neither do I. Somehow, it seems unlikely his father will return from wherever he is, and I think all three of us know that.

"Look, you gotta keep it." A nervous desperation enters Fitch's voice. "Keep it. Make it your signature thing, your thing everybody knows you for, okay? They'll be like, who is that coming? Oh, look, it's Ronnie. He's got his Abercrombie hoodie."

Ronnie looks skeptical, as if anyone would recognize him, but since Fitch isn't taking back the hoodie, his arm finally begins to drop.

"Look, keep it. I'll come back on the what—?"

Fitch looks at me expectantly.

"Second and fourth Fridays."

"I'll come back two Fridays from now. You wear that hoodie and I'll give you... I'll give you fifty bucks."

Ronnie smiles, not a genuine happy smile, but a sad one, as if he's not willing to believe another lie. "I'm sorry," he says.

"One hundred dollars," Fitch says. "Just be wearing the hoodie and I'll give you one hundred dollars."

Uh-oh. This is serious.

I say, "Kevin, don't—"

"*I know what I'm doing*," he says in a sharp aside to me. He turns to Ronnie. "One hundred bucks. Two weeks. You can do that. You can hang on that long."

Ronnie drapes the hoodie over one arm and extends his free hand in slow motion, as if giving this offer great deliberation. Fitch raises his hand at the same slow rate—though I doubt he's mimicking Ronnie consciously—and miraculously, their hands meet at the same time somewhere between, engaging in a solemn shake. You'd think this was a business deal for millions. Perhaps for Ronnie, it is. A hundred dollars is a lot of money.

Business concluded, Ronnie dons the oversized hoodie.

He stares at Fitch in his tight T-shirt. "How did you get all your muscles?"

Fitch says, "I lift weights."

The answer must satisfy Ronnie, who nods several times as if Fitch's words were wise. He turns and steps away with a slow gait, anticipating being called back.

When he disappears under the dirty concrete overpass, Fitch raises his face to the emerging stars. It's light enough to see quite far down Jackson Avenue and even see Raspberry Island in the middle of the Mississippi. But high above, night begins to assert its influence.

After looking around, Fitch says, "I hate this place."

I see the veteran with the lame leg leaning on his cart as he pushes himself away. He gets confused. He sometimes drags himself here on the wrong Friday. On those nights, he goes hungry.

I hate it here, too, Fitch.

Which is why I keep coming back.

FOUR

We arrive at Rainbow Village in south Minneapolis close to nine thirty Friday night. Our first stop is the men's room, where we scrub our hands clean. I supply antibacterial soap and insist we both use it. We need it for the next part of the adventure. I make sure Fitch sees me washing my lips as well. We return in silence to the crowded foyer.

The bamboo-themed entrance includes a four-foot-high prayer house for Buddha with food offerings on tiny plates borrowed from a child's tea set. A tiny egg roll, a few spicy noodles, and a teacup of steaming soup. Candles flicker around us, casting shadows thrown against the stark red walls and green bamboo leaves, giving an impression of garish Christmas. Employees speaking Mandarin chatter around us, seating guests, discussing orders perhaps, preparing for the next wave of hungry patrons.

Fitch smiles, not a wide grin, but a softer smile. "I like Chinese food."

I think he's apologizing.

"Good. This place is amazing."

"Yeah, I've heard good things. I've never been here, though. It's funny how when you live in St. Paul, you don't cross the river much to visit Minneapolis. Seems so far away, but it's only fifteen minutes, you know? I mostly eat at places close to home."

I agree with the sentiment, but that's not me. I'm someone who travels for food. Good food.

When the hostess catches a moment between seatings, I go to her and speak quietly. She nods and disappears into the kitchen.

"Do you think he'll show in two weeks?" Fitch asks. "Ronnie?"

"I don't know. I haven't seen him there in the past."

"Do you think he's homeless?"

"Maybe. Probably not, though." I correct myself after seeing the worry appear on Fitch's face. "I bet he's got a difficult home situation, a parent who doesn't cook or forgets he needs to eat. St. Paul has a good record for keeping kids off the street, even if they can't help all the adults."

"Okay," Fitch says, mulling this over.

A moment later, the bright-red kitchen doors with gold dragon handles burst open, dramatically, and a handsome man our age, Greg, appears from within. On his heels, a rush of shrimp and ginger aromas escape, comingling with meats and fried smells making my mouth water, even if I can't identify the richness of each individual dish.

"Oh, man," Fitch says. "My stomach is grumbling."

Greg stops before me, and without smiling, holds out his hand. I place mine in his, and he turns it over, exposing the pink underside. Greg kisses it, as I did the veteran's. The king's kiss.

Fitch says nothing.

I smile big. "Hi, Greg."

He nods at me, nods at Fitch, and without a word, leads us into the kitchen, past the screaming fryers, the hot cloud of steaming water hovering over the double sink, past clanging pot and pans, wielded by a half-dozen cooks who see us, and give us as much regard as they would a head of cauliflower.

Greg leads us from the grill line to the manager's office. Papers are strewn everywhere, invoices on the floor and stacks of bound papers piled haphazardly on the edges of the desk. Empty cardboard vegetable boxes stack atop dented filing cabinets. Seeing the scattered papers, I have the distinct impression a filing cabinet threw up, violently. However, the most notable feature is the large, two-way mirror, looking out over the cooking line. I'm assuming Greg's parents—or whoever sits in this office—spend more time watching the kitchen than completing paperwork.

In the middle of this disorder sits a small bistro table with two wire-backed chairs. On the white tablecloth, a single red candle flickers in its glass holder. Greg seats us here and then gently shuts the door as he exits, closing us in.

"I take it you know this guy well?"

I say, "I do."

"What did he say to you when he kissed your hand? Sounded like mai chang, mai chang. Was that Chinese?"

"It was not."

When I do not elaborate, Fitch says, "That was the same as you did for the veteran. Why? What does that signify?"

I smile at him and study his face.

He's more handsome than ever in this feeble light, his confused features soft and vulnerable. Our experience serving dinner to the homeless has softened Sullen Fitch into someone new, someone curious. Someone open.

A giant flame leaps from the kitchen grill, and we both turn to the great glass window as it dies. One of the men claps for his coworker, while others nearby yell in Chinese. Though I don't understand the language, the tone is what I would assume is friendly, cajoling. Someone throws a shrimp at the grill chef, and he complains loudly. It doesn't matter we can't understand the words. Kitchen hijinks transcend language.

Greg returns and pours from a champagne bottle into long-stemmed glasses, but when we read the label, I'm pleased to discover it's fizzy water, apricot flavored. Perfect. I told Greg I wanted Fitch sober. He leaves us again.

Fitch says, "I'm not a bad person. I want you to know that."

I do not answer him but work my face into a puzzle.

"I mean, yes, I've done some shitty things..."

We stare at the kitchen employees, madly fulfilling orders. They move with coordinated, orchestrated effort. It's impressive.

"I just—"

He looks at me longingly, as if he wants me to finish his sentence, but I say nothing. I'm not letting him off the hook.

"Did you pick me because you thought you could change me?"

"Change you how?"

"I don't know," he says. "I can't figure it out. Why me? Why would you pick me for this...this thing you're doing."

"Why not?"

"Don't be a dick. That's no answer," he says. "I'm not like you. I don't do volunteer stuff with homeless people."

"You do. I was there. I saw you."

"Yeah, but you had to drag me. That doesn't count."

"Are you going to go back in two weeks to meet Ronnie?"

Quietly, he says, "Yes."

"Am I going to have to drag you? Call you and remind you?"

"No."

"Huh. I guess you are that kind of person who goes to feed the homeless after all."

"Not naturally," he says. "I'm—I'm selfish." He seems relieved to have said the word aloud. His face relaxes. "I am. I spend most of my time working out and doing stuff for me."

"What if I picked you because of who you were already—not who I thought I could change you into?"

"That doesn't make sense."

"Why not?"

"Because I'm kind of a prick," he says. "I don't like being an asshole, but people always want something from me. They want me to be their best friend, and it's not because they know anything about me...they just—they're attracted to me. I know this sounds conceited and it is, I know. But it's true. It's easier to brush people off than to explain to them that the reason they're being nice to me is they think I'm...I'm..."

"Say it, Fitch."

"I'm handsome."

The declaration makes him blush.

"Feel better?"

He frowns at this. "Is that why you picked me? Because I'm good looking? We both know it's not about my sparkling personality."

"You don't know that."

"Yes, I do," he says earnestly. "I need to know. Did you pick me because I'm handsome?"

"Are you even listening to the story, Fitch? The Lost and Founds? Every man is the one true king—*every* man. Not exclusively the handsome ones. Not only the ugly ones. Veterans who can barely walk on a badly healed break are the one true king. Foul-mouthed Father River is the one true king, and so is the man who demanded more stew. All men are kings. All women are queens. You're not better or more worthy because you're handsome, Fitch. You're worthy because you're *worthy*. Quit fighting it."

"I'm not," he says, hotly, trying to wipe away a tear popping out of his eye. "Jesus, don't get all worked up. I just asked."

"I saw that tear, by the way."

"So?" He crosses his arms and wipes away another tear. "You're really irritating. Do you know that? All your half answers and ignoring my questions."

"I've been told."

Greg saves our conversation by returning with a bowl of hot peanut noodles. The rich, thick peanut smell reaches us both at the same time, and we both inhale deeply, like in a cartoon.

"Oh god," Fitch says.

"Smells amazing, Greg. Thank you."

Fitch inhales deeply again. "Oh, *god*!"

Greg bows and leaves in silence.

Fitch indicates him with a jerk of his head. "Your ex-boyfriend isn't much of a talker."

Funny, because Greg talks for a living. He works as a translator when he's not at the restaurant. *Demure* is not how I would describe Greg. He's the life of the party. But he obviously decided his role tonight is to be seen and not heard.

Fitch studies the table. "And he forgot to drop off silverware. Or chopsticks." He meets my gaze and reads my silent intentions. He says, "You're kidding me. Please tell me you're kidding."

Steam still rises from the bowl between us, delicious tendrils aching with peanut-buttery goodness, cut by the crisp smell of steamed scallions.

"With our hands?" Fitch wrinkles his nose. "That's disgusting."

"Do you want to wipe your hands again with antibacterial gel?"

"No, I want a *fork*."

When I reach into the bowl, I find the noodles too hot, so I dance around them, stirring them slightly until I feel I can touch the top ones without scalding myself.

"Open up, Fitch. This has to happen quickly because they're still hot."

"Ugh, no thanks."

He glares me down with the Nightclub Fitch attitude, the bored disdain I witnessed quite often. But he's already a different man than a few hours ago, cleaner in the soul, so his expression melts like wax, and he looks deeper into my eyes, demanding an answer to the unasked question, *can I still trust you*?

With my eyes, I communicate back, *Yes. You can.*

Fitch opens his mouth.

I bring the warm noodles to him quickly, and several don't make it, the squirmy little buggers, jumping back into the bowl or landing in his lap. Four or five make it to his mouth. They slap against his chin on the way in, and he mutters a short, uncomfortable laugh at having peanut sauce whipped against his face, smeared over his lips. He sucks them in like spaghetti.

"'S good." He runs the words together, eyes arching in surprise. "*Really* fucking good."

I nod and pick up more.

Hot! Hot! *Hot!*

Like a baby bird responding to momma, his mouth opens again, and as I struggle to corral noodles into my fingers long enough to feed him, he chuckles at my effort.

The noodles are slippery. It's a strange experience to be slapped with a hot noodle. Pretty soon, he's got a peanut-butter chin. Soon after that, we're both giggling.

Slippery, sloppery, his mouth makes quippery, quoppery, funny little words dancing off his tongue, asking me how I know Greg, as another slippery noodle, noodle, *noodle*—

"The word noodle itself is a funny word. *N* isn't particularly hilarious until you pair it with those goofy brothers, those *o*'s, and then it's nooooooooooooooooooooooo, slipping right past that *d*, just giggling around it, and jumping off *le* slide, with noodle! *Noodle*!"

"If you say so."

"Say it."

Fitch laughs. "Noodle!"

Pull it together, Vin! Don't let this nooooooooooooooooooodley, slippery, sloppery—no. No. My latest coping technique is to drop a Honduran forest on the words, trees and bushes popping down on my visual horizon, landscaping themselves into passable trails lined with flowers and trees, so I can breathe, breathe, breathe out the crazy. The letters are making me crazy. I drop flowers on the scene, orange and gold-throated marigolds, but only because I don't know what kind of flowers they have in Honduran forests. I need to breathe, and get out of this letter trap. Forest and flowers, and not a noodle to be seen, nothing slippery—stop.

Watch him.

Fitch's face is smeared with peanut-butter paste, and not exclusively around his mouth. He insists on feeding me next, and we laugh outright as he discovers how hard it to capture noodles with your fingers. Noodles, noodles—*stop it*. He guffaws at the effort, claps his hands together—the parts not covered in sauce, and I must look ridiculous to him, sucking down his latest offering, because he bursts out laughing, a deep belly laugh, and I respond in kind, chewing and laughing at the same time.

Fitch grins ear to ear, and it's not the practiced, seductive smile I've observed him flash potential conquests. This is stupid and loopy, unaffected and unrehearsed. He's laughing and doesn't care about the squiggly noodle fallen to his chest.

Do not get started on *squiggly*.

I announce a new game: feed yourself.

"This is our entire dinner, Fitch. I don't want us overly full for what happens next. So, the goal is to eat your fill before I eat your share."

"Bitch," he says with a serious nod. "It is *on*."

We both dive in, fingers first, spending more time slapping each other's hands away than succeeding in drawing out a single noodle. When he gets a handful, I snatch them from him, watching them fall mostly back into the bowl, which makes him roar. During a particularly long laughing jag, he catches his ghostly reflection in the two-way mirror and freezes at the unfamiliar face. A shock of pain races across his features, gone almost instantly, but I had been watching for this, a moment of recognition, so I catch it. Fitch doesn't live like this, his boyish joy unlocked and free. I suspect he just saw a version of himself long forgotten.

The moment passes, and he returns to the competition with me, but the fight in him has faded. Soon, we are both calm in extracting noodles and eating them thoughtfully. I catch him gazing at his reflection several more times, seeking traces of the ghost he recently witnessed.

I want Fun Fitch back.

I pull out a noodle and flick it into his hair. It sticks to his forehead, and he laughs again. He leaves it sticking there, a fat noodle almost between his eyes. He chuckles a few more times, and with an archness in his voice he says, "I'd throw one at you, but these are too fucking delicious to waste."

I agree. We finish dragging every noodle from the bowl and spend a minute or two licking our fingers.

I knock on the glass, leaving a slight peanut smear. I hand him a paper towel from the roll on the desk, and we take a moment or two to make ourselves presentable.

Greg appears, wearing a sequined red shirt, reflecting rubies everywhere around us. While he serves us, the dark office sparkles. Fitch watches with wonder on his face, as if we are visited by a celestial being. Greg leaves us a plate of sticky rice and fresh mango, our dessert, and this time, forks.

Fitch gawks and makes a flattering comment, but Greg remains ever silent. This is so not the Greg I know! But when I proposed dinner here, he said he would be deeply honored to participate in a King Weekend. He got very quiet and serious. I should have known he would treat this experience with reference. He is a beautiful man.

When he leaves, Fitch picks up his fork, poised over dessert, and says with a mischievous smile. "Another competition?"

"Not this time. This is about gratitude. Let me serve you. Let me show you how grateful I am you showed up this afternoon."

Fitch watches me carefully as I slice through the fresh mango to prepare the first bite.

He says, "I sat in the car for about twenty minutes, because I was early. But also, I wasn't sure if I was going to come in. I was debating. But your house looked surprisingly normal. Well maintained."

He opens his mouth when I present the fork. He accepts what I offer, and as he closes his mouth, with my free hand, I cup his strong jaw. I feel him chew, and he stares at me. His green eyes, so bright in their reflection, seem confused again, and soon, tears brim along the bottom lids.

He says, "This is amazing. I mean, I've had mango and sticky rice before, but this is so tender, so juicy..."

In silence, I feed him two more bites. He chews slower. I graze his cheek with the backs of my fingers, and he winces. As I prepare the next bite, he sits back.

"No. No more. I can't take this anymore." He wipes his eyes, a futile gesture, as the tears continue to roll down his cheeks. "Why did you pick me? What are you doing to me? Why does every fucking thing make me cry? Who are these kings?"

The hurt on his face suggests I called him a string of derogatory names, not lovingly fed him one of the best secret desserts in the Twin Cities. It's not on the Rainbow Village menu, but you can ask for it.

He crosses his arms. "Tell me."

I sense an impasse.

"I will answer one question, but not all of those. One. Which question?"

"Why me?"

I wait in silence until I am sure he is ready to hear me.

"Roughly four weeks ago, outside a coffee shop on Selby, a boy dropped his ice cream cone. Maybe four years old. Red jumper. It was an exceptionally warm day in early April—felt like summer. While his mother cleaned up the sidewalk and scolded him, he kept staring at the ice cream stain in disbelief."

Fitch's gaze grows distant and then he focuses again and looks at me. "I bought him another ice cream cone."

"Yes. Before his mom had even finished cleaning it up, you appeared with a new cone and handed it to him before she could protest."

He waits. But I have nothing more to add.

"That was it? It was just ice cream."

"It was compassion. Kindness with no expectation of return."

Fitch looks away and wipes his eyes again. "I spent two dollars. Not even two dollars."

"I was sitting outside reading a book. Drinking tea. I saw the look on your face when you handed that kid his new ice cream, and I knew. You were one of them. But lost. Sometimes, I will see a man and the words vibrate strong inside me, *king him.*"

Fitch opens his mouth to argue, but says nothing.

We feed the dessert to each other in total silence.

When the mango and sticky rice is gone, we thank Greg and leave.

Downtown nightlife in Minneapolis is so different from my town, St. Paul. As Fitch and I amble down Nicollet Avenue, the city screams. Literally. I hear screeching a half block away, a group of kids shoving and tugging various members of their crew. Dozens wander the city streets tonight, not a crowded Minneapolis night, but bustling. A hundred people in view? Seventy? I love this city, alive, uncrowded, energized by spring. Life gushes down every street, trees happily reunited with their favorite green cardigans. Though local wisdom suggests not planting flowers until after Memorial Day, joy for spring makes us rule breakers, so flowerboxes brag purple petunias, pink impatiens, and strong, red geraniums, eager to spread their roots and flourish.

When I first moved to the Twin Cities, I inquired about the rivalry between the two. Someone from Minneapolis told me, "St. Paul? You mean the ugly twin?" Someone from St. Paul told me, "Minneapolis is nice. And when you grow up, you move to St. Paul." Jabs aside, their sibling rivalry seemed more jocular than spiteful. St. Paul is gorgeous, no denying that. And plenty of folks from St. Paul enjoy the Minneapolis nightlife. They are truly sibling cities—full of criticism for each other as well as deep affection.

Fitch rubs his arms a few times, because it's quite chilly now, not cold exactly—not by Minnesota standards—but without his hoodie, definitely chilly. I'd offer him my jacket, and I will once we reach the roof, but I want him to experience the consequences of his generosity. He's earned this discomfort. If he plans to be compassionate, he must understand there is a cost, even if it's temporary, even if it's merely a chill.

As we near our destination, the tallest building in downtown Minneapolis, Fitch puts his hand on my arm.

"Stop for a second." He pauses. "When I first met you, I didn't understand the appeal of you."

He does not speak, yet I sense he is not finished. "I didn't understand—"

I see his Adam's apple flutter in his throat.

"I do now," he says, focusing on my eyes. "I get the appeal of you. I'm sorry I was rude to you when we first met."

"No apology necessary. I'm not everybody's type."

"But you're a type I didn't know existed," he says earnestly. "You're so—you've flustered me tonight, and in case you couldn't tell, I don't enjoy feeling flustered."

I smile. "I noticed."

"May I kiss you?"

His words surprise me, but so does his attitude, nervous, shy, unsure. This is not the Fitch I've stalked through sticky jungle nightclubs, the tiger seeking prey throughout the Twin Cities. This is not the confident muscle queen who wouldn't give me the time of day.

"Yes. I'd like that."

He leans down, for I am few inches shorter than he, and our lips connect. Our first kiss is infused with the great tenderness he feels, as if he retells the story of our night, but backward, beginning with the intimate mango and sticky rice, the peanut butter noodles, then the homeless shelter, and as the kiss elongates, I imagine us bound together with invisible twine. He is skilled as a kisser, and his hands find my face, holding me close to him. I find myself swimming in his love.

"Get a room," a man in his twenties says as he passes with a buddy.

We break our kiss and chuckle.

I love that this is possibly the most homophobic thing I've heard on the street in a long time, and it wasn't even homophobic. That was a PDA admonishment. Another plus for the Twin Cities. Homo-friendly.

Fitch grins. "You're a good kisser. I knew you would be."

I nudge him forward. We're almost at the IDS tower. "So, you've been thinking about kissing me."

"I have," he says, falling in step beside me. "Since the string and the blindfold."

"Do tell."

"Several times, I thought you were actually kissing me. I felt kissed, listening to your strong voice and feeling your closeness. I'm sure I was being kissed and held by your warm hands. At some point, I realized I had only imagined it."

"You seemed to experience intense hallucinations."

"I did," Fitch says. "I only remember fragments. I thought the room was crowded with people. I sort of remember you assuring me we were alone, but you said it across a crowded room. I can't explain it. Flashes of color. Names. A dude with a question mark over his head. Crazy shit."

That's the most he's said about the experience in a few hours.

I knock on the revolving door to the IDS Center. The reflective building is gorgeous, one of the most distinguished landmarks in Minneapolis's skyline. I always picture this skyscraper as an elegant lady, a tall drink of water in her shimmering, slimming mirror dress. If there were any way for a skyscraper to hold a bubbly mimosa, she would. She would toast this city for honoring her, bringing her spirit to physical form.

The security guard approaches, a tall man. Six foot two, thick gut, bald, with an enormous black moustache, too large for his large frame. He wears a thick black jacket with a coms system attached to the arm, and he tugs on his white security shirt in a few spots. He looks at me, then Fitch, and with a silent nod, motions us to the left side of the revolving door, a regular door, which he opens.

I enter and Fitch, reluctantly, follows suit.

Fitch nervously says, "Vin."

I do not answer.

Our security guard friend trudges toward the elevator bay, and since he doesn't speak, neither do we. Fitch scans the empty lobby, anticipating something—a surprise which does not come. Inside the elevator, Nathan uses his key to unlock the top button, and our ascent begins inside the elegant lady.

Nathan leads us down a series of elongated hallways, a maze it seems, until we come to the stairwell leading to the roof door. At the top of the stairwell, he sticks his key into the lock and faces us. Without saying a word, he opens the door and leads us into the night.

Minneapolis is stunning—impossible and spectacular—from this perspective. The street lights far below, like distant Christmas tree lights, and the not-quite-as-tall buildings nearby, illuminated with their own challenge to the dark night. The many-voiced winds rip through us. But those impressions are replaced by the dominant and unexpected impression of trees, thousands and thousands of green trees in every direction, huddling in the city's glow and beyond, suggesting Minneapolis happens to exist inside an enchanted forest. Driving the city streets, or bicycling around the lakes, you notice trees, sure, but up here—this high—all you see is trees. They've been hiding in plain sight all along, the cold wind energizing them, making them swing their branches in dancing tribute, and you never noticed how much they love it here, our cold, refreshing state.

"My god," Fitch says, daring to take a few steps away from me.

The roof is enormous, like the building is enormous. Twists and turns of the building's shape, the metal communication tower rising from off-center, everything conspires to block a three-hundred-and-sixty-degree view. But it hardly matters, because everything in sight is remarkable. To want to see more seems downright greedy.

"I've never seen the city like this." Fitch is wide-eyed, and possibly terrified as people can be when facing a landscape without limitation.

He holds his arms and rubs them, turning away from Nathan and me, daring a few more steps.

"Don't go too close to the edge," Nathan says, the first words he has spoken.

Fitch turns in surprise and addresses him. "I won't. I promise. I'm too scared. But thank you for the warning, and—" Fitch stumbles. "I—I don't know how to say *thank you* for letting us see this once-in-a-lifetime...I'm...I lived in Minnesota my whole life and didn't realize the trees..."

Nathan removes his security jacket and unhooks his radio. He offers the jacket to Fitch.

"No, I couldn't," Fitch says.

Typical Minnesotan response.

Nathan continues to hold it in front of him without speaking.

Fitch says, "No. I don't—I'm fine."

Why must Minnesotans decline something three times before they'll finally accept it?

I say, "Take it. You'll need it."

Fitch defies local customs—not waiting for that third offering—and with a nod, thanks Nathan. As he pulls it on, I remember how Ronnie looked a few hours ago, pulling the sleeves up on a jacket too large for him.

"I really appreci—"

Fitch stops.

Nathan continues to strip, unbuttoning his white uniform shirt. Under this shirt, he wears another. It is gorgeous light purple, almost light blue, threaded with delicate plum-colored flames, arching up and down the sides. A delectable find, if I do say so myself. The shimmering material doesn't wrinkle easily, so instead of disheveled, the impact is to make Nathan suddenly appear glorious.

Nathan looks right at Fitch. "The Found Ones realized that Lost Kings could be reawakened. Restored. If only they could be made to remember."

Fitch takes a step back in surprise, glancing all around him. He says, "Oh shit."

Nathan continues. "The best chance of restoring a lost brother was to take him to greet the dawn. The kings of the ancient tribe did not know why they met the dawn, they just did. But greeting the dawn was more than symbolic. Greeting the dawn played an important role in the awakening. The Found Kings met the dawn in their most stunning raiment. To recover a Lost One, you sent him to the dawn alone, wearing his king shirt, and he would awaken, remembering who he was always meant to be."

Upon finishing this speech, Nathan turns to me. With almost sorrowful eyes, he takes my hand and turns it over, bringing the underside to his lips. He imbues his kiss with his deep gratitude, and through the softness of his lips, he communicates all his love to me in this delicate expression.

He picks up his white uniform shirt and leaves us to our privacy, pulling the door closed.

I look at Fitch and see he's pressed his hands against his face, crying into them.

He wipes his tears on the jacket. "What's happening? Who was that? Is this a secret society?" He doesn't wait for an answer. "I haven't cried this much in a year. More. I mean, never. Every little thing tonight sets me off. I can't—"

We are silent while the wind slaps us, and the trees below pass electricity through their branches, a secret green message to which we are not privy.

"We're not alone up here," he says sadly, meeting my gaze. "Can you feel it? They're crowding in around us, all the time."

"Who?"

"All of them," he says crossly. "Every time you start talking about them. Or your ex-boyfriend, when he started talking—"

"Nathan? He's straight. I fix his SUV."

"I don't care who he is," Fitch says. "I'm serious. Do you understand we're constantly watched by a thousand eyes? When you talk about them, you're inviting them. It's exhausting. I'm exhausted. Can't you—can't you feel it?"

I've never felt what he's describing—being watched. But that's not important. I need to switch this direction of conversation. I need him to focus on himself.

"Exhausted? That's too bad. Because I was hoping to have sex here."

Fitch takes a few steps closer, and the concern melts from his face. "I mean, not *that* exhausted."

"What about all the eyes watching us?"

He grins at me, a dirty little grin. "I can be an exhibitionist."

While I retrieve the sleeping bag, wedged under the lowest rung of the communication antennae, he explores the rooftop, not wandering too far, nothing approaching the edge. From the backpack tied to the outside door handle, I retrieve bottles of water. I unroll the sleeping bag, make it comfy. When I finish, he calls me over.

"Look at those dark spots. No lights. That must be Lake Calhoun and, farther out, Lake Harriet."

We point out additional landmarks almost unrecognizable from this perspective never witnessed before, regaining our bearings to the city around us, below us. We command the city tonight from this towering vantage. We are its kings on its highest throne.

"This is terrifying," he says, gaping around. "Exhilarating too."

After another minute discussing the forceful wind, the blackness of the night, and the terror spinning in our stomachs, our conversation draws to a natural close.

"Strip."

"Uh-oh," Fitch says. "Been here before."

"Lie down on the sleeping bag. Wear Nathan's jacket to keep your upper body warm."

Fitch takes my advice and soon wriggles naked on the sleeping bag, looking sexy with the uniform jacket unbuttoned and his sculpted chest exposed. He could pass for a cop in a porno, leering at me, beckoning me to do my worst.

"Will you get naked? I'd like that."

"I will. Not yet. Right now, it's all about the Fitch Dick."

He laughs. "Nice."

Without answering, I drop to my knees and wrap my mouth around his soft cock. Densely scented, it tastes fresh but with a tang of his personal musk and a hint of sperm. Somehow, it's a perfect match for this fragrant May evening, the stars gleaming and fresh, but tainted with the musk of humanity.

"Oh," Fitch says in surprise, "oh my god."

He groans, and his right hand finds my shoulder, whether to fight my luxurious strokes or to encourage them, I can't say. He doesn't know either. But I understand how—as a man—when this much sensation floods your cock, hands instinctively react, ready to intervene.

I suck. I slobber. His dick is big, so it takes all my concentration, at first at least, to open my throat to accommodate this fat monster. As much sex as Fitch gets, I'm guessing he doesn't get deep throated as often as he'd like, based on the surprised utterances he keeps making.

"All of it," he gasps at one point. "Oh god, you've..."

For all our bragging and porn star capabilities, we real-life homos can be quite naïve about cocksucking. Seriously. Stroking a man's dick with your throat presents so many opportunities, from light feathery glides meant to tickle the shaft, to hearty throat-gripping tugs, convincing him your goal is to separate his cock from his body. Variety is the key.

Fitch cries out and cuts himself off almost immediately.

I pull off the Fitch Dick.

"Suck it," he cries. "Please. *Please*. Do what you just—"

"One condition."

He whimpers. "Anything. *Please*."

"Make noise. Any noise. Lots of noise. Whatever comes out of you is cool. Growling, panting, yelling, whatever. Don't hold back or I'll hold back. Based on that limited sucking, you know I can give amazing head. Or, mediocre head. It depends on how vocal you get. I don't care if you hum the national anthem. Just make sound."

"Yeah, yeah," he says. "Get back on it. It's cold exposed to the wind, and your throat is—*oh my god*."

Fitch groans as I engulf him again. He arches his back off the sleeping bag as if only he could get *just* an inch deeper, every life problem would be solved.

He screams.

I jerk my mouth off him, and bark at him to keep his eyes open.

He shouts when I focus on the thick purple head, the crown of his massive dick, sucking it with the strength of my lips.

"The *stars*," he cries out loudly. "Stars!"

I'm delighted he noticed. Although I can't see them myself right now, I observed moments ago how the sky blessed us with a cloudless night. Far above the city's bright lights, we are witness to a few thousand extra stars, the private ones reserved for first class.

I scrape the head of his dick with my teeth. Most men assume *teeth bad* when it comes to cocksucking, and that's mostly true, from an amateur perspective. *Teeth good* if you know when to use them and how, gentle nibbling or gnawing with the right amount of pressure. It's not for everyone, but Fitch clearly loves it.

His butt humps off the sleeping bag regularly, fucking his cock into my mouth with long strokes, screaming his swears and yelling unintelligible words.

I edge him farther down the path, making sure plenty of my saliva drips onto his nuts, so by the time I start stroking them with my free hand, he howls as if I'd punched him, and his whole body jerks and twists, like earlier when he was bound with string.

He's getting closer.

But he won't come. I'm going to edge him closer and closer, nearer and nearer, until he cries for release. In the meantime, I will dog-throat him hard to bring him close to orgasm. I attack his cock with gusto and a low growl, barking on it, sucking with an intensity that makes Fitch string together curses like threading popcorn for Christmas garlands. Making noise is no issue for him.

As I attack him, he begins laughing, howling, and laughing between howls.

He laughs while staring at the thousands of stars, laughing while getting his mighty Fitch Dick worshipped. He laughs without reserve because nobody sees him here, nobody in the green kingdom below hears his jubilation. I hope he remembers what I told him earlier, about the kings who laughed at the stars while they made love.

FIVE

"I can't believe you edged me for so long and didn't let me come," he says as we clomp up my front steps. "Unbelievable case of blue balls."

I laugh, he laughs, and we're quite merry together, returning to my home close to one a.m.

He wasn't quite so chipper when I announced our Rooftop Suck-Fest had reached a non-explosive conclusion, but he begrudgingly acquiesced. He now consents to his submission, even if he doesn't always enjoy it.

Once inside, I point to the circle of unlit candles. "Strip. Stand in the center."

I leave him alone so I can arrange a few small details in the bathroom and my bedroom. I do not bother looking back to ensure he complies. He will. He gets it now. When I return, he smiles warmly, hands on his hips, naked in the middle of the room.

"Come!"

He chuckles. "You're good, but you're not *that* good. Warm me up a little first."

Snickering, he follows me into the bathroom, and if he's surprised to see the oversized Jacuzzi tub gurgling and frothy, he does not say so. I switch off the light so he gets the full effect. In curved, twisting boughs, green mesh netting swings from the shower rod to the medicine cabinet, back to the shower rod, then to the window, to a hook near the corner of the ceiling, crisscrossing everywhere, sometimes dangling straight down, to create the illusion of a green forest above us and everywhere around us. Tiny white Christmas lights crisscross through the mesh to illuminate our fairy woodland, as well as the white tile, bouquets of white roses, and a dozen white pillar candles flickering. A bottle of champagne in a silver bucket with crystal-fluted glasses awaits our pleasure.

His good humor from the living room vanishes.

"Hey," Fitch says, and the short word comes out of him strangled and quiet.

His face is serious, although he tries to smile. I had hoped the impact might be something like this. My bathroom isn't anything spectacular—though it has been scrubbed clean, which in itself is pretty spectacular. As ordinary as these decorations are, I wanted the effect to be like a homemade card drawn by a child. The effort matters. The details matter. There's something endearing and heartbreaking about a crayon dog with two stick legs and an enormous sun wearing a crooked smiley face, waving at said dog.

I don't doubt men who've admired Fitch have made great efforts to impress him. Probably spent a lot more money than I have. I admit, my effort is calculated. After an evening of heart-opening activities, this personal effort matters more.

He nods, and in a thick voice, he says, "Roses."

I invite him into the tub, and he lowers himself gingerly. The bubbling water accepts him, and his body disappears beneath its surface. With a few clicks of my remote, Celtic folk music—remixed as slow trance—plays over the skillfully hidden speakers, an energetic yet subdued beat. Twilight in an impossible Celtic jungle.

He watches with curiosity as I strip, and I think the muscle man is taking notes on my form.

"You've got a great build," he says. "You could really pack on serious muscle if you wanted."

"If I wanted..."

"Sorry," he says. "I didn't mean it as criticism. You've got solid definition already, hidden under your baggy clothes. Great shoulders—really thick. Your body would take well to bulking up if you were into that sort of thing. I'm jealous."

As I strip off my boxer briefs, he nods at my cock and says, "Nice piece. Looks fat."

"Thanks."

I climb into the Jacuzzi facing him, and he scoots back to accommodate me. He asks me questions about my workout routine, and I reply in short answers. I want to discourage conversation without making a thing out of it. While he asks, I use a lavender gel soap to work his neck, his shoulders, and soon his words disappear. I work my way down his left arm, soaping every fat muscle curving into the next. When he puts his head back and moans, I trace around his nipples, concentric circles arcing wider and wider until I cover his entire chest. When I do his fingers, he twitches, and his legs jerk, perhaps remembering earlier tonight and yet forgetting he is not bound and obligated to spasm.

When my hand reaches for his nuts, he almost jumps straight up.

"Sensitive!"

"I know," I say softly.

"They're sore," he says. "You blue-balled me, man."

"I know."

I manage to clean his legs, the mighty Fitch Dick, and eventually, while he leans back, I saw my index fingers between each of his toes. While in this tranquil state, he asks, "What happens with the Lost Kings? How do they get home?"

"They don't."

After a moment, he opens his eyes and leans forward. "What do you mean, 'they don't'?"

"Story's over. Some kings are lost. Some are found."

He sits up and pulls his right leg away from me. "There has to be more. You can't leave it with all these Lost Kings running around."

We're joined by a tension not present a moment ago.

I say, "I'm going to stand up. You scoot forward so I can sit behind you and massage your shoulders."

He reluctantly obeys. After a few seconds of sloshing, I sit behind him. The tidal wave caused by our movement diminishes. His arms are bigger than mine—hell, his whole body is bigger than mine—so I hold him as best I can, wanting him to feel safe and comforted, even while I try to make him uncomfortable.

I massage the back of his neck. Right there—there is the tension.

"What about Vladimir, the beauty guy?"

"The Finder of Beauty."

"Yeah. He's still lost?"

As pleased as I am with his concern, I do not answer him. Instead, I work his neck muscles where they merge with his shoulders. I scratch the backs of his shoulders with my goatee, tracing letters and patterns into him, secrets of the story not yet revealed.

After another moment, he says, "Seriously? Nothing?"

"Just bits and pieces. King Vladimir the Finder of Beauty was reportedly wandering around Europe. Of course, he'd be in disguise so nobody would recognize him, physically. King Andrew the Singer of Souls was seen in some nameless corporation's accounting department, courting numbers and spreadsheets because it was too painful to remember his gift of music. The Lost Ones disguise themselves well. Very often, they do not want to be found."

"What happens to Lost Kings?"

"The same thing that happens to Found Kings, eventually. They die."

He jerks, creating a smallish tsunami.

Damn it, I almost said, *we* die. I have to be careful. I have to protect him from knowing too much about me. I am poison. I can assist him becoming found, but if there's one thing I've learned from my years of kinging men, it's the price they pay. Their joy is not complete because of who crossed them over. I am a thorn in their paw. I always inserted myself too much into the process. I didn't understand the damage I had wrought by ingratiating myself in their hearts. I simply had to know all their secrets, *had* to know, didn't I? But I didn't need to know. I only insisted on knowing their secrets because I was weak and unskilled.

How much do I know about Fitch? I don't know about his parents. Childhood traumas. I don't know if he hates his career as a graphic designer. Ex-boyfriends—other than the one he mentioned cheating on. Coming out. I don't know much about his life circumstances at all, really, yet I do know the man, Kevin Yonnick. His resistance, his power, his submission. I know what he needs, and I have witnessed his great love. I know what he doesn't want in his life. Turns out, that's enough information to king a man. Malcolm always called it the truth behind what is true.

"Before we get out of the tub, Fitch, is there anything you want to say?"

"Yeah, are you ever going to quit calling me Fitch and use my real name?"

"I didn't invite you to ask a question, I asked you if you wanted to say something."

"Like what?"

"Dunno. Get quiet and go inside yourself. See if there's anything you want to say. To me, to yourself, to release into the world. If no words come up, that's fine."

"What am I supposed to say?"

"Nothing."

We sit for a moment or two longer, and I instruct him to put his arms on his knees so I can work different back muscles.

He says nothing.

I say nothing.

After another few minutes, I start to rise. We should dry off.

"Wait," he says. "Just wait. This isn't easy. Sit, okay? I don't want you to look at me. I want to stay like this for a moment, okay?"

I return to my sitting position and put both hands on his upper back, feeling him breathe in and out.

"Thank you," he says. "I want to thank you, I guess. I don't know. I don't know what's happening. I'm all inside out."

He glances around the bathroom, as if looking for help from the forest.

"I don't understand how you know to push—how you'd...Jason, my last boyfriend, was Chinese. Chinese American, I guess. Did you know that?"

"No."

"Well, he was. He would cook for us, these incredible wok dishes. Healthy. I don't go to Chinese restaurants anymore. They all taste greasy and unsatisfying, not like Jason's food. I miss eating his food. And I miss him. But tonight—"

He stops talking. The words get choked off.

"Thank you," he says. "There've been parts of tonight I didn't like, but thank you. And not just thank you to you personally, but thank you to...them."

"Them?"

"Them. Watching us."

I want to ask more, to understand what he sees or senses. But isn't that just me inserting myself more into his process? Aren't I committed to less of that? Less damage? I admit, I hoped he might confess how he knows the story of the Lost and Founds. Maybe he visited my website and lied about it. I'm not getting that vibe, not with the intimacy we've created. He would have confessed.

He stands, so I stand too, and like titans emerging from the sea, we create typhoons and wreak destruction upon the porcelain shores. The tub drains while we shower, rinsing ourselves clean. We step out. With thick fuzzy towels, I dry him in long strokes, neither of us speaking. He mostly avoids eye contact with me, though occasionally, I catch his mournful expression. Fitch is sad. He doesn't know why. He doesn't understand something crucial—I never removed the string.

Sure, the physical string fell away, but that binding was the first of many. I've been squeezing his heart all night, pulling from different angles, from volunteering, to the surprising night guard who revealed his lavender beauty. The regal glory of Minneapolis's kingdom, the wild-stallion feel of sex on the roof, everything conspired with me to break Fitch's spirit, his psyche, in ways he doesn't see and can't understand. He doesn't recognize how it's all related; though his sorrowful gratitude in the bathroom suggests he understands on some level. He thanked *them*.

I lead him from the bathroom to my bedroom, and he pauses on the threshold, putting his hand against the doorframe. Mine is an average bungalow. The bedroom is modest, hardwood floors and exquisite molding, which I refinished myself, gleaming chestnut against the cranberry walls. A heavy, mission-style bed dominates the room, a thick mattress and flannel-covered comforter suggesting snuggling warmth, a bed hard to leave in the morning. On top lie two white roses, one stem crossing the other as if they'd recently finished fucking in that position. The room is illuminated by soft, white Christmas lights.

"You went to a lot of trouble," he says.

I do not respond.

He faces me with his sadness. "Do you go out to the bars on your own?"

"No."

"You were there looking for me."

"Yes."

"Only looking for me. All those times I saw you, week after week."

"Yes."

"Did you ever go home with anyone while you were out there?"

"No."

"Why not? You're a stud. You don't show off your body, but you got game. And a thick cock. Why not?"

"Because I was there for you."

Fitch's eyes clench tight when he hears this answer. He turns from me and picks up a rose. "You must think I'm a total whore."

"I don't."

"Why not?" He faces me angrily. "You saw me go home with different guys. You saw that."

"Few times."

"Well, what the fuck? Were you jealous? Did you want me?"

I recognize this shift in tone. It's easier to express anger than sadness.

"Did I want you, *yes*. Was I jealous, *no*. We had no agreement. You get to fuck who you want. As often as you want. There's nothing wrong with loving sex. I have no problem with that."

"What about making me apologize to all those guys in the candle circle. You were judging me, then."

"You directed that conversation, Fitch. Not me. I asked you when you had sex last. You lied to me at first, and then started telling the truth. Then, you took over the conversation and I followed. Think back and remember it. What did I say that made you feel judged? What did I do?"

He splutters for a moment, formulating answers that don't emerge. He sits on the bed next to the remaining rose and looks at the floor. "I don't know what's happening to me."

"I do. Do you trust me?"

"Yes."

"Then let me worry about what's happening to you, and you just be present with me. Okay?"

He wipes his eyes. "This is so confusing."

I sit next to him and put my hand on his neck.

He chuckles. "First time I've been with a hot guy in his bedroom and started to cry."

"So, I'm a hot guy, huh?"

He turns his gleaming eyes my way. "Absolutely."

We kiss.

This kiss tells another story, a story about Fitch's softness, his vulnerability. This kiss is not Nightclub Fitch, swaggering through the darkness, knowing he looks great in whatever light hits him. This kiss is warm, sticky, and hesitant. It's an invitation to stand by his side while he trembles before the unknown. And like most kisses, it evolves into something more physical. More wet. I love sucking his tongue, and suddenly, this kiss is about sex.

"Let's pull back the comforter."

"Uh-huh," he says, grinning as we pull apart. "Let's do that."

Sexy Fitch is back.

Once the comforter reveals the shimmery, hunter-green satin sheets, Fitch says, "Oh, wow. This is kinky. I *love* this. I mean, feel this."

His hands make ripples he chases across the bed.

"Lie down," I say. "Facedown."

We pull back the covers more so this is possible, and he crawls into bed like a jungle cat.

"This feels so erotic," he says with delight. "I can't believe I don't have sheets like this."

With a click of the remote, I switch the music to a group from India named Kali, their wet thrusting beat and sensual melodies gifted to me by Ryan, who once loved me with all his love. Ryan. Talk about great cocksuckers. Kali's beat is hypnotic, pounding, suggesting faraway kingdoms and life's unsolvable mysteries.

I trail my fingertips over his bulging shoulders and down his spine, lightly enough for him to spasm uncontrollably. All those fat muscles come in handy as he flexes and releases, each hyperdeveloped neuron supercharged and eager to deliver the sensuality to its muscle neighbor. I trace the outline of him for a few minutes this way, making him shiver.

"You better be careful," he says. "You might put me to sleep."

"Feeling sleepy?"

He answers as if I'd chastised him. "No, Vin. I won't sleep. I don't want to miss this, whatever's happening between us. My heart is on fire."

Yes! This is his true voice. He's not playing games. He's transitioning from Fitch to Kevin. Authentically, Kevin.

His muscle ass meets regulation-pale standards for all Abercrombie & Fitch wannabes. I trace it, running my finger down the smooth and yet stubbly crack, listening to him change his breathing slightly when I come closer to touching his anus. He clenches and unclenches.

"You know I'm a total top." His voice sounds apprehensive.

"And tonight?"

"Tonight," he says, and I sense he's stalling for a few more seconds to decide whether he's going to go through with this. "Tonight, I'm yours. I'm...I'm yours. Be careful with me, okay? I don't get fucked."

"Do you hate it?"

"No. Happened once or twice. But it never felt great, and I prefer to fuck, so, why bother?"

This is good to know. I must ensure Fitch loves tonight's experience, especially if he may never get fucked again.

He says, "You? Get fucked?"

"I'm a total top as well."

"Ever been fucked?"

"Yes."

Well, *raped*. I was raped. That's not the same thing. Also, once I was fucked with love. I needed it once, to balance out the horror. This is not the time for my deep sharing. He doesn't need to know about my rape issues.

"It doesn't do much for me, either. Fitch, my intention is to fuck you. Let me try to make love to you this way, and if it's something you just can't endure, we'll stop. We will find another way to play. But unless you say stop, I'm gonna keep going."

"Fair enough. Let's give this a shot."

I begin kissing his beautiful ass, soft, dry kisses in appreciation for the hard work he does, the thousands of squats—I'm guessing—to arrive at this perfection. Millions? The mind boggles. I introduce my goatee to this way of honoring him, and finally, slow moans escape him. I start at the bottom of his butt and drive my chin north, eventually finding his spine. He twists, and his leg jerks to the side, like when he was tied. Everything remains bound together, all the sensations. On the rooftop, I ensured his cock became the center point—the unconquerable knot—for his binding, sucking it for almost two hours inside a snow globe with falling stars instead of snow, while he laughed and screamed.

Soon, my king. Your destiny is manifesting.

I could spend an hour on his ass alone, loving it, worshipping it, but I have greater plans for him, so I introduce my tongue in long strokes, and soft laps at the top of his ass, suggesting further wetness is coming his way.

He twists.

He groans.

When I actually begin to slobber down his crack, a sizzling hiss leaves his mouth, and he jumps against the satin sheets and then trembles in aftershocks.

"These sheets," he says huffing, "every time I move, the sensations..."

I know.

I dig my tongue into his pink, and Fitch yells a few choice religious words in a tone both blasphemous and reverential. I lap him with basset-hound tongue strokes and also short nippy strokes like a Yorkshire terrier. Fitch cries out during these terrier nips, their surprising intensity unnerving what little nerve he has left.

When I sense he can't stand this anymore—the satin zipping along his skin, and my wet, gurgling dives—I bite his white butt cheek and then suck hard on the spot.

"Hey," he cries out, but it's too late.

I've already left a hickey. Might be awkward to explain the next time he's at the gym.

He laughs. "Didn't expect that. You got me." Fitch squirms against the sheets. "My cock is rock hard again. I mean, I figured you planned this, but I am right back to where we were on the roof."

"Good."

Now that I feel his full submission, it's time. He's ready. We've got two hours to fuck, but I suspect a total top like him won't be able to take it very long. He might get a nap tonight. I flip him over and the mighty Fitch Dick rises to greet me. Thick. Strong. Oozing precum as if he gets paid by the ounce.

He licks his lips and pulls me to him, squeezing my biceps.

"Nice," he says, and smiles shyly at me. "You're a stud, Vin."

"Thanks."

He tries to pull me into a kiss, and when I resist, he growls at me. "C'mere. Don't be a dick."

He adopts a tone to hide the fact his eyes are pleading. He's begging for me to kiss him. Fitch is not someone who begs, I'm guessing.

I drop my lips on top of his. He's a good kisser. He's got well-practiced lips, sensitive and strong, and a tongue that knows the goal isn't to stab me to death. He manages several different styles of kissing, which means he knows the best kissing isn't always accomplished the way you prefer, but rather finding your kiss together.

I let my hardening cock rub against his abused hole, and he grunts when we make contact. His throat vibrates against me when my cock pauses—just there—ready to press in. He pulls back with surprise, asking me with his eyes, *are we doing this*? *Are we really doing this?*

Yes. We are.

I drop to his side to grab the lube from the nightstand and a small washcloth, getting my index finger ready to insert. He watches me with fear, anger, and trust. Would I label the combination resignation? The anger is a curious ingredient, harkening to a betrayal in his life long ago, something I know nothing about. But he was betrayed. By someone important. His submission—his trust in me—offers me a chance to make it right...my lovemaking may counter some of the damage, and I won't even know what it was. What matters is he's aware of it.

"Someone hurt you," I say, making my gaze soft. Nonthreatening. "A long time ago. I don't think it was around sex. It's older than that. Someone told you they would take care of you, look out for you. They didn't. Remember it. Can you do that for me, Fitch?"

"I'm not sure—"

"You are sure. You know. I saw the anger in your eyes a second ago, a flash of recognition your trust had been betrayed. The gift of trust you offer me right now is a big deal. You can handle a little physical pain, but you're worried if you say *stop*, I won't. It's hard for you to trust I will."

"I don't know—" he says, and tears fall from both eyes. "—what you mean."

"Maybe I guessed wrong." I smile. "I thought it might be a big deal, this level of trust."

His eyes look even more hurt now than a few moments ago.

"That," I say. "What happened inside you just now. You don't have to explain to me. But notice it. Remember how it felt to trust and be betrayed. And now, years later, to trust so big again."

While my finger dances around his most vulnerable spot, his head thrashes to one side, then the other, and he clenches his eyes. He doesn't want to see the connections.

Oh, Fitch. The connections are swirling all around us like twine. A mysterious note delivered with his favorite beer. Surprise inner truths revealed in crowded nightclubs. The immediate stripping, the dawn of his deeper trust in me. The orgasmic grid, his weeping, his generosity with Ronnie. Peanut-noodle laughter, and being lovingly fed mangos and sticky rice. Satin sheets, a generous River, the rooftop of a modern-day castle, and a thousand shimmering stars above the home he's always known. Bubbling Jacuzzi in the center of an enchanted forest lit by firefly candles. A security guard who sheds his familiar skin to reveal flaming plum curls, a magnificent man disguised as ordinary.

He doesn't understand how it's all intertwined in his heart, but it is.

It's a fairy tale.

Despite the digital clock's assertion of 2:32 a.m., it's 11:59, and the stroke of midnight is seconds away, symbolically at least.

The crown jewel—the missing element from this fairy tale—is a king under a dark curse.

I take my time, but after a few moments of hungry kissing and me tweaking his nipples, Fitch is surprised to discover three of my fingers have burrowed inside him. His face registers a certain pleased surprise—as well as pleasure—as I twist them gently.

"How?" he asks, gasping. "How?"

Not every question gets an answer.

I retrieve the condom I set aside for this fuck, and in silence, unwrap it, then sheathe my cock, hard and ready for service. I love him. I've been loving him for weeks, despite the fact he dragged me through nightclub after nightclub.

"Go easy," he says, keenly observing my preparations. "I'm impressed by the three fingers, but go easy, okay?"

"Of course, my king," I say.

His eyes fill with tears, spilling over. He throws his head back on the pillow. "Is that what your friend, Greg, said in the restaurant? 'My king, my king?' And you said it to the veteran..."

While Fitch cries, I kiss his forehead and touch his tears with my fingertips.

When he stops, I begin making small circles on his anus again, causing him to switch almost instantly from mournful to sensual. His legs shoot out, and he groans. I know which strings to pull.

"Wait, I'm not ready," he says, eyes closed.

I stop. I watch. Someone didn't respect him, didn't keep their word to protect him. Although I don't sense it was sexual, trust is trust. I must right this wrong.

He unclenches, everything relaxes. I feel it in how his hole responds to my presence.

Fitch opens his eyes and sees me evaluating him.

"How are you doing?"

"Okay. I'm ready. I'm ready now."

I nod.

We groan in twin when I enter him, easing into him, watching his face. When I see tension in the corners of his eyes, I slow or pull out—just a little—so he understands we move at his pace.

Fitch is warm. Warmth pulsates from the center of him.

I pull all the way out, then re-enter slowly, causing his entire body to flail against the sheets, a whole different level of distress. Pleasurable as the sheets are, they're also driving him nuts. Distracting him from what's happening in his ass.

I'm deeper.

I find a steady rhythm inside him, not pounding him—I could never pound him the way he undoubtedly pounds some of his men—but asserting myself in a strongish way. I give him as much as he takes, and by the incredulous look on his face, it's more than he supposed. But he can't sustain this for terribly long. He's not a bottom by trade.

Is he ready to come?

I grab his dick, and he screams, jerking himself farther onto my cock as his arms shoot out in opposite directions.

"Oh my god," he screams. "*Oh my god!*"

He's ready.

"Hey Fitch, guess what? I just remembered part of the king story. An update."

Fitch pleads with me in slobbering, mouth-open silence, *don't do this*.

I attempt to look bashful, while driving into him. "Sorry. But it's been so long since his last reported sighting. The Found Ones had never deserted the hope of reclaiming him; they could never give up on the one true king. But he himself had given up."

I use my eyes to assure him. It was always about you, Fitch. The whole night—the stories—they were always about you.

He cries out and pushes on my chest, as if to push me away. But in the next deep stroke, he pulls me into him and lunges at my lips, his passion driving the hunger in him, the squirming, twisting, writhing, ravenous hunger squeezing him, inside him, and surprising him all at once.

When he breaks the kiss, he says, "I have to say this. Or I will go crazy."

I try to observe what's happening, what's boiling in him. All seemed good a second ago, seemed like we—

"I love you," Fitch says unhappily, or at least with anxiety. "I'm terrified of where you're taking me, but I love you. *I love you.* I love you."

He repeats the phrase, which I like hearing, and he enjoys saying the words as I fuck my cock into him. Over and over, he repeats this mantra. "I love you, I love you, I love you."

Until he spends himself, I will listen and take it in, this love, and try to push it back into him.

When I speak again, I see my words imbued with pink and orange sparks. "He was seen in eastern Russia, possibly Kazakhstan, in a museum dedicated to preserving the native language. King Vladimir Vitchnokker was spotted again, traveling through Europe, searching a dumpster, looking for patterns in food splatters. Rumors suggested he spent two weeks watching the waves crest on the Aegean Sea. Nobody recognized his true identity, but reports circulated that a stranger was near, one who might show you a rare cobalt rose or perhaps invite you to consider the elegance in a sloth's tail. He found beauty everywhere."

"No," Fitch whispers.

"Yes." I nod and stare down at him.

His legs wrap loosely around my torso, and since he never bottoms, he's not sure what to do with them. I grab his calves and hold them upright.

He screams.

But he didn't say *stop*, and by the sounds he's now making, I can tell he still possesses words. So I keep pounding him.

"As a Lost King who wished to stay forgotten, Vladimir did his best to hide his hideous—and very recognizable—appearance from anyone attempting to find him. They say he got plastic surgery so no one would gawk and remember his face. He got his teeth fixed. Compassion toward his ugliness was the gateway into seeing someone else's beauty, so he became well muscled and always followed the stylish trends. He made himself gloriously handsome, the perfect disguise for someone who both loves and hates beauty."

Fitch clamps his ass around my cock as if he could fight the story that way— fight me into not revealing the last few lines. His green eyes, so wide-open and terrified I could fly deep inside him.

Silently, I communicate, *I have a message for you. It's too late for you to fight this.* When you wept in my arms, spent after your big orgasm, did you not hear the king love I whispered into you, the pink and orange sparks binding your heart?

Tears pour from both eyes. He sobs my name.

"I wouldn't worry, if I were you." I say the words harshly, glaring at him.

He will not escape this. He will not deny this.

I continue to batter him.

"To remain hidden, the lost King Vladimir would act nothing like you did tonight, giving your favorite hoodie to a homeless kid. To remain lost, he would never accept your peanut-smeared face with noodles in your hair. You howled with laughter into the deep black night. He could not do such things and remain hidden among the Lost Ones."

Fitch screams, and his legs jerk in my arms.

Be strong, Vin. Hold on.

My orgasm approaches.

"Then again," I say, maintaining my intensity and my rhythm, sliding in and out of him. "Nobody called him King Vladimir. No, that name was for history books, and used when he presented papers at conferences. After all, there were at least seventeen Vladimirs among the Found Ones, so that would be confusing."

"Don't," he cries. "Please don't..."

I speak louder and use my true authority, commanding my voice into his body. I need him to absorb this. "They used his last name, Vitchnokker, and made a nickname. They called him *Vitch* for short."

I fuck him harder, and he screams—a noiseless scream—staring into my eyes.

"Of course, the Vitch got altered when he arrived in Sweden—"

He screams again, this time with sound.

I fucking knew it—he's *Swedish*!

I give him my best jabs—nailing his prostate with all the force he can handle.

I yell, "They called him King Fitch the Finder of Beauty. All hail the one true king. *King Fitch*!"

The first arc of his splattering load flies through the air between us and nails his forehead and beyond, down his cheek, and another fat stream lands inside his mouth, which is forming an enormous, cavernous *O*. His green eyes show more white than emerald, his surprise engulfing everything. All of this happens in silence, the *O*, the first arc, until sound explodes everywhere.

Fitch bawls, eyes wide. He howls, and every part of him screams, every cell giving up its normal responsibilities to contribute to this sound. Arc after spoogy arc splashes against him, his chest, rivulets flowing into the valley between his overly built pecs.

Each time he clamps his ass, he forces out more cum, and my dick definitely digs this brutal handshake, so I respond by spitting out my furious load, deep inside his butt.

The next few moments are lost between us, intensely focused on ourselves, each other. We kiss. Fitch cries. I allow his legs to come down as I pull out of him, and he cries when I do that too. After I unroll the condom and set it next to the bed, he holds me most desperately, unwilling to let go, unwilling to release the fairy tale he's now part of. Even I don't understand this one, how he gets a king name from someone else's story. When I visualized the Finder of Beauty as a king name, the attached name was always Vladimir Vitchnokker. I never suspected this king name fit a man currently alive. Is Kevin the reincarnated version of this man? Is there some connection between these two kings I don't understand? Every other king name came to me a very different way. Is Kevin special? Who is Vladimir Vitchnokker? Once again, I must accept I simply don't have everything figured out.

He cries. He falls back. He stares at the ceiling—through the ceiling, perhaps—seeing heights I cannot fathom. He pants, his lips moving.

I kiss his left pec, and he looks at me, not at me, because he's a thousand stars away, surfing eternity.

His eyelids touch together, and he says, "Vin."

And, he's gone. Asleep. Snoring gently.

Well, he's earned it.

In the Finder of Beauty, *B* is for binding, muscles bound up tight, and *y* is for questions answered and unanswered, like "why am I here?" Why is my life the way it is, a bouncing beginning, an unresolved ending, with mystery in between, a slew of *eau*, the verb that sounds *oooooooooo*, so open and longlicious, a bouncy beginning, the *b* beginning to bounce around, the *oooooooeau oooooooeaus* elongating gracefully, skating into elegant patterns—*stop it!*

The forest!

Trees! Shrubs! Trails littered with flowers and skittering creatures, maybe a snake would be welcome, who knows? I'll have to get used to snakes if I move there, the forests in Honduras. Stop this insanity with words. Drop a forest on it.

I need to get up. Do something. Get the word *beauty* out of my head. He's gorgeous, so amazingly beautiful, inside and out. I extricate myself with exaggerated slowness. I don't want him to wake.

From the edge of the bed, I take a moment to study him, spread-eagle and unconscious on the satin sheets, rippling like green ocean waves crashing against the mass of his island body. He's perfect and gorgeous. Although not his preference, he welcomed me inside him.

King Fitch.

I'll let him sleep for another hour or more. He needs it.

I move with stealth into the bathroom and extinguish candles, then wander to the kitchen. I'm hungry. I should eat something. Sandwich? Still debating, I move to the living room and consider disassembling the circle of candles. Who knows? Maybe we'll need this tomorrow. And I'd probably make noise. I will leave this as is. Instead, I'll check email quickly before returning to him. Maybe make myself a sandwich.

By the early morning glow of my laptop, I discover a reply from Mr. Persistence in New Jersey. He argues saving his virginity is a perfect example of his maturity and ability to delay gratification. How much more mature do I want? He's got a point. In fact, he makes several good points in his long reply, including calling me an "ageist" for not considering him an equal. I finish reading.

He attached another photo.

In this one, he's frowning at the camera, mouth parted, beautiful, full lips. The sun behind him creates a halo effect on his chocolate, dark hair. Buzz cut, which makes him look military. Hot military. His eyes are golden brown—sharp in this photo. Obviously, he's smart. Sometimes a photo reveals that.

I reread Mark's words again, impressed by his well-reasoned arguments and his passion. He's in New Jersey. Distance doesn't bother me. Is he truly a virgin? Maybe. Seems unlikely, one of those Internet lies. Maybe he considers himself a virgin because his partner pulled out before five minutes had passed. Who knows what the New Jersey rules are around virgin status. Does it matter? No, I guess not.

I suppose I could meet him for sex—give him a positive first sexual experience, if he really is a virgin. No, I couldn't do that. Not my scene. And I'm done kinging men. Hell, none of that even matters. He's twenty-four. I'm so much older. I can't get around that.

I delete his email.

I read a few others, respond to my older brother's demand to know when I'm next visiting Chicago. He instructs me to bring my tools because his Lincoln needs work. I write him a snarky reply, telling him it's his own damn fault for buying a Lincoln—a used Lincoln at that—suggesting two weekend possibilities for my visit. King Malcolm the Restorer. As I click Send, I feel a flood of affection.

I should go back to the bedroom. Gaze at my beloved and watch him while I can. Soon enough, he will greet the dawn and be out of my reach forever.

I already miss King Fitch the Finder of Beauty.

The last king.

SIX

When we arrive at Witches' Tower, the east is deeply purple, still bruised from nightfall. It's dark enough my headlights were necessary on the drive over. Fitch says, "I know this place. Witches' Hat."

Everyone calls it something like this—Witches' Hat or Witches' Tower—the abandoned water tower in the Prospect Park neighborhood. The stone stronghold perches atop the highest neighborhood hill, surveying the tree-thick neighborhood. The cone-shaped black roof with a wide brim lends itself to the obvious moniker, which is perfect, because the entire vicinity seems designed with autumn in mind. Every September, old maples explode in glorious color, dusting the neighborhood's mansions with oranges, reds, and yellows to contrast their muted exteriors. Golden leaves and glowy jack-o-lanterns seem perfect on the twisting, winding roads, manifesting a perpetual sense of Halloween's mischievousness, no matter the season.

Despite the autumnal magic at Witches' Tower, spring casts its own powerful spell, especially premorning. The dense tree cluster at the base of the hill conspires to block entrance to the hidden pathway, the brick walk leading to the tower. I smell seductive lilac, though I cannot see them beckoning. We can see the tip of the hat from the parking lot below, but no more. As far as I know, the tower isn't haunted, but then again, Fitch has been sensing the presence of kings around us. Maybe Halloween magic lasts the whole year around here.

"Meet me at the back of the truck."

Fitch wipes his bleary eyes and fumbles to open the passenger door.

When he reaches me, I'm already holding the purple box tied with wide purple ribbon. Even in the semidarkness, I watch his spicy green eyes wake up fully, darting at me with uncomfortable surprise.

"What's this?"

I hand the gift to him. He takes it reluctantly, turning it in his hands and staring at it from several angles. "What is this?"

"Open it."

Gripping the present, his reluctance is palpable. He shakes it, toys with the ribbon until he can delay no more, and he rips the paper. Once liberated from the box, the cobalt blue silk spills into his hands. He refuses to make eye contact.

He stares at the blue shirt in the predawn light, and though we stand at the back of the truck, flecks of diffuse illumination from the headlights make the irregular surface sparkle and shimmer in the dark.

I say, "Greeting the dawn played an important role in the awakening. The Found Kings met the dawn in their most stunning raiment. To recover a Lost One, you sent him to the dawn alone, wearing his king shirt, and he would awaken, remembering who he was always meant to be."

He says nothing.

"There's a bench at the top of the hill. Go there. Sit. When the sun rises, if you're truly a king, you'll know."

He runs his fingertips over the fabric. "Come with me, Vin. We don't have to talk. Just sit."

"I can't."

He finally raises his eyes to me, and I find a casual smirk. "This king thing is fun—hot role-play. But nothing's going to happen. I mean, it's a fucking sunrise. Happens every damn day. Today isn't special."

We stand in silence.

With extra casualness, he says, "Man, you take this king thing way too seriously."

I say, "Do you ever wonder how your life would be different if you hadn't been so inflexible? Would you still be with him?"

He's startled by the words, the words from my napkin note. His eyes get wide, like a ten-year-old who skinned his knee: old enough to resist bawling but young enough to want to. His teeth click together.

"Go find out if you're truly the Finder of Beauty."

"What if nothing happens?" Fitch's voice betrays the slightest tremor. "What if I'm just me?"

I let him see my eyes, loving and firm. "Then, you'll finally know."

He pleads with me once more, this time in silence.

"I'll be here when you get back."

I resist for as long as I am able.

Which is not long.

The *b* in *beauty* comes to me first, brave and bouncing, unabashedly brash in its insistence that it belongs, boldly braying its bloom as one of the highly desirable consonants. Soon after, *U* follows, because without a relationship to an observing party, what is beauty but an inert and possibly undesirable concept? No, you need *u*, an admirer, for beauty to exist, for what is *b* without *u*? *T* tests the *y*—

Stop it.

I can't stop it.

That's the point. I can't stop it anymore, the craziness inside me, manifesting in letter and word obsessions, berating, betraying, belittling, bemoaning, between and betwixting the—*stop it.*

It's getting worse.

Why? Why is it worse? What's behind all this madness I can't seem to see? *Y*? Why? Or is this the price I pay for breaking into the kingdom, a Lost King's reward for wandering into a clubhouse marked PRIVATE? Maybe. I don't know. It's my fault. I've never been good at keeping away from off-limits places. I see a locked door, and I get obsessed with having to know what's on the other side.

I try to calm myself, reduce the trembling in my arms, thinking about the forest, a Honduran forest, but even that doesn't help this time, the letters in *beauty* swimming around me, giving me no peace. Is it any accident that *eau* in *beauty*— the very staple of it—is French for water? Is not beauty the water of life? Without beauty we die of thirst, we wither. I thought I would die from lack of beauty, but I found books. I was dehydrated and fading fast, and then beauty in books. The letter *y* is a vowel, and sometimes not, because beauty doesn't mean the same thing to every person, *eau* must figure out what it means to *eau*. *E-a-u*, or *ea-u*, or *ea-u*, 'cause *e-a-u*—

Stop it!

I try harder, imagining trees and earth falling atop wispy fonts that cannot defend themselves, and like a mass murderer, I bury them all in an unmarked grave, signified by a few tasteful shrubs.

There. Light.

The sun is rising.

Mentally, I keep relandscaping, replacing hostas with juniper bushes, because I love the smell, and they're more durable, but will junipers grow in South America? I should look that up. I need to get serious about moving. Well, now that the last kinging is almost done, I can. No reason to stay.

I can escape my life at last.

I don't know how long I've been behind my truck, rocking back and forth on my feet, fighting these mental images and the accompanying words, words, words. I'm aware of light in the sky, the exact second of daybreak already forgotten by daylight. Around me, trees begin to assume shades of green in place of mysterious black, and I can see the path leading to—

He's coming.

I don't see his shadow, or any movement, so how could I possibly know?

I *feel* him, like a giant, pounding each footstep into the earth with brazen authority, a man who knows his place in the world. My heart beats faster. This is it. The king is coming.

Fitch appears at the end of the path, his whole body gleaming in shimmering sapphires, spinning around him, outlining him, and while completely defining his physical form, the blue light also frees him from the pedestrian constraints of humanity. He is...he is a Greek god, awakened from marble perfection, rising from Poseidon's lapis lazuli kingdom. I wince and turn my head. I can't stand to look at him, not directly, as I feel him approach. It's like the sky is walking to me. My knees get weaker. If he was gorgeous before, he's unbearable now, my god, the luminosity—

"Vin."

I squeeze my eyes shut. I don't dare. It would be like staring into the sun.

Why do people proclaim love is more powerful than hate, stronger than all the violence and misery so prevalent around us? It's moments like this, when you suddenly see a person glowing, radiating what is possible, all at once "of the kingdom." You see this power and humbly think, "Of course the light trumps everything. Of course."

"Vin," he says softly.

His voice is blue sky, invisible, refreshing, impossible. I feel the heat of him next to me. I am also drunk on blue oxygen.

"Kevin, I'm afraid to open my eyes. I can't bear the light."

"Then, don't," he says.

He cups my face with his thick hand and pulls me to him. I feel his cool breath against me, crisp and yet woodsy, the smell of a creek in June, the smell of breeze when you ascend a mountain—

His lips touch mine.

Without touching myself, without an erection, I gasp and come in my pants.

It's the last thing I remember before I pass out.

I'm awake.

I'm groggy.

I'm grasping the pillow I hold when I sleep, my body covered in sheets.

Oh shit.

I bolt straight up.

I was supposed to take Fitch to greet the dawn! Did I oversleep? *You fucking moron idiot, you overslept!* How the fuck am I going to fix this? It *has* to be the dawn. He's got to be alone at dawn!

Peppermint reaches my nose. Warm peppermint.

"Relax, bear," Fitch says at my side, his voice strong.

"*The dawn.*"

I struggle to speak. Words sound thick and unwelcome in my throat.

He kisses the back of my head. "Yes, the dawn. I have many questions for you, like, how does it work, exactly? How did you know it would work? That I would remember?"

Details come back to me, standing near my truck and slumping to my knees, Kevin grabbing me as I slid into black oblivion. Did we meet the dawn this morning at Witches' Tower? Didn't we? Did I dream it?

"I made you some tea," he says. "The peppermint kind from your cabinets."

I inhale deeply, and the smell calms me.

I'm in my bed.

Fitch throws an arm over me, pulling me to him.

He's naked. I'm mostly naked. How did I get mostly naked?

"I apologize for that kiss," he says. "I was...unprepared for how excited I felt to see you. I couldn't tone myself down. I didn't know how at first."

Tone myself down? I don't know what that means.

He says, "It's all very new, very...surprising."

Neither of us speaks for a moment.

"Have some tea, Vin."

I obey. I reach for it, and he shifts, moving one hand to my hip, allowing me to stretch across the bed toward the nightstand.

Fitch asks, "You know about the sunlight?"

With the mug halfway to my lips, I freeze. They aren't supposed to tell me anything about what happens to them. The King of Bargains once warned me, many years ago.

"I shouldn't say anything," he says. "Got it. I mean, I'm getting it. There's so much to learn, and I don't know how to take it all in. I shouldn't speak of this, should I?"

Aric told me the more I know, the less likely I am to cross over myself. Well, what the fuck do I care? I'm never going to be a Found King anyway.

I say, "Sure, go ahead. It's not a big deal."

"It *is* a big deal. And you're wrong. Just because your path hasn't opened before you, Vin, doesn't mean it's not happening."

What path?

He doesn't elaborate.

I take a few deep sips from the mug, and he's right, the tea relaxes me, allows me to come back to my body. He brought me home. He drove my truck to get me to my house, carried me up the steps, undressed me, and snuggled in. Wow. He carried me. I'm not exactly light. Finally, he had a real use for all those big muscles. And somewhere in there, he made tea. Holy shit, I was unconscious a long time.

He kisses the back of my neck.

In a low and rumbly voice, he says, "I want to show you my love, *all my love.* How important is it to you to not get fucked?"

No!

I don't want to get fucked.

"Okay," he says, kissing my naked shoulder. "Okay. No fucking. You don't have to answer this next question, but I'm going to ask anyway, Vin, to give you the opportunity to share something with me. Share your ugliest hurt with the Finder of Beauty, and we could, together, bless that part of you."

My insides panic. I don't like where this is headed.

He asks, "Why don't you want to get fucked?"

I have two or three answers ready for this—I always do—so there's no need to panic. But my heart beats faster as I contemplate telling him something that does not come easily for me—the truth. The real truth. There's no need. He already told me I don't have to answer. However, he is the last king. Maybe, just maybe… it would be okay to say it aloud this once. To let someone in the world know what happened, someone besides Malcolm.

Okay. Do it fast, before you change your mind.

"When I was younger, I was raped. Like you, I didn't feel like I wanted to bottom anyway but that—that experience confirmed it."

I don't know what I expected him to say in response to this, but he doesn't respond at all—he says nothing. He leans in and kisses my shoulder, and his right hand wraps around me, finding my hairy chest. He squeezes. His shoulder kiss becomes a second, then a third, then a soft caress of my neck with his chin.

His cock is getting harder. The mighty Fitch Dick awakens.

Uh-oh.

Is he going to try to fuck me? Will he try? Do I stop him, or is this what I'm supposed to do?

Panic rises in me. *I don't want to get fucked.*

"Trust me," he whispers, his mouth right at my ear. "Trust my love for you, Vin."

I can't! I can't!

His lips keep finding my tense shoulders, my tense neck, and each time his lips touch me, he communicates "You can. You can trust me." With each kiss, the words spiral outward through my skin. *Trust me.* I don't want to… But. He is the Finder of Beauty. *B* is the letter which brightly begins—No. I can't get into that now.

He guides me onto my stomach, which terrifies me, but his attention is careful, measured. He understands what he asks of me as he does this—he gets it. He knows I'm freaking out? Yes. He knows. I sense it. I feel we're engaged in a full conversation through touch alone, his gentleness and attention compensating for absent words. *Trust me.* He massages my back in long strokes, tracing along either side of my spine with his thumbs, occasionally lowering his weight onto me, so I understand how strong he is, how capable. This dance horrifies me—the inherent possibility of fucking between us—and yet he relaxes me, he honors me, so when tension manifests, he kisses or massages it into begrudging acceptance.

I hate not being in control.

I have no idea how long he continues this—massaging my back, legs, neck, and shoulders. He accepts with patience and love whatever tension I throw at him, rubbing it into something softer and more vulnerable. It strikes me at some point, my body feels almost fully relaxed, the closest to relaxed I might ever become.

He kisses my ass cheek.

Oh no! Does he think—

He dives into my ass with his mighty Fitch Tongue, slobbering and lapping the soft folds of flesh. Other men love this, I know from experience, but I feel I might scream, the intensity that's two parts pleasure and three parts terror. *He knows, doesn't he?* He must understand how terrifying this is for someone who was raped.

The sensation rippling through me at this second is definitely pleasure. I spread my legs a little wider. *I didn't mean to do that.* The sensation isn't exclusively his tongue, but his attitude, his undeniable hunger for me, to worship me, to show me I am a king through this delicate sexual act. He honors me, the Finder of Beauty, and some part of my angry confused brain understands this—this honoring—and commands the rest of me to relax.

I can't.

But I try.

After a few moments of this exquisite torture, his lumbering frame—all those honey-baked muscles attached to his skeleton—climbs my body, and I feel his hard Fitch Dick align with my ass.

Oh my god. *Oh my god.* Do I throw him off me? Do I scream "no"? Can I do this? I don't want this, but can I refuse a king? What if this—this is what I need to do to become a Found King? But would the Found Ones want me to do something I desperately hate and will always hate? That's not how it works. But is that their price of admission? For me? It can't be—*my god, what do I—*

"Relax," he says, his strength slicing through my internal screaming. "I'm not going to fuck you, nor will I try. Breathe with me."

Okay, okay, okay, okay.

We take a deep breath together.

"I want you to trust me," he says. "Trust in me. I'm going to show you all my love without fucking you. But you must trust me, and let yourself receive this love. Will you do that?"

Though I'm not sure I trust anyone that much, I squeak out the word "Yes."

One of his muscular arms slides around my chest, the other around my neck, and in a few seconds, I am immobilized in his arms. My body squirms against the slippery satin sheets, wanting to slide off the bed, but he holds me in place. I feel his cock against my butt crack, moving slightly, gyrating.

Trust him.

Trust him!

My panic is rising. How can I trust anyone this way?

Fitch says, "Trust me. Trust the love you brought into my life, the capacity for greater love, to bring—"

His voice breaks. Finally, words emerge from him, vulnerable and trembling. "You changed me."

The words, or his tone, relax me—him using his king voice—and I remember how I felt when he returned from the Witches' Tower. The sapphire light. His emerald eyes, impossible and piercing. I relax further. He loves me. He promised me. It's confusing, growing trust. I do not trust these circumstances, but I trust him, but I do not trust being immobilized, but I want to trust him. The mental backflips weary me more than the night without sleep.

Fitch picks up his pace, rubbing his cock against my butt, the mighty Fitch Dick ready to show me his true power, *but I don't want to experience the Fitch Dick,* he'll—no. He said he wouldn't. I hear his breathing get shallower, the harder he slaps his body against mine. He does not attack me with the ferocity of a hungry lover, but of a king who wishes to convey a message—power. Ownership. He owns me. He conveys he owns me, not in the property sense, but he owns the responsibility, his love for me, the way he ensures my safety.

Something in me wants to trust him more. Don't trust him. *Don't trust him!*

I will. I do. I'm terrified but I push back.

I can't believe I did that, pushed back, pushed back into him. Why would I do that?

His body is slick with sweat, mine, too, the weight and heat of him cooking me beneath him, and I feel his grunting—his power—as one of his strong hands wraps around the underside of my neck, stroking me as you might slowly caress a thick cock. He kisses my skull, my shoulders, the whole time rubbing his big dick in my wet ass crack with serious determination.

Did I just see lightning?

Fitch is now what pornos imitate so poorly, raw masculine energy, muscles ripe with power and stamina, a tightness in his body given over to an ecstasy found only on the ancestral fields.

He grunts.

I am freaking out he will accidentally penetrate me—despite his promise— what if he cannot stop his momentum? No. *No!* He promised. I—I don't like trust, it's stressful to trust, but I'm doing my best.

He shifts his body, grabs his dick and angles it downward, so his hard cock punches my nut sack, and he slams his hips hard against me several times, and this gesture is proof—*proof*—he will not, physically could not at this point, accidentally slip inside. This position is overwhelming evidence he loves me so much, he never intended to—

Blue lightning crackles all around us.

I scream.

My legs clench together as my orgasm screams out of me, my balls collapsing, and he cries out at the same moment, locking my throat and head in his arm, his chest against my back, and fucking my legs harder. He spills his sperm onto my nuts. It's warm. I feel it.

The satin sheets are almost torture, a thousand ocean textures rippling and wrapping my cock, my torso, god, my damn elbows feel twitchy and intense, as my head spins, drowning in this blue, and at the same time, skidding across the universe in blue lightning. I suck in air, gulping it down, hoping it provides some sanity for my exhausted brain and overworked body.

He pants on top of me, his grip as tight as ever. "Do...you...trust me?"

"Yes," I say, gasping for breath.

"You trust...me?"

"Yes."

I do. I really, really do.

"You are...beautiful," he says, still catching his breath. "So...beautiful..."

Maybe because I shared with him a secret.

Maybe because he is the last king.

Maybe the intimacy between us is that strong.

Whatever the reason, for a moment, I believe him.

We wake, early afternoon. We lie in bed, stroking, touching, reliving. I want to ask him what he meant when he said "tone myself down." He won't tell me. I'm sure.

We kiss.

I admire his muscles and ask about his workouts, but he doesn't seem interested in answering, so I let my questions drift away. Something is on his mind.

"Tell me," I say.

He props himself on his elbow and kisses me on the forehead. "It's kinda weird."

"I bet I can handle weird."

He chuckles. "No doubt."

He pauses again. "It's a family story, one of those stories from when you're a kid. My parents like to retell it, especially because it involves elderly relatives, you know? When I was three years old, our family took a vacation to Sweden, so mom could reconnect with distant cousins and see her grandparents. I don't remember any of this. We visited my great-grandfather, this ancient guy named Benke Dett. I kept insisting he hold me, reaching my arms up to him. I called him *Benke*, which made everyone laugh. So I'm told."

I suddenly realize he's Kevin, no longer my Fitch.

He's Kevin.

"According to my folks, on the final day of our trip, he seated me in his lap and told me a long story. In Swedish. My mom barely spoke any Swedish, so she couldn't understand the words, and our Swedish relatives said it was 'old language,' some heavily Finnish and small-town dialect from where Grandpa Dett grew up. Even the Swedish relatives couldn't make out most of what he told me. I sat there, captivated by every word, nodding when he paused, and apparently, just, really into it."

Kevin chuckles, which makes me chuckle too.

"I have no memory of this. But when he finished, my mom asked something like, 'Did you enjoy Benke's story, Kevin?' and I said, 'Yes. It was a story about the old ones. The kings and queens.' My mom and dad started laughing because I was so serious, but my other relatives—the Swedish ones—got quiet. They had recognized random words in Benke's tale. They confirmed it was a story about kings from an age long ago."

We take a moment to consider what this means.

Kevin stares into my eyes. "What do you think of that?"

"Do you remember any details?"

"Nothing. I mean, I don't even remember the trip. I hadn't thought of that family story in years, not until last night in the circle, when you started talking about them. But now, I'm not sure. Is it possible Grandpa Benke knew of the Lost and Founds?"

"Possible? Yes. It's an old story. It survives through retelling, handed down over many generations like an heirloom. The king names often change depending on the storyteller. But some names stay the same."

We are quiet together, naked, touching, contemplating. I might have seen a written copy once. At the Met in New York city. The Greek tablet. But I barely remember what happened. I remember being terrified out of my balls in the security office. Then, we were escorted to that private room and, well, I don't remember much until we were outside looking at the food trucks and I really wanted a street gyros.

"In the bar," he says, "you yelled at me to 'remember the king.' I felt like you'd punched the air out of me. I couldn't breathe."

"Yeah."

"You knew."

"Yeah. I did."

I get squeamish talking with kings about how I knew they were one of mine—a Lost King who I was meant to cross over. These are prickly conversations, embracing the intersection of common sense, intuition, non-verbal cues, and my own personal madness. But hey—this is the last time I'll ever have this conversation. After today, no kings. Life will be easy.

He watches me with expectation.

Crap.

Well, I can share something. "These days, the men I target are ready to cross over. They don't know it, but they are. Years ago, I used to invite men who were less ready. That made for some difficult weekends. I mean, they were ready, too, like ninety or ninety-five percent ready. But there's a huge difference between ninety-five percent and ninety-nine percent ready."

"And me?"

"Ninety-nine percent."

"How can you know when a man is ready? How is that possible?"

"I can tell. I don't know how to answer that, other than to say, I can tell."

"How many men have you kinged?"

How do I respond? Does he want the total number, or will he next ask for their contact information? It hurts to talk about them and their fabulous lives. I miss them. All of them. There's nothing I need to tell him. If he wants, he can find them. A couple of the men I've kinged always seem to know when a new man crosses over. Michael from Atlanta dreams about them. I wonder if he already dreamt of the Finder of Beauty.

I say, "There are things I should not tell you. Not because I am forbidden, but because it would rob you of the discovery."

He nods. "As well as some things I should not tell you. Okay. Got it. One more question. What about women? Have you queened anyone?"

"No."

"Any particular reason?"

"Yes. A kinging is dangerous. Always. Lives can be ruined. Or transformed. Men, I understand. Women are a mystery. I've come close to failing men in the past, and I'm not willing to gamble ruining some queen's life to satisfy my curiosity. I've met amazing women I would consider candidates, but I didn't get the extra nudge inside me that said *queen her*. I wouldn't risk it without that nudge."

His eyes fill with tears. "You kinged me. I will always love you, Vin Vanbly. You know that, right? This weekend, you stole a piece of my heart, irretrievably lost to you forever. Tell me you understand this is true."

Now it's my turn to have my eyes fill with tears. I know far too well what it means to be in love with someone you'll never see again. I will be in love with Kevin for the rest of my life.

We kiss tenderly, over and over, good-bye kisses, until my doorbell rings.

I timed the food delivery for midafternoon, figuring we might sleep. Well, assuming we would sleep. I knew I'd be exhausted. Plus, I wanted to sleep next to him, in his arms or him in mine. I assume that's half the pleasure of a relationship, sleeping with each other. While I will never enjoy a relationship myself, on these weekends, I sleep in the arms of love.

Kevin is surprised the food is from his favorite Korean restaurant and includes a number of dishes he loves. We're unpacking the steaming mandu and barbeque when the doorbell rings again, probably with our Indian food. Kevin laughs uproariously when the bell rings a third time, and he races through the house wearing my only sweatpants as if he expects Santa at the front door. Over his shoulder I spot an instantly infatuated twenty-something woman with dark eyes, doing everything within her power to extend their conversation. To her disappointment, he thanks her profusely and zips away behind me, eager to unwrap the treats inside this latest delivery. I tip her generously to compensate for her loss.

We spend the next hour or two on my couch, him against my chest, sampling his favorite delicacies, laughing, telling stories of amazing meals, reliving every thought from last night. Toward the end of our feasting, I promise a surprise and return from the kitchen with homemade funnel cake.

He jumps up and dances around, explaining this is the one indulgence he permits in his normally strict diet.

"What about the rest of this?" I indicate the food containers and our used plates.

"Today, calories do not count," he says, beaming. "Today I am a king."

He asks if we can cuddle by firelight, so while I arrange the wood, he cleans up the remains of our smorgasbord, humming in the kitchen. When we're back on the couch, having exchanged the obligatory kisses, reflecting how we missed each other during our brief time apart, he says, "You followed me. To know I loved these foods."

"I did."

He nods.

"Does that bother you?"

"No," he says with surprising energy. "I find it immensely comforting. Even though I was an arrogant prick to you the first time we met, still, you loved me. You already loved me."

He stares into my eyes in a way that makes me uncomfortable. The light inside him is hard for me to witness. Inside him, the blue lightning is endless. Eternal.

"Don't go," he says.

"Kevin, our time together ends—"

"That's not what I mean," he says. "Don't go, Vin. You shouldn't go."

"Go where?"

He gazes into the fire. "Don't go."

Does he mean Honduras?

We watch the flames as they flicker and dance for us, each one living for less than a second and then erased from existence, a chemically explained flicker in time, unsung and unnamed, yet seared into my memory as an essential ingredient in our most intimate experience as a couple.

Our final shower together is almost mournful. We wash each other with great affection, and I say good-bye to the Fitch Dick with one last blow job, but this one isn't raunchy so much as a final good-bye. Breakup sex. Fitch sucks my cock, but I can't come. I'm too sad.

We hold each other, heads touching under the rainforest shower.

We are in love.

We're saying good-bye.

I've heard the arguments love isn't possible between two people unless a certain amount of time passes. Or unless you commit to spend the rest of your lives together. I don't bother arguing those rules because it boils down to a simple truth: if you haven't experienced it, you assume it's not possible. And if you have experienced it, you don't need to argue reality. This is our love. Kevin and I are in love.

We dry ourselves, and I feel sick to my stomach.

Good-bye is the only possible option for me, but I hate it nonetheless.

Kevin insists on wearing his king shirt, which seems appropriate for clubbing. Given it's almost ten on Saturday night, that's exactly where he should be heading. The clubs. I altered my "leave exactly at noon Sunday" rule because I wanted our time together to end on Saturday night, forcing him into an interesting decision. There's nothing wrong with a life spent clubbing, if that's what you truly want. Is that what he wants, or has it been an easy substitution?

We stand in my foyer.

Fitch says, "We could watch a movie, you know. Hang out. No king stuff, no sex. Just two friends."

I give him my answer with my eyes.

"Fine." His growl is tired, but I suspect he knows it's best to make a clean break.

He must leave, or I will fall deeper in love. I cannot handle any more heartbreak. I'm already staggering under the weight of the magnificent men I still love with all my love. I can't handle one more. Not a single one.

He touches my face, caresses it, and without words, opens the front door.

Kevin hesitates on the top step, facing the street, carrying two bags of leftover food.

He says, "Most guys see me as this collection of body parts, and I know, I encourage that. You saw me as more, even when I demonstrated how shallow I could be. You always saw me as more. Your beauty is you see men for who they truly are."

His earnestness touches me, and I'm surprised to feel how deep this blessing sinks.

He turns to face me. "People think you're weird, Vin. I asked about you in the bars, asked the bartenders. Few people knew you, and those who did thought you were a weirdo. Now that I've spent time with you, I agree. You are weird."

He gazes at me with his full love.

I smile, and tears form. I know he loves me. I know. But it hurts sometimes to live as such a freak.

"Someone is coming for you," Kevin says. "Some dude is gonna fall in love with you, like I have, and he won't let go, because to him, all that weirdness is the most natural, most beautiful thing in the world. Everything's gonna be okay after that."

I can't speak. I have no counter to this.

For reasons I cannot explain, I tell him my name. My real name.

Kevin laughs and wipes the tears from his eyes. "You're shitting me."

After watching him drive away, I close the front door.

He almost fucked me this morning. But he didn't. And thank god for that, I didn't want that. But I can admit the frottage felt amazing in those moments when I allowed myself to feel it. I almost denied that experience because he encroached on one of my rules. Am I too rigid? I remember the note I wrote to Kevin the night we met, back when he was Fitch. *Do you ever wonder how your life would be different if you hadn't been so inflexible? Would you still be with him?*

What if I'm too inflexible?

What if—to find greater love in my life—I need to do something that makes me uncomfortable?

I flip on my laptop and dig through my deleted emails until I find the one from the New Jersey guy, the one from Mark. I study his face. He's very handsome. I mean, stunning.

What would you risk to find a Lost King? And what if he doesn't remember you? Maybe I need to be more flexible.

Hello, Mark, I type in my reply. *Do you IM? Perhaps we should talk further.*

Epilogue

As soon as I spot Kevin hiding behind a tree, I realize more than a full year has passed since I last saw him. It's July, so, yeah. A year and two months. We are both at the wooded dog park on the banks of the Mississippi River. This is heaven for dogs—six acres of forest paths, dog smells, and shallow banks for splashing and swimming after tennis balls. My pooch is busy smelling some other dog's butt. He takes after his father.

Joy and deep pleasure rush over me, just seeing him. I am filled with the love we once shared.

I see Kevin's boyfriend, well, the man I assume he's dating. He's thirties, mostly bald with a slight peak to his skull, and he pretends to attack his dog with giant arms and claws, making ridiculous faces. His young terrier yelps in pleasure and speeds away, returning seconds later to face the same monster threat. I smile watching the love he feels for his animal friend. Kevin jumps out from behind the tree, surprising the happy woofer, who rushes right to Kevin's leg. They both chase the dog, who chases them, and they chase back. The dog darts away to nearby new dog friends, barking, probably bragging about how great these men are, and how lucky she feels to be so loved.

They pant and laugh at their charge, calling her name.

Kevin straightens up when he spots me. His face acquires a strange, fixed expression.

I nod to him, smiling but serious.

He approaches.

His boyfriend follows Kevin's gaze directly to me.

The two of them cover the thirty yards distance, Kevin leading without talking.

Kevin does not hesitate to stand close to me, kissing distance. He takes my free hand in both of his and turns it palm up. The boyfriend arrives just as Kevin raises my hand to his lips and kisses the meaty part under my thumb. I forgot Kevin's beautiful green eyes. I forgot how they are gorgeous and clear.

"My king," Kevin says. "My king."

"So weird," his boyfriend says with forced casualness. "Kev did that to me on the night we decided to move in together. He kissed me on the hand like that."

"He would," I say, still staring at the Finder of Beauty. "He is of the kingdom."

"Uh-oh." The boyfriend pretends to laugh. "Should I be jealous? Is this one of your former lovers?"

Kevin and I relive our old love, letting it be true again in these seconds. For a moment, blue lightning crackles around me.

I ask, "What if your boyfriend is jealous?"

Kevin says, "Then, I will show him my love. I will show him all my love."

After our time in the dog park, Romero leaps into my Prius as if he's never seen it, never been on a car ride. He scoots around the back seat with genuine excitement. If I offered to let him drive, no doubt he would accept the challenge. While he reacquaints himself, I smile at his investigations and pull out my phone to check for messages.

One text. From home.

From him.

Mark's message reads, *We're out of eggs.*

I check my wallet to see if I have cash. Out of old habit, my fingers rub the edges of the note—the one he tossed so casually at me from our motel room the weekend we met. I pull it out, unfolding it gingerly. I have folded and unfolded this paper so many hundreds of times since that Sunday I stood in the parking lot, unable to wait more than five minutes before reading it. The paper is now fragile from all my attention. Standing next to the car, I read it again, again, and again. My eyes skip over my original all caps message, my attempt to dissuade him, and fixate on his angry scrawl, just below.

I AM A LOST KING.
Then I am lost too!

THE LOST ONES

The events of this story take place in 2008

One

"**Y**o. Mark."

He catches me staring into space, clutching my socks.

Kevin frowns and opens his mouth to ask me a question, but doesn't. "Smoothie shots?"

I nod. "Five more minutes."

He saunters from the humid locker room, the scent of male funk and wet towels trailing him. Well, also a dozen wistful stares. The gay men around me study his ass, and the straight men study the rest of his frame. Kevin's got a great build. Men always ask him to become their personal trainer, but he won't. He only trains at-risk teens the local agencies send his way. It's his thing.

Kevin knows something's up with me. We've been friends long enough he can tell when I'm not lifting to capacity, and he's right. For shoulder-and-back day, I didn't push hard enough. I skipped my final set of lat pulldowns. Did I want him to notice and ask? Or maybe, I got distracted, thinking about Vin.

Oh, Vin. Why can't you just let it go? Why can't we stop fighting and get beyond this?

"Hey, Mark, good to see you."

The voice addressing me comes from the mirror, and I look up to catch his leering gaze. It's Davey, who always hits on me. *Ugh.* I've told him I'm in a monogamous relationship, but he doesn't care. He doesn't show me—or Vin—respect. Despite my continuous rebuffs, he still tries. I remember the night in the steam room when he jacked off in front of me until I left, which was immediately. He won't quit.

I nod in his direction, a curt, *Yeah, I see you,* but I want no conversation. I have important things to work out in my head. How much am I going to tell Kevin? He probably guesses Vin and I are in a rocky place. Am I betraying Vin by talking about it with one of our best pals? We do a lot with Kevin and Roger. Should I talk to someone else? I need to talk to someone. This is getting serious. Vin wants us to break up.

It's ridiculous to think of breaking up with Vin. But how do I convince him?

Vin looks at me mournfully these days, as if my bags are already packed at the front door, and a taxi waits at the curb. But I'm not going anywhere. He's the one who wants to end things. When he puts his mind to something, he usually makes it happen.

Vin Vanbly, you're a real pain in the ass, you know that?

I look up.

Davey's still at the mirrors, shirtless, but at least wearing jeans, shaving extra slow while scoping out asses in jockstraps. I estimate twenty or so men changing clothes, average crowd of familiar faces for a Tuesday night. Well, I'll stand a few sinks away from him. Maybe he'll leave me alone. I don't find him attractive, but that's more personality than appearance, I guess. He's trim, with muscles, a face you'd find on a billboard advertising clean cut products. His smile is smug, so certain of his handsomeness. Not like Kevin, who is so beautiful, and his smile for everyone is so big.

I study the mirror, and my face looks sad. *Vin. How can I convince you? How can I ever convince you?*

Davey says, "Good workout, Mark?"

"Sure."

I should have never told him my name. Of course, the first time he asked, I thought he was friendly, not Creeperville. Why won't Davey leave me alone? Is he this relentless with everyone who shuts him down?

I add product, enough to structure my high and tight, now that it's growing out. I make the tips spikey. I groom my sideburns trailing down the side. Vin and I are meeting in an hour, and I want to look good.

"Looks like you're working your triceps. Good bulge."

Involuntarily, I glance his way in time to see Davey rub his cock mound against the sink a few times, to make sure I pick up on his not-subtle hint. As if his ogle wasn't enough. I've fucking had it with him. *No more, Davey.*

"If my boyfriend Vin was here," I say, before I know where this is going, "and he saw you hitting on me—"

"Yeah, yeah. He'd punch my lights out. You forget, I've seen your mushy, older lover, and he couldn't—"

"Don't interrupt, Davey. You're wrong. Vin would never hurt you. The opposite. He would tell me to think of you with compassion. Think about how lonely you must be, to hit on men you know are happy, because you want a taste of that happiness for yourself. Vin spent a lot of years unhappy, so he has a soft spot for people like you."

Davey's trademark smugness drops away. I'm not exactly speaking quietly.

"Vin would urge me to remember you were once a kid with big dreams. Or maybe you're an adult with big dreams, still. Or maybe he'd tell me to consider you had a hard day today—the world treated you shitty—and maybe trying to impress me by bumping your cock against the sink tile is your small, defiant gesture to take control. To not feel vulnerable and completely lost."

Davey isn't smiling now.

"I'm not Vin. Vin's not here. So let me assure you, once again, Vin and I are together for life. Even if we had an open relationship—which, again, we do not—I'd have no interest in you 'cause of how you operate. You're skeevy. Rude. You've ignored every request I've made for you to stop. But let's not talk about the past. Let's talk about your future. You work out Tuesdays, Thursdays, Fridays in the evenings, and Wednesdays late morning."

His face slowly melts into alarm.

I don't know for sure if this is true. Doesn't matter. Vin taught me how to make guesses about people after observing a kernel of their truth. As long as Davey thinks I know his schedule, this will work. Come to think of it, I saw him here one Wednesday. Maybe my guess is more educated than I thought.

"See? I learned your schedule so I can better avoid you, Davey. Anyway, I was saying, I'm not nearly as good a person as Vin. He's not here to help me be a better man. If you ever talk to me again, I will drop a forty-pound barbell on your foot during your squats, and I'll make sure to smash every toe. The little toe is surprisingly important to vertical balance. Also, although I'm a Minnesotan now, I'm originally from New Jersey. We don't waste time with threats in New Jersey. We only state future intentions. So, this is not a threat. This is my future intention. Do you understand?"

The changing-room crowd watches, half-concealed behind their wooden lockers or staring openly from the worn benches, facing us with undisguised curiosity. This is a weightlifter's gym. Mostly seriously bulked-up guys here.

He eyes them and then me nervously, "Sheesh, calm d—"

"Do you understand?"

I'm not afraid to yell. I can make noise.

Davey glances around and says, "Yeah, okay. Yes."

"Great," I say brightly. "So we're agreed, there's never a need for us to speak, not ever again. You can nod hello if we pass in the gym. I will nod back, to be polite. But this was our last conversation."

He nods at me the way I did a moment ago, not wishing to chat more. Good.

I finish working my hair, because I won't be hurried by Davey, who just became someone I used to know. But Kevin is waiting for me, and I'm done anyway, so I pack my final items into the duffel bag and leave the humid wet-towel smell behind. I feel better, yelling at Davey the way I did.

Crossing the equipment area, I nod to a few regulars who Kevin and I know, women and men with whom we share tips and whom we sometimes spot. I should go say hello to Mary Elizabeth, but I wave instead. I'll talk to her Thursday. Kevin's waiting.

Despite the marketing posters around the gym, showing people totally loving smoothies and flax seed energy packets, the gym's healthy bistro area is always underpopulated, and tonight is no exception. Only two people at the polished silver tables: Kevin texting on his phone, a lady with a towel around her neck two tables away.

As I approach, I see Kevin made good on his threat and purchased us smoothie shots. Something with kale, I'm guessing. Nope, it's pink.

I drop my bag and sink into the chair across from him. "No kale?"

"I would have, Mr. Mark, but you're not quite yourself. I thought maybe you needed a treat. You'll like this one. Grapefruit and egg-white protein powder. Plus strawberries."

"Thank you."

"But seriously. Dark leafy greens."

I chuckle. He says this every now and then, trying to get Vin and me to eat better. It's more longstanding joke than actual advice. A year ago, for Christmas, Kevin and Roger built us a three-foot replica of a snowman made from spinach, romaine, and kale. That was funny. Kaley the Snowman.

I flick the smoothie cup with my fingers, not wanting to taste it yet.

Kevin says, "Skipping the small talk, what's going on? What's wrong with Vin?"

I sigh. "You know me."

"Mark, it's the only time you get upset. You're cheerful and upbeat. If you're not happy, something's wrong in Vin World. Spill."

I still haven't decided how much to admit, what I can share without betraying my lover. But since our relationship is on the line, maybe I'd better tell the whole truth.

"He wants us to break up."

I see the shock on Kevin's face, and he sits up straight.

"You're wrong. He would never want that. He loves you."

"Yeah, I know. That's why this is so stupid. But...he thinks I'm not...I'm not—"

It's hard not to blush. *Just say it.*

"He wants me to sleep with other men. Vin thinks, if we stay together, when I reach forty I'm going to resent I wasted my entire youth on him and not fucking other men. He thinks we should break up for a year or two and then see about getting back together. *Maybe* getting back together. He feels he's stealing my youth."

Kevin takes a moment to absorb this. "He's an idiot."

"I know! I told him I'm right where I want to be."

"And his response is..."

"Vin says, sure, I'm happy, right now. But when I'm older—his age—I'll regret not having more notches on my bedpost."

I make my *whatever* face.

After a long silence, Kevin asks, "Does it cross your mind? To sleep with someone else?"

"Are you kidding? I can't imagine sex with anyone other than Vin. He's...it's..."

Kevin says softly, "I know. I remember."

I look deep into his green eyes and see his affection. He really does know. He exactly knows. I forget sometimes they shared a weekend together, and Vin loved him with all his love. The Finder of Beauty. Of course Kevin understands sex with Vin is the most intense, physically exhausting, insanely intimate—it's everything. Sometimes, Vin teases me until I scream. Other times, the rough, animal fucks we—*I'm blushing*. I know it. I don't need sex with thirty strangers to know I found the best. I may be twenty-five, but even when I was a virgin, I could always tell the difference between a Davey and someone like Vin.

Well, that's not true.

I never met someone like Vin until Vin.

Kevin says, "I had sex with a lot of guys before Roger. A lot. Some of it was amazing—well, a lot of it was amazing. But Vin...Vin makes you feel like nobody else exists in the world. He immediately knew all my hot spots because he studied me with loving attention. When he touched—wait, is this weird? Describing our sex?"

"No. Go on."

I like hearing about Vin having sex with other men. I don't know why—but it turns me on. Kevin's never talked about their weekend together, not the sexual parts. Of course I want to know more.

Kevin considers and continues. "We bathed in your Jacuzzi tub. Vin had decorated the whole room with white lights and this green bunting, like mosquito netting or something but...better. He had cut shapes like leaves, and the ceiling looked like treetops. White candles. White roses. It was...he called it 'an enchanted forest.'" Kevin's eyes fill with tears. "It *was* enchanted. I—it was an ordinary bathroom. But the care...the lovingness...it's... Next to one of the vases, two fallen rose petals had been arranged to overlap, touching in this intimate expression. I don't know how I knew, but I immediately understood Vin had artfully placed them as a deliberate symbol for the two of us, a miniscule expression of his love for me. That weekend, I felt loved on a cellular level."

Kevin looks away.

"After Vin, it was three months before I could have sex with anyone else. He changes the goal of sex. Instead of blasting your nuts out, you want—you just want to be with Vin. Just be loved by Vin."

I wipe away my tears. I know. I know how true this is.

We are both quiet, absorbing what Kevin said.

He smiles. "You know, I tried to be friends with him. I called him a half-dozen times. He never returned my calls. Did he ever tell you that?"

"No."

"I wanted us to be friends." Kevin's face softens. "Which, thankfully, we are now."

He gets quiet, contemplating this.

I say, "It's not surprising he never called you back. You know Fredi? She's been at a few of our parties. She works at the garage with Vin."

"Yeah, of course. Gorgeous weave? Grew up in Denver?"

"Right. One night about four months after I moved in, he came home from work and casually mentioned Fredi had invited us to dinner. Again. He shook his head like, 'Can you believe it?' I asked him which night we were going, and he looked at me all puzzled and said he'd declined. Vin explained Fredi'd only invited us because he was her boss, and she felt obligated."

Kevin wears the same puzzlement on his face as Vin that night.

I don't think he's getting my point, so I keep babbling. "I marched Vin over to the phone to call her immediately and say, *yes we'd love to come to dinner*, which was awesome beyond awesome because she's an incredible cook, and she makes cakes as a side business in addition to working as a mechanic, which is cool, isn't it? She made us this gorgeous orange-flavored white cake, with orange frosting and flowers all over it, to celebrate Vin had finally said *yes*. She had already asked him seven or eight times. He always said no because he couldn't believe she wanted his company. He thought she was just being polite."

Kevin nods, but I'm not sure he understands the point I'm trying to reveal.

Am I betraying one of Vin's secrets in telling this? I don't think so. I believe it will make Kevin feel closer to Vin.

"When I moved in, I told Vin I wanted to meet all his friends, but he never introduced me. At first, I thought he felt ashamed of me because of my age, but I soon realized I was wrong. He didn't have any friends. Not one."

Kevin nods. "I'd have been his friend."

"I know. He had opportunities—like with you and Fredi—but he would get...shy."

Kevin chuckles. "*Shy* is not a word I'd use to describe Vin Vanbly."

I won't elaborate on the extra shades of meaning hiding behind *shy*. That would reveal too much. Whether I call Vin *insecure* or describe him as *low self-esteem* doesn't matter. It's a very specific pocket of low self-esteem. He is impossibly shy when it comes to friendships.

Finally, Kevin says, "If he's so shy, why did Vin call me after we ran into each other at the dog park? I gave him my same number and suggested we get together, but I assumed I'd never hear from him."

"Oh," I say, feeling myself blush. I thought the answer was obvious. "When he got home from the dog park, I asked him if anything special had happened. He showed me your phone number, but he didn't want to call. He said you were only being polite. It was me. I made him call."

Kevin's smile widens. When he smiles so big, I feel like I see angel wings expanding behind him, aglow with unseen light. Kevin's smile can do that.

I blush again.

"Of course you were behind it, Monkey Mark. How did I not realize that?"

"Duh," I say, covering my embarrassment by sipping my smoothie shot. "Also, I had been training him for a real friendship. I convinced him we needed a dog to complete our family, but secretly, you know, the dog was just for Vin. A shelter dog is a starter kit for making friends in the real world."

Kevin laughs and claps his hands.

"But you can never, ever tell him I was training him."

"Scout's honor." His smile fades. "How serious is Vin? About you two breaking up?"

"He's getting more insistent. I can't find a way to show him I could never want anyone else."

"This has been building?"

"For the past six months. Not a lot at first. It's only in the last month has it gotten intense."

"Why now?"

"Vin's birthday. It's in two weeks."

Kevin says, "Uh-oh. The dreaded Saint Patrick's Day birthday."

I know the guys—Roger especially—still feel bad about last year. It wasn't their fault. They had no idea how much Vin hates his birthday.

"Last year was not your fault. It was fun of you guys to put all those flamingos in the backyard. Romero and Chipotle both loved it. Those two hooligans raced around and knocked over every single one, you know. But Vin..."

Kevin's half smile makes me stop.

He says, "You got a tough nut with Vin Vanbly, Mr. Mark. How do we help? Can I talk to him? Roger's good with Vin. Maybe we can convince him."

"I don't know. Let's keep that option on reserve. I think Vin and I need to work through this ourselves, but I don't know how. If I can't convince him by his birthday, then, maybe, yes. How about that?"

"Okay. We love you guys too much to sit on the sidelines for long. As soon as I tell him, Roger's gonna call you with additional questions. I'll try to hold him back, but you know him. He worries."

I smile. "We love you guys too. You're family. But give me a couple more weeks to work this out."

Kevin looks like he has more to say on this topic, but he obviously changes his mind. "Drink your shot."

I lift my glass. "Cheers."

We stay silent while sipping the pink-tinged foam. I'm thinking about Vin, and I'm sure Kevin is too.

Ironically, the problem started with Kevin.

The night Vin laughingly suggested I should sleep with Kevin—just to see what it was like—I didn't laugh in return. It wasn't funny. It was rude. What about Roger? Hell, what about *us*? Vin tried to play it off as a sexy, half-joking suggestion, but his overly casual tone betrayed his insecurity, a subtle worry buried three layers deep. How could Vin suggest that? Why would he suggest that?

I got mad. I yelled.

I refused to talk to him for hours until I cooled down.

When we made up, Vin apologized. I felt better because I thought it was settled. But seconds later, when I sat in his lap with my arms around his neck, I could hear his heart beating faster, and I understood this was not over. Vin was afraid. He hates to feel afraid. That's when I began to understand the grief boy I had seen in his eyes.

Vin's grief boy says, "You'll leave me too, right? Eventually?"

Kevin says, "As long as we're trading secrets about your big bad lover, what's the deal with his older brother, the cop from Chicago? We met him at the same party where we met Fredi."

"Malcolm."

"Yeah, Malcolm. How come Vin's brother is a black guy who is, like, twenty years Vin's senior. What happened there?"

Considering we've been living together for three years, I feel I should know the answer to this, but I don't. "I honestly don't know. They adopted each other a long time ago. Not just as friends. They really consider each other to be oldest and youngest brother. There's a third brother, Vincent. He's the middle one. He died in prison long ago."

"Okay...?"

"I know everything about Malcolm and Vin from after December of 2005, when I moved in. Vin doesn't hide anything from me. But he rarely talks about his past and never about his childhood. Once, we visited Malcolm's family in Chicago over the Fourth of July. At the party, I discreetly asked a few of Malcolm's relatives, but they couldn't tell me anything. They said that, one year, Malcolm brought Vin home for Christmas. Then he started showing up at family events. That was all they knew."

"Vin is quite the mystery man."

I feel like I have to defend him. "He volunteers things in his own time. I could demand answers, I guess, but that's not how it works with Vin. Whenever I hint he should tell me about his past, he gets this scared deer-in-the-headlights look."

Kevin smiles. "I know that look. I saw it on his last birthday."

We smile at each other.

Vin brought Kevin into our lives, Kevin and Roger, whom we love.

"Kev, I can't stay. I'm meeting Vin soon, and we fought instead of eating dinner, so I'm gonna get a burrito first."

Kevin leans across and touches my shoulder. "Go easy on the rice and beans."

I laugh at his goofy expression of concern.

He looks over my shoulder—in that way that makes me realize someone is approaching us. He nods a cautious hello at our visitor.

Davey appears at our table and says, "I apologize for how I've treated you. I won't talk to you again."

He pauses as if he wants to say more, but instead, turns and walks away.

We watch him leave the club.

Kevin says, "You finally told him off."

I sigh. "Yeah."

He says, "Long overdue. Don't forget we're grilling out Saturday night. Bring a fruit salad. Neither Roger or I will mention this conversation. And nobody will mention Vin's upcoming birthday."

"Good. Thank you. That's best."

Sometimes it's best to do as Vin wants.

Two

I stop for a burrito, and leave it on the front seat of my car. For later. I drive to Camp, the bar where we're going to meet. Well, meet and do a little fantasy role-playing. I love how Vin never finds my fantasies weird or stupid. He knows how to coax them out of me too. Whenever I arch my eyebrows at something interesting, or he catches me listening intently an intriguing story, I usually find his intense gaze fixed on me with his naughty smile. Then, I redden, because he can read my thoughts, how I was thinking sex-wise, it might be fun...

I love Vin's Naughty Smile. The one which reveals he's getting ideas.

Tonight, he's gonna find me sitting at the bar, cool and casual, acting like we're strangers, like the first night we met. I won't make tonight easy for him. I'll pretend I'm not interested, and make him win me over. Maybe he'll buy me a drink, and I'll refuse it. Or when he introduces himself, I'll say I'm busy and pull out my phone. I don't know. I enjoy getting him worked up.

First, look for parking.

Camp is tucked inside a giant warehouse block, the building exteriors all industrial looking and totally working class. I'll use the club entrance everyone uses, through the back parking lot, next to a cluster of giant pipe shafts running up and down the weathered brick. All the nearby buildings turn their backs on this grubby space, like homophobic real estate that doesn't want to see *the gays* entering and leaving. There's always steam coming from the street, billowing out of a manhole near the corner, which makes the entire area look rough and sexy. I wonder why there's always steam coming out. I bet Vin would know.

I ease into a spot and shut off the engine.

I'll leave my jacket in the car, but I need to change shirts. I pop the trunk. Gotta change quickly—it's really fucking cold tonight! I thought it was supposed to start getting warmer by March. I jump out of the car and exhale white steams into the dark trunk. I smile when I see it, still unwrinkled on its hanger. He bought me this crazy orange shirt while we wandered through the Castro neighborhood. Yard sale. A dollar-fifty. Orange with tall sailboats drifting across it, headed toward an overly red-and-yellow sunset on the back. We both like it because it's the opposite of me, and so cheap, this was totally worth the gag. He'll chuckle tonight when he sees me wearing it. I save it for special occasions when I need his laugh.

We both need his laughter tonight.

I pull my shirt over my head, and while it pains me to not hang it on the hanger, it's too damn cold to be proper, so I toss it into the trunk. Shivering, I yank the orange sailboats over my head, congratulating myself on how I snuck it out of the house without him noticing. My fingers tremble but work nimbly over the top three buttons.

I smile.

Of course we won't break up. I'm ashamed of my doubt back at the gym. Vin is stubborn, but he's not unreasonable, and he knows we're the perfect combin—

What the fuck?

Panic floods me as a hand covers my mouth, and my arms are both locked behind me—I'm being dragged from my car.

Holy shit, I'm being dragged away! I'm being dragged away!

It's over before it's started, because I'm lifted off the ground and flung onto a mattress, one of the last things I see is the mattress. My eyes are covered, and I hear duct tape, all of it happening so fast, I can't react or realize—

Holy fucking shit. Vin!

I can't handle this! I feel myself falling asleep. No, no! This is the worst time! …I'm back.

I have no idea how long I slept, but I don't think long. My hands are duct taped together behind me. Holy shit, fighting my wrists against each other, I feel the tape refuse to give. Holy fucking shit!

A door slams shut with metallic finality. I'm in the back of a van on a mattress or something. Definitely, that was a van door slamming shut. And I'm not alone. I hear the heavy breathing.

He says, "Stay quiet and you'll be fine."

Vin! Oh god, Vin!

Help me!

I take some deep breaths. My mouth isn't covered. Oh, right. My mouth isn't covered! But I've been too freaked out to scream, trying to understand why I was dragged and couldn't see, why my hands don't move the right way, and only now when he says not to scream it dawns on me I should scream.

I open my mouth to scream and screaaaaaa—too late.

Shit, too late.

Something is stuffed in my open mouth, something more fuzzy, like a bathrobe tie, and my mouth is forced open around it. He wraps it twice, ties it tight, wait— there are *multiple hands on me*, someone tying the mouth guard and someone else going through my pockets.

"Where's his cell phone?"

"Hasn't got one."

Is the second voice English? Is that an English accent?

The first voice says, "Of course he's got a fucking cell phone. Check his car."

"No," says the Brit. "We should go. People are coming. His boot is open. Let's get the fuck out of here."

Panic, panic, panic. I've got to control my panic.

What would Malcolm do? Malcolm the cop, think of Malcolm right now, the one who taught Vin how to work with people, how to get them to do what you need. What would Malcolm do? Nothing. I bet he was never tied up in the back of a van on a mattress in a parking lot. C'mon. What would Malcolm do?

Fight like hell.

I squirm and scream.

A rough hand pushes me into the mattress harder. "Quit fighting us. Grab his other leg."

Instinctively, I fight them, trying to free both legs, but they've done something, tied them to something hard and it feels roundish—some kind of bar, it feels like—and now, they're raising it to the roof of the van? Is that possible? My chest is pressed into the mattress, and my legs dangle in the air. What the fuck kind of weird angle is this?

Calm down. Think this through. This isn't happening. It's not happening.

It's happening.

My heart pounds.

You can handle this. You can *handle* this.

With a big commotion, they leave me alone in back, hopping out, swinging wide the van's back door and slamming it shut again, so hard the metal rings in my ears. Could it have been three men? No, no...not possible.

The driver's-side door opens, then the passenger's-side too.

Slam! Then, slam!

The van takes off, leaving my legs and ass swinging from side to side. The feeling of being this ungrounded is terrifying, like I'm in a perpetual state of falling down. I hate this.

I hate this!

Don't panic. Stop panicking. Remember everything. What would Malcolm do? What would he say? He would say to stop panicking. This isn't real. This isn't real.

Don't panic and don't fall asleep. *Don't fall asleep!*

I do my best to recall Malcolm's face. His short black hairs lie tight against his skull with plenty of pure white, black hair and white hair, but never gray. He's got a cluster of brown marks on his left cheek, high, like Morgan Freeman. Bottom front teeth are crooked, not much, but a little. He's strong. Wiry. I bet he was built, when he was younger. Malcolm watches you while you talk, you're always watched, always under observation, which is what I have to do. I have to pay attention to everything, any sound which may be a clue. Every single—

My body swings hard to the other side. Did we leave the parking lot and pull into the street?

I fight hard again, squirming my arms and my useless legs, but I gain no traction, make no movement, and I scream—not because I think it will do any good, but because I need to scream.

Vin, oh, Vin! Why did this have to happen tonight? We fought earlier. This is not a good night for this!

Don't think of that. Think of *this*, of now. Malcolm would say to observe. What do you hear? What clues give away the situation?

The driver speaks. His voice is sharp. "Next corner, I pull over, you get out. Go get his cell. We need it."

Brit says, "Why me? You go."

"'Cause I'm driving, you dipshit."

The driver's from Chicago—he's got a thick Chicago accent. Vin told me how to recognize the vowel-crushing sounds of a South Sider—that's where he grew up. Vin trains me in some of the ways Malcolm originally trained him. Stay present. Follow the man. Make the connections. Leap and read. Vin calls these the four pillars of kinging. He trains me to look for the truth behind what's true.

Chicago says, "Take his car keys. And for fuck's sake, don't make any calls from his phone."

I hear a jingle. They took my keys! I can't check my pocket to confirm it, but I know it's true.

The Brit says, "You coming back to retrieve me, then?"

"In the van we used to snatch this guy? Are you a fuckin' idiot? Go four or five blocks away. Call from your own phone, and I'll come back in another car. Jesus Herman Christ, you're dumb."

The Brit says, "Fuck off."

The van jerks to a halt, and my whole lower body swings to the right, to the left, like a pendulum. I hear the passenger's-side door open and slam shut, fear shooting me with adrenaline. I don't know why I should fear any more than a minute earlier, but I do. I'm alone with Chicago.

The van pulls away, less ragged and jerky than a moment ago. He's calming down. Maybe.

When the van door opened, I strained to hear every sound, but nothing. *Nothing!* I collapse against the restraints, and the sudden release makes me aware how much I had strained against them. This is exhausting work, this waiting, anticipating, listening. I wouldn't have liked being a cop. *Stupid Malcolm.*

We were cautious with each other the first time we met. Vin was panicked while pretending to be chill, because he wanted me to like Malcolm, and he wanted Malcolm to approve. Malcolm and I were polite, sniffing each other like dogs. Malcolm could tell I felt nervous because he started doing things to make me relax, and then I realized he liked me enough, because if he didn't, he wouldn't have made the effort. We made peace with each other, accepting that each of us owns a part of Vin.

Chicago swears at another car. I hear him mutter under his breath.

Not being able to see while in a speeding vehicle is terrifying. My whole body contorts and swings in this unnatural way, exhausting and confusing me. I twist my wrists but they remain taped tight behind my back. My only hope is to keep working them back and forth, eventually wearing down the duct tape. But this isn't like television. I'm not three twists away from breaking loose.

Malcolm was a cop. He trained my man, and my man trained me. I can endure this. I will endure this. I will win.

Holy shit, I'm tied up in a moving van!

I'm going to keep freaking out sometimes—*holy shitting* every now and then—because this is terrifying, and I need to remind myself it's okay to be terrified. It's okay.

I hear a bit of crushing static, and then Chicago says, "Got the package."

Hearing I am *the package* makes me fight more, makes me want freedom from this nightmare. I twist. I jerk my body from side to side. I use my energy to fight this. The van turns, but it's not a hard turn like earlier, and I get quiet, panting, listening for telltale signs of something outside, some clue. Nothing. We're just driving.

He puts on music, the radio or something, something by Rihanna, and he mumbles the word *bullshit* or something like it, and turns the volume lower. He switches to another station a half minute later, and wait—

What's that? A sound I recognize!

Outside the van, a cop car sound, a siren. Are we passing a police station or— is a cop passing us? The siren gets louder, shriller, and it's not going away, which means—Chicago's getting pulled over.

He's getting pulled over!

Is that possible? Do I stay quiet or, oh my god, this is my big chance to get help!

For no good reason, I imagine Vin explaining his philosophy of blueberry pancakes while we shower, of him lecturing Romero on world politics using dog treats as European countries, *any* memory to remind me how much I have to lose if I miss this opportunity.

The siren gets louder.

Romero ate Greece and Italy in one chomp. Vin cried out, "The euro!"

From the front seat, Chicago spews a whole stream of "Fuckin' unbelievable" as he decelerates—I feel the van slowing down—and I know for a fact this is happening. Seeping under my blindfold, I see tiny flashes of red and blue light.

My heart pounds.

We stop.

The siren stops, and Chicago flips off the radio.

I lie still, waiting for the sound of the policeman's footsteps. Is this really happening?

"Okay, listen up, faggot," Chicago says. "Do *not* make any trouble for me, do not. You understand? This is big. I don't want to have to kill a cop, but I ain't goin' to jail for kidnapping, so keep your goddamn mouth shut. This van is soundproofed anyway, so fuck your little rescue fantasy. There is no rescue. Don't be stupid."

I'm shocked by his language but barely have time to register it when I hear something slide shut—whether it's a panel or not, I can't tell. I can't see the hint of blue and red lights anymore, so maybe it's true. Maybe the van is soundproofed.

What do I do?

Do I risk a policeman's life to get rescued? Or did Chicago bluff me? What do I choose? What person am I? Who am I right in this moment? *Who am I?*

I admit, sometimes I get caught in the frenzy with Vin, and I forget to be me. I forget who I am. Never for long, but it's moments like this you wonder: Am I the idiot who doesn't scream for help? Or do I risk someone else's life, an innocent cop's life, on the off chance I might never—

No. Don't overthink this. Not tonight. I'm not dying tonight. I feel the resolve forming in me, solid, like a block of stone. Fight to live.

Fight to live!

Ever since Patty's death, I've always known I was going to die young. I don't know why the conviction is so strong, but I know what I know. It's why I couldn't wait the full nine months to move in with Vin. I showed up on his doorstep three weeks after he left me in New Jersey, eager to begin our life together. I knew I had to live every possible minute with him. I couldn't miss out on a single day.

I may die young, but not here, not now. Not tonight.

He's bluffing. I'm calling his bluff.

I will make noise.

But first. *Listen.*

I can't be sure—do I hear conversation between Chicago and the police officer? I'm not sure, so I scream. I scream as loud as possible with my mouth full of fabric. I jerk my body as hard as I can to the left, to the right, but I barely move. If I could swing my torso off the mattress, would I bang against the metallic van bed? Maybe. I don't know if it's carpeted or muffled somehow, but the point is moot because no matter how hard I fight, I'm still not moving, not enough to rattle the chains hoisting me. I swing my legs, like I'm some sort of acrobat—Monkey Mark, Kevin called me tonight—and my eyes fill with tears, thinking of Kevin, of Roger, and all our other friends.

I don't want to die.

I want my life with Vin.

I fight.

I fight, remembering the weekend we bought a new vacuum. I fight, remembering Korean Pizza Night, and the night Dad yelled at Vin on the phone for an hour; Vin just accepted Dad's yelling because he loves me so much. I fight, because I need Vin's giant gorilla arms wrapped around me at night, and because of how when I narc out, he's always right there. Corn Cob Night. Apple Picking Tuesday. Tuxedo Night. I fight for all our times together!

After a while—who knows how long—I surrender. Nothing. I can't make a sound. All I hear is my heart pounding hard. Sweat pours down my forehead, trapped by the blindfold. I thought I was exhausted before, but now I'm truly exhausted, having spent my last reserves attempting escape, but with no results. My body is limp. I want to cry.

Everything is fading. No! Each time I fall asleep, I die. Don't fall asleep! I die... Awake.

I can't hear talking anymore. Just my ragged, drooling huffs into this mattress, trying to catch my breath and to stop freaking out. I know the first thing I'm going to do when this gag is removed, which is to scream Vin's name as loudly as I can. I will. I'll do it.

The van starts moving again, and I start to cry.

I shouldn't do this. I know I'll be all right. I know.

All of tonight's insanity reminds me of Patty's death, the helplessness, the inability to change one detail, one single aspect. She was just gone. Patty taught me to dance so I could go to homecoming. She lied to Mom for me so many times, I appeared as the golden child, and she accepted tarnished second. When I had my appendix out, she read me Harry Potter for five days until she figured out I was lying about being "too weak" to lift the book. But after she died, every prayer I prayed went unanswered, every request of the afterlife to let her visit *just once*— denied. She's gone.

I cry because I still miss her, I miss talking to her, and I'll never, ever get to hear her voice again. Patty will never meet Vin. The enormity of that still shocks me, the considerable timeframe of never, ever. Never, *ever*.

I swallow my tears.

Concentrate. What would Malcolm do? What would Vin do?

Fuck them. *What would I do?*

I hear a noise, that muffled sliding sound.

"Hey faggot, the cop is gone. You can make all the noise you want again, not that it matters."

A moment later, I hear him turn on the walkie-talkie, and the telltale static.

"We had a delay," Chicago says into it. "Fucking cops pulled me over. Expired tags. Fuckin' Richie, that dipshit."

He is quiet, and another voice answers back.

Who is that? Who is *that* voice?

"I know. Just got a warning. I'm five minutes out. Less."

We can't be far out of St. Paul. Could we be in Minneapolis? Maybe, but I don't think we drove far. I can't tell. We're arriving at the destination soon, which makes me breathe easier until I remember, holy shit, I'm restrained in a fucking van. *Holy fucking shit.*

My every muscle feels individually drained by trying to escape during the cop pull over. I feel like I can't do anything, not even freak out properly, because I have no energy left. If untied, could I run? I don't know. I don't think so.

I want him to talk again, give me more clues about where we're headed. On TV, people listen closely and hear distinctive, important sounds, like the foghorn from the shipyards, or a church bell, something they report to the police with novice optimism, saying "Does that help?"

I get nothing. I hear nothing.

I feel irrational anger at Malcolm. He should have done more to prepare me for something like this. I still don't know how he knows Vin, their mysterious connection, and now, here I am—in danger—and it would be fucking nice to know how those two know each other. Vin has darkly hinted several times that he's been in jail, but for what? Jaywalking? Drugs? Extortion?

The van stops.

I hear metallic grinding and churning. I feel I should recognize this sound, but I'm exhausted and feeling utterly defeated, so my brain can't figure out what it means. Did we arrive?

How did he—no, no time to think this way. Think of the situation. Assess the situation. Get out of this situation. I'm not calling out Vin's name when my mouth is free. I'm stronger than that.

The driver revs the engine again, creeping forward, and I hear someone slap their hand against the van's exterior. My body should have reacted, a jolt or something, but I honestly have no energy left. Nothing. This slow-driving sensation is more terrifying than speeding, because it makes me think the van is about to go over a cliff. Which it's not, of course. The mind plays terrible, unholy tricks.

Vin taught me that phrase: *the mind's unholy tricks.*

He thinks I don't know about the nights he lies awake staring at the ceiling. I do. I learned to recognize the grief boy who lives behind Vin's eyes—and when comes to visit—on those days—and even weeks—when Vin thinks he is nobody, deserving nothing. He tries to hide this insecurity from me, but he cannot. On those nights, we lie sleepless together, me grasping his balls in my hand to symbolically prove I will protect him. I pretend to sleep, and even snore lightly, trying to seduce him into sleep. He stares at the ceiling. I know.

The grief boy in Vin's eyes has been visiting more and more in recent months. He's the one trying to force me away.

Chicago answers someone else, saying, "No, you ass," and gets out.

It's obvious he's frustrated because he slams the van door much harder than necessary, which makes my skull throb. Vin would never do that, pay no attention to my potential discomfort. Vin is thoughtful.

Vin was shocked to see me park my car with a U-Haul trailer in front of his house, only three weeks after we first met. Ha. I had prepared paragraphs of explanation for why I appeared so early, but he didn't care. He ran out of his house and leapt down his front steps, telling me he loved me. Nothing mattered after that.

Oh god, Vin! Where are you?

The back door of the van flies open.

My heart pounds again.

Why tonight? *Why tonight?*

Chicago's voice has a sneer in it when he says, "Hope you're ready for the boys, faggot."

A thrill of terror races through me.

So sleepy.

The world is fading again, and I am without Vin.

THREE

I'm awake. Okay, awake again.

What's happening?

The back of the van is open. I hear men, and a new voice. Someone who is not Chicago, says, "Get it done. Over there." I hear footsteps move away, a shuffling sound. Get It Done's voice is lower, quieter than Chicago. I don't like it.

Footsteps move slowly toward the back of the van...no, not footsteps. These are distinct. They are precise. They sound crisp, like—boots. I hear boots!

The boot sound stops. After a few seconds of concentration, I hear that distinct sound when someone twists their shoe over a concrete floor, and I realize Boots now stands still at the back of the van. Without seeing, I know I am being studied. His fingers touch me, and then come to grip my jeans. I flinch, jerking my leg away best I can, but the hand remains on me, and I hate it. *I hate it!* This isn't Vin's hand! There is something cold and calculated about the way this hand moves down my leg, from calf to ankle, then to midthigh, as if he's a butcher deciding how to achieve the best cuts. *There is no kindness in his touch.*

I'm panicking. I'm definitely panicking.

Who the fuck is this?

He unhooks whatever holds my legs and butt aloft, and they fall to the mattress, landing with a dull, thudding hurt. My legs are still spread apart, attached to a bar or board something, maybe a metal—dragging! Oh shit! He drags me from the mattress—

Holy fucking shit! What's happening?

—and throws me over his shoulder, my head bouncing off his back. Oh god, he reeks, sickly sweet, thick and disgusting. The worst cologne ever.

I cough.

I cough harder. It's horrible.

After he readjusts me, I hear those same awful boots scrape the pavement when he pivots. I bounce against him, though he moves in an inexplicable, controlled way. I can't describe it because I can't see him, but it's creepy, the way he carries me, both conscious of my weight and somehow unthinking of me as a burden. Is *unthinking* a word? I don't know what I mean anymore—I'm trying to understand the bouncing sensations, the feelings. You can't think like a normal person when your sight is stolen—nothing makes sense. Everything feels foreign and cold—*oh god, that's so cold*! Vin has carried me fireman style in the past, but he was always careful, making sure—I cough hard against the fabric in my mouth. This thick cologne is revolting. He's slathered in it.

My body is twisted, lifted higher, and...*what's happening*?

Is this my last breath? Am I being murdered—no. No, I am not. Don't think that way. Don't freak out against the fabric in my mouth. Don't do anything to provoke—

Turned over, then over again, so I'm on my stomach, and I scream because it's so goddamn cold, this unfamiliar texture—it's padded. Okay, it's padded, it's a cold padding on a stool or a bench, more like a raised bench. Weightlifting bench at an angle? I'm facedown, panting, huffing, as if I'd done all the work. I don't know what I'm on, exactly, but that's what it feels like, so cold, which makes me—

Oh my god.

He lifts the back of my jeans and slides something under my belt. I fight it— squirming hard against him—but with his hand, he pushes me back down onto the bench, pushes the air out of me, nonverbally communicating *don't fight this*. I hate how he doesn't speak, I hate how he says *don't fight this* with his hand. Motherfucker! I feel the cold against my skin first, before I hear the ripping sound, before I understand the almost-silence of my jeans being cut from my body. But that's what's happening—he's slicing the jeans off my body. The knife is so sharp, the fabric rips like wrapping paper, and my left leg is fully exposed.

I scream.

He pushes my back down forcefully, and I gasp because this shove proves he's not fucking around.

He has no kindness in him!

My leg gets cold, and then—now that I know what's happening—the knife returns under my jeans on the right side. This can't be happening. Don't black out with sleep—stay awake!

Remember! Remember something good!

The cologne.

The day after I moved in with Vin, I made room in his medicine cabinet for my things, which wasn't hard because he didn't use any products, not even exfoliating cream. I stood shirtless in the bathroom, wiping down the little shelves, happy my little bottles would live next to his for the rest of our lives. Vin found me and stood behind me, watching, hooking his thumbs in my belt loops, saying nothing, observing me as I completed this satisfying chore.

When I got to the bottle of Versace cologne, I said, "Brian gave me this last Christmas, because he knows I like fashion."

Vin closed the medicine cabinet, before I could place it, and looked into my reflection.

"Do you wear this?"

I shook my head no, a subtle movement, because he stared so intently I didn't need to respond much, just a twitch. His intensity is something I had gotten addicted to in our short time together, and now I experience it every single day. That day, I shivered.

I shiver now.

In a quiet voice, Vin said, "You like the smell?"

I stared back and talked to his reflection. "No."

"What smell do you want on your body?"

I tried to say the word "you," but it came out mostly a whisper.

We didn't speak.

Vin finally said, "You won't need this anymore."

While staring into my eyes, he dumped the cologne into the sink. He kissed my—

Wait—not my shirt—*not my San Francisco yard sale shirt*!

Too late.

The asshole's knife glides through the orange and yellow sailboats with what seems like pleasure, and the shirt falls off my back and bunches around my taped wrists. I've made no progress. My arms remain immobile.

I hate this man! *I fucking hate him!* He sliced it off with no regard, not a single thought of what this shirt might mean to me, how important that particular trip was, how this shirt commemorates Vin taking me to Alcatraz for the first time!

Before I can get more outraged about the shirt, I feel a familiar probing around my underwear, and *noooo*! This is Vin's favorite underwear of mine—I wore Vin's favorite underwear tonight! Silky, baby-blue briefs hugging my ass, giving shape—

The hand lifts the fabric from me, and within seconds, it's all gone, cut off me.

I scream again—he had no fucking right to do that, no fucking right!

I twist my torso, trying to knock myself off this bench apparatus, show some form of resistance, but I stop immediately when I feel his boot on my ass. On my asshole, specifically. The boot is cold and feels gritty, the way the underside of a shoe does, with tiny granules acquired by just walking around.

I calm myself.

Breathe.

I gasp because, my god, this is horrible. I had no idea.

The knife slices the duct tape, and my hands fall to my sides. I want to fight, I want to use them to push him off me, but they hang limp, refusing to obey my brain's commands. My shoulders are sore. Heavy. I feel the remainder of sliced shirt slither off me, and since I feel the fabric still touching my fingers, I guess that means I'm not far off the ground.

With every ounce of my remaining energy, I turn my head to one side.

Talking—there's *talking* coming from the other side of the room. I hear distinct voices. Nobody I recognize, but who's here? Where's here? I could guess, but—

The boot drags itself off me, thank god. But the awful sound of those distinctive boots clacking against the hard floor means he's moving around my body. I'm dizzy. Disoriented. When he comes to my head, a wave of the thick cologne assaults me, forcing me to cough again. I've never smelled anything so strong and conflicted. The boot sounds—I feel I should be able to get some clue about these boots, just by the sound. Malcolm or Vin should have taught me how to guess the age and weight of the wearer, or some magicals tricks like that. Maybe Vin can't do that either. I don't know. He can do a lot of things I can't explain.

My right hand is now handcuffed to something, a padded handcuff, and I feel I should fight this more. I know I should. But I'm so exhausted, my brain feels so exhausted, it's all I can manage to stay awake, let alone, well, fight. By the time my left hand is shackled as well, I know it's a board. I'm handcuffed to a board, and by maneuvering, I can get my fingers over the top of it, grasp it.

The board is raised. It's raised? I hear chains clanking. My arms move up higher, until it feels like I'm trying to peer over a fence, my torso almost vertical. The clanking stops, and I sway a few inches in either direction, swinging.

It's the exact reverse of the van, where now my torso angles up, and the rest of me lies flat on the bench, my ass sticking up and my legs still bound and hanging over the end. My feet don't touch the floor, which makes me feel dizzy when I consider how ungrounded I feel, how lost and confused.

I'm naked.

Trapped.

Breathing hard, and I'm sweating and cold. I shiver—no denying it, I'm terrified—but I refuse to be intimidated. Only one man intimidates me. And only sometimes...when I let him.

A sound happens farther away, two dozen feet away, far but not too far, musical and strong, a piano key plunked extra hard, but that's not it because it's a stronger, higher pitch, followed by metallic clattering, echoing all over the place.

I know that sound.

Thomas is clumsy with his tools. He's always dropping them. That was the sound of a high-quality wrench hitting a concrete floor.

The boots leave me, pointed in the sound's direction, their unhurried pace not changing in the slightest, and as glad as I am to feel him go, I almost feel bad for whoever he's going to see. I picture alligator boots now, ugly snake-patterned alligator boots. I know this makes no sense, they're only a sound, but I hate these boots, and I hate Gator, the man wearing them.

But more importantly, *I know where I am.*

I'm in Vin's garage. I'm tied up in Vin's garage. We never left St. Paul. Well, we're in South St. Paul, but same difference. That wrench sound came from Fredi's work area. Gator better not have fucked with one of her tools; she's gonna be pissed.

Gator clip-clacks his way over to them, and I hear the voices rise, but I can't make out any real words in a meaningful way because they're too far away. Of course we're in Vin's garage. I should have guessed immediately.

I hate being blindfolded and tied up like this. I hate it. Things I should have thought of, logical things, don't make any sense. I didn't even understand my jeans were sliced off until I felt the cold air, because I didn't understand the sounds. Vin sometimes says Malcolm taught him to "find the truth of a thing, not just what is true." Vin says everything has a true name beyond its name. It's hard to find the truth of a thing when your senses lie to you.

The arguing gets quieter, and then Gator clomps out the far door, the one leading into the customer waiting area and Vin's office.

I struggle against the board, my handcuffs, twisting my ass, trying to see if there's some way to pull myself off this bench and wrench myself—no. I can't. I'm stuck.

I can't do anything, so I start remembering.

When we met. When we fell in love.

I didn't want to go into Romero's dressed as a gay stripper with two loads of Vin's jizz in my butt, so I insisted on staying in the truck, realizing I was failing him, the man I already loved. But I didn't care. How could he ask that of me? In my own hometown? Hell, my parents could have shown up, though I knew they wouldn't. They were at home, terrified out of their minds I'd be killed by a psycho from the Internet. I assured them over and over...but they worried. I showed them the paperwork that Vin owned a garage. The fact that he was findable on the internet made it better. But I didn't dare show them Vin's king life. Ha. So I sat in the truck, feeling bad.

And that fucker tricked me with a note.

Vin knew I'd watch from the truck, so he wrote me a note and put it next to him. Began chomping his pizza. He knew the note would drive me crazy. He knew it! Sure enough, I stumbled inside, my heart pounding. When I sat next to Vin and read the words he'd written to me, I saw his block letters, and nothing else mattered. I stopped questioning why he did what he did, and everything inside me started singing, like a new color was born, one with musical abilities, a new spot on the spectrum of light. I reread the note, and knew I would do whatever he said. Because I loved him. We ate pizza together, and I thought about love, how love was like a whole box of new crayon—

"Hey," says a voice in my ear.

I scream in pure terror. I never heard anyone approaching.

Holy fucking shit! Holy shit!

"Maybe you can scream better with this gag off."

His hands work quickly, freeing the gag, and I gasp at the freedom, beautiful freedom to breathe and speak and scream. I scream again.

"Yes, scream," the voice says directly into my ear, in a patient, understanding tone. "Cry for help. You'll feel better."

I stop.

I hate the voice in my ear. I hate the layered intonation, demanding and supplicating, like the way women at Mom's church used to speak to me after they found out I had gotten arrested, their mournful condescension masking a secret glee, as if the key to rehabilitating me was talking at me like a six-year-old. "Poor thing," they used to say, and my eyes blazed with rage.

"Fuck you," I say with as much snarl as I can muster.

"Aw, Poochie. Is that any way to begin our relationship? Hmmmm? I haven't even introduced myself."

He speaks quietly, like someone who gently admonishes chatty relatives before the funeral, saying, "The service is about to begin."

He strokes my hair, which makes me cringe.

This undertaker says, "I understand if you're in a hurry. We don't have to exchange names. Quick couple of questions, and then you're on your way. Does that sound fair to you?"

He strokes my hair again, and though I jerk my head away, his hand follows, thinking he can calm me down by petting me. Tied down in this freakish way, I feel as though I'm kenneled, but I am not his fucking dog.

Or if I am, he'd best beware.

I bite.

"First question," Undertaker says. "Can you confirm your boyfriend's name? His real name? We're old friends from Chicago, and he didn't use the name Vin at that time. Of course, he's all grown up now."

I say nothing.

"Don't pout, Poochie. It's only a name. We're pretty sure already. We just want confirmation."

He moves around me, I guess, because I feel a slight shift in his presence, a breeze almost. Thank god, no cologne. He does something to my board, pushes it, and my arms and torso follow, a caricature of dancing, me swinging to the beat.

The movement stops, jerking me toward him.

Ow.

He says, "I started with an easy question. You should be more accommodating."

"If it's so easy, you don't need me."

I shouldn't speak. Shouldn't engage. But when could I ever keep my mouth shut?

When Vin told me not to talk to Thomas about breaking parole and driving to Chicago to see an ex-girlfriend, did I keep my mouth shut? No, I did not. I yelled at Thomas. Yelled about how Vin got him a third chance, after he'd blown his second chance, and Thomas was throwing it away for a woman who didn't want him. That was a year before he and Fredi became an item. Did I keep my mouth shut when the new neighbors across the street asked—in a sideways way—if any black people lived in the neighborhood? Nope. I'm not good at shutting up.

Undertaker says, "We know his real name isn't Vincent. But he named this place Vincent's Garage. Why?"

I know the answer. But I will keep my mouth shut.

He tugs a lock of hair. It hurts. Not much, but enough to make me jerk.

"I'd like an answer. Our English friend isn't back yet. He usually asks the questions. Of course, he's not much of an interrogator. His thing is to repeatedly punch the kidneys, over and over, until you eventually tell him what he wants to know. He's a one-trick pony. I'd suggest answering me before he returns. We might be able to keep this civilized."

Say nothing.

Think of Vin.

I was mad when he left New Jersey, mad at him for his dumb-ass rules, because it sure would have been nice to chat with him while I packed up my whole life, or while I investigated Minnesota schools, or even when I wanted to hear his sexy, dirty voice as a distraction from my parents' massive tirades against him.

When I arrived at his home, tired and crabby from two days' winter driving, and he ran from his house because he felt such excitement to see me, I felt my anger melt, and I realized the three weeks apart had been hard on him too. Still, I refused to let him kiss me and snarkily suggested we wait eight more months before we got physical, but my resolve lasted all of twelve minutes before he dragged me into his home, and we made love for hours and hours. That night was definitely in the Top Five. He was all over me, and I was all over him, so we stayed up all night touching, talking. He took me to his favorite bench in the Twin Cities so we could watch the sun rise at the Witches' Tower. I thought to myself, "I'm here. I'm with the man I'm going to be with for the rest of my life. It begins right now."

A few hours later, we lay in bed, exhausted, and my butt felt this throbbing sensation I would come to associate as kind of regular with Vin. We were falling asleep facing each other, my head pressed against his hairy chest, mid-December sunlight streaming in, and me trying to snuggle closer to him, if it were humanly possible.

In a mumbly voice, Vin said, "You can't move across the country to be with someone after one weekend."

"I know," I said, because, yeah, that's totally insane. You can't do crazy shit like that.

"Good," he said, and kissed the top of my head, but it was only a half kiss because he was fading.

"How did you know?" I slurred the words and didn't finish the question, because I was as exhausted as he was. More so. He kept trying to fuck me into unconsciousness, but I kept staying awake. I couldn't miss a second. I wanted to ask him how he knew it was me—I was the one.

"A king...said...you...were coming."

Clearly, we were both out of our minds, crisscrossing that bridge between sleep and reality, but I never asked him that question again, because even though he was asleep, I liked the answer he gave me. A king said I was coming, so Vin waited for me.

When we finally crawled out of bed, sore and groggy, we ordered two pizzas and moved in my stuff. All of his closets were fifty percent empty, just as I'd instructed. Even the floor space.

"—wouldn't you?"

Oh. Undertaker is talking.

"Sorry," I say, trying my best not to sound sorry. "Could you repeat that? I wasn't listening."

I feel the movement of him, but his shoes are so silent, so impossibly quiet, I can't be sure where he went.

His fingertips touch my ass, causing me to squirm and bark out a noise.

"I overestimated you," he says in the same even voice. "I thought you might know something useful. But you don't know his very name. You don't know anything about his garage. Perhaps you don't know Vin Vanbly as well as you thought."

Say nothing.

"We watched. We assumed you two were more than butt buddies, more along the lines of a gay lover. But if he tells you nothing, maybe he doesn't love you as much as you think."

A low blow. "You asshole. You should not have said that."

He says nothing in response, and the gentle whir of breeze suggests he travels again, completing his path around me.

"He loves me," I say, with an extra bit of defiance.

Undertaker's voice is in my other ear. "How much do you actually know about Vin Vanbly?"

His condescending church-lady voice is back.

Well, fuck you.

I know Vin Vanbly.

I know he hates romantic comedies because they make him sad. He won't watch movies where animals get hurt, though he likes movies where cities get destroyed. When we walk through forests, he gets silent, except for when he talks to the trees. He took me deer stalking once, which is about the dullest thing I've ever done in my life, standing still for three hours in case a deer wanders up. Vin being who he is, I thought they would stroll over to him and start nuzzling his face, but they didn't. Three hours in the early morning mist and then rain, waiting for deer. Then again, spend three hours in wet silence deep in a green forest, and you know a person in a way few people ever will.

He likes noodles but not white sauce. He won't eat cookies, not ever. He juggles bananas for me, to make me laugh when I am upset. He is chatty with strangers, until they say something racist, and he ends the acquaintanceship. He will wear the same shirt five days in a row if he thinks it's "clean," but now he changes socks and underwear every other day. I've trained him on that.

On our walks, if he finds a dead bird, he buries it. He makes a little pattern with stones over the dirt to honor its short life. When neighborhood gossip reveals a neighbor in trouble, he asks me to bake a dish so we have an excuse to visit. Then, he asks subtle questions to figure out what they need. He bought an expensive hospital bed for Linda's husband when he came home from physical rehab. She never found out who paid for it.

I know everything about Vin Vanbly, but only since the day I moved in. I can piece together about six years before that, and a few details from the ten years before that. Then, there's this sea of fog blocking the years with Malcolm towering above, standing gatekeeper to Vin's early life.

My whole body shakes and twists, as if the ship I'm on was tossed in sudden waves.

The jarring makes me a little nauseated, especially when it stops as suddenly as it began.

"I said, I *expect* an answer." Undertaker's voice sounds less patient, though still quiet. "How many ex-cons work in this garage? How many?"

"I don't know."

"You do."

"I don't remember who is and who isn't an ex-con. Between current and past employees, it gets blurry."

"Lies, little Poochie," he says, stroking the side of my face. "We've seen you here in the daytime. You walk your precious dogs over here. Oh, yes, we've been watching."

"Why?"

"Vin recently popped back onto our radar. Many years ago, he left Chicago in a bit of a mess, so now that we've found him again, we came to pay our respects. We discovered this garage. We like it. His little parade of ex-cons and freaky mechanics working side by side. Perfect place for running drugs. Ex-cons have the connections, and assorted weirdos—who aren't from prison—have the customers. The shop is well-enough integrated into the community to not arouse suspicions. Lots of minivans pull in here for tune-ups, which is good. This place is an untapped gold mine."

"He'd never—"

He puts his hand on my upper back. "He will. I can be very persuasive."

I twist. No. *No.* Even talking this way is wrong, talking about his mechanics this way. He works so hard to reach them.

I remember Ex-Con Suck Off night, when I was sucking Vin's dick after he put in a long day at his garage. He had fired one of his ex-cons—Clark, I think—who had been stealing parts to sell on the side. It was his third and final chance.

Vin was majorly distracted and not himself, angry about firing someone he wanted to trust. He always believes the ex-cons will come around, and he's such a good judge of character, he's right almost all the time. He thinks the *x* in ex-con will give them extra strength to return to society. That night, he wasn't concentrating on me, he was angrily fucking my mouth, mad at work, mad at people.

I guess I should have been insulted.

But he loves me so much I don't need him to see me every single second. I knew what he needed.

Me.

I loved him with everything inside me. Not only my wet mouth and sucking throat. That wasn't enough. I adored him. I worshipped him. I fixated every cell in my body on him. I knelt for him, humping forward for him, groveling for Vin as if he were my personal god, and I felt blessed to serve at his altar, worshipping every fat inch of the power he fucked into my throat.

After a time, his gripping my head became less angry and more about me, and his fingers brushed my hair, and he made sounds of pleasure. When I looked into his eyes, I saw this recognition, like, "Hey, it's you!" And I knew he realized I had been loving him the whole time, even while he was angry at Clark. I am our anchor, and I pulled him back into himself, into us. He watched me with surprise, then joy, because no matter how we drift apart, we always find each other again. We just do.

When he fired down my throat, I eagerly devoured his love. When I swallow him, I feel the color again—the new color I first saw at Romero's when I knew I'd do whatever he said. If I were to guess, I'd say I must believe all his fire—all his passion for life—lives in that milky fluid, because how else would you explain him not constantly overloading with excessive smoke and flame? There's got to be a release valve inside Vin Vanbly. When he puts his power into me, for a moment I'm as wild and fierce as he is, sucking his cock and milking out all those squirts. Suddenly I am on fire and unrelenting.

During that moment, I am Vin.

He gets soft, his eyes full of love. He is me.

Czzzzzk.

Holy shit! The walkie-talkie buzz scares the fuck out of me.

The sound of voices drifts away as Undertaker moves, creating that weird air current. Mumbled talk as far as I can tell.

A moment later, he's right back at my side. I now recognize the mini air currents announcing his presence. He—or anyone else—won't be able to sneak up on me again.

"Well, isn't this interesting," Undertaker's even tones suggests it's not all that interesting. Does he ever break inflection?

"It seems Vin has been joined by two friends in the gay-club parking lot. A handsome, muscular one, and a pasty fellow. Your absence has been noted by the Hardy boys."

"Vin is better than you," I cannot resist saying. "He's smarter and stronger, and he can make things happen better than you."

Undertaker says, "Interesting."

In a breeze, I feel him leave. I never heard his shoes, not at all. How can he walk so silently? Sneakers?

With him gone, I feel my body sag in relief. Not too much relief, because every part of me is getting sore. My arms. My legs. I could scream, demanding to be untied, but I'm proving how strong I am, how much I endure. Vin taught me to be strong.

But where are you, Vin?

I'm not sure how much more I can take.

FOUR

I remember last spring, when Vin got it into his head to make us fried chicken, even though he hadn't cooked it for years and years. He scrunched up his face and studied the *Betty Crocker Cookbook* Malcolm had given him, and it seemed easy enough. I teased him while I made us a blueberry pie for dessert. Vin insisted on making the entire batter from scratch, because once he decides to do a thing, he overcommits. He decided to flip off Betty Crocker and add his own spices and ingredients, assuring me these substitutions shouldn't matter. He burned himself on the oil in the pan, not realizing it would splatter, and despite that, he wouldn't stop touching the chicken as it cooked. I had to coax him to put his burned thumb and index finger in a cup of ice water. Of course, he burned the chicken.

We each ate three pieces of blueberry pie.

After dinner, I studied against him on the couch, and he watched reruns of a cop show he'd already seen, when he should have been doing his accounting books for the garage—which I reminded him of, and to which he grunted. Later, Malcolm called, and then later than that, Fredi called. While I emailed my mom, I heard Vin say "Fredi, you're wrong. I bet you ten dollars. Verbal handshake. No, no. Don't try to change your story now. You said—" They spend all day together and still bicker on the phone at night. Before bed, we walked the dogs, holding hands, talked to Cheryl and her son Jerry, who were exercising Nickels. When I first moved to Minnesota, I didn't realize two men could hold hands out in public, but yeah, you can here. We do.

An ordinary, unremarkable night.

In bed, I teased him about the fried chicken and kissed his blistering thumb.

Our giggling turned to sexy talk, and soon I was on my back, and my legs wrapped around my man's waist, and his chubby cock inside me, oh, he was *inside me*, and we both smelled like burned chicken, because the whole house did.

He stared at me. I stared back at him.

Vin said, "This is our life."

Suddenly, the whole night was remarkable, important and sparking alive. I cried because he was right, this was our life, and I was so happy. I tried to fix every detail in memory, in case someday I needed to remember how good life could be. He kept humping me with these slow, luxurious movements, stroking my insides,

212 | EDMOND MANNING

and this was *our life*, dirty dishes in the sink and dogs panting on the bedroom floor. Who would ever think after Fried Chicken Night there could ever be trouble between us?

When I stopped crying, which was only a little bit anyway, I said, "Do you ever wish we could make a baby?"

Vin frowned at me, as if he didn't understand.

I repeated the words. "A baby."

He frowned harder, puzzled, and never stopped his dick from moving inside me. "But we do, Marky. Every time."

I twisted his right ear, which I do sometimes.

"Oh, you mean a physical baby," he said, pretending to get me at last. "No. Too much poopy."

I laughed. "What did you mean?"

"Spirit babies," he said in a quiet voice, "are made by two people in love."

I waited. You often have to wait for Vin.

"When two people make love with intention and light, they create something new which didn't exist in the world, bringing it alive, a force of nature. For some couples, this spirit baby is made flesh, and for others, like you and me, the spirit baby rises out of us, the best of us, and flies to where love is most needed."

"Where," I say, losing myself in his sparkling voice, the quiet one he uses when he wants me to listen. "Where?"

He doesn't answer immediately, concentrating on my body and leaning down, so our noses touch.

"You tell me."

My brain swims in possibilities, flying through space and time, like Vin has sent me on a mission. When words come from my mouth, they are as much a surprise to me as the notion I'm speaking out loud. I sometimes think I talk right into Vin's brain.

"Seattle," I say, closing my eyes. "A woman misses her daughter, and our spirit baby comforts her."

"Yesssssss," he says, and he gets harder because I know what he likes. People finding comfort and love. "And what about two nights ago, where did that go?"

"To Baltimore," I say, though I don't know why. "A trans woman is about to ask someone out on a date. First time ever asking. She's scared."

Shit.

Time to stop remembering, because the air currents around me change suddenly, announcing that someone stands near, and nobody makes any noise, so it's got to be him. Undertaker is back.

"I know you're here."

Undertaker says, "Yes. I'm back. We're running out of time. Soon, he'll figure out where you are. Or, maybe he won't. Maybe you'll be found by the first ex-con to open shop in the morning. We could call Vin and tell him you're here. You won't spend all night dangling, which is probably a good thing."

Say nothing.

"But you've got to help us. Where are the employee files? We need to know more about the ex-cons. We need leverage."

"Maybe you should call HR in the morning."

Undertaker strokes my hair, which disgusts me, but at least this time, I don't jerk away. I need to show him I don't care.

"All the goddamn filing cabinets are full of children's toys. We checked them all."

Say nothing.

Vin and the mechanics hide toys in the cars they fix, at least inside the cars they know have kids.

"We need those files."

His hand traces the length of my spine, and the feel of his casual touch is spidery, so I shiver. His hand stops right at the top of my ass. "I wish you would cooperate."

I hate the threat in his casual words.

I will remember times with Vin and get through this. Fried Chicken Night. Flat Tire Night. Fredi's Attack Mouse Night. That was a good night. We laughed so hard.

The voices start up again on the other side of the room, and the change in current around me suggests Undertaker moves away.

From a few feet away, Undertaker roars, "*Shut up, goddamn it!*"

The fury, the loudness of it, terrifies me. I shake. I didn't hear wrath in anything he said to me, even the buried possibility of this vehement explosion. It's hard to cry with a blindfold on, the tears get pressed back, which is about the only good thing about this situation. I hate this. *I really hate this.*

The walkie-talkie static breaks through. A faraway voice says, "They're coming."

They're coming!

Hope!

Undertaker returns to me, and I feel his closeness, feel his body crouch next to mine.

"We should go," he says softly, right into my ear. "We could probably stay and chat with Vin ourselves. Or, whoever he thinks he is these days. But we'll save that for another day. Tonight, we'd prefer to give him a message. A calling card to let him know we're in the neighborhood and looking for business opportunities."

Through gritted teeth, I say, "I'll be sure to mention it."

"No," Undertaker says. "Those are just the words. They aren't the message."

He walks away, talking loudly, telling them to leave everything as it is.

"What's the message?" I yell.

What message? Where is he going?

"What's the message!"

No answer.

I keep telling myself it's stupid to be afraid. Stupid.

I twist, but I'm tired of twisting. I can't get free. What's the message?

My heart beats.

This is my moment. This is it, right now, to use my magic power, whatever it is—my king power—to make this right. But I don't even know my king name. Vin says he doesn't know it, either, and it bothers him. He says he doesn't understand why he can't find the name—he can always find the king name—but he can't uncover mine. Once, in a bratty voice, I told him I knew *exactly* where mine was—trapped under his. He caught the reference I was making to his shirts being all over mine in our bedroom. I was snotty because I was afraid Vin didn't think of me as a king. Maybe I wasn't good enough to be one of his king men?

He said, "Not knowing someone's king name doesn't prevent them from being a king. A name doesn't define you or make you something you're not. Your king name is true, but not the truth." I figured he knows about these things. But I wish he knew what my king name was. Maybe it could make me powerful, or help me think of a way out of this.

Wait, what's that sound?

No.

The regular clacking, evenly spaced, starting across the room.

It's Gator.

Shit, it's Gator's boots!

No, no, no, no.

I find the fight in me to squirm, to fight this. I have to get out of here. He has no kindness in him!

He's coming.

I hate this. I *hate* this!

I'm trying to remember anything, anything Malcolm said to me that might be useful, any little tidbit or detail about police work or being strong, but the only thing racing to mind is the last time I saw him in person, and we spoke about Vin.

The mechanics were over while Malcolm was visiting. Big cookout. He and I sat on the back porch, watching them throw a football at one another's crotches. Fredi screamed at someone to stop moving his damn ass, and when she nailed him, everybody clinked beers. We all might have been a little buzzed.

I was buzzed enough to ask Malcolm why Vin never talked about growing up in Chicago.

Malcolm turned it around and asked me why I thought he did not.

"Because he's ashamed."

"True," Malcolm said. "And..."

"He thinks it will make me love him less."

"True," Malcolm said. "And..."

"And because Vin's an idiot."

Malcolm smiled and said, "True."

Gator's bootsteps are almost here! My heart starts pounding again. I can't do this. *I can't.*

Malcolm said, very seriously, "So what are you going to do?"

"Wait," I said. "Until he tells me. When he's finally ready."

Malcolm said, "He loves you."

"I know."

There was a lesson there from Malcolm, which was to trust the love, to trust it all the way, even when it's super hard. To trust the Fried Chicken Nights, the Tuxedo Nights, Vin's Naughty Smile, the night we—

The sound of boots walks behind me. Gator's hand is on my ass! Caressing my ass!

I hate this!

Bad Shrimp Night, when I was sick for hours, and Vin could do nothing but sit next to my side of the bed, watching me mournfully, the grief boy in his eyes, afraid, so afraid—

No, no! *No!*

I scream, "*Get your goddamn hands off me!*"

I'm freaking out. I'm freaking out. It's not Vin! It's not Vin!

I hear the zipper of his jeans go down, the most horrifying sound I could possibly imagine from this freak of a human who has no soul. I hate him! *I hate him!* Then, the unmistakable soft *thud* of his jeans hitting the cement floor, a tiny metallic *clink* giving it all away.

The horrible cologne—I smell it. It's so thick!

He pulls apart my ass cheeks, and he spits, a great glob of Gator spit. I can't feel where it lands.

In a low, gristly voice, Gator finally speaks. "*I'm the message.*"

I scream. I scream as loud as I can.

I can't go through with this!

I scream out Vin's name—his real name—the one we never say aloud.

FIVE

The blindfold is ripped from my eyes instantly. Then my hand is freed, and now both hands are free. I long to yank the remaining sticky, gray tape while he unchains my feet. Can't. Not handcuffed, but arms are still bound. He works efficiently and silently, as if the garage were on fire and every second mattered for life or death. My feet touch the floor. He frees my arms and chest.

In less than one minute—maybe a minute and a half—I'm free, standing wobbly on the garage floor.

I'm free.

I rub my diminished wrists, and crumple the used duct tape, tossing it.

I lean to one side.

He catches me.

Not until he wraps himself around me, squeezing me tight, do I feel my freedom. I held out for as long as I could, but now that it's over—it's *over*—my body starts shaking uncontrollably, and I order myself not to bawl my eyes out.

He senses this and rocks me. He now understands my bravado was an act. I was terrified. I couldn't even think right in the head. I tried to hold on as long as I could.

After all, this was my fantasy.

I told Vin I wanted to try an abduction, a forced sex scenario, because I thought it might be super hot. We agreed I had to be genuinely surprised, preferably a night when I didn't have early classes the next day, or we hadn't devoured Vin's three-meat lasagna—or something equally heavy—for dinner. I guess tonight met our guidelines. But it was not sexy like I had hoped. I truly felt abducted.

I can't help it.

I start to cry, clutching him tighter. It was horrible. I almost got fucked by Gator.

"Mark," he says with anguish, repeating the word over and over, rocking me. "Mark. *Mark.*"

He doesn't need to say anything, he just needs to be Vin. The memory of Gator will fade. Eventually. Right now, I need Vin.

I need *Vin.*

"I'm so sorry." His voice is full of grief. "I thought you were into it. You didn't say anything."

I pull myself together. I'm still trembling, but it's over. It's all over. It was role-playing.

"No, don't," I say. I pull away from him so I may take a few deep breaths. I keep my hands on his chest. I don't want him far from me.

"Sit in the chair," he says, indicating the metal chair behind him.

"No."

He eases into the chair himself, pulling me with him, and says, "Okay, *now* sit in the chair."

I chuckle, because he knew—he always knows—what I really need.

I ease onto his lap, feeling chilly and naked, and he wraps his arms around me again, pulling our chests together.

"I'm so sorry, Marky."

"No, don't. Don't apologize. I wanted to try an abduction fantasy. This was my idea."

"I went too far."

"Vin, I knew whatever you'd pull together wouldn't be half-assed. Something insane like this is what I expected. I just didn't react like I thought I would. It was horrible. Not sexy."

He says nothing to this, giving me the chance to look around the garage. I need to see familiar things, the working bays of friends I know. Thomas's, Fredi's against the wall, and the one shared by Deshawn and Linda. Mex used to work over there, Joel here. Joel. What a sweetie. I hope he still loves living on an island. Vin's truck is parked twenty feet away, and there's the white van. I wonder whose he borrowed. I don't recognize it. *Transformers*, the movie poster from last year, hangs near the kid-fenced-in area Vin installed so boys and girls interested in cars could watch from a slightly closer vantage. Vin would make an excellent dad.

Looking down, I can't see Gator's boots because Vin still wears them. But I know they're still there, under his jeans, which were at his ankles when I sat on his lap. I hope he doesn't like those boots, because they're never coming back to the house. He can wear them here at the garage, but Gator must never come into our home.

"Babe, would you please kick off your boots? Then, kick them away from us?"

"My boots?"

Vin shrugs off the first one before I nod. He kicks it a clattering distance away. He bends over to free the other one, and with me in his lap, we bend together, awkwardly, chuckling, restoring a little humor. As the second one goes skidding away, I realize I don't want them at the garage either. I want them gone forever.

There's the wrench, lying near Fredi's station. I'm guessing Vin threw it from here so it would make big noise over there. Makes sense. I check out the stereo speakers on the far side as well—the light blinks on. I guess he played a podcast or radio show so I heard real conversation. He's good.

The walkie-talkie. The fake English person in the car, who he made "jump out" at the corner to go back for my cell phone. He did enough voices and fake personas to make me question we were truly alone. He's like a professor of psychology, my Vin. He never went to college, I know, but I've never met anyone who understands people the way he does.

I push back from him. I'm calmer now. My body has stopped trembling.

"You okay?"

"I am. I'm better. Just freaked out for a moment."

He watches me with worry, but he doesn't say anything.

I need to hear his voice. "That was you doing an English accent?"

"Yah."

"But you sounded really different."

"I called John. He coached me. John Robertson."

Right. John.

John came to our house a year and a half ago, his fedora in hand, looking like a 1950s door-to-door salesman. Before he could introduce himself, I knew immediately. I said, "You're one of the kings," and I invited him in. I can always tell.

Within ten minutes, I texted Vin we were having a surprise guest for dinner, and to bring home any hungry mechanics, because the secret guest and I were hand-rolling pasta into noodles, enough to feed a crew. John fascinated me all afternoon, talking about his legal adventures in Latin America, organizing workers, and spending months in a Mexican prison to fight for their rights. By the time Vin arrived home with Fredi and two others—Who was that? Mex and Deshawn? Mex and Joel?—John and I had moved on to sauces. Despite Vin's initial surprise and discomfort, by the second glass of red wine, it was obvious how much he had missed John, and they hugged for a long time while John cried in Vin's arms. Kevin and Roger stopped by for food, bringing Roger's mom. I think that was the same night. John's Pasta Night.

Through John, Vin reconnected with Helena and Alan and their two girls. They're all coming to Minnesota this summer for a reunion, along with other Burning Man friends.

"Was there really a police car?"

"No," Vin says.

"The siren?"

"From a CD I played."

"But you switched radio stations and the siren continued." I pause to figure this out. "It was layered into the—how did you manage that?"

"I asked Jerry to do it."

"Jerry? From the down the street?"

Vin chuckles. "I didn't explain it was for sex role-playing. I said I wanted to scare you in the car."

"*You* talked to one of our neighbors? And asked their son for help?"

"I did."

I'm wildly impressed. I'm the chatty one in our family. I'm the one who borrows butter, their cheese grater, vinegar, or takes them gingerbread muffins from when we bake too many. I invite neighbors for Sunday-night beers on our deck and Friday card games with pizza. Vin never initiates those interactions. Well, I guess that's not true anymore. Vin asked Jerry for help. How about that? People can change.

In my body, I feel relaxed. Better. I'm okay. It's all over. The garage is just the garage again.

"Why did you pretend the cop car pullover?"

Vin hesitates. "I'm not sure I want to say. It's pretty dark."

"Tell me."

Vin pulls back and looks me in the eye. He wants to watch my reaction. "I wanted to take away your hope. Even though this was all fake—and you knew it— the mind can't be sure, even when it's sure. The police represented your last chance to get free. I knew you'd struggle and exhaust yourself, physically and emotionally, which would make you more pliant when we reached the garage. I watched you struggle yourself into exhaustion."

I show him no reaction. "You're right. That's pretty dark."

He says, "I know. I'm not proud of that. But I think that dark, sometimes."

I move my hands up to the back of his neck, but I am careful not to alter my expression. He thinks he can scare me away. He can't. Everyone thinks dark sometimes. Everyone worries the darkness inside them cannot be contained. But that's not who he is. How does he not realize that?

"Gator's cologne?"

"Gator?"

"The boots. That was my name for the man with the boot sound."

Vin says, "Ah. Necktie. Over there on the floor. I soaked it in three different kinds of cologne. Wore it when I wore the boots."

"It was horrible."

He nods. "I thought so too."

We stare into each other's eyes. It's so good to see him again, to feel Vin again, after spending all evening separate from him. There's one more question I have to ask.

"Tell me again, why you bought this garage?"

"Good investment."

I do not react. I will wait for his real answer.

"I was tired of getting fired from garages, or begging the owners for time away for travel, then begging for my job back. Over the years, I stopped cultivating my high-end clientele, which means I didn't have as many lucrative side gigs."

"Why?"

"I didn't like dealing with rich people. So, I bought a garage. I'd been thinking about it off and on."

I arch my eyebrows. While it's true, it's not the truth.

He watches me, considering. Does he think I don't know the truth?

"Vin, I talk with every mechanic. They're part of our lives. Do you really think I don't know the truth?"

He says, "Why are you asking?"

"I want to hear you say it."

He considers me.

"They fired Thomas," Vin says at last. "From A&J Auto. They fired him because they couldn't uncover the real cash register thief, and Thomas was an ex-con. That was fucked. Next, they fired Deshawn for standing up for Thomas. *That* was fucked. I knew I had to quit."

"So you used all the nickels and dimes you'd saved for twenty years to buy a garage and hire your friends."

Vin says, "Something like that."

"Even though you hate working as a mechanic, and you never dreamed of owning your own garage. You mortgaged yourself to this giant ball and chain to ensure you'll always be stuck in this world."

We stare at each other, unflinching.

He thinks he can scare me by revealing his dark side? *Gimme a break.* I know everything about his light, the living sun inside him. He cannot deny his light is stronger, not to me. I'm just as stubborn as he is.

Another reason I love him. We can be soft and tender, yes. But we can be hard men together too. Unyielding. We do not apologize for our strength. We do not shy from it.

He asks, "Are you really okay?"

"I am. Now."

Vin pauses, "If you're sure, can I ask you something? About tonight?"

"Shoot."

"Why did you end the scene? If you hated it so much, why didn't you end it sooner?"

"Let me think about this. I need a second."

I search the dark corners of Vin's garage, knowing the answer is not out there, but I like seeing familiar surfaces, familiar memories. A month ago, I dozed on the napping couch near the back. Fredi and Vin's yelling woke me up. He'd eaten her purple frosting, stored in the employee fridge, which she needed to show a client for color matching. With purple lips, Vin argued it wasn't his fault.

"I wanted to see how long I could last," I say, the words surprising me because I haven't planned out my answer exactly. "All the work you put into this was incredible. If you could go through with it, so could I."

"But you didn't..." Vin says carefully. "You didn't go through with it."

I nod. "Because I couldn't handle getting fucked by Gator. It can only be you."

"But it was me." Though he uses a softer tone, I hear the challenge.

"No, it *wasn't*. It wasn't even you pretending to be someone else, it was completely *not you*—someone with no kindness in him."

Vin looks at me with skepticism. "I can be someone who thinks in dark ways."

"You can think that way, even plot out strategies. Sure. But that's not you, Vin. We've done all kinds of role-playing, and every character was a variation of you. But not Gator. He wasn't you. And it can only be you."

Look into my eyes. Don't you understand, Vin? Not Davey. Not Kevin. Not a locker room full of hot weightlifting men. Not anybody but you. And not even your physical body while you pretend to be a man with no kindness in him.

There—*there he is*! The grief boy who lives in Vin's eyes is now exposed, the lonely ghost who holds him back from everything. Grief boy makes Vin doubt everyone around him. He whispers in his silent, mouthless voice, *Please don't lie to me. Please.* But he never believes the truth.

Grief boy will kill our relationship if I don't kill him first.

Vin says, "But—"

"No."

This is it. Now that he's exposed, I've got to make my words sharp, and sink an arrow right into Vin's pleading eyes. I've got to love Vin with everything inside me, and show no mercy. I will not share Vin anymore with you, grief boy. He's mine.

He is *mine*.

I grip Vin's neck. I stare him down. "It has to be you. Only. *You*."

I see the words leave my lips, black and sharp.

This is the moment.

Right now.

This is the moment.

If Vin believes me, sees my love for him, we survive. Vin Vanbly, do you believe in Fried Chicken Night?

There's a rumbling sound, like the trembling in my body—my leftover adrenaline—got transferred into him. But inside him, it's not fear. I think whatever love he was holding back—waiting for me to eventually leave him—is vibrating to the surface. *All* his love.

Holy shit.

Holy shit!

I'm up in the air again, still wrapped around him, one muscular arm clamped on my opposite shoulder, his other arm holding me up against him. He kicks the jeans from his ankles with almost angry energy, but not angry, just intense, *very* intense, and he dazzles me with his stare. He strides across the cement, long strides, and you'd think he was late for a corporate meeting the way he's moving with confidence and purpose, staring at me, staring into me—

He's gone!

The grief boy is gone.

Suddenly, I'm pressed hard against the back of his truck, next to the back wheel well, and he grabs me tighter and pulls me next to him. I feel his hard cock, the one I love almost more than my own. I've witnessed Vin in his power before, but this—this is new. This is a new flavor of Vin's power.

Maybe it's one of our spirit babies coming home, a dream born of love, a dream rising from being both awake and asleep, strong and soft, yielding and firm, all in the same moment, and maybe it means we're never going to fight again about breaking up.

Oh, man, I'm right. I see it in his eyes! Vin believes! He believes in me!

He kisses me hard, demands I accept him.

I do, Vin. Now and always, I do.

We neck in this hard way, faces mashed together, and while his torso pushes me against the truck, with his free hand he unhinges the gate, and it slams down, the sound bouncing hard around the cement walls. The dying echo sounds rough, masculine, impatient. Needy. I need him. He needs me. This is what it's like when men need each other. This raw hunger.

He jerks back from the truck, still holding me, carrying me over to the gate, carefully laying me flat, the cold *cold* cold! Against my skin, his feels almost like it's burning, so strong is my desire to jerk away from it. The sensation is tingling and uneven, but I don't care. I don't fucking care.

We're done fighting about breaking up!

We'll fight about other things, sure, but never that again.

I glance down at the cock he's aligning with my ass, and I scooch closer to the edge. His glittering gray-blue eyes bore into me as if he finally recognizes me, a virgin offering for him. His cock is soaked in precum, so much it looks like he's already finished himself off. I've seen him precome before, and I love it, but my god, nothing like—Oh!

His cock disappears from sight, but I feel it next to me, pushing against—pushing, he's almost—

There.

He's inside.

Vin glowers at me, demanding, pleading, insisting, begging, diving into me as his cock slowly drives deeper.

The blaze in him, the sparks of orange and pink almost, a trick of the light maybe, as he grabs the back of my neck and pulls me to him, pulls me, oh god, oh god—that feels amazing.

I think I'm drooling.

All of his cock is inside me, and my eyes open wider. I don't understand how he does this, makes me feel I am a virgin again, our first night together, but some nights, inside me, it's like a new part of Vin shows up, discovering me and freeing me once more.

I gasp.

Vin makes his dick feel thirteen inches long when he decides to. And those extra, imaginary inches...well, those are power—that's how the power inside him manifests. What he feels like right now is an ancient Roman warrior. A battle-weary bruiser who fucks his way into me, throwing his spear—

Ow! Oh, that feels amazing when he—ow!

Like—ow!

This is the man who juggles bananas when I need a study break. He filled out as much of my graduate school paperwork as I did. Vin loves my meatloaf, my garlic curry, my thousand baking experiments, and he loves when I surprise him home early with takeout, and he loves—ow!

He loves.

Oh my god, his cock feels huge!

He's brutal, my Roman soldier, my banana juggler, the wild man inside me, bringing all this power to bear because I can take it—I will take it—this power he culls straight from the earth, into his legs and up to his balls, this power he uses to–ow!

Each *ow* is bliss. It makes me indescribably proud to have my strength tested, to be loved so deeply, to know he won't pull out until he's satisfied himself, which he knows will satisfy me.

Oh my god—

I throw my head back and scream.

I'm still panting. Still coming down.

Wow.

How much time has passed since we started fucking? Fifteen minutes? Don't know. Don't care.

Though it was only a half minute ago, maybe more, my brain replays him coming, my handsomest bear screaming as if he were birthing a fully formed stag, something huge with antlers. I grabbed the sides of his head and pressed my fingers into the scars along his hairline, ones he once told me were "made by a mob." That scream of his was totally inflamed, like ripping flesh, and although it was unearthly, it was totally human, the most common male experience we share.

The mind-shattering orgasm.

I myself screamed, partially out of terror, because his sound was so scary, but also so very beautiful. I screamed at how lucky I am to be a man who gets fucked.

He chomped on my neck, and I spurted next, screaming an echo of his raw surprise. I could only hear drumbeats and chanting. I think the drumbeats were us, pounding the flatbed, and I might have been the one chanting, though I'm blushing to recall the exact words. But I thought I heard drums.

Breathe. *Breathe.*

Okay, this is better. I'm recovering my breath.

As I came, I hallucinated every single color, and a few extra shades, all of them wearing sparkling shirts, every imaginable color screaming circles around us, loving us. In an explosion of rainbow mist, the colors blasted everywhere, and I was getting pounded up the butt in the semidark garage on the back of Vin's truck.

My lips curl into a smile.

I imagine the craziest things when we have sex.

And he's worried I might regret not having sex with someone else?

Yeah, right. Like I would ever give this up.

Vin takes in air, more like himself, gasping and pulling back for me to see the wild in his stare as it fades, the beast retreating, and Vin stepping up to look out of his own eyes again, brows raised to express incredulity. He huffs, in almost apology, and grimaces as he slides each inch out. The sensation is excruciatingly tantalizing, for him and for me, until at last, with extreme relief, he gasps, and his Roman soldier is outside of me again with a limp but convincing promise: "I'll be back."

When he can get enough air, Vin says, "Top Ten?"

I smile big, like Kevin's big smile, to show Vin how happy I am to be here with him. "Top Five."

"That good?"

I close my eyes and drift into happy sleep. "That good."

When I open my eyes, he's where he always is after I fall asleep, staring at me from inches above. I want him to be the first thing I see when I awaken. I barely have to raise my chin to kiss him.

"Hi, babe."

I smile stupidly, still dazed. "Hi."

I'm exhausted. This night...oh, this night was worth it. But I'm feeling dead. I'm going to be really sore tomorrow. I can already tell. And not from the weights Kevin and I lifted.

I stretch, and he straightens up, giving me space, tracing the length of my arms with all his fingers. I love lying here, feeling the biggest weight off my shoulders, but I suppose we had better start getting home, to the dogs. To our ordinary lives.

"Help me up?"

This is going to hurt.

He pulls me forward, and as predicted, I'm sore everywhere. My legs, my arms, my shoulders especially, right now. Wow. Extra strength aspirin, tonight, you will be my best friend. I'll ask Vin to massage my shoulders. I inch forward on the flatbed, and my ass tells me sex was longer than fifteen minutes. I took a pounding.

Vin kisses me.

Tasting him reminds me I'm pretty sure we made a spirit baby. So while Vin chews my lower lip, I make this wish. I wish Vin would tell me his real name. Not his birth name, I know that, of course. I want to know who he was when he was twenty. The name of him, so to speak, when Malcolm found him and changed his life direction. Who was here before Vin Vanbly emerged? Find out, spirit baby.

Then, come back to us.

Oh, and hurry. I'm not going to be around forever.

When we break from the kiss, we're panting again, and my mouth feels like the sticky residue of sperm, because I guess he caught a few globs of mine on his face. I see it in his hair and on his cheek. I love feeling sexy and raunchy.

"Sore?"

I close my eyes. "Sore. Yeah. Everywhere."

"Aw, puppy," he says in a pitying murmur, adding a cooing sound which means I'm definitely getting my shoulders rubbed when we get home.

He helps me climb off the gate. We walk toward a pile of clothes where I was tied up.

Sore, sore, sore, sore...

"I'm so fucking hungry," Vin says with energy. "We have to stop somewhere open late and get food."

I'm happy to have this covered. "Burrito from the Chipotle Grill. It's in my car."

"You're kidding."

"Steak, with extra corn salsa and guacamole. Kevin suggested 'go easy on the rice and beans,' but I ignored him."

Vin makes this big goon dog face at me, one of the faces I love.

"I assumed you would forget to eat because you were upset."

He says, "I didn't forget. I just couldn't. Please tell me you're not kidding about the burrito."

"Not kidding."

"I love you," he says eagerly. "And also, I'm not sharing."

He knows what to say to make me laugh.

Ow. Hurts to laugh. *Everything hurts.*

Vin kisses me again, a happy and in-love kiss, the kind you give when you have no more doubts. I've been kissing him like that for years. Maybe I will never understand why he is—oops, *was*—so nervous about loving this deeply. I couldn't live without it.

With him leading me by the hand, I arrive where our clothes are. I see a familiar green shirt and jeans laid out for me. Too bad we lost his favorite underwear of mine tonight. But I'll go shopping for another favorite pair. I'll take Kevin with me. We'll have fun.

"You destroyed the Castro yard-sale shirt."

"I know," Vin says. "I'm bummed about that. You didn't leave the house wearing it."

"I was trying to surprise you." As I pick up the fresh shirt he brought me, my gaze wanders to the other side of the garage. "You better not have thrown one of Fredi's wrenches."

"Are you kidding? I like my testicles attached, thank you." He indicates the Gator boots. "I'm assuming you don't want me to put those back on."

"We're burning them. I'm serious. Don't even donate them, Vin. Those are evil juju boots."

He does not answer this insistence of mine, but I don't need him to say "Yes, sir." He will do as I request. He understands how important this is to me.

Once his jeans are on, he sits on the metal chair to put on his white tube socks. Before he can finish, I sit on his lap. I don't want to go home just yet. I want to soak in this moment, for him to soak it in too. Does he understand what happened here tonight? Of course he knows. He's Vin.

He puts his arms around me and bounces me twice until I am pressed against him, my butt right over where his cock lives. He smiles at me, a tired dreamy smile, and we kiss slowly, leisurely. *Remember it all*, I tell myself. *Remember this night.*

With his chin, he indicates the back room. "You sure you don't want to clean up?"

I shake my head and offer him a devilish smile. I know he likes it when I carry his sperm inside me. I have to, especially tonight.

It's our wedding night.

Tonight, he gave all of himself, especially the part he'd always held back because he was terrified I'd eventually leave. Tonight he revealed his biggest fear: that he is a monster—and Vin Vanbly is an act. But I wasn't fooled. I know who he is. I may not know his life story, but I know who he is.

Our wedding night. Huh. I should capitalize our Wedding Night in my head, like Vin says you can do with important days. Oh good. I just did. Good job, brain.

It's important things have names, like special nights in your life, or your man's favorite smile. Maybe the two of you name things together, like spirit babies made with love, and you watch the love come true. But then again, Vin is best at naming some things on his own. He named Romero just right, and then almost nine months later, he named Chipotle just right too. I admit I was totally doubtful, because he said he wanted to name our dogs after restaurants. Oh, and king names. That's Vin's job. He hasn't found my king name yet, but he will. Vin says you have to be patient and wait for the right name to reveal itself.

Wait, that reminds me.

"We need another dog."

Vin says, "Are you serious?"

I lean in and kiss him on the nose. "Yes, they need an older brother. A big, quieter dog to show them how to grow up. A blue-collar dog, working its way into retirement. Maybe an old police dog, one who wants to take naps and be lazy all day."

He frowns at me with his eyebrows furrowed, like he's working through a problem. He's always working things through with his brain. He thinks way too much. But that's okay. I'm training him on that too.

"A third dog? You're sure."

"Yes."

My confidence is important to convincing him. On some level, he knows this is my wedding present. I had always hoped my wedding would mean us in tuxedos surrounded by our friends, but this is Vin Vanbly. Nothing works out normal with him. You just have to go with it.

Vin kisses my neck with the slightest brush of his lips. "I love you, Marky."

I snuggle into his chest and feel his sweat soak into my shirt.

I whisper, "I love you, Melvin."

He flinches when I use his real name, because we almost never say it aloud. Nobody calls him Melvin.

He hates his name.

That's why it's perfect as the safe word when we play out our fantasy stuff.

King Malcolm the Restorer

The events of this story take place on Thursday, March 17, 2011

ONE

I dread glancing at the red digital display, but I do anyway, and it glares an angry 4:30 a.m. with crisp numbers. Damn. Twelve minutes have passed since my last look. My eyes feel raw and heavy, but I cannot sleep. Not a great beginning to this shitty, *shitty* day.

I attempt breathing techniques we mastered during tantric explorations, but they aren't helping. Makes me think of Mark's and my first try—when after half an hour of deep inhales, Mark whispered, "Is it working? 'Cause, I'm not boning up." We giggled, which led to laughing, which led to groping, and then to kissing, and we decided to go tantric another day.

Good, that's good. Remember something good.

No.

No fun memories. No getting mushy and wistful. Nothing good will come from today. I have to brace myself. Mark may never leave me, but today is the day he stops loving me, which makes this the worst day of my life.

Dammit, it's only 4:38.

I have to quit looking.

When Mark's phone vibrates, I feel the muffled tremor through the mattress. He ends it almost immediately, and if I had been sleeping, it would not have woken me. Mark always stuffs his phone between the mattress and box spring on nights when he's the doc on call. But he's not on call. Nobody at the clinic should be calling him this early. Could be an emergency. He gives out his number to favorites, and there's an elderly bulldog not doing well, the one he told me about Tuesday. Mark is everyone's favorite vet.

He eases out of bed, sliding to the floor in liquid form—the transition is so smooth. The man moves with jungle-cat ease when necessary, sleek and strong. He's trying not to wake me. The clinking of metal dog tags can be heard from three different spots on the floor.

"No," he whispers to Chipotle. "Quiet. Guys!"

All three stand, shake themselves off, everyone curious as to why Mark rose so early. They can't help it. He's the leader of their pack. Mark attempts to quiet them. Through my closed eyes, I sense him watching, to see if their movement wakes me.

I do not move.

When I hear him padding across the floor, I twist my head enough to squint and watch.

Mark leads a naked parade of three medium-sized dogs, all of whom wonder if this early morning expedition involves food. I don't think this is clinic-related. He wouldn't try to sneak out if it were. He'd kiss me good-bye. Which means he'll come back to bed.

Shit.

Mark will want to have sex this morning. But he also knows—from previous years—I can't perform. Not today. He makes it a personal challenge to tease an erection from me every year on this day, but I stress out thinking of him working so hard with such limp reward. I'll tell him not to bother.

Here he comes.

I close my eyes. Feign slumber. Whatever his scheme, I don't want to ruin his surprise. Clearly, he's got something up his metaphorical sleeve, because the rest of him feels awfully naked, sliding into my arms, nuzzling against my front. He pulls my arm over him like a blanket.

This position reminds me of vacation two years ago, renting a small yacht and lying naked on the mattress we'd dragged up from below, far enough from land we felt isolated. Hours and hours we spent this way, under the striped awning's shade— until nature demanded food, sparkling wine, or piss breaks—and then right back into this position, rocking together against the blue, shimmering love of the Aegean sea. In sight of Greece's distant shores, we rose and fell to white-crested swells, and in hushed tones, I revealed the story of the first pirate kings.

Once there was a tribe where every man was the one true king...

Okay. Awake.

Awake now.

The alarm bleeps and bleeps and bleeps and bleeps—

Mark hits it.

Oh, hey, I slept. Good for me. Without needing to check, I know it's now 6:00 a.m., which means another hour and some minutes more of this horrible day have passed, and I wasn't conscious. Good. That's good. Let's get this shithole day over with.

Mark rotates in my arms so we can kiss. He always wants our kiss as his first experience in the morning and the last one at night. Every day, I oblige the best I can. He truly is waking, which means he fell back asleep. I feel something odd brush against my arm—pointed but curved—and pry my eyelids open to investigate.

A cone hat?

"What day is today?" He yawns for effect, but it's too dramatic, and I recognize his fake-waking. He keeps his eyes closed as his grin curls into itself. "Oh, right..."

He grabs my arms.

"Happy birthday!" Mark screams into my face. *"Happy birthday!"*

His screaming makes the dogs bark. Mark lunges for my face, and the pointy, silver hat on his head juts from him at a funny angle. The tip is crumpled, bent in his sleep. We kiss, the first kiss of today, serenaded by a chorus of barking.

"Happy birthday," he cries again, eyes popping wide. "The boys made you a card. It's on the dining room table with their gift."

Mark makes them sign birthday cards with ketchup pawprints.

"Is it a bone made from bacon?"

"No."

"Is it a bone made out of some food?"

"No. Guys! *Guys*! *Quit barking*! Bone sculpting was last year. And the year before."

"Is it..."

"Quit guessing. No more guesses. You'll see soon enough."

He scolds Chipotle, one last time. That dog. Ha. What a goof.

The silver party hat makes him look like a stripper I brought home last night, one who didn't quite get out of costume. If I weren't so sick to my stomach, I'd love how much he wants me to celebrate this day, to get excited. I shouldn't complain. My life turned out pretty great. I've had more than five incredible years with Mark. I had no idea I could ever be so happy. If I get hit by a bus tomorrow, I'll have no cause for complaint. But I think the bus is more likely to hit me today.

Stupid, shitty, Saint Patrick's Day.

Mark grabs my limp dick. "Thomas opens the garage. Fredi is bringing in muffins. They will be no-particular-reason muffins, so nobody will mention your birthday. Jenna's covering my early hours at the clinic. We get a leisurely morning. I'll make us bacon and eggs and pancakes. Right now, I'm gonna let out the monsters. Don't leave the bed."

He tugs my cock one final time.

I say, "Still limp. You don't have to try this morning."

He smiles. "You'll know when I'm trying."

He throws on his morning sweats, University of Minnesota colors, and it's the only thing he wears outside this morning. Weather warmed this week. Snow covers the ground—and plenty of it—but to Minnesotans, a high-thirties day in March is a welcome heatwave. Spring feels imminent, but I can only see dead tree branches.

I watch the backyard through the bedroom window, and within another minute or two, the whole circus comes into view, the dogs chasing one another, chasing Mark, him waving the purple ball high over their heads—threatening to throw it, then actually throwing it—and they drive themselves crazy with joy. He packs a snowball and throws it at Romero, who dodges and leaps, barking happily.

Wow.

When he first arrived in our home, Romero would have taken a hurled snowball as confirmation: *we no longer love you.* He would have sulked in the hall closet, his eyes sad and worried. Romero used to hide all his toys under our bed. Every time I'd attempt to toss Mark onto the mattress, Mark would cry out, "The bed! Under the bed!" Kind of a mood killer when the sad dog under your bed is mourning with his best friend, the rubber chicken with the chewed-off head.

After four months of this, Mark sat Romero down and said, "We need to talk." I happened upon them at this exact moment, Mark sitting on the living room floor, Romero obediently attentive. Mark said sharply to me, "Go away, Vin. This is private."

I turned on my heel, and left. Sometimes it's best to obey Mark.

After that mysterious conversation, Romero quit dragging his toys under the bed. He stopped hiding in the hall closet. Romero understood we would never leave him. I have no idea what Mark said. Some things are private. Mark's hold over Romero seemed absolute, well, until earlier this week.

The play war outside continues as Mark hurls snowballs at three happy dogs, and the scene feels oddly familiar. A déjà vu moment. Huh.

Romero's toys started disappearing this week, and I checked under the bed. Sure enough, there they were. Chewed Ears Bunny, Droopsy, the latest rubber chicken—a descendent of the original, many generations removed—and Pig Doll. All of them regarding me in silent accusation, like ancient, evil statues.

It was an omen of doom.

Dogs can smell disaster approaching. They know. They get nervous.

Plus, my birthday present was hidden under the bed, an eight-disc series about the Civil War, narrated by Shelley Long.

Another omen of doom.

I made a comment months ago about not knowing enough about the Civil War. Despite all the reading I do, I never delved much into that chapter of US history. Too bloody. But Mark remembered, and soon I must endure ten hours of Shelley Long narrating battles and cheerfully describing amputated leg stumps— okay. That's enough imagining or I'll get sick.

Mark returns, panting, and closes the door on clumsy attempts to sneak in behind him.

"No," he says. "C'mon. Your daddies need some time alone. Out."

They whine for a few seconds until Mark says, "*Hey.*"

The toenail brigade scatters for other parts of the house, clicking and clacking against the hardwood floors. Sometimes, it's best to obey Mark.

To me, Mark says, "Stay there. Listen. I'm going to hop in the shower. Listen to me shower."

"Yes, sir."

He disappears into the bathroom.

I am pleased Fredi will show up this morning. I miss seeing her every single day. Thinking of her makes me chuckle, remembering the day we finally smashed the glass in her framed twenty dollar bill, her wager she'd never marry a fellow mechanic. She kept promising it could never happen and pointed at that damn twenty as if it were proof, so when Fredi and Thomas finally announced their engagement, we used that twenty to buy a bottle of celebratory champagne for $19.99 and told her to keep the change. They got engaged the same night Mark and I did that abduction scene a few years ago. An odd coincidence.

Three years ago.

Man, what a bizarre night. I've never been able to puzzle out exactly what happened when he screamed my name, so loud and strong I felt small in the face of his immense power. No, not small exactly, but smothered, like his scream exuded pure light, and I could not breathe. Sometimes, I don't understand his power, and yet I know him better than I know myself. I wonder if he named that night, like he did Fried Chicken Night or Elvis Impersonator Night.

I hear the shower running.

Fredi still comes around plenty, which is good. She is my oxygen. Until Fredi, I didn't have a friend who was not Mark or Malcolm. One day I realized how hard she had been trying to befriend me. Nobody who had tackled this futile chore had ever kept at it for so long. *Not true, Vin.* Various kings have tried over the years, reaching out, attempting to persuade me to visit for a weekend—a non-sexual weekend—movies and talking and great dinners out. I always resisted.

I'm not easy to befriend.

Fredi is happy being a mom, and her cake business is booming, so she may never come back to the garage. That's rough to contemplate. But when she was pregnant, she promised I could be her nanny while she fixed cars. I should remind her again today. Tell her my salary requirements.

It was exactly one year ago, on Saint Patrick's Day, when we fought about the baby's name. He was an abstract concept back then, and we were both frustrated we would very soon find ourselves out of constant daily contact. We argued for hours that shitty, shitty day. Fredi got loud, explaining she was not going to lose the opportunity to name the baby Melvin and then boss him around for eighteen years. My stomach ached, but she felt strongly about his name. She told me, "I don't care what kind of wrecked king you think you are, you do not step in on the queen's realm, which includes giving her baby his name."

It comforts me to think Fredi never forgot she is a queen. It was Thomas who first spoke her queen name aloud, quite accidentally. Six months before those two dated, we all watched her leave the garage one night as she carried out two bags of new baking pans. "There goes Fredi," he said. "The Rose Maker."

Although he meant frosting roses, the truth of his words silenced us all. She is both thorns and intricate layers of petals, dancing in hot pink and thick red blossoms. The world vibrates when she is near. You must respect her proud elegance or get pricked. As soon as he spoke, I jerked my head to Thomas and witnessed his gloomy secret. He loved her. He was waiting for her to notice. "Love me back" he might have said, if only he weren't so shy.

Last Saint Patrick's Day, Fredi countered my every evasive argument. She even threatened to cut off my frosting supply, but she finally conceded I had sufficiently persuaded her to consider another name, also in homage to me: *Dumbass*. With no fight left in me, I said, "Melvin is a horrible, horrible name. Please don't do this to my godson."

During one of our icy time-out silences, Mark showed up with the dogs, and suggested a compromise. And it was beautiful, just like Fredi and Thomas's actual son. I get to see my godson today! Okay, that's three good things for today: frosting, Fredi, and baby time. And bacon. Four. I wonder if I could be a full-time nanny? Baby vomit wouldn't bother me.

I hear Mark humming or singing song bits in there, the words echoing off the tile. I guess he wants to make sure I hear him, so he sings a little louder, getting me to imagine him soaping his meaty chest, his round muscle butt, all over his gorgeous skin—a gift inherited from his Italian ancestors. His small black thatch under each toned and pleasantly shaped arm. I like imagining him naked.

But today's imaginings are swirled with despair. This life, this glorious life I've cherished for so long, ends today. It's okay. It's more than I ever deserved. But I will miss the way he looks at me.

The water shuts off.

I wonder why he told me to *listen*. That meant something. He's up to something.

I underestimated him on Alcatraz, the night I brought him to meet Jerome. We had successfully avoided Jerome for two hours after dark, Mark shadowing my every move as if he were born to be an Alcatraz ninja. We stayed flat against the rocks while Jerome's powerful flashlight swept nearby. I bragged I knew the island so well there was nowhere Mark could hide from me, especially since he couldn't get inside the prison without me. Mark said, "Let's find out," and slipped away.

I gave him a fifteen-minute lead.

I searched for an hour, every known island hiding spot, and during the second hour, I started to freak out, afraid he'd slipped while climbing a wet boulder. When I could not find him—was no longer capable of suppressing my panic—I screamed for Jerome, allowing my terrified fantasies to win. As I raced toward Jerome's flashlight, I discovered the one place on Alcatraz I had never considered searching for him—standing next to Jerome. The two of them were chatting when I raced up, sweating, wheezing, wiping away tears.

"Well, well," Mark said in a dry voice. "If it isn't our favorite escaped criminal, Vin Vanbly."

Jerome and I locked eyes in shock. I forgot about being terrified. Mark had done the impossible, breached a chasm neither Jerome nor I would ever have crossed on our own. Mark revealed my name. After so many years as the Human Ghost,

Jerome and the other guards had forgotten I was a person. While I panted, my heart thudding louder than the ocean, Mark said something like "What's wrong? Why are you two being so weird?" We stuttered, neither of us able to explain why I had never revealed my name. I'm twitchy about revealing any part of my name, that I know.

Mark insisted we exchange contact information, which meant Jerome possessed not only my name, but my phone number. I couldn't justify this in my head, not after so many years of anonymous friendship. But when Jerome called eight months later, and with strangled words, revealed his Cynthia had double breast cancer, I was more grateful to Mark than I have ever felt. We flew to San Francisco the next day to be with him. Mark knew what he was doing that night on the island. Right? Maybe today will work out as well?

No.

Not possible.

I promised Mark he would learn from Malcolm how we met. Today, Mark meets the one person I hate more than anyone else in the world.

Melvin the Rat.

Mark appears in the master bath doorway. "Hey."

He dries his hair with a thick green towel, taking his time, giving me a chance to appreciate his beautiful curves, the body I love so well. He tosses the towel to the floor.

"This is the soap I used," he says, holding a small beige bar aloft.

It's not our normal soap, but as far as surprises go, I'm not particularly overwhelmed.

"Only five bars of magicals soap exist in the world."

"Oh yeah?"

He nods. "Magicals. This is one of the five soaps I took from the Hotel Indigo the weekend we first met. Many years ago."

I sit up. Lust for this beautiful, powerful man courses through me. He saved our soaps? He *saved* them.

"We used the first one when I moved in. We both used it for almost a week. I washed off my old life, and rinsed in my new life with you."

I glance at my naked body and feel I'm seeing a miracle—my dick is getting plumper. Thicker. Is it possible? These tingly feelings signal *erection*, but is that even possible on my birthday? Maybe! He used *magicals soap*!

"The second bar I opened the first night we fought about me sleeping with other guys. I was so mad. You were so apologetic. But I insisted we shower together, and I used the second soap. You complained it wasn't our regular Irish Spring. Remember? We needed magicals soap, to get through that thing, that ugly door that had been pried open."

He takes a few steps closer.

"The third bar, I used on our Wedding Night—not only to get Gator off my skin, but to scrub out those sad memories of our almost breaking up. Down the drain went all the grime and fears, washed away."

Mark! Mark! I love you!

"This is the fourth soap. Because you agreed to let Malcolm tell me the story of you. Tonight. You need to shower with this today, Vin. I showered with magicals soap, this love from when we first met. At the time, I remember saying 'Who needs five soaps?' I didn't realize they were for us, for our life together, necessary whenever we needed the magic of our first weekend together. The weekend you took my virginity, and you kept it."

I rise.

"Stay," he says with a gleam in his eye. "I'm in charge today."

Okay, now I'm surprised.

Wait—did he say we had a wedding night?

Mark leaps and tackles me to the mattress, which is ferocious, and also adorable. He pins my forearms and snarls, this lion king. He locks his lips onto mine, and his teeth grab my lower lip, tug it faux-roughly, as I have often done to him. His power has only grown since I've known him. So, why can't I discover his king name? Why won't the name reveal itself to me as so many others have?

He rubs his cock against mine. My stomach hairs tickle his warm body, and I inhale the scent of the Hotel Indigo. The memory of him—of us—triggers my dick into lengthening. I'm very, very surprised by this, but in my defense, he's used magic soap against me.

Mark chomps onto my left tit in one strong motion, and his teeth clutch it hard, tugging with more edge than normal. He knows how to read me, how to read my body. My cock makes one final stride to fully hard. Yup. I'm hard.

He lunges at it like Chipotle attacking a pig's ear, sucking, slobbering, using enough teeth to scrape jarring sensations from me, a skillful trick I taught him years ago until he mastered the ability far beyond my teachings. I once worried sex might get boring after years of living together. Turns out, keeping sex interesting is not challenging when you treat each other as kings, honor the gift of this man, when you—oh god, oh god! His throat! Mark performs king worship right now, sucking the trunk of my cock, his eyes open and staring at me, helplessly, lovingly. A tear streaks out of his right eye, and my cock jerks in response.

Holy shit—he got me hard on my birthday!

Only Mark could work this miracle.

You want to hear the whole sordid story of Melvin the Rat? Fine. Malcolm can tell it; I will grieve later. But right now, you have awoken the fire of my king. You win. I submit. I tilt his skull and fuck his mouth in long, majestic strokes, the tip of my dick head pausing for a second on his rosy lips before disappearing into the warmth I have come to love and know so well. His eyes glaze over as they often do when in the trance, the glowing sticky haze of our mating. I feed him my precum, a few wet drops racing down the sides of the mushroom-thick head, and he gurgles in his throat.

"Lie down."

He does with alacrity, as ready for me to be inside him as I am.

Within seconds, I am balls deep in him. We are not novices; I know he lubed up in the bathroom, for I was welcomed with ease. I rest here, my nuts on top of his, and groan. There's no danger of my losing my hard-on, not now. Not after we've found each other on the ancestral plane and have acknowledged each other's kingdoms. I am safe here. I am alive.

I belong here.

Mark purrs with his entire body, his sternum buzzing.

"I can taste you," he says, murmuring.

God, I love the word murmur. Murmur, murmur, murmur...

I want to see his eyes when I come. This might be the last time he loves me.

No!

Don't think that way!

It's no longer the middle of the night, when the worst, darkest thoughts bone dance with skeletal glee around the bed, promising horrors and grief. Maybe he will love me anyway.

Maybe, maybe, maybe.

Maybe is the most hopeful word I know.

I stop fucking him and rotate his body without pulling out, flipping him over as I have so many times before. Sometimes I crave pushing his face into the mattress as I howl in excruciating relief. But this morning I want to see his dark eyes as I pulse semen into him.

He scrambles to accommodate, as desperate for me as I am for him, and within a half minute, I'm pushing hard inside him, grabbing his cock, which makes his mouth open wide. I fuck him as deep as I can, every inch, and maybe a few more inches beyond that. His arms grip my shoulders as if I'm trying to get away and he must stop me. My foot kicks the yellow sheets—lemon-yellow, the shade of his dress shirt when Roscoe served us champagne—and I force my face into his armpit, where I smell him, the musk he can't shower away, and the soap—the magic soap!

I took Mark's virginity.

I pull back and look into his eyes.

He stares at me, and with vulnerability, says, "You'll always be Vin."

Oh god, oh god, it can't be this strong, but it is! I scream. All of me racing out the quivering steel that is my cock, splattering warm bursts inside him.

Mark joins in my scream, a different musical note, and the dogs hear our screams and complete the chord, barking from elsewhere.

I jerk him into a frenzy of twisting flesh, and while I finish my orgasm, he begins his, thrashing, yelling at me, staring into my eyes and then jerking his head away.

I come down, sweating, panting, pulling him to me, and he offers no resistance, none whatsoever.

In fact, he's snoring.

I love this. I love these few seconds—infrequent as they are—when he sleeps in my arms, and I have done this to him, fucked him into another state of consciousness, another realm. I made this life, this world, so overwhelming he had to leave. I pull out, lay him flat, and position myself so I'm an inch away from his eyes. I want to be the first thing he sees when he comes back to life. He looks so beautiful, so peaceful, still breathing harder than normal.

I'm still gasping.

I will never understand how I earned the right to this much love.

"And that," he says, before his eyes flutter open, "is how we do things in Jersey."

We kiss.

We stare for a moment, happy and in love.

He reaches out his hand to indicate he wants the silver cone hat from the nightstand, so I lean over and grab it. He tucks the elastic under his chin, my private stripper, and puts his hand on my cheek.

"Today's going to be okay. You'll see."

"Okay."

"You have to trust me, Vin. I'm strong."

"I know that."

"And you love me?"

"Always."

"How much?" He asks this with a smirk.

We sometimes play this game. I have loved him more than blueberry pancakes. I have loved him more than the scent of April breezes. I have loved him more than a lazy Saturday TV marathon and deep-dish delivery pizza ten minutes away. He once claimed to love me more than rock-star parking in a crowded lot. But today is not a day to joke around.

I say, "I love you with all my love."

He touches my eyebrow. "It's going to be okay."

No. It's not. Today does not end well.

Two

I hate this beer-stinking hellhole.

Green cardboard clover leaves link in spangled garland, dancing along the length of the bar, a shitty attempt at frivolity and temporary glee. Some of the clovers are bent, the boughs are uneven, and in some places, the naked string is visible where clovers have been broken. The ceiling's emerald crepe streamers might have appeared fresh and party-ready a few hours ago, but they've been ripped from their holdings—most likely by drunks—and now hang limp, enduring this night until tomorrow, when they can be laid to rest. Gritty tables, sticky with the previous beer-guzzlers' spills, and random fried mushrooms stomped into the tiled floor. This bar is disgusting.

It's not super crowded, but more than I thought it would be. I'm not sure I was thinking clearly, suggesting we meet in a bar on Saint Patrick's Day. I picked a dive I assumed would be emptyish, considering more legit taverns are within walking distance. I didn't count on the A-list bars spilling over, and the overspill staggering to this dump. The place smells like armpit. And not the good kind of armpit.

My brother says, "Vin, why the fuck did you pick a bar?"

He glares at me across the table. He's the only person who dislikes Saint Patrick's Day as much as me. Of course, he worked as a beat cop in Chicago, assisting people sick all over themselves, and dismantling drunken brawls.

"No particular reason."

Malcolm huffs. "You're lying." He watches me before answering. "You brought us here—both of us—because you don't like this place. You want me to tell Mark the story of how we met, but you don't want to do it in your living room because you don't want your home tainted."

All true. He knows me well.

Under his power, I have no option but to say "Correct."

Mark squeezes my hand under the table and says, "Well, I don't mind. My burger was good."

Malcolm casts his gaze around the room. "It was all right."

I look at mine. I haven't eaten any. I can't. I'll vomit. Hell, I just might vomit anyway.

The drunken partiers occasionally burst into Irish song a few booths away, and the drinkers at the bar raise their glasses, joining in. While they carouse, Malcolm folds his fingers before us on the table, like a schoolteacher waiting for an explanation. I study his creased expression, the shades of ginger skin above his eyes contrasting a deeper brown on his chin. I know what he's waiting for, permission to begin. The Irish song falls apart after another half verse because nobody knows the words. Or they're drunk enough to not care.

"No point in delaying," Mark says with cheer. "They're just going to get drunker and sing louder."

He's right. But I want to run. I want to excuse myself to the bathroom and return to find this conversation over. For a fraction of a second, I even regret meeting Mark—because if I'd never met him I wouldn't have to deal with this right now. I will die if he stops loving me. I will die.

With cautious eyes, Malcolm questions me, and I nod.

It's time.

He dips his head in return, almost imperceptibly. I doubt Mark noticed.

Malcolm raises his gin and tonic, clinking the remaining ice, and takes a deep sip. "Saint Patrick's Day, 1987. Vin's green birthday."

"Bullshit," Mark says, interrupting before I can. "The real story, Malcolm."

While staring at Mark, Malcolm waits for my confirmation.

I drop my head and say, "Yes. All of it."

I feel so goddamn old.

"Unedited," Mark says. "We've got time. You don't have to be at your retired cop thing for a few hours. So, not the twenty-minute version."

"Yeah, what time does the Policeman's Ball begin?"

I don't care what time it starts. I am delaying. Every wasted sentence is a reprieve.

"It's not a ball." Malcolm's tone scolds me. "It's retired farts getting together and telling cop stories. And it's not until around eight thirty, so we've got time. What the fuck are you doing now?"

I'm embarrassed to be caught, but there's no escaping Malcolm. He sees everything.

"Smelling my arm."

Mark leans his head against my shoulder.

"I showered with magic soap," I say, hoping this explanation will suffice, because I don't want to explain more. I want to delay, but I haven't got much left inside me at this moment. I'm dying. Dragged back to *his* miserable life, the one I've spent a lifetime trying to forget. I hate Melvin the Rat. Today is one of the few days I allow myself to even *think* his shitty name.

"Well, magic soap or not, we don't have to do this on your birthday. We could do this tomorrow before I drive back to Chicago. Or I can stay another day or two."

I mumble, "It's not my birthday."

Mark's head snaps toward me. "Wait—today's not your birthday? What do you mean?"

Mark jerks his head at Malcolm, expecting confirmation, but Malcolm won't tell the story out of sequence. I know him. He's methodical to a fault.

Malcolm says, "I met Melvin three days before he committed his first murder and two weeks before his young death. Melvin was destined to die, and he didn't know it. I found his rap sheet in the precinct stalls, and decided I needed to meet this little punk who had already—"

My heart sinks. My big brother is still trying to protect me.

"No, Malcolm. Start at the real beginning. Start with Vincent."

I love he's trying to protect me.

Inside, I'm dying.

I die today.

But Mark deserves the truth.

"Okay," Malcolm says slowly, watching me for confirmation. "The real beginning."

THREE

I say, "I met Melvin three days before he committed his first murder and two weeks before his young death. Melvin was destined to die, and he didn't know it. I found his rap sheet in the precinct stalls, and decided I needed to meet this little punk who had already—"

Vin interrupts me. "No, Malcolm. Start at the real beginning. Start with Vincent."

I study him. He's so much older than when we first met, twenty-four years ago. He was only nineteen. The weary bags under his eyes now, the wrinkles. He wouldn't have slept much last night, of course. That's why he looks like shit. His whole body sags. He used to live like this, sagging all the time. Of course, back then he was almost done being human. Though he's more muscular than ever, more in-shape, on his birthday—always on his birthday—he returns to the sad lump who was once Melvin.

"Okay." I say the word slowly, watching for his confirmation. "The real beginning."

Vinsmark watches me with great attention, to see if I'm lying. He sees more than Vin realizes. Or maybe Vin realizes? Not sure. Vinsmark has been with Vin for, what, six years? Five and a half, I guess. It's hard for me to imagine Mark without Vin, or separate from Vin. I realize Mark's his own person. He's got a career and friends, and he's a real doctor now. I recall his graduation celebration fondly. But he'll always be *Vinsmark* to me. He just is. Vin is a favorite blanket wrapped around him.

Mark smiles at me, pleasantly, encouraging me to begin. I'm not fooled. That man is ruthless in his defense of Vin. And he's been waiting for this story for a long time. I guess Vin meant it when he insisted I tell the whole story.

It's the right thing.

I just hope Vin can handle the backlash.

"I had been sleeping in a jail cell. Which is amusing, considering I was a cop. What can I say? I've lived a curious life. I found the confinement and lack of distractions calmed my troubled mind. When I needed alone time—or, as was the case that day, to cry hard—I would seek out an empty cell. In our precinct house, we had general holding cells, drunk tanks, and a half-dozen more apart from those, housing the truly dangerous or those who needed to find their calm. I would lock myself in one of those, the cell farthest from the hallway entrance, and lie on a bunk, arms under my head. Even if I could hear the yelling of desperate men, I felt soothed. They were locked up. I was locked up. For a few minutes, the world felt safe.

"That day, I awoke. Instinctively, my body tensed, and my internal alarm screamed at me to be silent. Something was happening. I attribute my never being shot to this instinctive quality—stop, listen, gather information first. Don't react. I heard noises. But this sound was intentionally quiet, furtive. Any locked-up collar would have made noise—a lot of noise.

"I could hear wet thrusting in the neighboring cell. 'Yeah, do it,' I heard one man say in a low voice. 'Fuck that ass.' I knew right away, by the Polish accent, it was Wolchek. Another man's voice with more bass, said, 'So tight...I could nut off at any time, man. I'm ready to breed it.' The second voice was his partner, Dominick Reynolds. They were going at it. Couldn't say I was entirely surprised. Not that they were big flaming gays on the force or anything. The opposite.

"See, they always shook hands good night, or good morning, whenever their shift ended, and when they did, dust crumbled around them. Lies. They would have preferred to stick their tongues in each other's mouths, but they would never do it. The lies were too thick around them for that kind of honesty. Funny, though. They were both single. It was the 1980s, so you know, gays were in the news and making some noise. I'm sure they would have been harassed, but they were tougher cops than most. Hell, those two were the ones who picked on others, so they could have handled themselves. But they never went for it. Maybe it was a cop thing. Or maybe, some men prefer to live in cages."

Mark says, "They never came out?"

"No. Nothing like that. But I could hear Reynolds fucking Wolchek, and I was shocked. I had pegged them both as too homophobic to make a move. Apparently, I was wrong. Sometimes, people will surprise you. Those two had a lot more in common than mere cock lust. They were both crooked as hell, almost openly following the orders of a South Side crime boss, some midlevel piece of garbage who murdered and betrayed his way to the top of the shit pile, and relied on crooked cops to keep him there. Those two worked for him, and they were not alone. This was a tough time for the city of Chicago. Tough time to be a cop. You didn't ask specific questions of colleagues about their latest arrest unless you wanted to know the answers. With those two—Wolchek and Reynolds—you definitely didn't want to know the answers.

"I decided to continue faking sleep. The sound became more guttural but not necessarily louder. Reynolds grunted a final time, and I imagined his black cock, two shades darker than mine, burping out this perfectly white jizz. I didn't want that visual in my brain, but it was hard to lock it out, considering I could hear the slick, wet sounds, and Wolchek whispering, 'Yeah, do it.'"

I feel as though I am betraying Vin. He and I have never relived this day aloud. Twenty-four years of silence. He hangs his head.

A fake Irish brogue rises above the din a few feet away, toasting family and friends in a convoluted tribute that's supposed to sound like an Irish blessing. Beyoncé is included in this blessing. His tablemates cheer.

Ignore them. Keep talking.

"Wolchek said, 'Hurry up. My turn.' That wasn't much orgasm-recovery time for Reynolds, who I could still hear panting. I would not like being a gay man if this is how the exchange goes down. This 'my-turn-bend-over' attitude seemed a little too much like 'business.' With women, it's less tit for tat. But hey, it's not like I chose to be straight. You don't get to choose some things. With other decisions, there's more flexibility. I heard what sounded like scuffling. Coughing. That, combined with my surprise by Wolchek's demand, made me realize something was off about my assumptions.

"Wolchek said, 'It's fucking wet in here.' 'Yeah,' Reynolds said, quiet-like. 'I came hard.' Wolchek talked low and dirty about filling this ass with cop spunk, and I finally understood a third person was in the cell. They weren't fucking each other. They *wanted* to fuck each other. Probably the closest they would ever come to screwing was to watch each other's dick meat slide into some poor woman.

"I couldn't hear any noise from the third party, not grunting, not pleasure, all was silent. Maybe it was a junkie. Maybe a pro, and they were gonna trade sex for a free walk. Maybe it was a civilian who got off on cops. Wolchek cried out, something strangled and muffled, and Reynolds encouraged him with a dirty laugh. I heard deep chest coughing, followed by vomiting. Then, gasping for air. Something was very wrong over there. I heard them zip up and open the adjoining cell door. Reynolds said, 'Thanks, Melvin. We'll make good and get you out.' I heard a wheezing, raspy reply. 'You *raped* me. You both raped me.' Wolchek laughed and said, 'I didn't hear *no*.' The third party, obviously a man, said, 'You choked me. I couldn't breathe. Speak.' He coughed again."

Mark's head jerks to Vin, who ignores him.

Instead, Vin stares me down with silent hate, demanding, "How could you reveal this?"

Damn you, little brother, for putting me in this position. Damn you for not telling him yourself. But it's not hate in Vin's eyes. It's never hate. It's always fear and self-loathing, baked together and frosted thickly with disgust. His favorite recipe. It wasn't his fault. It was never his fault. But he never quite believed that. I remember the birthday more than ten years ago when Vin came to Chicago, got very drunk, and passed out on my couch. Just before unconsciousness took him, he said, stinking of beer, "I should have struggled more."

Vinsmark doesn't know what to make of our stare down, the silence between us, as Vin and I face off over this dangerous memory. Our brotherhood was forged that horrible day, a day we've never discussed. But now, it's been said. The thing Vin didn't want Mark ever to know.

Vin was raped.

Mark touches Vin's hand, and Vin jerks it back, looking away from both of us, his eyes scanning the green patrons all around. Someone who had been singing "Danny Boy"—loudly—and then burst into peals of drunken laughter falls silent. His tablemates cheer.

Oh, Vin. Why do you make life so hard on yourself, picking this shithole bar for your most intimate story?

Vinsmark turns to me. "Go on. Tell me what happens next."

I nod.

He's right. The only way through this is forward.

"Wolchek said, 'Won't do you no good to claim rape. You helped us. Now, we're gonna help you.' The raspy voice said, 'You promised me if I came here with you, *willingly*, you wouldn't touch me.' Reynolds said, almost cheerfully, 'We'll be back soon.' With no further conversation, the two cops slammed the cell door and strolled back toward the front of the house. I could hear their casual gait. At the end of the hallway, I heard Wolchek laugh at something Reynolds said. As far as they were concerned, nothing significant had happened. The door buzzed open and then slammed."

This part is hard. Must be said. If my little brother can reveal his horrible truth to his beloved, I can reveal my horrible truth too.

I speak slowly. "I must say this aloud, Mark. I am not proud of this moment in my life. Now that I understood the circumstances were rape, I pondered what power I had to influence events. If I turned them in, what punishment would they receive? A temporary suspension? Any punishment at all? You'd think this was a fireable offense, but not in those rough days. Deep corruption within the force. I would win their animosity and the attention of others on the force who didn't like the straight and narrow cops."

Vinsmark says, "There wasn't anybody you'd tell?"

He asks a hard question. You'd think I'd be ready to answer it, having pondered it for twenty-four years.

"I trusted a few cops. There are always good men and women on the force. But we were all trying to avoid death on a daily basis. Wolchek and Reynolds had enough influence to ensure I'd be repeatedly sent on the worst, most dangerous calls. Both had less experience than me, less time on the job, but they were connected. Or, higher-up officials would assign me a corrupt partner, someone who could get me killed through negligence or withheld intelligence. Whichever clean cops I told, I would put in danger as well. Maybe I'm justifying my actions. I've had years to contemplate what I could have done different. In the end, you never know. You're just surrounded by a million empty questions like discarded peanut shells."

I can't look at Vin.

I never fought for his justice. That's on me. I carry that regret.

Mark does not nod in agreement. He does not judge me either. His eyes and face remain stoic, not wanting to influence my narrative. I see how this kid works. He would make a helluva interviewer, getting criminals to tell their story and think it was all their idea.

"I listened for sounds from my cell neighbor. Crying. Sniffling. But after a couple more coughs, I heard nothing. I experienced the prickling awareness whoever crouched in the cell next to mine had somehow sensed me, and now he listened for me, just as I had listened to him. He felt my presence. He knew he wasn't alone. He knew.

"I waited two minutes and—without sound—rose from the cot. I slipped through my open cell doorway, turning my back and dipping my head as I darted past, hopefully preventing him from seeing my face or the color of my skin. I did not want him to be able to identify me. I did not want to see him again. Ever.

"I buzzed out the door at the end of the hallway, confirmation to the raped man he was not alone, but he couldn't see me. As I strode the halls nodding to other officers and service staff I knew, I thought about quitting. I had to. This was the last straw. I used to believe I could do good—any incremental amount of good—despite the corruption around me. But now? I was compromised. I listened to a *rape*. If anyone asked me why I didn't stop it, I would say I didn't realize it was a rape. I thought it was consensual, so I didn't intervene. My testimony would end up supporting Wolchek and Reynolds's story.

"I entered our changing room, dreading it, because I hadn't seen Wolchek or Reynolds anywhere in the station. They could have left the building, but I doubted it. The stench of feet and mildew overwhelmed me as soon as I pushed open the door, and standing there, half-dressed, were the rapists."

Vin stares at the green beer in front of him. Mark's hand is on his arm, having won—in the past few minutes—the right to touch him again.

"Vin," I say.

He doesn't look up.

"Hey. I'm talking to you."

He gazes at me coolly. I want to tell him how unfair it was to put me in this position, his biographer, but I know he cannot speak of this experience. I know he spent much of his childhood trying to avoid being raped by adults—and it happened anyway. Mentally, he replays it endlessly. Physically, he remembers details that he does not wish to remember. Triggers are many. I can't be mad at him for wanting me to tell his Mark this story. I can't stay mad at Vin, no more than I could stay mad at my Vincent, for committing the crimes that sent him to prison.

"Vin, do you want to hear this? What they said to me in the locker room?"

Vin says, "I don't care."

"You're lying. You care very much. Do you want to hear this or do I skip ahead?"

Vin opens his mouth and then closes it.

"Okay. I skip ahead."

"No," Vin says. "Tell it all."

Vin sags again into Melvin, and for the first time ever, he looks truly middle-aged, weary with life. But then again, aren't we all? Vinsmark watches our exchange, assessing the dynamic between us.

"I'm going to keep talking." I measure the words carefully, making sure Vin looks me in the eye before I continue. "But you say the word and I stop."

Vin gives the slightest indication of a nod.

I taught him that. Communicating with minimal expression, minimal movement. Using subtlety to your advantage.

"Okay. I asked them if they were off-shift in another thirty minutes, and they said no, they were just freshening up. Pulling a double shift. They passed each other a sly glance, like they were proud of something. I opened my locker and turned away, not wanting further contact. While I changed into my uniform, I contemplated my next move. Quit my job? Threaten them?

"'Hey Malcolm,' Wolchek said, 'you like fucking pussy.' Reynolds snickered and said, 'Even if it's rat pussy?' My loathing for Reynolds rose inside me. Punching him would provide relief, short-term, but I considered another variable—I might need whatever influence I possessed, meager as it was, to help my brother Vincent in prison. He wasn't surviving well. Another reason to ignore them.

"'Should still be pretty tight,' Reynolds said. 'Well, less so after Wolchek's big dick.' They snarked, and I tried to tune them out. I was terrified of what I might do to them. These evil pricks forced me to witness and participate in a rape. I didn't realize it was rape until Melvin said those shocking words. But still, I participated. I was guilty."

"No," Vin says softly. "You didn't know."

He stares at me with wet eyes.

I say nothing.

Vinsmark wipes his own eyes and holds back whatever he's feeling.

I have never asked for Vin's forgiveness. Yet, I have always felt I betrayed him almost as much as his rapists. I cannot speak, stunned by how much his words mean to me, how much they matter when I did not realize I desperately craved them. Vin forgives me. I saw the truth of his words. He forgives me.

Ten feet away, a college boy screams, "I'm a lucky leprechaun! I'm a lucky leprechaun, and I be granting wee little wishes."

I hate Saint Patrick's Day. The obnoxious, false cheer around us celebrates nothing of value. This celebration is no more about the Irish than Christmas is about Jesus. This is a drinking festival, resulting in bad judgment and, undoubtedly, lost lives. A terrible night to be on duty. It's only six thirty, and the place, already crowded, will surely grow packed in an hour or two. Hell, this dump isn't even an Irish bar.

For now, I must swallow little brother's forgiveness. Let it become part of me. Return to the story.

"Wolchek and Reynolds told me their story. They arrested a homeless teen for possession with intent to sell. It was common to give up-and-comers in drug trafficking a few small trial runs. If they proved trustworthy, they earned the right to a larger run. Melvin had auditioned for a bigger role, carrying a half pound of cocaine. These two took his drugs, and promised they would 'do him a favor.' They would get him released without any charges, if he provided a small service for them. They indicated he had to suck them off. He fought them, tried to escape through a window of the burned-out house where they had cuffed him—throwing himself through broken glass—but they beat him down until he could be dragged to the station.

"I couldn't stop myself from asking about the confiscated drugs. Reynolds said, 'To help this punk, we had to make the drugs disappear.'"

Mark says, "But they lied."

"Yes. Lies were always crumbling around Reynolds, every time he spoke. If they hadn't already, they would hand over the confiscated coke to their master. Melvin would be forced to confess he had 'lost' the drugs. He would be killed. He was homeless and young. No one would care. But it would send a strong message to those auditioning for the now-open role of drug courier.

"'He let us fuck him,' Wolchek said. 'He wanted it. He said he'd do anything to get out of being arrested.'"

"I never said that."

The surprise of hearing Vin's voice startles both Vinsmark and me.

I look him in the eye and say, "I know. I always knew."

"I jumped through a glass window to get away. I *never* said—"

"I know." My voice conveys finality.

A quick glance at Vinsmark reveals he shares in this misery, and for Vin's sake, is doing his best to just listen, to not let himself sink into horror and grief.

"They tried to get me to go fuck him, this homeless teen, telling me how much he wanted it, and how it wouldn't make me *gay* because it was merely using a hole, which didn't count. I thought I would choke on the dust from all their lies. These two assholes, who had always treated me with formality, now acted like old chums, telling me how great it was, how he would accommodate me.

"After changing into uniform, I left them, sick to my stomach, wondering what career would follow if I quit my job. I should have walked to the Assignments Desk. Guzzled a shitty coffee. Started gathering intel about that day's crimes prior to briefing. Instead, I searched for his file and found it right on top. Corrupt as they were, these two cops knew how to bury their actions with legal paperwork. Paperwork said they brought him in for questioning and figured some time alone would scare him into talking. They were making good on part of their word—they'd let him go with no charges. Of course, sending him back to the streets without his drugs was a death sentence. They knew that.

"Flipping through the meager arrest record summarized the short life of Melvin Vanbly. Typical story for many of these South Side boys before their early, anonymous deaths. In and out of foster care for years. Hospitalized for extensive rat bites a bunch of times. Illnesses related to the infections. Bottle glass removed from his skull when he was eight. There were odd annotations around one foster home, listed on Thropp Avenue. The address was circled and starred, but without explanation. Why did I know that address? It wasn't part of my beat. But I knew I'd heard of it. *Thropp*. Then, I remembered. Foster parent scandal made the nightly news years back. Whole lot of abused kids and a basement full of rats used to control the children. It was a nightmare. Melvin was one of those Thropp Avenue kids, I assumed.

"A couple fights with other juvies, and then it got interesting. Stolen cars, minor possession—mostly pot—and 'excessive loitering.' That was code for cruising for sex. Melvin might have been a rent boy, which would not help his claim two cops raped him. This nineteen-year-old hovered between stupid kid mistakes and bottom-tier career criminal with no future."

Vinsmark hangs his head, unable to face either of us. His guy—his true love—almost didn't make it. Vin's eyes are glazed over, nervously watching people near us, though I can't imagine why. He can't escape this retelling.

"A former teacher had made notes, stuffed into Melvin's folder. They may have been part of a plea for leniency on some charge probably dropped, not even present in what I held. Her words explained how Melvin kept away from other kids. She said he could be sweet. Whenever a child found themself thrown into the foster system for the first time, Melvin would visit them in their room, trying to make them feel better. Her words concluded, 'Please show mercy. His life has been hard. The other boys call him Melvin the Rat.' Yup. He was a Thropp Avenue graduate.

"I finished reading his file standing in front of his cell. My feet had been walking toward him the whole time I was reading. I looked through the bars into the furious, beady eyes of Melvin the Rat. He was backed into a corner, like a kicked and mangy dog. A smelly, wet dog with a ragged, uneven Mohawk. He raged at me in silence, very angry and very afraid. Blood had run down the side of his face and dried, and there were drops of crusty brown under his crooked, swollen nose. They had broken it, obviously. His shirt was ripped open, and he massaged his collarbone. I could see red marks. That's why he'd been silent during the rape. They'd strangled him in a choke hold."

Mark looks pale. I can guess what he's thinking. Your neck being squeezed so tight your skin gets burned red, and the bones inside you hurt. Or how many rat bites you would sustain before you were hospitalized? Or maybe he's thinking of the tiny scars crisscrossing Vin's head near the hairline. Or his broken nose.

Vinsmark looks like he's going to puke. Well, he's in the right place at least. Nobody will notice in this bar.

"Anyway," I say, with a slight edge of Cop Voice to pull them both back. "I stared at Melvin the Rat in his jail cell, and he glared back. The boy had smart eyes, blue-gray, gleaming. Though he remained fixated on me, I could tell he'd also worked the escape angles, how to attack me and get away. He was a smarty, but not smart enough. He had gotten himself into an impossible situation.

"If he couldn't pay for his missing cocaine, he would be killed—or—offered a deal. He could murder a competitor to pay off his debt. Drug runners sometimes offered a 'kill it forward' option to those they were going to kill anyway. And who doesn't want to stay alive one more shitty day? He would die in two or three weeks when some drug thug wanted revenge for the murder Melvin had not yet committed. I was confident that within three weeks—if not sooner—this kid with the smart and angry eyes would be found shot in the head. Kids like him were easy to use, easy to lose."

"Stop," Vinsmark says, covering his face. "Just stop. I need a break."

His voice is shaking.

"I can't believe this. I can't believe I suggested we do this today, your birthday." He faces Vin, full of anguish. "I'm so sorry. Oh, Vin, I'm so sorry to make you relive this. On your *birthday*!"

Mark cries.

Nearby, revelers croon "When Irish Eyes Are Smiling." They don't know the words.

Nobody pays us any mind.

Vin puts a hand on Vinsmark's upper back, meant to comfort, obviously, but Mark flinches, and he cries harder. Vin now looks at me with anguish, because this is what he feared—Mark would see him differently. Instead of invincible Vin, Mark sees the weak, abused kid who came before Vin Vanbly.

Mark wipes his eyes. "I should be comforting you, not you comforting me."

Vin looks confused.

"It's your birthday, and you have to relive this horrible thing—"

Vin says, "Mark, babe. Don't worry. It's long over."

Lies.

It's never over for Vin. He relives this every year, every birthday. Hell, though we've never discussed it, I believe he relives it most days, not exclusively on his birthday. Today, for the first time ever, we speak of it aloud. That's the only change.

"What a horrible birthday present," Mark says bitterly.

"You've gotten me worse," Vin says in a soothing tone. "Remember?"

Did Vin just make a joke?

He flashes me a *follow me*, and I will follow, because he is family, and with family you jump in first and ask questions later.

I say, "I seem to recall a subscription to Golf Digest."

"Right. See, Mark? Remember that year? That was an awful birthday present. Tickets to that version of *A Chorus Line* adapted to the 1800s? That was awful."

Mark pushes Vin away. "Don't. It's not funny today."

My turn. "No, he's serious, Mark. You're a terrible gift giver. And not just for birthdays. Three Christmases ago, you gave me a full year's subscription to the Tie-of-the-Month Club. I'm fucking retired."

"Don't," Mark says, wiping his face. "Not funny. Not now."

"A little funny," Vin says. "Honey."

I'm not sure humor is the right tone. I wouldn't have played quite this angle. But this is Vin's relationship. He knows Mark better.

"No. Not fucking laughing," Mark says, refusing to give ground. He looks to me. "Malcolm, I'm ready now. Go on."

We take a moment to sober ourselves and share silence together. The humor passes without succeeding. Vin still worries. Mark's not making eye contact with him. When the waitress returns to conclude our dinner transaction, Vin asks if we might stay at this table, and hands her a roll of twenties to cover any tips lost by our remaining. After accepting Vin's generous donation, she's cheerfully agreeable, announcing drinks are on her the rest of the night. We all take a pass on more booze. She is confused but promises to bring us all waters. Some idiot nearby summons her as a bar wench, and he's immediately chastised by another voice, which snaps, "That's the English, you twit." She leaves, and our mood sinks back to somber despite the liveliness around us. We must continue our journey.

"While I contemplated what to say, the kid behind bars spoke first. 'My name is Mal,' he said, snarling. Electricity jolted through me, from the top of my head to my feet. In truth, I wanted to forget everything about him, but I couldn't now, not ever. *Mal*. We shared the same name. He said, 'You should know the name of the man you're going to rape. Because that's what this is. It's *rape*.'"

"I was still fixated on our sharing the same name. I grew up known as Mal. When I discovered it was Latin for *bad*, I figured a black teenager in the 1960s had enough trouble without his name announcing it. I chose to go by Malcolm. Fit the times. I said, 'Why Mal?' He said nothing. 'Why not Mel, which is short for Melvin. You should go by Mel, not Mal.'

"I repeated my logic. He said, 'The fuck should I know? It's just Mal. It's Latin for *bad*.' Electricity sparked through me again. '*Just do it*,' he cried, lunging toward the middle of the room. I didn't flinch. '*Just get it fucking over with*.' He paced nervously, preparing to fight me, but instead he turned and threw up. The cell was covered in vomit. The hallway reeked.

"Without knowing where I was going exactly, I said, 'Let me tell you about Joliet State Penitentiary. You won't have to offer your ass for rape. They'll just do it. Regularly.' He spit at me, seething. I could see he was almost done being human. I said, 'The Joliet infirmary sets aside four beds, permanently dedicated to first-time rape victims. The beds are always full. The first gang rape is really to grab your attention.' Mal said nothing, but watched me with narrow eyes.

"I said, 'I know this because my brother Vincent killed a man in a bar fight. He's in Joliet. They told me over the phone today Vincent got raped. He didn't get a first-timer bed, because this was his third rape. He's now breathing through a tube. Unlike you just now, he didn't volunteer to be raped.' This sobered Mal. I said, 'So here's what we're gonna do.' Spontaneously, I outlined a plan whereby he'd come to live with me in my home in Logan Park on the North Side. He had to get a job within one month and pay rent within two. Gone within a year. He said, 'Oh, right, your personal butt pussy to rape, right on the premises.' I said, 'I do not rape teenage boys. I do not rape anyone. You will not be harmed in my home. But you will treat my belongings with respect and obey my rules. Rules will be few, but you will follow them.' He kept raising objections. 'I'm not going to be a narc for you,' he said. I said, 'I know.' He said, 'I won't do any police work for you.' I said, 'I know.'

"I did not want Mal as a roommate. I had intended to say something about finding him a group home, some charitable place to live, but my mouth surprised me, continuing to make the offer of my home. I repeated my terms to him, and his face remained contorted in disgust. I kept thinking about how a former teacher pleaded for mercy toward Melvin the Rat. She said he could be sweet.

"When I moved to unlock his cell, he shrank toward the back corner, slipping and falling in his vomit. I said, 'Are you always clumsy?' He didn't answer, just scuttled backward, seeking a weapon to fight me. I said, 'Because I have nice things. I'm not rich, but I don't want you to break them. You'll have to be careful.' I unlocked his cell and immediately moved into the adjacent one, which caused him great relief. Not the cell I napped in, but the other side. I wanted to give no reminder of that man. Mal gave no indication he knew that man was me.

"I explained the trouble he was in, returning to the streets without his cocaine. He swore at me. I said, 'Trust me, I'm not exactly thrilled about having a greasy little weasel, like yourself, as a roommate.' With a certain smugness he said, 'They call me Melvin the Rat.' I told him I found the name distasteful, and I refused to use it. I would only call him Mal. This humbled him, my outright refusal to call him the name he both bragged on and hated.

"We argued. We were silent. He grew angry and said, 'The last cops I trusted raped me.' I said, 'I know.' I explained how they'd bragged in the locker room and had suggested I go take my turn. This terrified him, learning his rapists had become carnival barkers, offering him to others. He cried. I then realized I had been talking tough with him, scaring him, and he had been traumatized less than thirty minutes before. Perhaps I was not who he needed. But I was the only one standing there. I asked, 'Do you want to press charges?' I was now ready to confess all I'd heard in the next cell. After meeting him, I had to. He said, 'No. No way.' He demanded to know why I offered him a home. I wasn't sure. I explained we shared the same name. I suggested because I could not help my flesh-and-blood brother, I had to help someone else. I also said, 'Because I've spent thirteen years trying to convince this community police are good and trustworthy. And my colleagues unraveled any good I've accomplished by raping—'

"He cut me off and announced his one condition. Non-negotiable. That we would never, ever discuss what happened. Not in two weeks. Not in five months. No casual hints about therapy or survivor help groups, no rape victim brochures left on the kitchen table. Never. I witnessed his unyielding determination. I reluctantly agreed, but this condition needed a loophole. I told him the day might come when he wanted to discuss it, and he would be welcome to bring it up with me. Mal barked harshly and said, 'Never. Starting right now. Understood?' We both left our cells and shook hands. Well, we would have, but his hands were covered in vomit, so instead, we bowed."

I look across the table at Vin, who appears completely defeated. But also in this moment, love pours from his eyes, the pure gold of Vin Vanbly.

I kept my word. Until today. Until he requested we speak of the rape.

I can see the words swimming in Vin's eyes. *I love you, big brother.*

With my eyes, I communicate back, *I know, little brother.*

After a moment, I turn to Mark. "He was a terrible roommate. Mal slunk around the house in silence and locked himself in the den. In there, he had a sofa bed, my desk, and a metal folding chair. Boxes from Vincent's and my childhood occupied a quarter of the room, another quarter piled high with belongings from my first divorce. Mal was forced to work around those. He rarely talked to me, and every night I heard him drag the metal folding chair to wedge under the doorknob."

Mark turns to Vin. "You didn't trust him."

Vin looks at me. "No."

"Why would he?" I ask. "He didn't know me."

A silence follows.

"We were cautious with each other. Sniffing each other out. He left copies of his job applications on the kitchen table. Then, he left me his new employee handbook to find, so I'd know he was working. Mal left me short notes constantly. If I mentioned I planned to make spaghetti for dinner tomorrow, I'd come home and find a yellow Post-it stuck to the frying pan that read NO ONIONS. On the bread bag in the fridge, he left another note ordering NO MAYO."

I chuckle. "I used to put mayonnaise on his sandwiches, trying to get the dumb fuck to talk to me. One week, he voiced a stumbling request to hang a band poster in his room. I said, 'Sure.' That was our conversation for the week. I'd find notes attached to the bathroom mirror, on my car windshield, and sometimes for more pressing issues, attached to the back door above the lock. We lived this way for three months.

"One day, the Post-it notes stopped. I remember changing clothes in my bedroom, realizing I had not encountered a single Post-it note, not in the garage, the kitchen, the living room. The day before, there had been no notes either. No notes? Something bad was unfolding. I searched the house and heard him moving in his room. With no actual evidence, I decided my radar was off, and I started cooking us tacos. But I couldn't shake the feeling this was a bad night. A very bad night.

"He couldn't be in trouble over the drug delivery. The day after Mal had moved in, I had made clear to Wolchek and Reynolds, threatened them, they needed to fix things. I told them I held proof of Melvin's rape. They doubted me—the cameras on those cells had been conveniently shut off—but when they called me out, I was able to quote each of them, lines spoken during the rape. I commented on details Mal could not have told me. They had no idea I'd listened from the neighboring cell. What else could it be but videotaped evidence? Two days later, I receive a note in my locker which simply read 'Fixed.'

"With everything headed in a positive direction, I couldn't understand why I felt so unsettled. I had become attuned to this punk kid. Melvin the Rat's nose was twitching, which meant mine was too. He never came out of his room for tacos. I barely ate. Around nine o'clock, he emerged and walked right toward the front door. This was it. This was the night—the one deciding where his life goes. I barked at him, 'Where are you going?' I never asked about his plans. I never demanded an answer. I was not his father. 'Out,' Mal said. But it wasn't Mal. Melvin the Rat was back. I yelled at him, 'You leave here right now, you never come back to this house. It's done. You never return.'

"Mal didn't bother to lie or pretend ignorance. He paused to hear my words, and without looking back, he left. I exhaled hard. I had not realized I'd stopped breathing. I thought the Post-it notes meant he was coming back to being human. Choosing life. But tonight, he had chosen an unhealthy direction, and I had to accept his life choices, like I'd had to accept Vincent's. Comparing Mal to Vincent made me wonder if I had done enough—in both cases. I wasn't sure. I decided to chase Mal down and offer him money to not do this thing, whatever it was. I assumed steal a car—he had fixed mine twice, and had skill in that arena. He had stolen cars in the past. I had to stop him. One more try.

"I went to the front door to see if I could still catch sight of him, but there he was. I could see him sitting on the front stoop, his head in his hands. He was thinking real hard. I crept away from the door and lowered myself into a chair in the front room, watching the wooden door, fixated on it, pleading with him. Come back. Come back inside, Mal. Say *no* in a way my younger brother could not. Come back inside."

We three are quiet.

I sip the water our waitress delivered.

"Around midnight—three hours later—the front door opened. He walked back to his room without saying a word. The criminal career of Melvin the Rat ended with the soft click of his bedroom door and the sound of the chair being shoved under the knob."

Mark exhales.

So does, Vin.

And I guess, so do I.

Vinsmark says, "What were you going to do?"

Vin says, "I was headed out for an RC cola."

Mark stares coldly at Vin.

"I was," Vin says, defensively. "And also, yes, to cruise a convenience store. One of the guys I worked with said we could clear four K if we rolled it on a Saturday night. The plan was for two days later. But we didn't do it."

Vinsmark is absorbing all this, the best he can. He wanted to know Vin's past. He's hanging in there. He's strong.

"I probably wouldn't have gone through with it," Vin says, nodding at me. "Malcolm way overreacted. Besides, could you see me robbing a convenience store with a stocking over my head? I'd knock myself unconscious running into a potato chip display."

Vin laughs.

I shake my head. I won't play. I won't joke about that night.

Mark isn't amused either.

But Vin is grinning. For him, the worst is over, remembering and reliving Melvin the Rat. Seeing the small, ugly world from his beady eyes. The garbage heap that was his life. And Melvin just scurried under the table.

The rest of the story is about becoming Vin.

FOUR

Our waitress surprises us with three green beers. She says, "I know you didn't order these, but you guys look so serious over here, I couldn't resist. Try to have some fun tonight, okay? It's Saint Patrick's Day. Everybody's Irish!"

We thank her, watch the unappealing green froth spill over the plastic rims, and look at each other.

Still, her appearance is timely. We're about to discuss his first birthday.

"Things changed after that bad night. He cooked dinner once. Burned the shit out of it, but he tried. I noticed books removed from the bookcase and then replaced. I left him notes at the end of certain books, seeing if he would find them. He did. This began a competition. He would sometimes leave notes in strange places, like my shirt pockets, or in the garage, in my toolbox, under tools he knew I'd use. One night, the dishwasher did not work, forcing me to tinker around to see what was broken. Inside, under the blades, I found his book report for something I recommended. I laughed about that one. He'd graduated from two- and three-word notes to actual mumbling sentences. He talked to me about the mayonnaise. One morning, he got up early for work. Instead of *me* making sandwiches for both our lunches, he made my lunch. He used chicken from the previous day's dinner with two slices of tomatoes, pepper shaken over it and mayonnaise on one side of the bread. Exactly how I made sandwiches for myself, but how did he know? I had never made sandwiches in front of him. Obviously, at some point, Mal had secretly studied me. He was coming back to human."

Vin reaches for his green beer and takes a sip.

Mark says, "But he stayed in his room? And still put the chair under the door?"

"Yes. I asked him once why he spent so much time there, white walls and boxes stacked high. Why didn't he watch television with me or listen to music in another part of the house? I told him we could rent movies, if he wanted. VCRs were still new technology—it was fun to see a whole movie in the comfort of your home. But Mal told me 'I like it in there.' His answer was true, but not the truth. His answer bothered me. A week later, I asked again, and reluctantly, he told me his deeper truth, that he never had a room all his own. Despite the smallness, the boxes, and the boring white walls, he wanted to enjoy it while it lasted. Before it went away."

Vinsmark groans into himself, and his heart bears a new kind of heavy.

Absorbing someone's story can do that to you—weigh you down. It can also free trapped parts of yourself, but first, you have to let it weigh you down. There's no escape. Vin was right to believe this night will change Mark, but probably not in the ways he expected.

"When Saint Patrick's Day came around, I got home and found a note inviting me to a bar on North Clark Street to celebrate. He had written PLEASE COME and underlined the words. All day at work, we'd answered noise complaints, party complaints, domestic complaints from people so drunk they could barely form words. I did not want to go. But he had never invited me out for a beer, and I could not pass this opportunity.

"Mal had secured a table, no small feat in this crowded establishment, and had my favorite beer waiting for me. It was warm by the time I showed up, but still, I was touched by this gesture. He nodded. I nodded. We drank in silence and watched the crazy people get drunk and drunker. Mal said, 'It's my birthday.' I said, 'Happy birthday.' Mal said, 'It's not actually my birthday.' He told me his birth certificate was destroyed in a hospital fire. He needed a birthday and he'd chosen this day. I was horrified, and I'm sure my expression showed it. 'It's a good day,' Mal said. 'There's always a party on my birthday, and people are always happy.' I said, 'They're not happy, they're drunk. Don't pick this shitty, shitty day as your birthday, Mal. You will regret it.' Mal laughed. This was a new sound from him—laughter. He said, 'I might be Irish, you know. I mean, look at me. Or maybe I'm German. Or Finnish. You know, blonds.' I realized at that moment, this was, officially, our first real, sustained conversation. But I couldn't talk him out of it. He had picked Saint Patrick's Day, and he thought it was genius."

"Preaching to the choir," Mark says with a serious expression.

His face is less filled with anguish. He has also returned from the dark side. He's Vinsmark once again. Good to have him back.

"I live with this Einstein," Mark says. "When he thinks he's right, he's insufferable."

"It's true," Vin says eagerly.

I pick up my water and tip it in Mark's direction. "Let's not get distracted by the topic of Vin's obvious and many flaws. We must save that topic for when we have more time. That night—Vin's first birthday—sorry, Mal's first birthday—we drank beer and engaged in conversation. We talked sports, though it held no interest for either of us. We were hunting for common ground. I did not ask questions about his upbringing or anything to do with his former life. We mostly stared at the people around us, and I shared a few observations. He made his own observations, and I discovered his talent for seeing people. We ordered corn beef sandwiches, because, that's what you do. Mal insisted on paying for everything."

Mark bumps Vin's shoulder in a goofy way, and I can see Vin's arm muscle tighten as he squeezes Mark's hand under the table.

Someone belts out, "When Irish eyes are smilin'..."

Again?

God, I hate Saint Patrick's Day.

"Mal left his room. We cooked dinner together when our work schedules overlapped. Mal discovered he could fix anything with four wheels, and changed jobs, now spending all day on his back under cars. He didn't care for it, but it paid better than working in a convenience store, and he didn't have to talk to people. We watched Little Rascals on Saturday-morning cartoons together, and we both perfected our Buckwheat face, to show our white-eyed, wild surprise. He introduced new recipes for us to try. I never understood how someone who loved food as much as Mal could be such a terrible cook, but he overburned and undercooked with true commitment. It's not easy to ruin corn on the cob, but he did. You boil it in fucking water, for God's sakes."

"Yeah, but for how long? There are conflicting reports."

"Well, you take it out before it ends up wrinkled, I know that."

"Conflicting reports!"

"Whatever. I tried to help Mal rediscover sex. I would shower and leave the bathroom wearing nothing but a thick white towel around my waist. I may not look it anymore, Mark, but I was a muscular man. Not too shabby in the looks department. I would chat up Mal while leaning against a doorframe, trying to remind him that he liked sex."

Vin says, "Wait, that was intentional?"

I make my Buckwheat face and Vin laughs.

"Surely, you knew I was posturing and posing for you."

"Never. Not once."

"Well, I wasn't any good at it. I wasn't trying to seduce Mal for myself. I just wanted him to remember he liked sex."

Vin tips his green beer at me. "You're a man whore, that's what you are. Trying to seduce your own little brother."

"We were not brothers," I say, and instantly realize that came out harsher than I intended. "Not yet. I thought of Mal fondly, but we were not kin."

Vin turns to Mark. "He was really stacked with muscles. I totally noticed."

Mark says, "How would he...what did he do?"

Vin pretends to be me, rubbing his biceps and saying, "Sure is *hard*, being a cop."

"Okay, okay. Enough. I wasn't that bad. The point is, Mal rediscovered sex. Every now and then, I found signs around the house suggesting he'd had company over while I was away. That made me glad. Remembering lust was good, another step back to being human. Once or twice, late at night, I heard some fumbling coming from the white bedroom. I would hear an 'ouch, go easy' or sometimes the sound of an elbow or knee crashing into the wall. I got the impression Vin wasn't so great at sex. Maybe I was wrong, but he didn't have many repeat visitors.'"

Vinsmark blushes. "He's much improved."

"Hey, speaking of which," Vin says, "we had sex this morning. Full-on butt sex and everything."

"How? You never have sex on your birthday."

"Well, we did today."

"Viagra?"

"Not even!" Vin beams. "We used magic soap."

Vinsmark smiles with pride. "I'd been saving magicals soap for a special occasion."

I sometimes envy these two and their life together.

"Please go on about Vin's terrible sex skills," Mark says. "I'd like to hear more."

"There's no more to tell. He didn't entertain often, and I wasn't listening deliberately. But he ate more. Left his room. We would go out together, and I would teach him how to watch people, watch for what was true, and then the truths behind their true. He already possessed this skill. I enhanced it. Vin always took it further than I would. He would intervene. Once we spotted a woman hailing a cab, and we both concluded—based on her clothes, her hairstyle, and the way she held her umbrella—she didn't much like her appearance. Mal crossed the street and spoke to her. She smiled. When he returned, he explained, 'I told her she looked beautiful.' Mal was beginning to find his way.

"As the end of the first year drew near, I told him he didn't have to move. I had not anticipated I would grow to enjoy this odd weasel, sneaking around my house, leaving me notes in surprising places. I did not know he would help me laugh, something I never did often enough. I did not know I would find in him a kindred spirit. The day I invited him to stay, he brought me into his room and showed me how he had already packed his belongings in two brown paper bags, so he could be ready to leave the minute I said 'Get out.' His readiness to leave made me sad. Again, I asked him to stay. Mal said, 'I have to move out sometime.' I said, 'I know. But not yet.'

"Months passed. Saint Patrick's Day came around again, and Mal insisted on taking me out to celebrate. He pretended to be buoyant, but the lie crumbled into dust around him. This year was different, a dissatisfaction was present. He shredded his beer coaster, and he wouldn't sing Irish songs like the previous year. Once more, I tried to dissuade him from celebrating this as his birthday, but he told me you can't change your birthday or else it's not really your birthday. This false birthday forged a chain from Mal's new life to his former life as Melvin the Rat. He didn't think of himself as that creature anymore, but he could not escape Melvin on this one day of the year.

"While we drank beer in silence, Mal said with cheerful desperation, 'Tell me a story.' I started talking about my marriage to Vanessa, but he interrupted and said, 'Not a bummer story. A good one.' I was surprised to realize my many years as a cop had pushed the good stories out of my head. Over my many years of service, I had killed three people in the line of duty. I stopped two suicides and couldn't prevent two others. I used force when necessary, and I felt justified, but that didn't mean it felt good. Those were the stories I remembered. I tried a game we sometimes played, where I told him the aspects of a crime, and he tried to solve it. But Mal wouldn't have it. 'C'mon,' he insisted. 'Tell me something different.' I couldn't think of anything. I didn't know the kind of stories you told to help someone stop feeling shitty about their former life.

"But Mal needed something beyond my normal skills, so I reached deep into memory and found an old story, one my Aunt Judy used to repeat when Vincent and I were kids. We would stay with her after school and sit at her feet, making faces, trying to force each other to interrupt her storytelling with laughter, earning her sharp scolding. But we did listen at times. She told us good stories. I recalled one in particular. 'Once there was an African tribe,' I said, digging for the forgotten words I'd heard so long before. 'A tribe where every single man was the one true king. Every single woman, the one glorious true queen. You may wonder how any work got done in a tribe where every person was the highest royalty. But these were not those kinds of kings and queens.'

"Mal already seemed bored. He kept scanning the room. I felt sure he had not absorbed a single sentence, still, my words served a purpose—additional noise to outshout the sorrows in his head. So, I kept talking. I had to improvise parts I could not remember. But I was surprised how much flowed into me, and how I could hear Aunt Judy's voice in my own. I started integrating names of men in my life whom I revered, men over whom I had wept. Malcolm X. JFK. Martin Luther. Uncle Joe. My father. These were kings who walked among us. Mal never commented on the story, just continued to rip his beer coaster to shreds."

"Two months later, a Wednesday, Mal was waiting for me on the couch when I got home from work. He wouldn't make eye contact. He said, 'I'm moving away. I can't be in Chicago anymore.' I had expected this. He wasn't Melvin the Rat anymore. He no longer needed me. This city was no longer his home. While this was a good thing—a very good thing—I felt sad. I tried to argue with him. 'What about your clients? You said you're handling these high-end cars?' He said, 'I'll find broken cars in other cities.' I said, 'You can't cook for yourself. You'll starve.' Mal gave me his best fuck-you expression, and I knew there was no more debate. He had decided. I asked, 'When are you leaving?' He wouldn't look at me when he said, 'Now.'

"I nodded and went to my bedroom. I returned with a thick envelope and handed it to him. Inside he found his birth certificate with his full name, Melvin E. Vanbly. Unbeknownst to him, I had ordered a new one, and through Illinois's corrupt bureaucracy, made sure his birthday was now March 17th. After acquiring his birth certificate, I ordered him a social security card, which had arrived the week prior. I knew this day was coming, his moving. I handed him the envelope, which included his childhood medical records—photocopies of only two ripped pages. That was all the documentation that existed. I included some emergency stuff I thought he should have, phone numbers and resources. While rifling through these meager documents, he pulled out a cashier's check made out in his name for ten thousand dollars. He studied it dispassionately. 'What's this?' he asked. I almost couldn't answer him. I waited several moments, swallowed and said, 'Vincent's parole was denied.'

"Mark, I had been counting on Vincent's parole. I had been saving money to help him start a new life without drugs. This was my last hope for my ever-hardening brother. Even then, a month after parole was denied, I could barely choke out those words. Vincent was going to die in Joliet. I told Mal, 'This was his start-over money. Now it's yours.'

"He said nothing about it, pushing it back with the other documents. Mal had already packed his car, a Ford Escort he had recently reconstructed and which looked like Frankenstein's monster. No two panels were quite the same color. In the back seat, I saw his brown bags filled with clothes, and a few books I had given him, and the most valuable thing he owned—a framed poster of The Who."

Vin says, "It was Foreigner."

"Oh, right. Those guys. I never much liked them. While we stood on the sidewalk, I asked Mal where he was headed. He didn't know. I asked him to contact me when he arrived somewhere. Call, or send a postcard. He shrugged and said, 'Sure.' Mal was not particularly skilled at good-byes. He just wanted to be gone. We shook hands. He climbed inside his crap car. He stuck his head out the window and stared at me, a curious expression on his face, and then he ducked inside. Drove away.

"Back inside, I turned on the news and then got a beer from the fridge, wondering how I would now live without my strange and lonely roommate. I hadn't drunk but one or two pulls when I heard the front door slam open."

Vin looks down.

To Mark, I say, "Mal had returned. And he was pissed. He kicked over an end table in a spasm of fury, sending a lamp crashing to the floor. He approached me with his fists clenched. He screamed, *'What do you want? What do you want from me, you fucking asshole?'* He swung this amateur punch at me, this twenty-one-year-old kid who'd developed a taste for my biscuits and gravy, and had once miraculously cooked us a perfect pot pie. Of course, I was surprised by his return and this outburst, but I was not threatened. Mal couldn't hurt me, not physically at least. I allowed one of his punches to land on my chest. I thought it might make him feel better. Apparently, it did not, because as soon as he hit me, he threw up on my carpet. After wiping his mouth, he raged, *'What do you fucking want from me?'* If Mal could've killed me with his sharp blue eyes, he would have. Because, physically, fighting got him nowhere.

"I knew why he'd returned. I had spent more than a year teaching young Mal how to listen, how to hear the truth behind what was true. How to watch the crumbling lies in a person's face and gestures. So, I knew. A broken kid who had only known the love of hungry rats did not know how to process human love. He understood life's beatdowns. Those made sense. But he could not fathom the caress of kindness. The money I had given him, with no expectations, confused him. Infuriated him.

"I don't know why I said what I said next, maybe because Saint Patrick's Day was only two months earlier. I had been thinking about my brother Vincent, and how we would never again go together for Demon Dogs, our favorite Chicago hot dogs. With all my grief swimming to the surface, I said, 'It's a terrible thing to be a Lost King.'

"Mal screamed as if I had broken his arm, and his eyes went wild. He was so insanely furious at me, and he didn't even know why. His face turned bright red, and his whole body shook as if he were manning a jackhammer. I worried he was having a seizure. At last, he screamed, 'I hate you!' He backed toward the door. 'Stay the fuck away from me! I hate you!' He fled. I heard his car start again and screech away. But I knew what he meant. I saw the truth behind what was true. That was the first time Mal had ever said the words *I love you.*"

Mark weeps into the crook of his arm, his head on the table, and when Vin tries to comfort him, Mark pushes him away. Sure, it's sad, but lots of people have sad tales. Some of them are worse than Mal's, and without a happy ending. Not everybody gets a Mark. But Vin is beside himself all over again, hating to see his guy cry, and to be the cause of it. He looks at me with desperation, and indicates Mark, begging me to do something, to make this right. He never wanted Mark to hear these rat tales.

I shake my head. I'm sorry, Vin. I can't help you this time.

Over the years, I've witnessed plenty. Sometimes the real vermin are people. Abusive moms and drunk dads who spew poison into their eager kids until those kids end up with hate as their flowers, and they never even think to blame the gardener. Best to let Mark hear it for what it is—the story of a pathetic life.

One Saint Patrick's Day, Vin and I spent three hours on the phone in almost total silence. During a brief conversational interlude, Vin said, "I didn't come alive until I was twenty."

I said, "I know. I was there. I was witness to your birth."

FIVE

"Three months later, I received a postcard from Kansas City with a single word: SORRY. A few weeks later, I received another post card, another city, with a whole sentence on it. Another postcard came later. Then, a phone message. A week after that, we actually spoke. Well, I spoke. Mal mumbled or was silent, which made for difficult conversation. But it was a start. Two months later he came to visit, and he brought me a gift—a lamp to replace the one he'd broken.

"After traveling around for a while, he settled in St. Paul. I asked him about making friends. He said, 'Yes. It's easier here.' Lie. Then, he bragged about how great he was doing at the garage that hired him. Truth. And how he was meeting all kinds of men to date. Lie. And how glad he was to be away from Chicago. Truth."

"You're wrong," Vin says. "I totally dated this one hot guy named Tommy—"

"Vin, really? It's *me*."

"Dammit," Vin says, laughing. "You always know."

Vin's jocularity right now is a lie, but I do not call him on it. I let this pass. Vinsmark attempts a smile, and his face is pale, but he's not dying inside anymore. He's just sad.

"Why?" he asks.

Vin pretends not to understand.

"Why haven't you ever told me any of this?"

Vin knows exactly why. But while he is eloquent on some topics, he's silent on others.

He says, "I don't know."

Mark says, "Bullshit. I deserve an answer."

Of course he calls Vin out. Yup. That is the power of Vinsmark.

Silence.

"Why haven't you ever told me anything about Melvin the Rat?"

Vin looks at me for the answer, but says, "I can't talk about it. I can't."

This answer is unsatisfactory, and Mark presses again, but Vin's truth behind the true is clear to me: he literally cannot discuss it. He's not lying right now. The stalemate between them is dangerous, growing worse by the second. I can almost witness the damage happening to their relationship. Mark can't understand the silence. Vin can't justify it. But I know why. I've always known.

Watching this tiny fissure become a crack, and grow the tiniest inches apart—those rare, first inches when the distance is fixable—I make a decision. I must intervene.

"Mark, he's telling the truth. He can't talk about it. Discussing his past is a form of violence, and you know Vin around violence. He literally cannot tell you why he would never explain his past. He'll puke all over you before he can get out a sentence. But I can explain his motivation, if hearing it from me is acceptable."

They stare at each other—discussing this nonverbally, no doubt. I've never understood their secret language, but I suppose all lovers have their own ways of communicating.

Weary-eyed, Mark turns to me. "Yes. Please."

"You've heard the details of Vin's former life, the secrets. But do you recognize the truth behind it? This is the story of a nobody. Someone who probably shouldn't even be alive. But luck, and a few good decisions, changed him into Vin Vanbly. His secret truth is that his background isn't exotic—it's ordinary. Do you know how many kids live in poverty? Get rat bites? Grow up through the foster care? Tens of thousands. Hundreds of thousands. Vin Vanbly is no one special."

Mark's eyes glower at me, insulted I would call Vin *a nobody*, but he also doesn't challenge me verbally—I think because he recognizes the truth in my words. I don't think Vin's nobody. He's my family. I love him. But we're not talking about my opinion. Vin closes his eyes to hide the fluttering and nervousness, these words said aloud, but his silence is also telling.

"Vin always makes such a big deal about his name, his *secret name*. It's goddamn Melvin. It's nerdy, sure, but no more than Francis or Neville. He would much rather you ponder the mystery of not knowing his true name than learn the truth: it's ordinary. He's afraid, Mark, that after today, you will no longer see him as special. He wants you to see only Vin. Not ordinary, plain Melvin."

With his fingers pressed into his closed eyes, Vin says, "Laying it on a little thick."

"Well, speak up, Champ. Tell Mark I'm wrong."

Mark has covered his eyes, too, but not to hide from the world, like Vin. He's attempting to hold in the feelings overwhelming him. Side by side, mimicking each other by accident, neither of them seems ready to let go and see how this unfolds.

What a day. I can't believe Vin and I talked about the rape.

I wondered if this day would ever come.

Mark made this happen. He broke Vin with nothing more than extreme patience.

Our table is nudged by new patrons arriving, wedging more people into the table behind ours as the bar fills up. It's only seven-thirty. We need to finish around eight, so I must push forward. No time for hesitation. But I don't love this next part of the story.

Take a deep breath.

"My younger brother, Vincent, got stabbed in the neck in the prison cafeteria. Two hundred men watched him die on the floor, wriggle his life away, kicking the air while he tried to hold in his blood. But apparently, nobody was responsible for it. Nobody came forward. They just watched."

Mark looks pale again, withered, and says, "Ooohhh."

New grief stings his eyes.

I nod, grateful for the sympathy.

"They sent us the remains, cremated, but I insisted on a real funeral service in a cemetery. I wanted him buried like family. I ordered a coffin with gleaming brass handles. I could not believe I was planning a funeral for Vincent. When we were in school, I helped him with his reading. He taught me to swear. I pinched him, punched him, wrestled him, tickled him, as much or more than he did me. It was the most physical contact I'd ever had with another man. I could not breathe when I thought about never again seeing him.

"The funeral was conducted on a crisp September afternoon, surprisingly cool for that time of year. All the relatives who would not visit Vincent in prison showed up to weep. I was mighty pissed about that, but grateful for their presence as well. It was confusing.

"By some instinct, I twisted around in my front-row chair and spotted Mal out of the corner of my eye, shuffling about, gently kicking tombstones not terribly far away. I had called him the night Vincent died. He watched the proceedings from a distance, wearing a disheveled black suit, holding a white paper bag with grease stains in the bottom, like maybe he'd brought his lunch. Although he had made some effort to clean up—he seemed to sport a fresh buzz cut—he looked unkempt. Others in the family spotted him as well, and word buzzed through our small crowd: 'Charity' had shown up.

"That's what my relatives called him when I dragged him to family functions. Charity. They would say, 'Hey Charity, you gained weight?' Or, 'You sure like Lucille's greens, Charity. You sure eat enough.' They were not kind. But Mal never said anything in return, he just looked at his feet when anyone in my family talked to him.

"While the pastor from Aunt Lucille's church praised our ultimate salvation, indignation grew. Charity dared show his face at an intimate family event. He'd never even met Vincent! They were equally outraged Charity had brought his lunch to the funeral. We were spoiling for a fight, angry mourners that we were, and someone had inadvertently stepped up. The nerve of this white trash! While this whispering escalated—partially for my benefit—I ignored them all.

"Personally, I was glad Mal had come. On the phone, he had given no indication he would. But I was frustrated he represented so poorly in his rumpled suit, holding a greasy lunch. Vincent deserved better than that. Maybe I was more mad at my family but focusing it all on Mal.

"When my Aunt Judy stood up from the white folding chair next to mine and took off her black glove, I knew what she was going to do. We all knew. You could feel it in the air. She strode right back to where Mal was standing, and the whispering fell silent as we listened for it. We heard the sharp crack of her hand slapping his face—it was so hard, so loud. Then, Mal heaved into the grass with such vigor, even the preacher had to stop speaking and pretend to wipe his glasses. I heard her hissing at him, and I could imagine Mal's blue eyes wide in surprise. Everyone could hear the crinkling of the white bag opening, and then the noise stopped. Next thing I knew, she dragged him to the front and plopped him down in the empty chair next to mine. She bent and breathed in my ear, 'Tell him I'm sorry.'

"Mal's left cheek was fire red, blazing heat, bisected by a long bloody scratch. She had rotated one of her rings. He touched the scratch gingerly. I felt sorry she'd slapped him, but still somehow mad because he sat there, next to me, and Vincent, who I could not save, was dead. How could Vincent be dead? I hated how much money I'd wasted on an empty coffin and cemetery plot, but I could not think of another way to show Vincent how much I loved him. Without bothering to whisper, I asked, 'What's in the bag?' Mal leaned over to me, and said, 'Demon Dogs. To go inside the coffin with the ashes.'

"I howled with grief. Before my whole family, I bawled with my fists over my eyes. I dropped to my knees and screamed with an animal rage I could not contain. That was the first time I had wept since the day Vincent got raped for the third time, the same day I met Mal. He knelt in the grass next to me, one hand on my shoulder, not knowing what to do. My strange friend Mal was nurturing his unique perceptiveness about people. He understood them very well, watching for all those years. But he couldn't quite figure out how to walk among them.

"After that day, nobody in my family ever called him 'Charity.' Not to his face, not behind his back. Eleven years later, almost to the week, Aunt Judy lay on her deathbed. Everyone hovered in her house for those final days, mourning, saying their good-byes. Vin walked among us like a ghost, comforting the devastated, cradling bawling babies until they were silent, and making piles of sandwiches. While she and I said our final words to each other, Aunt Judy asked someone to bring in Vin."

I find myself choking up.

"'Take care of Malcolm,' Aunt Judy said to him. The disease had made her voice ragged. 'And don't bring any of those nasty hot dogs to my funeral. I'm having it catered.' Vin knelt at her side and kissed the inside of her hand, just under the thumb.

"When Vincent's funeral service ended, I was so physically devastated I needed Mal's help stumbling to the limo. Mal got me inside. When Aunt Debra approached, wanting either a hug or to provide Jesus-comfort, Mal looked into my eyes and knew what I wanted but could not do for myself. Leading her by the hand, he walked her away. Though I could not hear them, he said soft words to her. The conversation ended with her touching his face, right where Aunt Judy had slapped him, as if to say 'Never again. We will never question your presence among us.' One by one, every aunt came to Mal. Even Aunt Judy. Each one left with a drop of his dried blood on her glove. A single, sticky drop. A permanent red reminder our compassion is what makes us human."

"Back home, Mal had to physically push me up the stairs to my bedroom, both hands on my back. I was weary, so weary in my heart as I hollowed out another chamber to carry this new weight. I loved Vincent so much, my heart was full of pockets of grief devoted to him, and other pockets too, for other griefs and loves."

I need a momentary break from telling this tale.

I focus on Vinsmark. "It's important a man make his heart bigger throughout his whole life, to create room for all the love in its many forms. The smell of Demon Dogs. The death of a dream. A new love, maybe. If your heart isn't constantly getting bigger, how will you store it all?"

Mark nods somberly.

Of course he knows this. Vinsmark understands what makes a man.

"I stayed in bed for several days. I couldn't drag myself out. Mal carried me food, lots of food, dropped off by anxious cousins. Morning, noon, and night, Mal brought me trays, hoping to entice me with family favorites. And always cold water with lemon slices. He felt the lemon was restorative, though he could not explain why. He sat for hours near me, watching, and pretending to read books. Every time he came into the room, I felt worse because his grieving over me reflected my own broken self. I wanted him gone, but he refused to leave. So, I talked and told him stories. Why Aunt Judy was so afraid of life. I told him about my father, and how he was almost beaten to death by a mob in 1924. My Kansas relations. Together, we wondered about Mal's parents and whether they were alive. Mal was clear he never wanted to find them. I told him about my second marriage, to Vanessa, and how she did not like being married to a cop, though during our engagement she had liked the idea of it very much.

"During those days when my marriage crumbled, and Vanessa was no longer interested in our making a child, I sat with my older cousin, Andy, at his deathbed in the hospital. Andy was always crumbling dust, his whole life was a lie. Supposedly, he was a great trombone player and could have made a real name for himself. But he didn't want to be 'just another stereotype,' so he became an accountant and shunned his gift. As he lay dying, I was shocked to see his eyes held the music, for he was bathed in soft brass wails and plinking piano keys. I discovered that two days prior, his best friend, DuRay, brought the old trombone to Andy's hospital room. DuRay insisted Andy play. A few solos later, Andrew wept. Impending death had softened him, helping him remember who he was truly meant to be. Andrew asked quiet questions about Vanessa and how I loved her. He was so beautiful, this dying trombone player, I felt compelled to ask him for advice. Andrew put his arm on me. His brown eyes glowed with life from beyond, and this singer of souls said, 'You must show her your love. Show her all your love.'

"Mal worried about the sad stories, worried they made my condition worse. He didn't understand grief is good, it's part of the dance. He knew that grief was hard—he knew that lesson well. But he didn't understand a man has to weep in order to love. On the fourth day, late in the morning, Mal quietly put a fresh glass of lemon water next to my bed. Another tray. He moved in perfect silence, because he thought me asleep, and his deep care was crushing me. My back to him, I sighed heavily. He made me feel worse, and I had grown weary of feeling worse. The grief peaked in its weight. I could bear no more.

"Hearing me awake, Mal put his hand on my back, the back of my lungs, as if he could persuade them to make me breathe normally again. His hand rested on an ugly beige blanket, one he fussed over every two hours. I heard his quiet voice. 'You showed Vincent your love. You showed him *all* your love.'

"I froze. Mal called forth my secret grief, the deeply buried shame harbored in the depths of my heart. Had I shown Vincent all my love? I had been worrying about this every hour since his death. Did he understand how much I loved him? These questions haunted me, incapacitating me. I could not stop Vincent's life decisions, the ones that got him in prison. That was his life unfolding, and I didn't have the power to make it mine. Yet, did I show him all my love? I was not sure. What if—what if I could have done more?

"Without making a decision—without thinking—words rocketed through me, like electricity. 'Not this time. Not this time.' I would show this little brother all my love. I flipped over to face Mal, and bounced up, surprising him. Kneeling on the mattress, I drew his head to mine and crushed my lips against his."

"Wait. Wait a minute," Mark says. *"You two kissed?"*

Vin and I look at each other. He's grinning.

I nod.

"Did you have sex?"

I say, "Just the once."

Behind his hand, Vin says, "Totally fun sex."

Mark's eyes get wider.

"It was one single time. That's it."

Mark crosses his arms and leans forward on them. "Well, you have to tell all the details. You can't skip anything."

"I have my retired-policeman event."

Mark says, "You can be late to that. This is more important."

Okay. If he says I can be late, I'll follow his lead.

Vin says, "If you don't tell him everything, I'll have to later, and my version will have me doing sex like a pro."

Mark nudges him.

Interesting. A few minutes ago, they couldn't look at each other. Now, it's all smiles and silliness.

I say, "It was a long time ago. Details might be hard—"

Mark says, "Was this your only time having sex with a man?"

"Yes."

"And you don't remember the details? Bullshit."

I look at Vin. He smirks.

Quietly, I say, "I remember every moment."

The smirk fades. The tenderness in his eyes betrays how much that day meant to him as well. We are brothers. This is our bond. That experience bonded us.

Mark says, "Okay, so don't skip any details. What made you think—"

"I won't skip details. But don't interrupt me. Agreed?"

Mark pretends to lock his lips with a key.

I chuckle. "Good."

"Although I am curious as to why you decided to try gay sex, I mean, assuming you're not gay. Or bi. No labels."

I tilt my head. "Sounds like a question."

He shakes his head and points to the imaginary key used to lock his lips.

Goofball.

"Well, I'm *not* gay. This was not about 'gay,' this was about love. This was about Mal. I knew I could teach him things. I had heard his sexual fumblings. I knew he wasn't much good at it, and in fact, during our first kiss, he kept jamming his tongue into my mouth. I pulled him back and said, 'Easy, Tiger.' Mal panted, wide-eyed, and said, 'Are we going to do this? For real?' I told him, 'Yes, but this is just for today.' I said, 'I need to show you how to love the men you're going to be with.' Mal nodded eagerly. I said, 'Just today,' in my strong Cop Voice. He growled back at me, 'Yeah, no duh. I get it.'"

"I'm not interrupting with a question," Mark says with great seriousness. "But I have a question. But I'm going to phrase it as a statement so nobody has to answer it. Though it should be answered. Wasn't this weird? You two being brothers, didn't this feel sort of, I dunno, incestual? Nobody has to answer that. I'm just saying to myself, 'Huh.' Also, Vin totally kept that attitude during sex. You didn't do a great job ridding him of *that* habit."

I frown. "*Incestual* isn't a word."

"Mark has his own opinions on what makes a word." Vin turns to Mark. "So now it's a bad habit?"

"I never said that."

"You just said, 'ridding him'—"

"I know." He nods at me. "I'm trying to distract Malcolm from noticing I asked a question. No more questions."

He relocks his lips with the imaginary key, the one that didn't lock so well the first time. He throws the key in his mouth and swallows. I love how it makes no sense, what he just did.

Vin says, "But you—you don't have a problem with my attitude during sex?"

Mark shrugs and points to his lips as proof he may not speak. We just saw him swallow the key.

Vinsmark, I do enjoy how you run circles around Vin. I do enjoy how you make him bark for treats. Okay. I'll answer your question.

Vin says, "Well, if my *attitude* is a problem—"

Enough.

"Listen, you frosted donuts, I'm going to make a statement which is neither in answer to a recently asked question, nor *not* an answer to a question recently asked. I don't want to encourage question asking by responding, but perhaps I can make a statement that is related, but not a question-answer."

Mark says, "Noted."

Vin says, "Hey. You can't talk."

"I'm not talking. I just said *noted*. Like an agreement to his not *not* answering the question recently asked."

I nod. "I'm not *not* answering."

Mark nods. "Let the record show."

Vin grumbles. "You two sound like senators."

Mark nods at me. "Go on."

"We were on the way to becoming brothers. But not yet. On this day, we were friends. This one-day-only sexual experience bonded us as brothers for life. Mal rescued me from my grief. He gave me an impossible distraction. And in return, I anchored him to the world, his first real family member. Sex was like signing the paperwork on our brotherhood, but better, because we would both get to come really hard. After it was over, I told him that the next day began our new status as family."

Mark turns to Vin. "This one-day sex-a-thon was fine with you?"

"Hell yeah."

Vinsmark looks puzzled.

Vin says, "I was young. Horny all the time. There was no one I loved more in the world than Malcolm. Didn't seem weird at the time because I knew it was just this once. He taught me some invaluable stuff."

"Did he teach you the thing with your tongue on my balls?"

"No, no, that one's all mine."

"What about your taint move."

"Which one?"

"The teeth—"

I hold up my hand. "Moving on." Amused as I am, I am not listening to this crazy taint talk, especially since Vinsmark used the word *teeth*. Moving on. My first and only Gay Day.

"Women, I understood. I used my cop skills of listening and talking low, my physical presence, my eyes, my observations about their bodies, my everything. I knew how to make a lady feel like a queen. And then turn us both into rutting, writhing animals, and get her back to queen before morning. But, men? I had no idea. I wasn't even confident I could get hard for this. But I was exhausted from nonstop grieving, and this odd experience intrigued me enough to forget mourning. I committed.

"I commanded Mal to strip off my boxers. He grabbed the waistband. I told him, 'Wrong. Stop. You want to take off my shorts, start at my neck. It's all connected.' I explained how dual sensation points are a good trick, parallel movements with the hands, one up high, one down low. I showed him what I meant. I explained how you wanted the removal of clothes to feel like the orgasm itself, because of the sheer exquisiteness in the tactile experience. I made him practice. I talked to Mal in a low voice, rasping to him and making him respond in kind. I spent an hour teaching him different ways to kiss, because as far as I could tell, the only method he knew was stabbing his tongue at me like an angry fish. Not sexy. Not at all."

Vin looks at Mark. "It wasn't that bad." Vin sees my expression. "It wasn't. Don't overdramatize."

"I showed Mal how to work the body slowly, finding the spots. It works just like finding the truth and lies in words—you look for the truth responses behind what is true. The body doesn't know how to lie. Only the brain lies. Mal soaked up each lesson hungrily. I taught him how to rub his chin against the inside of my thigh, slow strokes, watching the rise and fall of my chest so he would know if this was especially sensitive. 'Always keep an eye on my breathing,' I told him. 'So you'll know what sensations strike best. Pay attention to the eyes, when they flutter. If I lick my lips, do what you just did again, to see if you might tease out the truth response a second time.'"

Mark's face folds with confusion and he says, "Yeah, but with men, don't you—"

"It was strange, I will admit. I had only used these techniques on women I had loved. For me, these were not 'get laid' tricks. To this day, I remember the name of every woman who offered me the gift of her sex. And I'm beyond counting ten fingers. These were skills meant to pleasure and honor a queen. Sex was always about her. I had never even considered if the same sensitivities worked on men. Never cared. Now, I was the teacher, and my mission was to prepare Mal for love, so one day, he would be ready. I needed to show him king love."

Vin's eyes pour love into me. He's back. The little brother I have loved all these years has returned.

Happy birthday, little brother. I hope you don't end up hating me for tonight.

Mark touches the backs of Vin's hands, and soon, their fingers intertwine.

"Already this experience created an odd solace inside me. I could not stand to see gloomy Mal cater to me anymore, wearing his sadness like an apron, and wiping his hands on it every ten minutes. But this grinning, goofy, happy-and-surprised Mal, well, this was heart medicine. His blushing smiles and eager slobbering created a tenuous bridge to a new space in my heart, fresh and clean. Mal spent an hour licking where I instructed him, and I'll be damned if he didn't find a few new spots on his own. He tugged on my nipples, and as I began explaining this waste of effort, I felt a stirring in my boxers, suggesting I might be mistaken. It was good to be surprised by something new.

"My surprise fed on itself, and pretty soon my boxers tented under the weight of my uncrumpling dick."

Vinsmark turns to Vin. "How big was it? Describe it."

"Hey. No questions."

"I can ask Vin questions. You didn't stipulate no Vin questions. Let the record show—"

I clear my throat. Cop Voice clearing.

Mark angles toward me. "Well, are *you* going describe your cock for me?"

"I hadn't planned on it."

He turns back to Vin. "How big was it?"

"It was a fucking beer bottle. Bigger, even. Same color as a Summit Pale Ale."

"Was it uniformly brown, or was any part of it pink?"

"The head was this brownish-pink. Some black guys have a bright pink—"

"Gentlemen," I say. "I'm right here."

Mark folds his hands. "Malcolm. *The gays* need to know these things. We *need* this. Vin, would you say it was as thick as my wrist? Grab around, right—"

"Hey! Let's not—"

"Huge," Vin says.

He does his Buckwheat face at me.

Ha!

Vin knows how to play me, how to get me to laugh.

Mark nods to me. "*The gays* are satisfied. Go on."

I chuckle twice more and sip my water. These goofy idiots.

"Mal finally released my cock from my boxers, and I offered him the option of backing out. I asked him if it was too much for him. He rolled his eyes and said, 'I've seen bigger.'"

Vin says, "I lied. It was huge."

Mark says, "Over ten inches?"

"Okay, okay. Enough size talk at the table. I couldn't give Mal any tips on how to suck cock, but I knew some things I liked, and I communicated them. I had him massage my right nut with wet strokes from a lone index finger, this slow repetition in a circular motion, the circle growing wider and wider, until my entire body shivered in response."

Mark says, "Yup. I know that one."

I laugh when he says this, all matter-of-fact. I never thought I'd be comparing sex tips with Vinsmark. "By the time my boxers were around my ankles, Mal eyed my cock like a snake charmer, following its lumbering side-to-side sway, his steely eyes gauging his next move. He pounced! My dick was halfway down his throat before I could react. He sucked hungrily, deeply.

"With his pink lips almost at my black curlies, he had managed to get most of my cock into his throat. I couldn't see his eyes, but I could see his face getting redder and redder from not breathing. He had impressed me, yes, but he couldn't keep this up for long, and I intended to last a long time. I asked, 'How you doing, Champ?' Of course, he couldn't answer. I could see spittle drooling out of his mouth. He couldn't even create suction. I said, ''Cause it looks like you're not breathing, and my dick will certainly get bigger from your attention. Then, what will you do?' Mal was turning purple. 'Maybe you want a few pointers, Stubborn Guy, on how to breathe?' Against the base of my dick, I could feel Mal nodding *yes*.

"I had been down this path before. After all, I have had a large penis all my life. I had trained more than one reluctant sweetheart who had pursed her cherry lips, communicating 'no way.' Her resistance never lasted long. Usually, forty-five minutes of my performing oral sex would woo her. But women needed to be coaxed and loved into that act. Men must show love first, before receiving love. This is not always true, of course. But it is one truth among the many. Although if Mal were indicative of how men approached sex, it would seem the goal would be to imagine the penis as your worst enemy and attack with gusto."

"Sometimes, that works," Mark says, rolling his eyes my way. "You'd be surprised."

"Not looking for pointers. May I?"

"Sorry."

"I grabbed Mal's neck and pulled him off my dick. He whimpered as if I were taking away his favorite toy. He panted heavily and grinned this goofy, sideways grin, making me laugh. I pondered how to give instruction. Sometimes, a woman wants to know she looks gorgeous while you're pounding her throat open, or that her lipstick is still perfectly applied. Were men the same way? Were they more concerned how they appeared to their partner, or did they just want suck cock? I tested my theory by thumping my hard dick against Mal's face. He laughed and tried to catch it with his mouth, uncaring about the spit splatters slapped across his forehead. Mal hungered for the no-holds-barred kind of cock worship a woman definitely gets into after sufficient warm-up.

"I had to first unteach him what he thought he knew about breathing through his nose. We tried several positions so he could assess the impact on his breathing, and soon he could take a strong face fucking using what I taught him. I had to admit, I enjoyed this workshop approach to sex, empirically comparing my experience with women to Mal while watching my dark dick pound his face. He surprised me a few times with suction, or a twist of his throat. He brought skills I had not anticipated to this situation."

Vin insists on a fist bump from Mark, who obliges with a sideways snicker.

"After a while, I started getting close. I could feel the tingling in my thighs which preceded the twisting in my nuts. Mal sucked harder, eager to claim his prize. I stopped him, pulled my cock out of his mouth, and held his head at bay, his lips stretching to reach my glistening head, covered in drool. 'C'mon,' he whimpered. I told him, 'Right now, you're full of cock lust. That's a good thing. I'm putting it back in your mouth, but don't suck.' I eased my rubbery head against his lips, and a few inches of the shaft followed, but he obeyed my command. I said, 'Cock lust is good. But you can take it further than this, Mal. You can grow a hunger in your partner beyond the physical sensations. Wanna explore further? It's fine if you just want physical lust. Nod *yes* or *no*.'

"Mal was torn. He was dripping sweat, and confused. He wanted my nut and wanted it now. I could feel the truth of that in his mouth. But I think he liked the idea of a lust beyond the physical level. He answered my question by sucking my cock slower, easing me back from the physical brink. He nodded *yes*. This pleased me. It meant Mal wanted more than good sex, it meant he wanted more than a decent job and a big television. He wanted to live. Mal wanted to be fully human.

"I spent the next hour guiding him, teaching him how the body, soul, and spirit are connected. How to rewire the connections during sex, when they aren't as melted together as they should be. I told him the words I say to women to stir something deeper inside them, and we discussed what you might say to a man for the same awakening. Mal described connections as he understood them, how sex was like a car's engine, how you tuned up the body while testing for circuits or wiring that had shorted out. I couldn't follow his detailed car talk, but it was obvious he had put some thought into this. It dawned on me sex might be the best way Mal connected with others. After all, we were well into our third hour of cocksucking and general training. He didn't appear to be fatigued in the least.

"By this point, he had brought me close a half-dozen times, and twice it was no longer under my control. Both times, he opted not to let me release. I recognized the student had already surpassed the teacher, but fuck it, I didn't mind if Mal took home the gold medal, because after today, I had no intention of returning to the Gay Olympics.

"He milked me. He used his throat to grapple my dick, forcing my nuts to knock under his chin on each deep stroke, which is to say, every stroke. My hands gripped his thick blond head, mashing the tiny spikes of his crew cut. My thumbs grazed the rat scars, which he had revealed to me only three weeks before he moved out. Mal jerked his head off my cock, looked up at me, and said, 'Go for it, big bro.' He inhaled my cock, all the way.

"He had done it—bound me in the way I had instructed him—energetically tangling everything inside me, the grief, my brain's worries, my exhausted and overtensed body, Vincent's soul—the part a brother leaves inside you—our physical bond. '*Go for it, big bro,*' he said. I came."

I take a deep breath. Sip my water. People over there are faking Irish accents again. Ugh.

"That's it?" Mark's eyebrows arch up. "*I came?*"

"I came. What else is there?"

Mark turns to his partner. "Vin?"

Vin says, "First two spattered right into my throat, but he jerked out and painted my whole face. He came like you wouldn't believe. Both eyes, running down my nose, all over my lips, and on my chin too. Gobs of it. Gushing."

Mark looks at me with disdain. "*That's* how you describe an orgasm. Amateur."

"My humble apologies. After I had exhausted myself, I fell back on the bed. I told Mal to clean off his face and get up there, next to me. Mal climbed on the bed with hesitation, unsure of the postcome protocol. I didn't know what to do either, but I was twenty years his senior, so I decided to be the grown-up. I guided him right onto my chest, kissing his forehead, then Aunt Judy's scratch on his face, already healed significantly. He told me that, while unpacking the food she left, he'd found a small container of vitamin E lotion, used to prevent scarring. I kissed him intimately, and could taste my salty jizz on his lower lip. That was interesting.

"I noticed something I never had. Mal was handsome. Maybe not drop-dead gorgeous, but he was a handsome man. Smart, blue-gray eyes, and a serious grin that made you want to smile in return. He was strong, solid, and yes, husky too. He possessed a scruffy, innocent quality making his confidence and ease somewhat surprising. *Innocent.* Not a word I would ever anticipate myself using to describe Mal. Or Melvin the Rat, at least. This amazing perspective, this wonderful side of Mal, I would have never witnessed had I not acted on instinct.

"Mal snuggled up into the crook of my arm, blinking his blue eyes at me, and I could tell he was considering what to say. Sweet, innocent Mal. He wanted to say just the right thing as pillow talk. I let him struggle for a moment. Finally, he blurted out, 'You eat pussy, right?' Not really what I was expecting. I said, 'Yes, Mal.' He said, 'I don't mean metaphorically, or once a year. I mean, you *like* eating out a woman's vagina, and you're good at it? With your tongue on her clit?' All class, our Vin Vanbly."

Vin puts his hands to his ears as if he doesn't want to hear this.

While Mark plays along for the sake of congeniality, I don't think Vin notices the slight differences in Vinsmark. This isn't over between them. Maybe I didn't heal the rift I saw developing. And Vin doesn't see it yet. I should finish this story soon. Give them a few minutes to process what we've discussed here tonight.

Should I warn Vin about what I see? Or am I butting into his relationship where I do not belong?

Mark says, "You keep calling him *Mal*. When did he start going by Vin?"

I nod. "Patience. Almost there."

Vin gulps down more of his green beer, which must be warm by now. He licks his lips with satisfaction. Oh, Vin. You really should pay more attention to Mark.

"Mal convinced me to let him eat out my ass, and sure enough, he needed pointers on that too. How to use the tongue as more than a wet paper towel, and how to recognize that erogenous hot zones were surrounded by more erogenous zones, radiating in concentric patterns. I can't say being rimmed was my favorite thing, but as Mal got better, I could see the appeal.

"While he ate out my ass, I thought about what would happen next. Who fucks whom? I did not know how gay men decided that. Flip a coin? First to 'call it'? Did they know when they first met, or was it revealed through conversation? Can't say I ever had much cause for deep consideration on this matter, but now it seemed awfully important. Could I fuck Mal, given what I had heard the day I met Melvin the Rat? No way. Of course not. I would not. But him fuck me? I didn't want that either.

"I thought of Vincent, and his being raped. He had taken dick in his ass when he did not want it. Same as Mal. Making that association solved the problem. I would get fucked. Another strand uniting the three of us. Granted, I was a willing participant; this was not rape. But I didn't exactly crave this experience either. Still, I would share this with my two brothers."

I read Vinsmark as surprised by this direction. Vin, too. He has never heard my reasoning, my rationale for how our lovemaking unfolded that day. Hearing my words, there is new grief in his eyes. Good. I wanted him to sober up. We're not out of the woods yet, Vin.

"I told Mal I wanted him to fuck me. He asked if I was sure, but he was already eager to comply. He rubbed his cock against my butthole—completely slathered in slippery liquid—and I asked him if he had already applied lube. He told me it was all precum. This startled me. I myself did not precome, and though I knew about it in theory, I had not ever had any practical experience in the matter. Today was becoming quite educational. I asked him questions. Was precum the same liquid as cum? Could he control how much came out? Under what circumstances would he see less or more of it? To my last question, Mal got rather snappish and said, 'Less, now that I have to analyze and measure it.'"

Mark nods. "Seems like maybe asking questions in a situation like this is totally normal, and to be expected, and other people—in general—don't need to make rules about that, huh?"

We exchange snarky smirks.

"Anyway. We stopped talking, and he resumed rubbing himself the length of my ass crack. It took a few minutes before we could begin. My mind and spirit had condoned a reluctant *yes* to this adventure; my body was not convinced. This wasn't an easy decision, even though it felt like the right one. Vincent endured this. Mal endured this. I could too. The confidence we three would share this bond allowed me to relax enough so Mal's wet cock finally poked itself inside me. I braced. The sensation was not what I anticipated.

Mark tilts his head, asking his question without words.

"No, I didn't like it. I didn't hate it either. It was an uncomfortable surprise, like finding a friend standing in your living room when you thought you were alone in the house. *What the hell are you doing here?* I got myself through it by coaching Mal how to read my body, my readiness to continue. I talked. I talked about how this intimacy was like magic—connecting head, heart, and body—and he must use the magic carefully. I spoke of attunement, and growing together, how Vanessa and I used to use the first five minutes of fucking to release the day's unique energy before we could truly find each other through sexual expression. Mal asked me, through clenched teeth, if I could please stop talking about my ex-wife while we were having sex.

"After a while, he was fully inside me. I didn't love it. I grunted. Endured. At that point, Mal said, 'I probably should have used a few fingers first.' And I said, '*You could have used fingers?*' Hell, I use fingers all the time with women. Why didn't I ask for that for myself? I had assumed, somehow, I dunno, that we were doing it the right way. The gay way. Fingers first would have been great."

Meekly, Vin says, "Sorry about that."

"Even so, it was less painful than I had anticipated. Vin was respectful as a top. I felt...violated, like through this physical act, he witnessed an intimate part of me I did not want seen. I have come to understand, through other gay friends, this is *exactly* the appeal. I didn't care for it. On the other hand, Mal was excited. He was the star of the football team back there, clearly in his element. He fucked me deep and slow, as if he were on the homecoming parade float and wanted to drink it all in, memorize every moment. He did not need much coaching from me once we had found our rhythm."

Mark says, "Did you feel closer to Vincent?"

"Yes. I did. The sensation inside me was...well... I could see how a man would enjoy this if his spirit and body leaned this way. I got that. But I also understood if not done with love, this experience would be horrific. The idea of hate and rage being only one thrust away, terrified me. I wasn't used to feeling terror. Mal loved me. He was gentle. But what if he hated me? Or felt indifference to my comfort? I finally understood the power of rape to change you. To change your whole outlook on life. With every loving stroke from Mal, I understood how thin the barrier is between love and abuse. How confusing that barrier could become in your head. All my years on the force had not prepared me for this."

I look at Vin, whose eyes are filled with tears. Tears? What did I say to provoke him?

"Vin, you may not have seen it, but I cried while you were inside me. I tried to hide it from you. But at some point, I realized I was saying good-bye to Vincent through this act, letting him know *this* was how far I would go to understand his life. Even those experiences he didn't want for himself. I would go this far, brother, to walk in your shoes."

Mark's eyes are wet and shiny. "Did you accept you had shown Vincent all your love?"

"Yes." The word is soft coming out of me. "I showed him all my love."

Mark nods and wipes his eyes.

A new chamber opens inside me, something in my heart, for Vinsmark. He has listened attentively and let Vincent's story—the little of it he knows—inside him. Vincent will now live inside another person, which makes my heart swell. See, Vincent? You mattered. You continue to matter.

Mark raises the green beer nearest him and nudges Vin to do the same. Apparently, we're toasting. Goddamn it. I never wanted to drink cheap beer in the first place, and now it's room temperature. But it's Vinsmark, and it's *today*, and we're toasting Vincent, so I pick up my plastic cup and do not look forward to the taste of this lukewarm swill.

"To African kings," Mark says slowly, staring me down.

I begin to repeat him. "To Afric—"

The look in his eye, the fierceness. He's toasting me. And it's not just "thank you" or "good job." It's wilder than that, stronger. There are no words for his piercing glare. Vin completes the toast and guzzles his, oblivious to Mark's message. The truth behind Mark's toast, his quivering eyes locking onto mine, says something more. *You saved my love,* he communicates to me. *You saved him. You are mine, now. You are one of mine, now.*

Just like that, in an instant, I now have three little brothers. Vincent. Vin. Vinsmark. I am surprised. For a man who was a cop so many years, this is no small thing, to be surprised. Mark and I do not break eye contact as we both raise the cheap beer to our lips, and we both take a mighty gulp. The beer is surprisingly cool and tastes good in my mouth. Sometimes, life can surprise you.

I have three little brothers.

I suddenly feel very Irish.

Some drunk on the far side of the bar has succeeded in unifying the patrons in song, and so, while the entire bar collectively crucifies "Danny Boy," we three are forced into reprieve. I sip my beer. Mark stares at me, making sure I receive the full intent of his message. I nod to acknowledge I do. Vin looks around with almost good cheer, so glad to have escaped the night with no consequences.

Vin, you have no idea, do you?

Mark is not done with you.

"Mal fucked me in several positions until I felt his body grow tense. I readied myself for what I was afraid would be the worst part, the coming. Mal roared like a bear, a word which, at the time, I did not know had a special meaning in gay world. He came inside me, and I found myself appreciating women even more. Mal collapsed on top of my back, and then it was over, the ass fucking. I could honestly say I had experienced much worse."

Vin toasts me. "Golly. Thanks."

"C'mon," I say. "I'm trying to explain to Mark what I thought on that particular day. I remember Mal's heaving breaths—happy, satisfied grunts—and I do not regret one minute of my sexual time with you. Better?"

Vin smiles, almost bashfully. "Way better."

"We talked about the experience, and he asked for pointers. I had little feedback to give. I was surprised at how masterful he was, well, from my limited experience. At one point, Mal snorted at me and said, 'What do you know about gay sex? You were a virgin a few minutes ago.' I was shocked by these words because of their accuracy. Mal took my virginity. I had always tried to live my life open to new experiences. New people. New ways of thinking. But I rarely thought of myself as a *virgin* to life experiences. Not after all those years on a corrupt police force. I felt jaded. Mal, in his crudeness, reminded me I could still—at my age and with grief in my heart—be a virgin to life in some ways, and that was the best consolation I had received since Vincent died. Virgin joys might await me if I remained open to their possibility. Let myself say yes."

Vin smiles.

Mark smiles.

"We drifted to sleep. I woke when he clobbered me with his arm. Mal was waking, and apologized before snoring again, then jerking upright in bed. He fell back immediately, and I thought he was asleep until I heard him groan the word, 'Fooooooooooood.' I ignored him, reflecting on my odd Gay Day experiences. But he persisted, moaning, 'Fooooooooooooooooooood.' I told him to go downstairs and get his own damn food. Mal said, 'I wasn't asking you to get up, you big baby. Just reach across.' Stacks of sandwiches were heaped on a platter, next to a lemon water. I had forgotten. A sandwich sounded good to me. I was remembering to feel hunger.

"Mal said, 'After the sandwiches, and maybe some Cokes or something, would you fuck me?' He said it casually, as if asking me to pass the salt. But it was definitely one of those 'true but not the truth' moments. True, he wanted it to happen. But I felt there was more to this request than the surface words. I could not puzzle it out. 'I don't know, Mal. I think I have to draw the line. I don't think I could.' He shrugged it off. Said it was fine. My truth was, I could not fuck Mal after having witnessed what I did with Wolchek and Reynolds. Although, technically, I did not see it, I heard every wet thrust and sloppy grunt. I heard Mal's choking and gasping when they released him. I was accidentally complicit in his rape. I couldn't fuck Mal.

"I could tell he wanted to argue my reply, but to what end? If I couldn't get my dick hard, what could he do—lecture it until it rose like a muddy tower? Instead, Mal explained the roast beef sandwiches. He babbled about the right kind of bread for roast beef, and then asked if I liked provolone cheese, which he had recently discovered. He said, 'Seriously, I didn't even know a cheese called *provolone* existed until about two months ago. Did you? I was like, what the fuck is this?'

"While I slowly munched my sandwich, savoring the taste of food, Mal talked. He asked me if I had ever eaten pizza with bacon and onions. A guy at work had told him it was really good, but to Mal, it sounded gross. We both ate a few sandwiches during Mal's unending monologue. Mal peeled a banana and handed me half. I asked him if there were any oranges downstairs, and he frowned. 'I've never seen you eat a fucking orange.' It's true. I didn't like the stinging citrus under my fingernails. But today I felt like an orange. Today, I was having different experiences. Mal offered to go buy one for me, but I didn't care. It wasn't that important.

"As the tray had been transferred to his side of the bed, I asked Mal to pass me another 'sammich.' I took a bite. A corner of yellow paper emerged from the bread, a right angle. I chewed slowly—and wondered what the hell was inside—until I tugged it free with my left hand. It was a Post-it note with two words on it: NO MAYO. My head snapped to Mal, who wore his best Buckwheat surprise face. I roared with laughter and hugged him to me, something between wrestling him and cuddling him, while he struggled to get free. I tried to shove the remainder of the sandwich in his mouth, and whenever I was close to overpowering him, he cried out, 'No mayo! No mayo!' and it made me laugh, weakening me. In revenge, Mal tried to force me to eat the banana peel.

"In that moment, I could feel the joy, the masculine freedom of two men in bed. Here I was trying to shove a sandwich down my buddy's throat, which was possibly still sore from sucking my dick. Neither of us cared about the breadcrumbs, the mustard stains, the crusty spooge in Mal's hair. I could see the appeal. On one level, I could admit it was damn sexy. I had another realization at the same time—I was going to fuck Mal.

"My cock had been growing harder as we fought because, well, I don't know why. Because he was my little brother. Because this sex was just for today. This was something he wanted, truly wanted, though I didn't understand why. While we wrestled, and knocked the platter of uneaten sandwiches around the bed, I let him get closer to winning. I wanted to tire him out, get the energy balanced between us so this went down the right way. I still had my reservations, but now my confidence in our brotherhood surpassed all.

"Once the wrestling had morphed into our gliding together, our taunts evolved into long, sensual kisses. I asked him, 'How do you want this?' Mal jerked his knees to his chest and said, 'Like this. So I can see you.' I nodded and said, 'As you wish.' We were both big fans of the movie *The Princess Bride*. He and I would watch it on the VCR over and over, quoting the lines and arguing over who had a more authentic sounding, 'My name is Inigo Montoya. You killed my father. Prepare to die.'

"I spat a few times on his pink little hole, and yes, it was oddly arousing. My cock was growing harder looking at the slobbery mess. The brown of my skin against his pale ass was beautiful and special because this would only happen once in our lives. I did push-ups against him, grazing strokes, previewing what was coming. I worked a finger inside him, then two. Whenever his eyes strayed from mine, I said his name with my Cop Voice, so he'd lock onto me. Whatever this meant to him, he had only this one chance to experience it. 'Mal,' I said. His gaze jerked toward me, and I used that moment to pop the head inside. Damn. He was tight.

"I'd assumed it would be, yet knowing this as potential did nothing to prepare me for the onslaught of sensations. Different than being inside a woman. Similar, too, in odd ways. With each small thrust, I tried to compare the sensations. Mal and I would surprise each other with our eyes and shallow breaths. Whenever I saw him wince, I worried I'd damaged him, but he would scoot his legs higher, and pull me deeper. I did not know how to read him during this experience. He told me, 'Don't hold back. I know you're holding back.' He was right. I was. I didn't think he could take the full weight of me, the full thickness. I pushed a little harder, but still held back. Mal grunted regularly, and I didn't think this was a bad fuck in his experience, because his eyes reflected more wonder than pain. But I couldn't imagine Mal enjoyed getting fucked. I wouldn't think he wanted that. That's when I started to realize what this meant to him."

Vin looks away from me, as if he cannot bear to witness me, this love he showed me. I focus my attention on Mark.

"This was a gift. Perhaps he thought it was the only thing of value he possessed. He did not like getting fucked. He did not actually want this. But it was the closest he could come to sharing everything with me. We gazed into each other's eyes with deep affection. And then, Mal said—Vin, do you remember what you said?"

Vin chuckles and looks down.

Yup, he remembers.

"Mal said, 'You don't have to worry. I pooped really good today, so I'm all clean.'"

Mark nods. "That comes up in conversation. It has to."

I grimace. "Yeah, I guess. Well, Mr. Pillow Talk reminded me I was fucking a shit hole. No way would I would ever visit Gay Town again. I told him, 'I won't talk about my ex-wife, but you can't talk about poop.' He grunted the word 'Deal.'

"I fucked him harder on the next few strokes, as affable punishment. Maybe he could take all of me—all my love.

"The rhythm we invented was slow and rocky. We lumbered from side to side as often as I knocked him straight up and down. My dick would fuck a new angle into his butt, and Mal's eyes would fly wide open. We maintained eye contact, me already sweating onto him and then kissing him. We were both getting close. I could feel it inside me. I held his arms down, worried slightly about this dominating position, but he had requested it. I lifted my hands from his biceps regularly so he didn't feel imprisoned.

"Mal said, 'I can take it. You can give...' His voice faltered for the last part, but I grunted and gave him, well, *almost* everything. I was close.

"I stuttered the words, saying, 'I'm c-close.'

"Mal stared into my eyes and said, 'I know it was you in the cell next to mine.'

"My eyes widened. We never—we *never* talked—

"'Thank you,' Mal said, and tears came. The almost-two years of living together flashed through his eyes: the Saint Patrick's Days, the meals we cooked, the times he lifted money from my wallet—hoping I would not notice—not ever commenting on the chair under the door. Giving him the dignity of pretending I had not heard his rape. All his gratitude passed from his eyes to mine, all the things he could never articulate, his deer eyes wide and full of love, whispering 'Thank you.'

"Mal pushed my right arm from under me, forcing my whole body to collapse hard on top of him, and I came. He tricked my body into blasting out my orgasm, my head crashing next to his, my cheek touching the long scratch on his face. Vincent's funeral flooded back to me while I came inside Mal. Every aunt left with a drop of dried blood on her glove. A single, sticky drop.

"It is our compassion that makes us human.

"After a moment, I pulled myself up on my elbows, and felt slickness on my stomach. That was Mal's doing. He had come too. My hands hovered over his chest. He took my right hand and dragged it to his lips. He kissed it, the space below the thumb. He said, 'My king.' I had never been loved so well by so few words.

"We lay together, panting, leftover sweat dribbling from my arms to his. By mutual agreement, we did not mention his 'thank you,' or what he truly meant. We both knew. I felt this immense sadness fill me, different from grief. This was sadness for Mal.

"When talking felt normal again, I said, 'I broke a promise to you. I promised you this would never happen, not within the safety of my home.' Mal was cheerful in his reply. He said, 'You didn't break your promise. You never had sex with him. You had sex with me. I'm not *him.*'

"What he said was odd, because it was true, but not the truth. Not exactly. Melvin the Rat was gone. Mostly. I wasn't convinced we wouldn't see him again. Saint Patrick's Day was his holiday to return and haunt Mal, pretending Mal was less than nobody. Maybe he deserved the life of Melvin and nothing better.

"Mal could see my silence and said, 'I'm not him. And sex with me was awesome!' I reminded him this could never happen again. His whole body stiffened next to mine. I told him to relax. I said, 'Be with me today, little brother, and tomorrow will begin our new life as family.' That was the first time I had called him 'brother' aloud. He cried, a little, because I think he worried I didn't feel the same way. Or maybe he believed such a thing as family was never destined for him. It stung a bit, as sweetness sometimes does. I kissed his square blond head, and he relaxed again, melted next to me. I felt quite affectionate with him and his kissing me. I was enjoying being gay for a day. Like I said, I've had a curious life.

"We both took the time to shower and then ate more sandwiches while air drying. We returned to the bed and he lay in my arms.

"We weren't speaking, just breathing together, when Mal announced he had some news. He said, 'I don't go by Mal. Haven't in a while. I don't like that name anymore.' I wasn't surprised, but I could hardly think of a name to fit him. Melvin the Rat. Charity. Even *Mal* was assigned by someone else. He was forever wearing someone else's hand-me-downs. The idea of him choosing his own name comforted me. It meant he was no longer on his way back to being human. He had arrived.

"'In St. Paul, I've been going by the name *Vin*. I even had checks made.' He said this with happiness. 'They still take checks in Minnesota. Isn't that weird? Anyway, I like it. Vin. *Vin Vanbly* is a cool name to say aloud. It sounds made-up, like I'm dangerous and had to adopt a false identity.' I said, 'You are dangerous. Mostly in the kitchen. And mostly to yourself. But you don't have to do this, you know. Take Vincent's name to be my little brother.'

"Looking at the ceiling, he said, 'I like the name *Vin*. It's half of my name. The first half of my life was the ugly part of Melvin. I'm going to reverse Melvin's curse. The second half of my life is going to be the winner part of my name. It's also similar to *fin*, which is like *the end*. Which matches what I was saying about the second half of my life.' 'Got it,' I barked at him. 'What a talker.' He giggled quietly. I felt merry with Vin, and he felt it too. Vin...*Vin*...I liked it.

"'Also, VIN stands for Vehicle Identification Number, which is pretty funny since I'm a mechanic.' He slipped this sentence out quickly before I could growl. I laughed out loud. We lay quietly for a while, breathing, and sometimes talking. I told him stories of joy in my family, first meetings of married couples, playful tricks my parents pulled on Vincent and myself. My father was serious with everyone, but playful with the two of us. I told him about family nights you name as special, and our inside jokes. I wanted to balance the picture I had given him earlier when I shared our family griefs. I did not want Mal—now Vin—to think I regretted family, despite the fact they were sometimes difficult. Looking out the window, I saw it would soon be night. We'd spent the whole day in bed. I asked if any of Aunt Lucille's lasagna was downstairs. I remembered it appearing on one of the trays of food I'd refused. 'Some,' he confessed. 'I ate a bunch.'

"This inspired another round of wrestling. Vin was no match for my strength, and was instantly pinned under me. My dick started getting hard again, another surprise on an already surprising day. I decided to let Vin suck my cock for a few more hours before Gay Day was officially over. I had a few more lessons to teach him. I said, 'One more time. You're not taking on Vincent's name to make me happy?' Vin responded with, 'Nope,' simply and seriously. Truth. It didn't get much cleaner than that.

"'Too bad,' I said. I started thumping my fattening cock against his chest. 'Because Vincent said his biggest regret in life was he left no mark on this world. No one would remember he existed.' Vin tugged on my bloated nuts, and I could see he wanted to suck dick. Good. He said, 'What if I named a car after him? Or something big I eventually own, like a boat? Would that make Vincent happy?' I laughed and said, 'Yup.'"

Mark says, "You sucked him off *again*?"

Vin laughs and says, "It was Gay Day."

Mark says, "Wow, what a whore."

"How does that make me a whore? He started it. He got hard."

While they quibble, I think about my last visit to Joliet State Prison, and how Vincent was despondent. He wanted his name on something to prove he mattered. That he was here. Even while getting amorous with Vin, I grieved for my other brother. Sometimes grief and love dance together like that. You open your heart to one kind of love and another slips in at the same time.

Years later, Vin told me my king name.

By then, he had begun his quest to find them. Bring them back. "Remember," he would tell them, "who you were always meant to be." I doubted his mission for many years. I fretted over the damage it caused him. But finally, I understood. He took Melvin the Rat's shithole of a life and used that compost to grow a field of mighty sunflowers. So strong. So tall. A field of kings with golden crowns, bowing gracefully to each other, proudly facing the sun.

I am King Malcolm the Restorer.

I am very strong.

And I have wept. I know how to weep.

SIX

This isn't good.

Things aren't right.

I thought things had worked out, Mark was okay. As we left the bar, before walking away, Malcolm said, "See you gentlemen for dinner tomorrow." He flashed me a warning and tilted his head slightly to Mark.

He was right.

The drive back to St. Paul has been exceptionally quiet. I've asked twice if Mark is okay, and he nods, grimacing. It's not okay. It's *really* not okay. This is why I hate Melvin the Rat. Shitty, shitty Melvin can never leave me alone. Now that Mark knows Melvin's story, will he ever see anything else? I'm fucked. Melvin ruins everything. In the bar tonight, I joked too hard. I pushed too hard. I have no people skills when Melvin is near.

I find myself growing angrier, the closer we get to home. Why? Why did I fucking agree to let Melvin's story be told? For being a weak, pathetic, nobody, Melvin somehow wields the power to destroy everything.

I have to fix this. I can fix this.

How?

Five blocks from home, Mark says, "Pull over."

Good. Good, let's do this here. I don't want Melvin coming into the house with us. I turn off the ignition. It's dark already, 8:20 p.m. The residential street is quiet, despite its being Saint Patrick's Day. For many, it's just another Thursday night in March.

Don't freak out. Fix this. Fix this *now*.

"Mark, Melvin is gone. Dead. We can wash off the stink of him with magic soap, okay? He doesn't have to ruin—"

"Unbelievable." Mark touches the passenger side window glass.

I am caught by surprise for in his quiet utterance—his tone, the underlying... what was that—anger?

"You're unbelievable," he says. He puts his hands to his face and starts to cry.

No! No, no, no, no, no! Melvin is doing it right now! He's ruining us!

Mark wipes his face. "I can't believe I'm married to such an *asshole*."

He cries harder after saying this.

Asshole?

My anger and panic hover near, each ready to skyrocket out of control once I understand what's happening. Mark cries against the passenger window, lets out a flood of emotion, and when I try to touch his leg, he jerks away.

It hurts, his jerking away, as if I were still that disgusting sewer boy.

I knew this is what would happen if he learned about Melvin.

Anger rising.

Take control of this.

With limited patience, I announce, firmly, "Melvin is gone."

"*No, he's not*!" Mark roars, and his fury staggers me. "He's not dead. Melvin the Rat is still sitting alone in his stupid room with his white walls and his one shitty band poster, waiting for someone to come be nice to him. You let him out every Saint Patrick's Day, and then you slam the fucking bedroom door shut. You prop a chair under the doorknob from the outside. Year after year. *He's still alone, you asshole.*"

Wait...wait...he's defending Melvin?

Through his choked sobbing, Mark says, "Of all the people who were shitty to Melvin the Rat, you're the fucking worst, because you know what he went through, and you're still horrible to him."

Mark cries harder after saying this, and the shock of it prevents me from doing anything but gripping the steering wheel tighter. What is this?

"*No more*!" Mark screams.

I open my mouth but am too shocked to speak.

He's defending a weak—

"No more," he says quieter, wiping his eyes. "Never again. I remove the chair from the white bedroom starting now. Melvin is no longer off-limits to me. I get to ask questions about him and you will answer. Not only on Saint Patrick's Day either. I want to know where he slept. How he learned to read. I want to know—" Mark chokes and swallows before he can speak again. "—who broke a bottle over his head when he was eight."

Rage races up my spine. My hair tingles. My toes tingle. *Never!*

Mark regains control. "He's never sitting alone in that room ever again. He is welcome in our home. We're moving that damn Foreigner poster from the basement and putting it above our bed. Do you understand?"

Rage boils in me. The *idea* we would discuss Melvin's exploits over dinner smashes against my skull like that bottle, and it hurts as bad. Never. I will *never*—

"*DO YOU UNDERSTAND!*"

The sheer volume shocks me. Mark has never screamed at me. Not before this car ride. Well, once, when in Room 1_1, he yelled good-bye, and I died hearing those words. I knew I would die without him. He has never, *ever* screamed. I don't—he has never screamed at me since then, until now. I hate that he's screaming at me over *him*. Over shitty, pathetic Melvin.

"You're going to stop being mean to Melvin the Rat, you damn bully!"

Bully?

No.

No, not me.

I couldn't be a bully, not like kids growing up, mean kids. There's no way. I'm not...

But is it possible he's right? Is it possible he's...my eyes fill with tears.

A sound, a wordless sound, escapes me.

I feel so lost. I *don't know what to do.*

Mark scoots over to me, and squirms his arm behind my back so he can hug me, under my arms, my fists still clenching the steering wheel. I hate this. I hate Melvin coming between us. But what if Melvin isn't the one coming between us? What if it's my own stubbornness? I've spent my whole adult life hating Melvin. Weak, ugly Melvin. What if Melvin isn't the problem? *I don't know what to do.* I hate the idea of talking about my childhood while we discuss our day, our friends, our plans, and dream our life together. But sometimes...sometimes it's just best to obey Mark.

This won't work.

I don't want Melvin back.

But my fury keeps melting as I try to sculpt it higher, dissolving around me, because Mark's fierceness for the forgotten always makes me softer, more filled with love. I can't even get angry like I want, because he loves someone I used to be. He has compassion for the one person in the world for whom I feel none. There's a thickness in my throat, a lump, as we sit in silence, breathing shallow breaths.

Bully.

He's right, of course, though I would never see it that way. But I guess I took over where the other kids left off. I've been bullying Melvin for twenty-five years, telling him it's a good thing he's dead because nobody wanted him around anyway.

How did that happen? *How did I become the bully?* I thought I was just being reasonable.

My heart hurts.

So I think of Mark.

Mark saw Chipotle through his first night of not peeing in the house. When I awoke the next morning, Mark was asleep next to Chipotle on the bedroom floor, being his friend. It was Mark who trained Romero to stop hiding his toys and become one of the family, using his stern, loving voice. Maybe I could be trained to tolerate Melvin. Could I?

Is it possible?

I take deeper breaths until I relax, soften a little more.

Unbidden, a picture from our future opens before me. In my mind, this fantasy, it's next Saint Patrick's Day, or maybe the year after that. We return home from a steak dinner, some restaurant not splattered in green. I will slap his ass at the front door, and he'll trot away, knowing what to do.

I will head to the back porch and let out the dogs, our mutts, each of them goofier and more wonderful than the next. I never knew I loved dogs until Mark. I will cut off the end of a cigar and give it a few deep puffs to make sure its embers glow orange. The bedroom door will be cracked open, and intermingling shadows from two dozen candles will dance around the room, a thousand shapes, a thousand men watching us, reveling in our love. Mark will be naked on all fours, ass raised. The soft illumination will bounce off his muscular arms, his strong chest, the curve of his butt, making him glow against the cranberry satin sheets, slippery to the touch. Making love against that passionate red is the raunchiest, most tender sensation I have ever known.

We stay like this, Mark presenting himself, and my cigar smoke filling the room. He will sniff the air, and know I'm watching him. In my imagination he growls and twists his head, and I guess it will be that kind of fuck, the kind where he ends up howling at the end, a howl which scared our neighbors a few years ago after they had moved in. Whenever Mark howls, the dogs echo their boss, and then I have to howl too because I don't want to be left out, saluting the moon and welcoming that strong, masculine energy.

Not all nights are like that.

Some nights are story nights, where he asks to hear about one of the kings. While I told Perry's story, scared on Alcatraz, Mark trembled. When describing running corn, with Farmer X, Mark gets tough, a hard look and a grin in his eyes. Although they've never met, Mark channels Mai Kearns. I won't divulge Kearns's name as long as he chooses to remain apart from the other men. As I describe the delectable virtues of Farmer X, he calls me a "damn bubba," a phrase he picked up in my telling. He knows it makes me fuck harder, and through Mark, I can love Kearns. I can love Burning Man all over again with Mark in my arms because Mark loves the Burning Man kings, too, agonizing over Alistair's lost night when fear stripped him into John. When I describe loving Rance, Mark assumes a commanding air, one of strong benevolence, riding me while I lie flat. But next year won't be story night.

Just Mark and me in bed together. "King Mark," I will whisper.

Who knows? By then, I might even realize his king name.

It dawns on me we might celebrate Melvin next year, light a candle for him. I'm not ready to concede that possibility, not yet. But maybe. Maybe. Perhaps that's the secret to our love, why it feels so new, always so new. Each time one of us exposes a little more shadow—more ugly truth of our fractured, human frailties—the other responds with, "You think *that* would make me stop loving you? You're so wrong."

It seems I am constantly stripping Mark's virginity, exposing a new layer of man, and he is constantly taking mine, both of us becoming better men in the process.

Mark flinches and says, "*Not sleeping*!" stirring me from my reverie.

Maybe I'll finish this fantasy later. Add a shower scene.

He rubs his eyes and looks at my crotch.

"Your pecker is hard."

Oh. He's right.

He scoots away, enough to free his hand and grip me through my jeans.

"Of course it's hard. I was thinking about you."

He squeezes it, as if trying to decipher the shape.

This erection is very good news because I saw my birthday present wrapped on the dining room table, the right size package for the Shelley Long Civil War DVDs. If I can't keep this erection, we may have to watch an hour or two tonight. On the plus side, Fredi snuck over a small birthday cake for two, smothered with frosting roses, and left it in our fridge for me to find after work.

I love Fredi.

Our drama is done—done for now. We have more to discuss with Melvin, I'm sure. But our relationship will not be ruined, and that's all that matters. I start the engine. Pull away from the curb.

"Oh!" Mark sits up straight before we reach the end of the block.

He's still working my dick with his hand, and he should be wearing his seat belt, but we're close to home. Nothing bad will happen.

"What's up, Sparky?"

He bobs on the seat, bouncing with surprising energy. We've had too much drama tonight, too much mothball misery. We've snapped back the other way, to Punchy Puncherson and the Punchettes.

"Damn," he says. "It's almost 8:40. Damn. The store's closed. I just realized I thought of the perfect gift for you this year. I'm not giving you the one I wrapped."

I laugh. This day has turned out *way* better than I expected. "Whatever you have at home is fine."

"No, no, this is better. I know exactly what to get you for your birthday!"

His glee is ridiculous, ri-dikulous, actually.

He's jubilant the rest of the way home, offering me teasing hints. Promising it will be better than the Pear-of-the-Month Club. All those goddamn pears. He's good at so many things. I find it refreshing he sucks at giving gifts.

I pull up right in front of the house. Easy parking.

"I know what to get you!" He grins at me and hops out of the car, slamming the door, running fast.

"Marky," I call after him, while opening my door. "I already got it."

I'm happy. I'm really happy. And best of all, no Shelley Long Civil War—

Wait.

Where are the dogs? Their faces are always mashed to the other side of the door the moment we arrive. Always.

"*I know what to get you,*" he sings as he runs up the front porch stairs and spins around.

Maybe they're investigating something in the backyard?

Mark unbuttons the top button on his shirt. "Oh, this is gonna be good. I can't believe I hadn't thought of this."

He slips the shirt off over his head, tossing it on an Adirondack chair covered in snow. He shouldn't do that. It's colder tonight than—wait, the dogs *always* come. Why is there no light on in the living room?

"Mark, didn't we leave a light on?"

Hand on the doorknob, he says, "I know what to get you for your birthday this year, Vin."

He twists and it opens?

I locked that door myself!

I slam the driver's door, yelling, "Mark, don't go inside!"

He slips into the dark.

"*Mark!*" My voice is shrill.

No dogs!

Door not locked!

Lights aren't on!

Not today. Not on my shitty, shitty birthday. Please, please—I am begging—don't punish him for my sins! This is it. This shitty day finally came.

Payback for the first kinging.

I scramble to get around the car, remembering every minute of our life together, back when we were astronauts lying in November grass, Fried Chicken Night, tuxedos and treasure hunts, and the night we argued in the backyard, why did we ever fight? No, *please.* I just found out we had a Wedding Night. Please, oh godsomeone, please, I'm begging, please, let him not be dead on the floor with blood gushing from his skull.

Vomit races through me, and I force it back down. I can't puke. Not now. Focus on him. Sprinting up the front walk, words fly into my brain. *What would you risk to find a Lost King?*

Anything!

Please!

Anything!

I would let the rats bite.

I would live it all again, the rats, every shitty moment in Billy's basement on Thropp Avenue, just to have one more day, one more night with him, *please.* For him to love me the way he does. *Malcolm, help me!*

I skip all three stairs and land loudly on the porch, which was stupid, goddamn stupid! *Make no noise!* While grabbing the doorknob, I realize I must go in low in case someone swings a weapon at my chest or head. *I'm sorry for the first kinging, Found Ones, please, please, punish me and not him.* I've got to get to the fireplace poker. I kick open our front door—

Please don't let him die on my birthday.

I jump into the front hall, crouched, ready to dive toward the fireplace, simultaneously hitting the light switch. Control this situation. *Don't vomit!* His life depends on—

All the people?

CHAPTER VIN

"*Surprise!*"

I freeze, legs crouched and fists curled, staring at the uncountable number of them scattered just beyond the foyer, standing around our living room and dining room. In the middle is Mark, shirtless, strapping one of those silver birthday cones on his head like this morning—

"*Surprise!*"

Cell phone flashes pop all around me.

Streamers run from the light fixtures and down the walls. Roger kicks a purple balloon in my direction with a happy grin, his arm around Kevin, who is busy blowing a horn at Fredi's nose while she laughs and bats it away.

What's happening?

Oh, right.

Today's my birthday.

Screaming and clapping begin. While my body pumps confused adrenaline through me, time seems to stand still, as if I'm reviewing a photograph instead of living this exact moment.

King John arches his eyebrows at me, offering two glasses of champagne, and even Michelle is cheering. Next to him, Helena rubs Alan's belly while he pushes it forward, his crooked grin confirming she's pregnant again. Both of their daughters are blowing horns. They've gotten tall.

Look at all the balloons.

Every mechanic from the garage screams in unison, crowded into the back of our dining room, clinking beers together, including Linda, who never goes out with us. They're already chugging one as a tribute. King Dewey stands among them, and Joel, the Puma King, who now lives on Whidbey Island. When he remembered his kingship, he remembered he loved the ocean.

I feel—I don't know what I feel.

Jerome grimaces, holding a yellow balloon like it's a bomb, nodding at me. *Jerome.* From Alcatraz. I should feel more surprise he's standing in my living room. Shouldn't I? His wife, Cynthia, claps her hands. She's beautiful. Even Mark's mom is here, nodding her approval, champagne flute raised. Bikers and dog-park friends. Kings and people from book club. Friends we have visited in hospitals and at gravesides, for cookouts, for yardwork, for birthday parties. Mark's brother, Brian, and his wife, Lisa, blow horns. They moved to St. Paul a few years ago, to be near us. Their younger daughter, Patty, jumps up and down. We all go for night walks together, where I hold Patty's hand and while we stare up, I whisper to her the secrets of the shimmering stars.

Fredi is pointing—my god, the cake! In the dining room, it's five tiers high, bigger than a wedding cake, slathered with pink and purple frosting roses, green icing vines climbing the edible candy columns higher and higher. Tears fill my eyes. She made this for me. She is my sister. I remember that day when I was four, at the gas station, when I watched a girl in her family car. We stared at each other and I longed for a sister. Now, I have one.

Streamers are thrown around the room, and glittering confetti showers me. Next to Fredi is her husband, King Thomas the Quiet Strength, and in his arms, my godson, Vincent. I love him as if he were my own. Next to Thomas—no—yes! Aric, the King of Bargains, sits in his wheelchair, weeping into his hands. How is he here? Travel is so difficult for him these days.

Aric! Father. *Don't cry!* Don't cry, father.

I start crying.

Aric has been my father for so many years, and like an ungrateful son, I refused to acknowledge his love. But it's not too late for us. Nobody's dying today. I can still show him all my love. *Father, beloved father, don't cry!* Behind him, stands my big brother, watching my face, studying how I'm handling this. He's always looking out for me. *Oh.* The retired policemen convention is a lie. He came for this. For me. And my father is weeping for me.

I—I don't know if I'm okay, Malcolm. I don't know. Do you?

What do I do?

Malcolm makes his Buckwheat face.

This makes me cry harder. I can't see. I can't breathe.

I hold out a quaking hand, because if I take one step, I will fall over.

Help me, Mark.

Mark laughs as he throws himself against my chest and wraps his arms under mine, knocking me off-balance. As he drags me from the foyer into the living room, I inhale him as I have done every one thousand, nine hundred, and fifty-two days I have known him. It's Mark. Mark is alive. He's not dead. My arms tremble, but he's okay.

"Gotcha!" Mark has to almost scream for me to hear him. "Didn't you realize the Civil War DVDs were a decoy present? I'm the one who asked you if you had seen Romero's penguin. About two hours later, you went and checked under the bed."

I squeeze him tighter.

Everyone's cheering.

"I may be terrible at gifts, but this year I knew what to get you for your birthday," Marky yells. "For you, Vin, and for Melvin the Rat. A family."

I—

I have a family of my own.

I can't hold myself upright. I sink to my knees, still squeezing him. He lowers himself to the floor with me. Tomorrow I will tell Mark his king name, because I know it now. I *know.* He is the King of Lost Dogs. A friend to those who cannot make friends on their own.

You found me, King Mark.

I inhale the smell of him, and I am home.

A few people yell random comments, mostly about the shock on my face. I hear Dewey's laugh.

Nearby, Patty yells, "Surprise, Uncle Vin! Surprise!"

Her dad says, "Baby, that part's over."

To scattered applause, I hear the toenail brigade, clipping briskly through the living room toward us, now encircling us, gently bumping with wet noses, reminding us they are here too. While sobbing, I laugh at their insistence on being included. Who are these creatures? Have they always been circling me, bumping me with wet noses? Of course. Yes. The King of Lost Dogs sent them to protect me. What am I saying? How—how is that possible?

What's happening to me? My brain is so faloopy.

Patty claps her hands together and yells, "Surprise!"

We are a family.

Through my bleary tears, I look up—right at Kevin—to see tears streaming from his emerald eyes, but he maintains his composure. He smiles, and the light around him grows brighter. My heart slams against my ribs, pounding over and over. What is this? *What's happening?*

Because of the laughing and yelling, I see him mouth the words more than I hear them. Yet somehow, the Finder of Beauty tickles the inside of my ear when he says, "It's time, Vin."

Instantly, all the prison cells in my brain swing open, metal doors creaking wide. All the memories I'd banished, names I forced myself to forget, everything bound with letters and word tricks and cleverly built acronyms locked up tight. Everything dissolves in ghostly clanking. The prisoners—all those memories—step out. Every smashed bottle. Every beatdown, every rat bite. All the ugly details from the first kinging. Things I could never forget but never wanted to remember.

Come out of your cells, prisoners of my former life. I was your prisoner as much as you were mine. But that's over now. I will love you. I welcome you. I will tell the story of the first kinging. I remember—oh. A face from long ago, a child's face, makes itself known. Other Kid, I honestly tried to save you from Billy and his friends. I'm sorry I failed. I tried so hard to forget your name, okay, OK, OK, okay? But I never could. Your name was Christian. I'm so sorry, Christian.

The applause is dying, and I can't quit weeping.

I will honor you, all of you. I will not deny you. I will serve you each a thick corner piece, rich chocolate with buttercream frosting, pink and purple roses. The Finder of Beauty says it's time.

Come back to me.

And allow me to introduce myself. My name is Vin Vanbly, the King of Cakes.

I really, *really* like the word *cake*.

EPILOGUE

POLICE REPORT

MARCH 18, 2012
43RD DISTRICT, CHICAGO, ILLINOIS

348: B&E
60441 S. THROPP AVE.

LAST NIGHT, 911 RECEIVED AN ANONYMOUS CALL REPORTING A BREAK IN, SUSPICIOUS PERSONS ON PREMISES IN AT 60441 S. THROPP AVE. OFFICERS MADDOX AND TAREN ARRIVED ONSITE AT 11:35 PM. DISCOVERED PLYWOOD FORCIBLY REMOVED FROM WINDOW OF ABANDONED RESIDENCE. PICTURE ATTACHED.

WALK-THROUGH REVEALED NO SIGN OF PHYSICAL DAMAGE OR LONG-TERM SQUATTERS. ONLY INDICATION OF RECENT OCCUPATION WAS TWO SETS OF FOOTPRINTS IN DUST LEADING TO THE BASEMENT. IN THE MIDDLE OF THE BASEMENT FLOOR, OFFICERS DISCOVERED A LIT-UP SNOW GLOBE OF SAN FRANCISCO.

NO SUSPECTS WERE FOUND.

WINDOW RESEALED AT 12:45 AM BY ON-CALL CARPENTER, UNION ID# 4335.

NO FOLLOW-UP.

Thank You.
Seriously.

Thank you for reading *Come Back To Me*. Feel like writing a review? Here's the deal: write a review and get a prize.

Doesn't matter if your review is one star or five stars.

As long as you write at least one sentence about your reaction, it counts. And you can copy the exact same review for each new site. After you your review goes live, email me at pickwickinkpublishing@gmail.com

- Write a review for Amazon and I will email you a document titled, "Secrets in The Lost and Founds." I offered a version of this for those who wrote a review of *King John*. With updates relevant to this book, this document is now roughly 24 pages, revealing Easter eggs throughout the series, like: clues to Vin's real name, how Vin's king name was represented significantly in every previous book, many harbingers of Mark's arrival...

- Write a review for Goodreads and I will email you a PDF version of the kidnapping in the third story, *The Lost Ones*, with commentary on all the ways to know the kidnapper is Vin, how the masculine archetypes interplay, and the real danger to their relationship in this story. More secrets! Remember, this can be the EXACT same review. Copy and paste.

- Write a review for some other website (your blog, Barnes & Noble, Amazon in other countries, ARe, etc.) and I will email you the first full chapter of my next novel, *Zacchaeus*.

Every review helps. So, please, let me thank you again. You've been patient waiting for this book—those of you who have loved Vin—so thank you. If you'd like to sign up for my mailing list, jump on board! http://eepurl.com/bYya6v

Facebook: Edmond Manning
Instagram: theedmondman
Twitter: @edmond_manning

Acknowledgments

Come Back To Me is a novel many years in the making. I wrote the first draft back in 2008, long before I published *King Perry*. I've been waiting many years to introduce these two as a couple. The people I met in 2008, sharing a rough draft of Vin's story, helped me believe in myself as a writer, which led to *The Lost and Founds*. I want to thank five of them specifically: Queen Fredi, King Joel, King Thomas, and the irascible King Ted, who admonished me in his very first email, stating, "I know what you're doing with the masculine archetypes. Be careful." The fifth, Tony Ward, was Vin's biggest cheerleader, and sadly, he's not around to witness the rebirth of this story. Damn it, Tony.

Thank you to my best pal, Ann Batenburg. You nurtured me from the start. When my writing was shitty, you read every word and told me I was good. You also were not shy about the writing's flaws, which is why we are best friends. Rhyss DeCassilene became my first editor. Though I was a stranger, she reached through the Internet to say to me, "I think you should try to get published. I can help" A.J. Rose and her wife, the talented Kate Aaron, are friends who loved me through rough drafts and final edits. Their beta-read feedback ensured my compass pointed due north. Jason Weidemann, I thank you for pizza while we wrote at your dining room table.

Explosive, heart-shaped emoticons to my most amazing editor, Jonathan Penn (Romantic Penn Publication Services). He does the hard work of a senior editor but refuses the credit. Did you like this book? He made suggestions that made it better. Thank Hercules he is patient with my over,us,e, of, comma,s. Excellent proofreaders Kate Aaron and Ashley E. found and corrected many "small fixes" that would ruin your enjoyment of the story. I am humbled by how many thousands of mistakes I make while writing. Shit. I need to get better at this.

I am supported by a community of writers. Kaje Harper, Marshall Thornton, Vanessa North, Lloyd Meeker, Posy Roberts, Brigham Vaughn, Helena Stone, Janet Cocklin Ellinger, Theo Fenraven, Barry Brennessel, Erica Pike, Brandon Witt, SA Collins, and too many more. I know I already offended someone by omitting their name. I'm sorry. Remember, I'm an idiot.

I have many, *many* readers to thank for suggesting to their friends, "Read this series." I thank you. I need you. I *thank you*, again. Also, I do that thing where you pour beer into the street before you drink it, while simultaneously appreciating my goofy and wonderful Facebook friends and other readers who delight and entertain me with love, cat videos, and proof of their own king- or queenship. All my love.

I end with a private note to the Bear Walker king, Theo Bishop. Come home, Theo

Also by Edmond Manning

The Lost and Founds series:

King Perry

King Mai

The Butterfly King

King John

AWOL (in the *Men of Honor* anthology)

Filthy Aquisitions

Hunting Bear: A Fariy Tale with a Very Hairy Ending (in the
A Taste of Honey anthology)

Non-Fiction:

I Probably Shouldn't Have Done That

ABOUT THE AUTHOR

EDMOND MANNING has always been fascinated by fiction: how ordinary words could be sculpted into heartfelt emotions, how heartfelt emotions could leave an imprint inside you stronger than the real world. Mr. Manning never felt worthy to seek publication until 2012, when he accidentally stumbled into his own writer's voice that fit perfectly, like his favorite skull-print, fuzzy jammies. He finally realized that he didn't have to write like Charles Dickens or Armistead Maupin, two author heroes, and that perhaps his own fiction was juuuuuuust right, because it was his true voice, so he looked around the scrappy word kingdom he'd created for himself and shouted, "I'M HOME!" He is now a writer.

In addition to fiction, Edmond writes nonfiction on his blog, www.edmondmanning.com.

For more book fun, join his mailing list: http://eepurl.com/bYya6v
Email: pickwickinkpublishing@gmail.com
Facebook: Edmond Manning
Instagram: theedmondman
Twitter: @edmond_manning